HIS GOOD SIDE

"Would you like to have your chemise stuffed in your mouth again, Tigress?" he asked.

"No, thank you."

"Then shut up and behave yourself. If you get on my bad side, I promise you won't like it."

"As if you have a good side!" Tempest sassed him.

Cord took a menacing step forward. "This *is* my good side," he breathed down her neck.

Cord didn't know why he did what he did next. Before he could control himself, he had grabbed her and his mouth came down hard on hers. His arms fastened around her, molding her soft curves against him.

"Why'd you do *that?*" Tempest asked when he finally broke the kiss.

"Hell, I don't know. Why'd you kiss me back?"

"I did not! The last thing I wanted was to be attacked by a lecherous scoundrel like you. I *hated* your kiss!"

"Then maybe you'll approve of this one," he murmured as his eyes focused on her mouth and his lips moved deliberately toward hers. . . .

Other Zebra Books by Carol Finch

Rapture's Dream
Endless Passion
Dawn's Desire
Passion's Vixen
Midnight Fires
Ecstasy's Embrace
Wildfire
Satin Surrender
Captive Bride
Texas Angel
Beloved Betrayal
Lone Star Surrender
Stormfire
Thunder's Tender Touch
Love's Hidden Treasure
Montana Moonfire
Wild Mountain Honey
Christmas Rendezvous
Moonlight Enchantress
Promise Me Moonlight

CAROL FINCH

APACHE WIND

ZEBRA BOOKS
KENSINGTON PUBLISHING CORP.

ZEBRA BOOKS are published by

Kensington Publishing Corp.
475 Park Avenue South
New York, NY 10016

First Printing: November, 1993

Printed in the United States of America

This book is dedicated to my husband, Ed, and our children, Christie, Jill, and Kurt, with much love . . .

And to Rebecca Wik, a very special lady whose friendship I treasure. Thanks for everything, Rebecca!

One

El Paso, Texas

Sunlight, like outstretched fingers, inched through the inky darkness, casting shards of gold against the shadows on the crumbling adobe walls of the jail cell. Cord MacIntosh shifted on his rickety cot. The creak of wood echoed in the silence. Cord greeted the dawning of a new day with a sour scowl. He came awake with the same cynical thought that had rumbled through his mind all night: *life is hell* . . .

While another bucket of sunbeams poured through the barred window, Cord rolled to his feet to work the kinks from his back. Restlessly, he paced the confines of his dingy prison, cursing fate and all mankind with every step. The creak of the cot in the adjoining cell brought a halt to Cord's pacing. His golden eyes darted to the twelve-inch-thick adobe wall that separated him from the other two prisoners in the cells to his right. Another foul oath fell from Cord's lips when he remembered what day it was—doomsday for the prisoner to his immediate right. Thinking of Dub Wizner's bleak fate, Cord reminded himself that his own life could be worse, though not by much.

"That you, Cord?" came Dub's hoarse voice. "I wondered when you'd wake up." A raspy cough rippled through the musty air. "I never did get to sleep last night."

Cord ambled toward the barred door and craned his neck around the corner. He could see Dub propped on his cot, staring unblinkingly at the ceiling where a black widow spider was tending her web. Cord had never been much of a talker, and he sure as hell didn't know what to say to a man whose hours were numbered. Dub had been tried and convicted of murdering his unfaithful wife and her lover. At ten o'clock this very morning Dub would be ushered to the gallows and . . .

"I still ain't sorry 'bout that bitch," Dub growled and then wheezed to catch his breath. "S'pose I should be, but I ain't."

With noisy effort, Dub heaved himself off his cot and shuffled over to prop his frail body against the bars. Dull, bloodshot eyes shifted to the raven-haired occupant of the adjoining cell.

"I'd rather they woulda shot me where I stood, 'stead of haulin' me to this stinkin' hole to wait the hangman's noose. Waitin' is the worst part. The end will be easier." Dub coughed and sputtered, ending with an audible sigh.

Cord braced his forearms on the bars and stared at the condemned man. Dub's spindly body and hollow eyes testified to his ill health, which hadn't improved under these deplorable conditions. His red-streaked eyes revealed his inability to sleep. Dub wore years of hard living like the lines of a road map—deeply rutted and creased with experience, not all of it good.

"Ya don't know what to say to me, do ya, boy?" Dub chuckled. "Well, I got a few words of advice for ya. So humor me. I don't have much time left."

Cord tucked his own frustrating problems in the

back of his mind and listened, though he wasn't sure the advice of a convicted murderer would do him a helluva lot of good.

"First of all, don't never trust a she-male," Dub lectured in a gravelly voice.

That was nothing new to Cord. He'd had dealings with two-timing women, but he had never cared enough about any female to let it make much difference. Women had only been a means of appeasing physical urges.

"Wimmin were put on this earth to torment us men. They lie, they cheat, and they use them curvy bodies to distract a man from their deceit. Wimmin only got one purpose for us men. Don't you never fall in love and don't waste one smidgen of sentiment on 'em. They'll tear yer heart out. I'm livin' proof of that." Dub raised a quizzical brow and peered around the bars at Cord. "You got one waitin' for ya on the outside, boy?" he rasped.

"No," Cord replied.

"Good. They're nothin' but trouble and don't ya never forgit it. You know damned well what lovin' a faithless bitch did for me."

Cord couldn't quite visualize this feeble, whiskered-faced old man in a blind rage of jealousy—spouting curses and spitting lead at his infidel lover and the man who had been in her bed when Dub returned unexpectedly. Obviously love made a man do rash, crazy things when he found himself betrayed by the one woman he thought he could trust. Since Cord had never become emotionally attached to a woman in all his twenty-eight years, he couldn't fathom what had motivated Dub to do what he'd done. As far as Cord was concerned, no woman was worth facing a hangman's noose.

Dub gasped and sputtered for breath. "You think you know the hunger for revenge after yer dealin's with Victor Watts, don't you? He's a crafty weasel, that one. But you never liked the son-of-a-bitch anyhow, now did you? Imagine how you'd feel if you had once called him friend. Now *that's* betrayal!" Dub broke off into another spasm of gut-wrenching coughs.

"You better save your breath, Dub," Cord quietly advised.

"For what?" Dub asked. "The noose?" He reached through the barred door to pat Cord's muscled forearm. "I'm tryin' to warn you against bein' as foolish 'bout gittin' revenge as me. If you git outta this rat hole and go after Watts, you better plot yer revenge, 'less you wanna follow me to the gallows. You'll wind up back behind bars, waitin' yer bad end, just like me."

"Shut up that yappin', old man," came the gruff voice from the cell just to the right of Dub's. "I can't get no sleep, what with you rattlin' like a damned preacher-man."

Cord glared at the cell door behind which Ellis Flake lay on his cot. Ellis had been wounded during a robbery at one of the stage stations west of Fort Davis. Although the other members of the gang had escaped, Ellis had ended up in jail, awaiting trial. His curt remark and lack of sympathy was his customary reaction to other folks' plight. The man had no respect or consideration for anyone but his bandit friends and himself.

"Aw, shut up yerself, Ellis," Dub flung back at him. "I gotta right to talk if I wanna. After this mornin', you won't have to hear my voice ever again."

Ellis grumbled, swore, and flipped over on his cot, but he clammed up just the same.

"As I was sayin'," Dub continued hoarsely. "Don't go off half-cocked like I did. If you want to even the score with Victor Watts, you gotta outsmart him. You gotta hit him where he hurts the most so he'll come after you. Then you can cut him down and make it legal-like."

Cord had to admit Dub was right. As much as he despised the shrewd *ranchero* who envisioned himself as the reigning baron west of the Pecos, Cord had to be cautious in his dealings with Victor. That scoundrel had seen to it that Cord was rotting in jail, awaiting trial for two tormenting weeks. Knowing Victor, he would find a way to make this trumped-up cattle rustling charge stick. Victor had friends in high places and he greased every political palm that could help him get what he wanted.

The echo of approaching footsteps heralded the arrival of the jailer. Cord muttered under his breath. This stint in jail had been intolerable, and the main reason for his, and the other prisoners', misery was about to make his appearance. Cord had come to hate the cruel guard as much as he detested Victor Watts. The jailer delighted in harassing, ridiculing, and tormenting his prisoners. After years of practice, Juan Tijerina was damned good at it, too. The mere sound of Juan's lumbering footsteps turned Cord's mood pitch-black.

Since Cord's arrival at this converted adobe house that now held four cells, a kitchen, and living quarters for the guard, Juan had goaded him unmercifully. Cord had very nearly been beaten to death before he was dragged to the hellish prison, thanks to Victor's vicious henchman and his army of *vaqueros*. Juan had seen to it that Cord was dealt even more misery.

Cord could almost feel the sting of Juan's whip on his back, feel the helpless frustration of being unable to fight back. Juan thrived on the hatred of the prisoners in his keeping. He teased them, dared them to retaliate, and then struck with his biting whip before tattling to the judge about the prisoners' disrespectful behavior. Now *here* was a bastard in every sense of the word.

The door whined open and Juan Tijerina's rotund frame filled it. His wild, woolly whiskers and rat's nest of hair partially concealed his homely features. The overweight Mexican moseyed inside with his twenty-foot-long bullwhip coiled under one arm. He balanced a breakfast tray in his pudgy hands. A crooked smile stretched across his froglike lips, displaying his lack of teeth. Cord sorely wished he'd have been the one who had knocked them out.

"I brought your last meal, Dub," Juan announced. His beady black eyes twinkled as he plucked up the shriveled grapes that lay beside the slices of stale bread. "Sour grapes for the condemned *gringo* who will soon march to the gallows to be launched into hell."

His scornful gaze slid over the frail older man who didn't appear to have much life left in him, even if he were allowed to die of natural causes.

Since Dub had nothing left to lose, he spit in Juan's mocking sneer. A furious curse curled Juan's lips as he set the tray aside and snapped his whip at the bars. Dub was barely quick enough to remove his hand before he felt the stinging lash. But the cell wasn't large enough for Dub to retreat when Juan thrust his arm through the bars to snap the whip a second time. Dub yelped when a burning sensation seared across his thigh.

Without provocation, Juan turned his attention on Cord who was agile enough to leap sideways to avoid the first assault. But Cord couldn't outrun the far-reaching whip a second time, either. He grimaced when the uncoiling lash bit into his shoulder like a striking rattlesnake.

"That's for cavorting with this *gringo* bastard," Juan snarled at Cord.

"I'll come back to haunt you, I swear to God I

will," Dub hissed as he collapsed on his cot to nurse the throbbing wound and gasp for breath.

Juan laughed at the threat. "You won't meet the Lord where you're going, you old buzzard. I've seen your kind put to death for years and heard those empty vows, but I haven't lost any sleep over the disgusting lot of you. Every time one of you *Americanos* or Indians die, I rejoice. It's what you get for bedding our Mexican women. I didn't blame Consuela for cuckolding you. She was young and poor and she only tolerated you for the security you brought her. But an old goat like you couldn't satisfy a woman like that in bed."

It was then that Cord was allowed to see—firsthand—the kind of murderous fury that must have motivated the ailing man when he turned his gun on his woman and her lover. With a growl that sounded almost inhuman, Dub hurled himself against the bars in an effort to get his hands on Juan. But Juan retreated a pace and burst into ridiculing laughter that invited even more animosity. The jailer had the most uncanny ability to draw the hatred of everyone in the room in record time.

"Save your strength for your stroll to the gallows, *gringo* bastard," Juan sniggered. "The priest and executioner will be here in an hour to take you away." Hurriedly, he scooped up Dub's last meal and tossed it between the bars, as if he were throwing scraps to a starved dog. "Eat your breakfast, Wizner. It's all you'll get before the hangman comes to fetch you."

Cord clenched his fists against his grimy breeches while he watched Juan degrade Dub. Day by day, burning hatred had begun to eat away at Cord like a worm into an apple. Juan constantly goaded Cord until the hatred, mingling with bitter thoughts of Victor Watts's cunning scheme, festered in his mind. Granted, life had never been easy for Cord MacIntosh, but the conditions had deteriorated so much the past two weeks that cynicism and animosity had poisoned what good there was left in him.

Cord knew he could do the world a great favor if he disposed of Juan Tijerina. If ever a man deserved to die for inflicting misery on humankind, it was this diabolical fiend. Juan Tijerina lived to give his prisoners their first taste of hell before the devil got his hands on them.

A wry smile, one of the few that had surfaced on Cord's lips in a fortnight, broke free when Dub scraped his breakfast off the dirt floor and hurled it into Juan's grinning face, leaving the taste of sour grapes on the guard's lips. Dub was expending his failing strength to exact what little revenge he could. Although Cord didn't approve of the crimes that had sentenced Dub to doom, he felt a certain affinity toward the sickly old man.

"You think this is funny, MacIntosh?" Juan jeered as he wiped away the food and glared in Cord's direction. "Maybe you should join your friend on the gallows this morning. The carpenters finished the spectators' stands last night so all of El Paso can watch this puny bastard swing. I'd like to see all you *Americanos* at a grand necktie party. And we'll send Ellis Flake out with you." He flung a mocking glance toward the far cell.

Ellis said nothing to provoke the guard, at least nothing Juan could hear. It was as if Ellis were trying to remain on good behavior in the guard's presence, biding his time, refusing to pick up the gauntlet and invite this fiend's wrath.

With a satanic smile Juan reached into the shirt pocket beneath the bandoleer that was strapped diagonally across his thick chest. Triumphantly, he waved an opened letter with Cord's name on it. "If you want your mail, half-breed *gringo*, you'll have to be nice to me."

Cord would have preferred to shoot himself in the

foot first. Juan inspired mutinous thoughts, not nice ones.

"It's about your papa," Juan said, purposely antagonizing him. "Haven't you wondered why the old codger hasn't been to see you since you were hauled in here?" Another taunting grin hovered on his thin lips. "Would you like to get your filthy hands on this letter, half-breed?"

What Cord wanted most was to get his hands on Juan's stubby neck. His tawny eyes raked Juan like sharp talons as he reached through the bars to retrieve the letter that dangled in front of him. Before Cord could grab the envelope, Juan snatched it out of his reach.

"Not so fast, MacIntosh," Juan said. "I have much else to tell you before you read the message, if you can even read at all. Being a half-breed bastard, you probably can't. Dumb Indian squaws and stupid *Americanos* sire only half-witted imbeciles."

"Get to the point, Juan," Cord managed to say without snarling.

"I thought you would want to know what Victor Watts has been up to since you've been rotting away in jail," Juan continued with a nasty grin. "You'll be pleased to hear that he's found himself a beautiful fiancée who can bring more wealth and prestige to his growing empire. Why, he's such a clever man that I can almost forgive him for being a *gringo*. He thinks like a Mexican instead of an ignorant *Americano*."

It was standard procedure for Juan to stab a knife in a man's back and then give it a few painful twists. Juan delighted in praising his race as superior and flaunting his power over his prisoners. Why, the scoundrel probably stayed up nights, inventing new ways to physically and mentally abuse his defenseless victims.

"While you grow skinny on prison rations, Victor is wining, dining, and wooing the daughter of a wealthy cattleman. Of course, you will have the chance to see the lovely lady at your trial. By then Victor will have taken many pleasures with his woman and you will be left without a soft, willing body to appease you. You will be rolling with the bedbugs while Victor takes his bride—again and again—at his leisure."

Juan certainly knew which strings to pull to make Cord hot under the collar. Victor was getting himself engaged and making plans to increase his wealth while Cord was locked behind bars, awaiting a trial—an *un*fair trial, if Victor had anything to do with it. That son of a bitch was as corrupt as they came.

"*Si*, the lady is a beauty by anyone's standards," Juan declared as he tossed Cord's meal to him in the same manner he'd flung Dub's. "I wouldn't mind spreading that female beneath me, even if she is a *gringa*. She would suit my purpose well enough." He shrugged carelessly. "But I have my own willing women, plenty of them. And you have none, half-breed. Victor Watts will not only have a prize piece of fluff, but soon he will also have everything that once belonged to you."

The baiting remark caused Cord to frown warily. He extended his hand for the letter, tired of the jailer's tormenting games, but Juan wasn't finished. He held the letter at arm's length and grinned wickedly.

"Patience, half-breed. There's more," Juan assured him. "Victor's fiancée has arrived at the hacienda to visit him. They're planning a grand *fandango* tonight. The whole community is invited, except for you, of course . . . and Dub. He will be good and dead by then."

"The letter," Cord demanded through clenched teeth. "Give it to me."

Juan snapped his bullwhip through the bars to

slash Cord's outstretched hand. When Cord flinched and instinctively recoiled, Juan guffawed.

"That will teach you some manners. Say *please,* or you will get nothing from me."

Cord would have cut out his tongue before he begged this oversized gorilla. *Caramba!* How he despised this brute who had allowed the power of his position to go to his head.

"Remember what I told you, Cord," Dub wheezed as he grabbed the bars for support. "You have time for revenge, but I don't. And when you have yer chance to repay this fat Mexican, you can give him hell for *me,* too."

Dub had purposely invited Juan's fury before Cord's temper snapped. When the growling guard rounded on the feeble old man, Cord struggled for hard-won composure. He winced at the bark of the whip and Dub's howl of pain. When Juan again wheeled on him, Cord snatched up his cot to deflect the oncoming attack.

"You want to know what's in this letter, half-breed? Then I will tell you in case you are too stupid to make out the words. Your papa is dead and gone," Juan said cruelly. "With any luck, you will join him in hell very soon."

The words cut deeper than Juan's skin-splitting whip. Cord dropped the cot and focused his gaze on the grinning guard.

"You don't believe me, half-breed?" Juan taunted. He waved the letter at Cord as he neared the bars of the cell. "It's all here in black and white . . ."

It was a gross oversight on Juan's part to think that Cord had lunged with tigerish agility only to retrieve the letter. Something inside Cord had snapped like a brittle twig. The news of his father's death stripped away what was civilized in him. He was lashing out at all life's injustices to quell the fury and grief that rumbled inside him. Instead of grabbing the letter as Juan anticipated, Cord's hands shot through the bars to put a stranglehold on Juan's stubby neck. The guard was too busy holding the letter out of reach to realize Cord's intent until it was too late. Before Juan could react, Cord jerked his head against the iron bars with a neck-wrenching jolt. Juan yelped when his forehead slammed against the unyielding metal a second and third time.

A muffled groan escaped the guard's lips as he teetered sideways and crashed to the floor in a motionless heap. Cord didn't regret hammering some manners into that brutal blackguard, not for one second. With lithe agility, he hunkered down to retrieve the pistol strapped to Juan's chest and yank the keys from his belt.

"Shoot that son-of-a-bitch while you have the chance," Dub demanded as he strained against the bars to watch the goings-on.

Cord did not respond, nor did he comply with the hoarse command. Hurriedly, he stuffed the key in the lock and let himself out of the cell. Still, Juan hadn't moved a muscle. He lay with the lower portion of his body sprawled in front of Cord's cell and his head and chest fronting Dub's small cubicle. Scowling, Dub kicked the fallen guard in the chin and cursed him.

When Cord stepped around Juan's limp body to free Dub, the older man raised an arm to forestall him. "You have to go without me. I'll only slow you down and you damned well know it."

"And you know what awaits you if you stay," Cord muttered before glancing at the door that led to freedom. With his luck, Dub's executioner would arrive any second.

"I've got nowhere to go and nothin' to live for, boy," Dub reminded him with a wheezy whisper. "My heart would give out if I made a mad dash for freedom with you. Now get the hell outta here while ya still can."

When Cord hesitated, Dub shooed him on his way. "I said *git!*"

Cord tucked the pistol in the band of his breeches and darted toward the door. He paused momentarily to glance at Ellis Flake, who was still lounging on his cot. The bandito seemed oddly content to remain where he was and more annoyed than relieved that Cord had managed to escape.

"You heard the old buzzard," Ellis snapped. "Get going. I got plans of my own and they wouldn't have included you. Now vamoose before you cause me more trouble than you already have."

Cord didn't spare the time to puzzle out Ellis's cryptic remark. His attention swung to the partially opened door that led into the kitchen. Hoping to bypass a confrontation, he inched toward Juan's living quarters. He zigzagged around the strewn whiskey bottles that formed a maze on the floor and then eased open the window. As Cord slid a hip over the ledge, his thoughts turned back to Dub, who had refused to prolong his life. Yet, the words Dub had spoken early that morning echoed in Cord's mind as he disappeared into the shadows of the sleepy community beside the Rio Grande River. *Never, ever trust a woman.* That was Dub's first piece of advice. *Plot your revenge, lest the sweet taste of satisfaction turns bitter and recoils upon you.*

Mulling over the information Juan had supplied, Cord considered his ongoing feud with Victor Watts. This time Victor had gone too far. Even when Cord took time to read the letter notifying him of his father's untimely death, he knew Victor was somehow involved. Victor had found a way to remove the second obstacle that stood between him and what he wanted. He had conveniently locked Cord away in jail while he disposed of Paddy MacIntosh. But now that Cord was free he vowed to repay Victor tenfold for all the torment, frustration, and this last infuriating injustice!

With a curse, Cord allowed the loss of his father to hit him full force. Suddenly, he became a man burning with vengeance. Life had always been difficult. Being a half-breed certainly hadn't opened any doors for him. To make matters worse, Victor had branded Paddy MacIntosh a dim-witted, good-for-nothing drifter who lacked integrity and respectability. Thanks to Victor's vicious rumors and damaging gossip, Paddy had become the laughingstock of the surrounding area, and Cord had been labeled a traitor and a scoundrel.

Victor was definitely shrewd with his plots. He had made certain he had discredited father and son before he moved in to take what belonged to the MacIntoshes. Victor may have thought he was about to have it all, but Cord had other plans for that conniving vermin. Cord intended to take Dub Wizner's advice and hit Victor where he hurt the most. Now Cord had only one mission in life—to avenge his father's senseless death, even if it was the last thing he ever did!

Dub Wizner was mulling over similar thoughts while he stared down at the toad of a guard who hadn't stirred since Cord had slammed him into the cell door. Dub surveyed the situation, then squatted behind the bars that separated him from Juan Tijerina. When Juan emitted a quiet moan, Dub scowled to himself. Quickly, he thrust his bony arms through the bars and clutched the bullwhip that had become Juan's trademark. With long-awaited anticipation, Dub coiled the whip around Juan's thick neck and tugged with all his might. When Juan choked, gasped for breath, and made a dazed effort to loose the coil around his windpipe, Dub put the finishing touches on his last revenge.

"I'll see *you* in hell, bastard," Dub wheezed before he pulled himself to his feet and stumbled toward his cot. But Dub never made it to his rickety bed. An unexpected twist of fate spared him from the gallows. Dub sucked air as his heart gave an explosive lurch. The old man collapsed on the floor, clutching at his chest, cursing the untimely attack. He died without having the chance to confide that it was *he* who had choked the life out of his malicious jailer, not Cord MacIntosh. Those were to have been Dub's last words as he stood on the gallows, waiting to meet his destiny.

"You okay, old man?" Ellis Flake questioned, still annoyed by the incident that had interrupted his own plans for escape. "Wizner, damn you, answer me!"

He was met with deathly silence.

"Well, hell's bells, you old goat. If you gave into that heart condition, you'll mess everything up!"

Ellis craned his neck around the bars to see Juan sprawled faceup on the floor, the whip around his neck. But the thick adobe wall that separated him from Dub Wizner prevented him from seeing the weather-beaten old man who lay facedown in his cell. Ellis had purposely refrained from rising from his cot during the struggle between Cord and Juan. He wanted no part of the commotion that could foil his escape attempt. But if Dub Wizner had collapsed, never to rise again, it was sure as hell going to throw a wrench in his scheme!

Cursing in Spanish and then in English, Ellis peeled off his shirt and waved it like a flag through the barred window. That done, he plunked back on his cot and stewed about his own future, or lack thereof. Dub Wizner was supposed to march to the gallows where the whole town awaited the hanging. Now there would be nothing but chaos!

"Hell's fire, a man can count on nothing in these parts," Ellis muttered.

With that disturbing thought, Ellis massaged his wounded arm and hoped everything would still turn out to his best interests. He sure as hell didn't want to end up like Dub Wizner and Juan Tijerina! They were accompanying each other to hell!

Two

Tempest Litchfield jerked back on the reins and brought her rented buggy to a halt in front of the grand hacienda. The sprawling mansion was surrounded by a well-tended bunkhouse and barn, plus several whitewashed outbuildings. Her astute gaze circled the countryside, surveying the purple hue of the mountains that skirted the peaceful valley. With a troubled sigh, Tempest clutched the hem of her gown and clambered from her perch. Since her exhausting five-hundred-mile journey from San Antonio to El Paso by stage, she seemed to have run into one obstacle after another. She'd had very little sleep the past few days, and the lack of rest had made her irritable. Her muscles ached and she felt a steady thump hammering at her brain.

After checking the gold timepiece her father had given her, Tempest sighed. "This trip is turning out to be an utter waste of time," she muttered as she headed toward the vine-covered veranda.

Her father, Judge Abraham Litchfield, had sent her on a wild-goose chase. *Well, I suppose I did ask for this,* Tempest amended. She had volunteered to take this legal case. Case? There was no case, no need for legal counsel. And just *when,* she asked herself, had there been a need for her legal skills of late? There had been scant few clients who were all that thrilled to learn they were to be represented by a lady lawyer. It was infuriating to be educated up to her ears without being allowed to pursue a successful career.

Since she had hung out her shingle, most folks had shied away from her because she was a woman. She had become the poor man's salvation, thanks to her narrow-minded colleagues and the antiquated beliefs of most of the citizens of San Antonio.

Her father supported her, and that usually brought her more ridicule because she was the district court judge's daughter. It had been difficult enough to obtain her law degree, even after she had graduated from Keachi College *magna cum laude.* The male attorneys she'd met in San Antonio and the surrounding area assured themselves that the only reason she had passed her bar examination and was allowed to practice in a court of law was because of her father. Not one pompous male attorney had given her credit for having the intelligence to enter a profession that had once been considered off limits to women. She easily understood the frustration Clara Foltz endured in her crusade to be admitted to the California bar.

Her thoughts screeched to a halt when a tall, sturdy man of thirty answered her knock on the door. Rumpled though she was after her rugged overland journey, Tempest combed her hand through the mass of wind-blown chestnut hair and drew herself up to a dignified stature.

"I'm looking for Victor Watts," she announced, mustering a polite smile.

Victor's green eyes made a quick appraisal of the shapely beauty. "You have found him, my dear," he purred with a suave smile.

Tempest had tolerated those probing stares dozens of times before. Men had an annoying knack of staring in a degrading way that inched beneath one's clothing to visualize and speculate.

The typical male response, she thought cynically. Men could never look a woman squarely in the eye without making a deliberate tour of her body first. Just once before she fluttered off to the pearly gates she would like a man to acknowledge her intellect instead of her figure. It certainly wasn't her fault that Mother Nature had been so generous. Tempest would have been perfectly content to settle for less. But men, she concluded, were more interested in a woman's body than her brains and that would never change. That was the one mistake the Lord had made.

"Won't you come in, my dear?" Victor invited with a gracious bow and an expansive sweep of his hand.

Tilting her dark head and lifting her chin, Tempest accepted the offer and breezed inside. Her quick inspection of the tiled foyer and walnut-paneled rooms that veered off to the left and right indicated that Victor Watts was a man of wealth and position. Her father's home in San Antonio was just as resplendent but not as spacious as this monstrosity beside the river.

"Victor?"

Tempest spun about to see a petite, timid-looking young woman emerge from the parlor.

Assuming an air of manly devotion, Victor scurried to the young girl's side to clasp her hand in his own. "We have a guest, my darling," he cooed. "May I introduce my fiancée, Annette Partridge. Her father owns the Sun Ranch near Eagle Mountain."

And Victor had given Tempest *that* look when he met her at the door? A woman couldn't trust any of them, Tempest thought. Unless she had misread Victor's intense perusal a moment earlier, he wasn't as devoted to his young fiancée as Annette was being led to believe. Given a month of wedlock, Tempest predicted, this rake would suffer from the inborn ailment that plagued the male population—roving eye.

Stop being such a cynic, Tempest chided herself as she checked her timepiece for the third time in ten minutes. Who was she to criticize this stranger? She had come in search of information, not to sit in judgment. Victor's personal life was not the issue . . . or was it?

"Forgive my interruption," she began. "I am Tempest Litchfield and I—"

"Judge Litchfield's daughter from San Antonio," Victor croaked. "*That* Litchfield?"

"Yes, that Litchfield," Tempest assured him. "I was sent to El Paso to speak with my client, Paddy MacIntosh. But upon my arrival, I was informed that he is deceased."

"*Your* client?" Victor stared frog-eyed at the undeniably attractive female. "I must say, I wouldn't have thought it."

Tempest overlooked the customary reaction to her chosen profession and tried to cut straight to the heart of the matter. But the dainty blonde clasped her hands in delight.

"A lady lawyer! I think that's wonderful," Annette piped up and then piped down when Victor flung her a disapproving glance. She lowered her eyes and the volume of her voice. "I am very impressed, Miss Litchfield."

"Thank you," Tempest replied, then focused on Victor. "I was told by the ticket agent at the stage depot that I should consult you about my client."

Tempest watched Victor press a devoted kiss to his fiancée's forehead before he steered her into the parlor. After he had seated Annette, he ushered Tempest into the room.

"Sit down, Miss Litchfield," Victor requested. "I'll have my servants bring refreshments while we discuss the matter," he added, reaching for the bell pull.

Tempest had been sitting in cramped spaces for days on end, bumping along the rough roads that carried her to the state's furthermost outpost of civilization. The last thing she wanted to do was sit, but she sat nonetheless.

"It is good that you came to me first," Victor said as he handed her and Annette their cups of tea. "I can save you a great deal of time and frustration."

That would indeed be nice, thought Tempest.

Victor flipped the coattails of his expensive jacket aside and sank down on the sofa. "The case that you have the misfortune of undertaking would be a waste of your talents, I'm sure."

He was patronizing her, and Tempest hated it. Men always had a way of speaking that indicated they thought themselves the superior gender. Hogwash!

"I must assume that Patrick MacIntosh tried to acquire assistance for his disreputable malcontent of a son because no respectable lawyer in El Paso would agree to defend that cattle thief—"

"*Alleged* cattle thief," Tempest corrected him.

"Cord MacIntosh was practically caught red-handed by my bravos," Victor declared emphatically. "He was riding herd over his father's cattle when my men went in search of our missing calves. The fresh brand that had been seared over my own brand was evidence enough."

Tempest reserved comment. She merely listened to Victor's explanation. If she did decide to take the MacIntosh case, it would be to her advantage to hear both sides of the story.

"Perhaps I should begin at the beginning," Victor suggested as he eased back to sip his brandy. "Paddy MacIntosh was not what one could call an upstanding citizen, not by any means. He was a rudderless drifter, a dreamer. He was a man whom most folks in the area considered a little crazy, in fact. For years he wandered hither and yon, prospecting and taking jobs as a horse wrangler at various stage stations along the route to San Antonio."

Tempest remembered that her father had mentioned meeting Patrick MacIntosh at a stage station more than a decade earlier. According to Abraham Litchfield, the way station had been attacked by a gang of Mexican bandits, and Patrick had saved the judge's life by knocking him aside before the bullet with his name on it found its mark. Abraham had felt himself indebted and he had insisted that Patrick let him know if ever there was anything he could do for him. Twelve years later, a letter had arrived, requesting Abraham's legal assistance in El Paso. Since the judge had been up to his neck in pending court cases, Tempest had volunteered to investigate the case, about which Patrick had said very little in his message, and now he was gone and Tempest was left to flounder around until she learned what Patrick MacIntosh had wanted.

"Somehow, Paddy stumbled onto a cache of gold, or so he would like everyone to think," Victor continued. "Some folks think he stole it since he was so familiar with the stage schedules."

"You included, Mister Watts?" Tempest asked.

"Me included," Victor admitted. "The man was worthless and so is his renegade son. Paddy had found himself an Apache squaw in the Delaware Mountains and together they sired a son. That should tell you something about Paddy's integrity and pride. Cord is no better than his father. The half-breed is restless, sneaky as an Indian, a born drifter who takes advantage of everyone else to get ahead in this world."

Victor scooped up a plate of pastries and offered

them to Tempest and Annette. Tempest eagerly accepted the nourishment.

"Cord MacIntosh was also a traitor to the Confederacy," Victor declared. "He joined the South at the beginning of the war, much to everyone's surprise. He is the kind of man who only looks out for himself—it stunned all of us to know he had any patriotic tendencies. Cord was captured and taken prisoner in Louisiana. When President Lincoln issued the proclamation that all Southern prisoners who wished to join the Union could take assignments with the Army of the West to battle Indians, Cord quickly enlisted. And until he was dishonorably discharged, he rode as a scout with a cavalry unit in New Mexico Territory, fighting his own kind! That in itself should give you some indication of the man's integrity!" With a disgruntled sigh, Victor continued. "He betrayed his fellow Texans to save himself from the prisoner of war camp and then he turned against his mother's people."

Tempest was sorry to say that Cord MacIntosh did not sound like the kind of man she preferred to represent in a court of law. To turn one's back on the South and join the enemy didn't say much for his character. And then to take arms against his mother's people? Cord did sound as if he were a scoundrel of the worst sort. He seemed nothing more than a mercenary, out to save his own hide and cheat everyone he could along the way.

Victor chased his mouthful of pastry with a drink, cleared his throat, and plowed on. "While Cord was off fighting Indians in New Mexico with General Carleton and Kit Carson, Paddy MacIntosh was buying up land with his ill-gotten gains—probably the gold nuggets from a stolen Wells Fargo strongbox," he added in speculation. "Since there were so few of us to ride herd over the hundreds of cattle left unattended during the war, Paddy gathered mavericks and claimed them as his own. I'm sure Cord learned his nefarious profession of cattle thieving from his father."

"You did not fight for the South, I take it," Tempest interjected.

Victor looked uncomfortable and apologetic as he toyed with the cuffs of his white linen shirt. "My father was gravely ill at the time and this vast ranch on the Rio Grande demanded my attention. I was a devoted patriot of the South, rest assured. But I could not leave my father, fearing I would never see him again. His crippling illness took him several years ago."

"I'm sorry," Tempest murmured.

"So was I," Victor replied. "I had the utmost respect for my father. He carved this ranch out of this lawless land. To join the forces of the South was to turn my back on his lifelong dream. I stayed to hold the ranch together. When Lieutenant Colonel John Baylor and the battalion of Texas Mounted Rifles rode through here on their way to New Mexico to attack Fort Fillman, I provided supplies and meat for our brave soldiers."

Victor smiled apologetically. "Forgive me. I have digressed. It is your would-be client who concerns you."

"I would still like to meet Cord MacIntosh," Tempest insisted.

Victor took one look at the stunning chestnut-haired woman and chuckled at the ridiculous idea of Cord MacIntosh and Tempest Litchfield standing side by side in a courtroom. They would make a most conspicuous pair with her eye-catching beauty and his wild, untamed savagery.

"I promise you that you will be uncomfortable in his presence and most hesitant to take his case, my dear lady. He is rude, surly, disrespectful, and as wild as the Apaches who raised him. But if you insist on defending that heathen, you will have to venture to the jail where he has been locked up since the cattle rustling incident. I strongly suggest that you decline the case. A man who refuses to live by any set of rules does not deserve your valuable time and effort—"

His voice dried up when a dusty, hard-bitten *vaquero* lunged through the front door, urgently calling Victor's name.

Tempest frowned when Victor stepped into the vestibule to listen to the stocky Mexican with harsh leathery features and a noticeable scar on his left cheek. She had no idea who the man was, but from the looks of him, he had led a hard life. His appearance was without redeeming virtue. His shaggy black mane was sorely in need of clipping; his full lips naturally turned down at the corners and Tempest wondered if the man hadn't contributed to the problem by never bothering to smile.

"What!" Victor exclaimed when Emilio Reynosa delivered his news. "When did this happen?" With a scowl and a muttered curse, Victor latched onto Emilio's arm and towed him into his private office.

"Cord MacIntosh escaped from jail this morning," Emilio repeated. "He killed Juan Tijerina by strangling him with his own bullwhip. When the priest and executioner arrived to take the condemned prisoner to the gallows, Dub Wizner was found dead in his cell and MacIntosh was nowhere to be seen. And while the citizens of El Paso were scouring the area, a band of thieves broke Ellis Flake out of jail. They robbed the bank on their way out of town."

"Damn," Victor swore vehemently. "Gather as many men as you can and meet me at the front gate. MacIntosh can't have gotten far."

The seasoned *vaquero* raised a thick brow and smirked at his employer. "No, señor? He is as slippery as a rattlesnake in molting season. He can be out of his skin and gone before anyone can catch him. I dealt with him once before, and I can tell you his abilities are not to be taken lightly." He called Victor's attention to the scar on his cheek, obtained when Cord lashed out in defense of the beatings he'd received to break his spirit. "I should have killed him when I had the chance, instead of dragging him to jail. MacIntosh is cunning and clever. There is a very good reason why the Apache call him *Lobo Plano*. Silver Wolf can move like streak lightning and he strikes with the same intensity."

"You managed to capture him with my herd of cattle, didn't you?" Victor reminded him.

"We took him unaware," Emilio clarified. "But now *Lobo Plano* knows he is a hunted man. He will make a most difficult prey."

"Just gather a posse of your most competent *vaqueros*, Emilio," Victor demanded irritably. "There's a murdering rustler on the loose."

While the Mexican scurried away, Victor composed himself and stared at the door that led to the parlor. He wasn't sure he wanted to inform the lady lawyer that her client had escaped from jail, though Victor wouldn't mind telling her that the charge had gone from rustling to cold-blooded murder. But Victor sensed a certain something about this confident female. She was the kind who would protest if the posse captured and lynched MacIntosh on the spot.

No, Victor decided. There was a different brand of law west of the Pecos—the kind this citified female attorney knew nothing about. Her interference would hamper frontier justice. Damn it, Cord MacIntosh should have been hanged already. The man was a nuisance. The less Tempest Litchfield knew, the better!

Tempest glanced up from her third helping of pastry when Victor reappeared at the door.

"There is an urgent matter I must attend to, Miss Litchfield," he announced in his politest tone. "Since you have traveled so far, I am offering my home for your rest and leisure."

He didn't want her tramping around El Paso where she could get wind of this manhunt. Here, Tempest would cause him no trouble or interference.

"I'll have one of my servants fetch your luggage and Annette can show you to a room to rest until I return."

"But—" Tempest tried to protest through her mouthful of pastry.

"I insist." Victor flung up a hand in a deterring gesture. "Please accept my hospitality. My fiancée and I are entertaining guests this evening and we would be pleased if you joined us, wouldn't we, Annette?"

"Oh yes," the younger woman replied. "I would love to hear what it takes for a woman to make a place for herself as you have done."

"Then it's settled," Victor said with a confirming nod. Hurriedly, he turned around and strode off.

Reluctantly, Tempest followed Annette upstairs. It would be best if she sought out her client and made her own decision about defending him. But when Tempest was shown into the spacious room that reminded her of the luxuries of home, she relented. She would feel much better if she washed away the trail dust and changed into clean clothes before venturing back to town. After all, a bath would come as a welcome relief after this tedious journey—one she had probably made for nothing.

From the sound of things, her father's attempt to repay a long-standing debt was ill-advised. A frown knitted Tempest's brow. Now that she thought about it, Victor never had said exactly what had happened to Paddy MacIntosh. She would have to remember to quiz him on the events surrounding the man's death. Her father would want all the details and her own insatiable curiosity would demand satisfactory answers.

Setting the conversation with Victor Watts aside, Tempest eased back into the tub and sighed with pleasure. Ah, this was exactly what she needed—the chance to relax and rejuvenate. Soap in hand, she scrubbed away the dirt that five hundred miles of traveling had left on her. Tempest wasn't sure when she'd enjoyed a bath quite so much. And this particular bath seemed to smooth the wrinkles from her soul after Victor Watts had painted a dark, sinister picture of Cord MacIntosh. It also did wonders for her aching muscles.

Tempest was torn between a professional and personal obligation, and the instinctive need to let the surly renegade defend himself against his crimes. Any man who turned his back on the South and took arms against his own kind could not possibly have any scruples. Tempest had the uneasy feeling that cattle rustling probably wasn't the only crime Cord MacIntosh had committed, even if it was the only one he'd been caught at. There was no telling how many offenses he had to his credit. Although Tempest had yet to meet the rapscallion she might eventually feel obligated to defend in court, she didn't like the man. And that was a shame, since she might be the only one who stood between that half-breed desperado and the hangman's noose!

Three

Cord MacIntosh pulled the wide-brimmed sombrero down on his forehead and straightened the concealing *sarape* he had confiscated from the evacuated bunkhouse at Victor Watts's *rancho*. Cautiously, he skulked toward the vine-choked lattice that led to the second-story of the hacienda. Cord had taken Dub Wizner's advice and carefully plotted his revenge. As Dub had suggested, Cord intended to hit Victor where it would hurt the most: he planned to take Victor's newest prize—his fiancée—for bargaining power.

According to Juan Tijerina, the greedy *ranchero* had set his sights on a wealthy female whose family could contribute to the empire Victor was trying to amass west of the Pecos. Not only would Cord kidnap the prissy little bitch Victor planned to wed, but he would embarrass and humiliate the pompous rancher. Victor would look the fool to his fiancée's family if she were stolen right out from under his nose.

Cord eased over the wrought iron railing and moved along the upper gallery like a fleeting shadow. Very soon, he would have Victor's fiancée in his custody and the grand *fandango* that was to be held this evening would become a disaster . . .

Cord's legs froze beneath him when he glanced through the glass door of the bedroom to see a vision of pure loveliness lounging in her porcelain tub. The midday sunlight sprayed through the chamber, bathing the gorgeous female in sparkling sunbeams. Skin the color of peaches and cream glistened with water droplets. The glorious mane of chestnut hair cascaded over bare shoulders in a wild tangle of curls, the thick mass seeming to catch fire and burn in the light.

The tantalizing sight struck Cord like a physical blow and he soundly cursed Victor's good fortune. Victor's fiancée was a veritable goddess! *Caramba!* The man did have the devil's luck. That bastard didn't deserve such a woman as this—beautiful and wealthy to boot!

Bitter and begrudging though Cord was, his hungry eyes absorbed the sight of this beguiling mermaid in her sunlit pool. Although he had stopped beside the river to bathe after enduring the unsanitary conditions at the jail, he was tempted to rip off his clothes and join this delicious morsel in her tub. If he hadn't been pressed for time, he might have yielded to such temptation, but he couldn't afford to linger at the hacienda a moment longer than necessary, lest he find himself dangling from a nearby tree.

Cord crept toward the partially open door. Noiselessly, he engulfed himself in the velvet draperies that hung just inside the terrace. Cord was thoroughly disgusted with himself for ogling this enchanting female like a love-starved schoolboy. And he was incensed that a scoundrel like Victor had convinced such a breathtaking nymph to marry him. But despite his irritation, and his need to abduct this woman and get the hell out of there—pronto—Cord longed to enjoy the pleasures a woman like this one could give. After all, a man was entitled to a few fantasies, wasn't he? Cord ached to stroke her satiny skin, to lose himself in the softness of her curvaceous . . .

What the blazes was wrong with him? Cord cursed himself soundly. He'd sneaked in here to take a captive. He wasn't here to rape and plunder, though the idea did have a certain animalistic appeal. All he wanted was to mete out punishment to Victor Watts, he reminded himself. Nothing more.

Clinging to that thought, Cord crouched in the drapes, prepared to pounce on his unsuspecting prey. Willfully, he dragged his eyes from the titillating sight to survey the room, noting the satchels on the end of the bed. As amusing as it would be to tote Lady Godiva off, just as she was, Cord knew his captive would have to have something to wear. She would attract too much attention if he took her with him as she was.

With her back to the terrace doors, unaware there was a man concealed in the drapes, Tempest rose from the tub and wrapped the fluffy towel around her.

Cord's heart slammed against his ribs and stuck there. He found himself gawking at five feet, two inches and one hundred and ten pounds of feminine perfection.

Tempest padded across the room, pushing wet strands of hair from her eyes as she went. She had just bent over the bed to pluck up fresh clothing when a body slammed against her, sending her sprawling facedown on the satin bedspread. When her assailant's body rammed against hers it was like being pinned beneath falling rock. Before Tempest could scream, a callused hand clamped over her mouth and lean hips straddled hers, holding her in place.

Like a wild bird, Tempest fought for freedom. A steely arm clamped around her waist, effectively restraining her. Before her terrified mind could conjure up an alternative method of freeing herself, the muscular giant took her lacy chemise and used it as a gag. Tempest found herself shoved to her back, unable to clutch at the sagging towel that barely concealed her breasts from this vile monster's gaze.

When Cord stared at his captive's enchanting face from point-blank range, he found himself cursing Victor a second time. Not only did this female have the body of a goddess but also the flawless face of an angel. Eyes as clear and blue as a mountain stream peered up at him. Those bright, intelligent pools were surrounded with a fan of dark lashes. To say this naked nymph was pretty was a gross understatement—she was the loveliest female Cord had ever seen. She was older than he had imagined, however, no babe in arms. She looked to be twenty-three or four, certainly old enough to know better than to tie her apron strings to a man like Victor Watts. Unless, of course, they were both cut from the same greedy scrap of rotting cloth, Cord amended. He also reminded himself that Victor could be suave and debonair when he wanted to be. Obviously he had poured on the charm to convince this shapely bundle to marry him.

Tempest lay like a block of ice, struggling to compose herself and shocked by the dark, bearded face that loomed above her. Eyes that sparkled like gold nuggets in sunlight bore down on her while the man effortlessly kept her plastered to the bed. A sombrero was set low on his forehead, hair as black as sin protruding beneath it. A colorful *sarape* covered the broad expanse of his chest and shoulders, but Tempest was starkly aware of the bulging muscles the garment concealed. Her wrestling match with this looming giant convinced her of his ominous strength and lightning-quick agility.

The man looked fierce and uncivilized, which he obviously was. There was a stamp of wild nobility in the angular lines of his face and a reckless daring in those tawny eyes. There was also an infuriating grin of male superiority, and Tempest hated that look as much as she detested being held down by this darkly handsome devil. She despised being restrained physically or intellectually and she was experiencing outrage as well as fear.

No doubt this was one of Victor's less-than-respectable hired hands who had sneaked in to molest and humiliate her while the master of the house was away on business. Did this lusty dragon think she would be too ashamed to point an accusing finger at him when Victor returned? Tempest vowed to drag this scoundrel to court and see that he received the kind of punishment he deserved!

To Tempest's amazement, her captor didn't yank her towel away and ravish her on the spot. Holding both her arms over her head with one hand, he fished into her satchel and randomly selected a gown. It happened to be one of her less expensive muslin gowns, which obviously indicated his lack of good taste. Hastily, her captor snatched up the garment and dropped it over her barely concealed bosom.

"Put it on and be quick about it," Cord ordered gruffly.

The rumbling threat in that deep baritone voice demanded no argument. But embarrassment and the inability to don the garment without exposing herself prevented Tempest from worming into the gown as quickly as Cord thought she should have. Growling like an ill-tempered tiger, Cord released his vise-like grip on her arm and roughly jerked the dress over the wild tangle of chestnut hair. His hand accidentally brushed against her breasts as he maneuvered the garment over her rigid body. A muffled shriek vibrated through the gag that covered Tempest's mouth and Cord forced himself not to dwell on the feel of her flesh beneath his fingertips. He had no time to dawdle.

Tempest had never been so outraged in all her twenty-four years. Not only had she never been treated so disrespectfully, but she had never allowed a man's hands to trespass on uncharted territory. Tempest had always prided herself in being in absolute control of situations and of her emotions. Knowing she possessed an explosive temper when she got her hackles up prompted her to attempt to keep her hackles down, and respond in a rational manner. Even so, her temper now came unraveled like a ball of twine on a downhill roll. Her hand instinctively rose to slap the whiskered face above her. Flesh cracked against flesh, startling Cord.

For a half-second Tempest feared he was going to hit her back. She knew it would only take one blow from this powerfully built giant to knock her silly. This was no gentleman, after all. Any man who would sneak into a woman's boudoir and manhandle her had no scruples whatsoever! But this ruggedly handsome demon didn't retaliate. In fact, the faintest hint of a smile quirked his lips.

"A tigress?" Low, husky laughter rumbled in Cord's chest as he jerked Tempest to her feet and yanked the towel away so he could tug her gown down to her ankles. As Cord watched the garment cling to her damp skin in just the right places, Tempest glared at him. "You beast! I will see you lynched for this, I swear I will!"

The spiteful threat lost its effect when it became muffled by the gag, but she felt better for saying it.

Cord snickered at the sassy little wildcat who was not at all like he had anticipated. She was a handful, to be sure. Cord had expected a whimpering, whining female who begged for mercy. Instead he found a hot-tempered, willful hellion who had slapped him for inadvertently touching her and then cursed him from beneath her gag. He had thought his unexpected attack would put the fear of God in this chit. He was obviously wrong. She didn't get scared; she got good and mad. This was no ordinary female and damn her for agreeing to marry a despicable louse like Victor Watts!

Casting his bitter musings aside, Cord tossed Tempest over his shoulder. He hadn't taken time to fasten the stays on the back of her gown, but he had bound her wrists with the pink satin ribbon he'd found in her luggage. In afterthought, he had snatched up her shoes and tucked them in his pocket.

From her jackknifed position over Cord's brawny shoulder, Tempest abandoned any thought of escape when her captor threw a leg over the railing. If she struggled during their precarious descent, she knew they would both fall to their deaths on the lawn below. Tempest found herself discovering a new facet to her character—a fear of falling. Hanging upside down in such a perilous manner stimulated her worst nightmares and she found herself clinging to her captor like a cat digging its claws into tree bark. A terrified gasp escaped her when Cord teetered on the lattice and then regained his balance in the nick of time. Tempest closed her eyes and held on for dear life while Cord skillfully maneuvered down the makeshift ladder despite the extra weight over his shoulder.

Cord landed on solid ground, then jogged toward the bunkhouse. The motion jabbed his shoulder into her hips and forced the air out of her lungs.

The instant he closed the door behind him, he put Tempest on her feet. His keen gaze circled the room for another sombrero and *sarape* to conceal his captive's identity. Since he needed provisions and cash for his cross-country journey, he would be forced to venture back to El Paso. The *vaqueros* who lived in the bunkhouse had very little to offer a desperate man. Cord did, however, confiscate a razor to clear the stubble off his face and change his appearance to avoid being recognized.

In stunned disbelief, Tempest stood amid the row of cots, watching her captor lather his face, then clear a path on his jaw. The man was obviously a lunatic. What the devil did he think he was doing? And what was she doing standing here like an imbecile when she could be making her escape? The thought spurred Tempest into action. She lurched toward the door, only to hear the click of a pistol behind her.

"Take one step, *chica,* and you're dead."

Tempest wheeled around to glower at the towering giant whose left cheek was devoid of whiskers. "I've had just about enough of this," she spat. "If you let me go now, I won't—"

Her mumbled words froze in her throat when a dagger the size of a butcher knife sailed across the room and stuck in the door—six inches above her head. Before she could even think to contort her bound hands, retrieve the knife, and plunge it into his rock-hard heart, Cord was beside her to yank the dagger from the wood and stuff it back in the leather *botas* that extended to his knees.

"Sit down," he ordered in a curt tone that defied argument.

If he expected silent obedience he was disappointed. Tempest tilted her chin and flashed him a glare that burned like flaming kerosene. Cord clasped his hands on her rigid shoulders and shoved her down on the edge of the nearest cot.

"And stay there," he added.

Cord went back to his shaving. When he finished the task, he peeled off his *sarape* and soiled shirt beneath it. His powerful muscles flexed as he reached for another shirt to replace the ragged one he'd been wearing since his stint in that hellhole of a jail.

Despite her distasteful situation, Tempest found her gaze wandering over the broad expanse of Cord's chest, marveling at his muscles and bronzed flesh. Although this scalawag was sorely lacking in manners and personality, he was physically devastating. Tempest wished she hadn't noticed the impressive architecture of his brawny body. He was more man, inch for solid inch, than anyone she'd ever encountered. It was a shame this half-civilized rapscallion had to be so blasted attractive.

Her silent admiration fell by the wayside when her eyes fastened on the red welts that scarred his shoulder and back. It looked as if he had been brutally beaten sometime in the not-too-distant past. She could not begin to imagine how painful those wounds had been. The crisscrossed scars looked as if they had been made by a whip. The man had suffered . . .

A shocked gasp bubbled beneath her gag when Cord reached down to unfasten his breeches.

Cord grinned when he gazed at this tangle-haired imp. Wide luminous eyes peered up at him like sparkling sapphires. He had noticed the woman staring at him when he shucked his shirt. He had also noted the way her gaze wandered over him in begrudging feminine appreciation. He could see the flush of embarrassment working its way up from the base of her throat to the roots of her chestnut hair when she realized his intentions. It was amusing to watch this feisty sprite become rattled by the prospect of seeing a naked man. It had been a long time since Cord had been in the company of such a naive female. Never, in fact, he amended. The women in his past were accustomed to bare flesh and modesty was something he'd almost forgotten about.

"You don't have to look if you don't want to," he teased as he eased the breeches down his hips. "You could look the other way, you know."

That humiliated Tempest all the more. Fuming over the dark, sensual arrogance this rascal wore like a second skin, Tempest jerked her head around so quickly that she almost wrenched her neck. She heard Cord chuckling at her naivete. She ought to swivel around and stare at him, damn his ornery hide! After all, he had watched her bathe and had practically dressed her. She shouldn't give him any satisfaction whatsoever. She shouldn't let him know he rattled, shocked, or frightened her in the least. Intimidation, she reasoned, was a two-way street.

Bracing herself, Tempest swung back around just as Cord's breeches dropped to the floor. He stood before her in all his splendor and glory, six feet, two inches and two hundred pounds of well-honed muscle. Why, this incredibly formed creature could have put a Greek god to shame! He was perfectly proportioned from the top of his raven head to his bare feet, and Tempest would have had to stitch her eyelids shut to keep from gawking at him.

He reminded her of a lithe panther. There wasn't an inch of flab on his sleek body, nothing but corded tendons and hair-roughened flesh. Her gaze slid downward until it focused on . . . Tempest's startled gaze flew back to those golden eyes that were fixed on her flushed face.

"Your feminine curiosity got the best of you, didn't it, *chica?*" he taunted as he donned a pair of *calzoneras* that were a mite too tight to be comfortable *or* decent. "You think we're even now, I suppose. I know all your secrets and you know mine, eh?"

"Go to hell, you ornery lout!" Tempest blustered beneath her gag.

Cord fastened himself into his breeches and cursed the erotic memory that still danced in his head after seeing this luscious beauty lounging in her bath. No doubt he'd carry that image around for a long time to come. He'd seen his share of bare females the past decade, but none of them compared to this one. She was refinement and elegance in the flesh. There were very few women who possessed perfect bodies, but this shapely sprite had one, and a face to match. A man could become hopelessly distracted if he didn't watch his step.

Cord had too much on his mind to become sidetracked—like staying alive, for instance.

When word spread that he had escaped from jail, Cord had accurately second-guessed Victor's reaction. Victor had raced off with every available bravo at his *rancho,* leaving the hacienda vulnerable to a siege. While Victor was scouring El Paso and its sister city of El Paso del Norte on the south bank of the Rio Grande, Cord made a beeline for the ranch.

It hadn't taken Cord long to realize why Ellis Flake had refused to become involved in the fiasco at the jail. Cord had been on his way to confiscate a horse when he saw Ellis waving his shirt through his cell window like a signal flag. Immediately thereafter, five bandits darted into position around the jail. While the executioner and priest spread the news of Cord's jailbreak, the desperadoes freed Ellis, then took advantage of the turmoil and robbed the bank on their way out of town, causing enough disturbance to allow Cord to make his getaway unnoticed.

The only thing Cord didn't know was what had become of Dub Wizner. He only hoped Juan Tijerina wouldn't take his wrath out on the ailing man. Cord had purposely left town before the scheduled hanging. That was one sight he preferred not to see, especially since he would be next in line for the hangman's noose if his plan went awry.

Unaware of Dub's true fate and Juan's death, Cord grabbed his *sarape* and sombrero and hurriedly shrugged them on. After making sure the coast was still clear, he placed a poncho over Tempest's shoulders and slapped an oversize hat on her head, then shepherded her around the bunkhouse to the spot where he'd tethered his horse. When Tempest refused to budge from the spot, Cord glanced at her sharply and frowned.

"This is no time to turn contrary," he scolded. "You're coming with me and that's that. You can fight me or accept your fate, but you're coming with me one way or the other. You got that, princess?"

Tempest would have told him she didn't know how to ride, if only she could have. But as usual, the gag got in her way. She had never thought she needed to learn to ride a horse when a buggy or carriage served her just as well. Despite her lack of equestrian skills, Tempest found herself straddling the sturdy animal while her captor clamped his arms and legs around her to hold her in place.

"If you don't cause me trouble, I'll let you live," Cord bargained as he reined toward the Rio Grande that separated Texas from Mexico.

It was to Cord's advantage that Texas authorities had no legal jurisdiction in Mexico. He could walk the streets of El Paso del Norte without being apprehended by police officials, but was vulnerable to Victor and his vicious henchmen who ignored boundary lines. Victor also had a tendency to make up his own rules as he went along, but Cord followed the same policy himself so he expected no less of his arch enemy.

There was a popular saying in this part of the country when discussing the whereabouts of renegades and fugitives from justice: *He is on the other side*. When a man was wanted by the Mexicans or Texans, he could quickly cross the border of the river to avoid a posse. And that was exactly what Cord planned to do—use the border to his advantage.

By now, Cord predicted, Victor had already searched the huddle of squatty adobe houses wedged between the river and the crumbling face of

Comanche Peak on the American side. Since the town consisted of only a few hundred people, two stage stations, a hotel, several stores, and enough saloons with free-flowing whiskey to drown a horse, Victor would have already made his search. He would also have searched the larger community across the river. Having found no sign of Cord, it wouldn't have taken Victor long to realize Cord wasn't in El Paso. Victor would then send out hunting parties in all directions, except back to the road leading to his own house. That was why Cord had gone to the hacienda first and to El Paso del Norte last. Victor would have come and gone, and there would be no confrontation until Cord was well-armed and ready to negotiate.

Cord's gaze dropped to the curvaceous female imprisoned in his arms. It still infuriated him that such a vivacious, attractive woman would agree to marry a man like Victor. Hell, Cord ought to marry this chit himself, just to spoil Victor's well-laid plans to acquire more wealth. That would really get Victor's goat.

As for this alluring bundle of beauty, Cord was actually doing her a favor. She would be eternally sorry if she married the likes of Victor Watts, and Cord intended to tell her so when he had the chance. In fact, she ought to thank him for abducting her so he could make her see the error of her ways! And for certain, Victor was going to see the error of *his* ways. Cord would make sure of that!

Four

When Cord bundled Tempest down a trash-lined alleyway in El Paso del Norte, she balked at taking another step toward the back door of the cantina. Enough was enough! She was not about to be stashed in some rat-infested storeroom while this scoundrel drank himself insane and then came back to attack her.

Cord muttered at his obstinate captive. "Look, lady, you're going where I say you're going so you might as well get used to the idea. If you keep your mouth shut, you'll be safe from harm."

"Safe from harm?" Tempest scoffed into her gag.

Cord quickly yanked the makeshift gag from her mouth to allow her to speak.

"Safe from harm?" she repeated for his benefit. "That? Coming from vermin like you? Don't make me laugh!"

Tempest knew she was really asking for it, but she was getting more frustrated by the second. Antagonizing this awesome giant was like prodding a coiled rattlesnake. But she would be damned if she stooped to behaving like a typical female who bawled her head off and begged for mercy.

Cord brandished a doubled fist in her face. "Scream and you'll be out cold, you got that? Now, you and I are going to stroll into the saloon and I'm going to invite myself into a poker game. If you open that mouth of yours, you'll get a taste of my fist. Do we understand each other?"

Tempest frowned, bewildered. "You *aren't* going to stuff me in a corner, get yourself all liquored up, and then rape me at your convenience?"

Cord did a double take. "Where the hell did you come up with that? Or is that what you wanted all along and were too ladylike to admit it?" he added with a smirk.

"Isn't that what renegades do? I demand to know why you're dragging me all over creation. And who the devil are you anyway? What do you want with me—and what time is it for heaven sake?"

Tempest hated not knowing the time of day. She had always been organized and methodical, and this unexplainable escapade was throwing her inner clock out of whack.

This female was firing questions like bullets—questions Cord hadn't the time or inclination to answer.

"Just sit where I tell you to sit and do what I tell you to do," he demanded harshly. "That's all you need to know for the moment."

"I'm half-starved," Tempest informed him. "It's been twenty-four hours since I've eaten a decent meal."

"How could you know that if you don't know what time it is?"

"I'm guessing," she retorted, irritated that he took her so lightly. "And besides that, I've had ten years scared off my life, thanks to you and your wild antics and I—"

"Would you like to have your chemise stuffed in your mouth again, tigress?" he growled in interruption.

"No thank you."

"Then shut up and behave yourself. If you get on my bad side, I promise you won't like it."

"As if you have a good side," she sassed.

When Cord took a menacing step forward, Tempest instinctively retreated two paces.

"This *is* my good side," he breathed down her neck.

"Somehow I knew you'd say something like that."

"And I knew you couldn't keep your mouth shut," Cord bit off. "You have an infuriating habit of wanting to have the last word."

"I do?" Another character flaw had just been brought to her attention.

Cord rolled his eyes and summoned his patience. Clasping Tempest's dainty hand in his callused one, he dragged her through the back door of the cantina. When voices mingled in a melange of English and Spanish, Tempest contemplated shouting for help. But the surly patrons in the saloon looked to be more trouble than assistance to a damsel in distress. She found herself clinging to Cord's hand for protection when she glanced around the smoke-filled room to see a dozen pairs of masculine eyes flooding over her.

Señoritas, puffing on corn husk *cigarittos,* were draped in the laps of rough-looking hombres. Dark, beady eyes gave her the once over as Cord led her through the maze of tables to take an unoccupied seat. Tempest had seen some scoundrels in her time, her captor included, but she swore they had barged into the lowest, most disreputable cantina south of the border. Men wearing bandoleers stuffed with an assortment of pistols and ammunition filled the dimly lit room to capacity. The smell of smoke, liquor, and sweat permeated the air. Tempest sneezed when her nostrils were bombarded by the noxious fumes.

In a place like this, it was probably best that she

kept her mouth shut. She could wind up raped on the spot, or at least fondled in the same degrading manner as the women all around her. Disgraceful! She'd never witnessed such carryings-on. A sorrier collection of ruffians and riffraff she had never seen in all her life. And she had seen plenty of them in her time—in the courtroom. Most of her clients were disreputable characters who could ill afford a lawyer and took whomever the court delegated to them. Tempest was often delegated.

It was unsettling to realize she could trade one intolerable situation for another if she dared to call even more attention to herself. In her worst nightmare Tempest never dreamed she would be forced to cling to a man like *this* for protection!

When Cord gestured toward an empty chair, Tempest begrudgingly parked herself in it. Leisurely, he folded his tall frame into the seat beside her and braced his forearms on the table. In fluent Spanish, he invited himself into the poker game with the motley group whose faces had undoubtedly graced WANTED posters on both sides of the border.

"You got money, *amigo?*" Miguel Díaz demanded.

A smile hovered on Cord's lips as he reached over to remove the sombrero from Tempest's wild tangle of chestnut hair, unveiling her face. He flipped the poncho over her shoulder to reveal the daring decolletage of her gown.

"This is better than money," Cord chortled rakishly. "If I win, I'll take your coins. If I lose, you can have my woman."

His woman? Unable to control her outrage a second longer, Tempest bounded up from her chair. This vile beast was wagering her against a stack of gold coins? Curse him to hell and back!

"You scoundrel!" Tempest spat, yanking her drooping gown into decency. "How dare you stake me in your card game!"

"Sit down." Cord's thundering voice echoed around the cantina.

Tempest had considered her captor dangerous from the instant he had pounced on her, but the look in his eyes now could have sent a lion cowering to its den. Despite her outrage, Tempest flounced back into her chair, tugged the *sarape* back into place and cautioned herself against reigniting this amber-eyed demon's wrath. He looked downright frightening when he was furious.

Miguel chuckled at Tempest's outburst and nudged one of his scraggly-looking companions. "I like a woman with fire in her, don't you, Antonio?"

Antonio Cardova nodded in agreement. His dark eyes flowed over Tempest like slow-moving molasses, lingering overly long on her bosom. *"Si!* Fiery *putas* are much better in bed than passive ones. I would like to have this one squirming beneath me."

Tempest's Spanish didn't fail her. She understood the crude remark. But before she could utter one word, Cord's lean fingers tangled in her hair, giving it a painful jerk. As much as Tempest prided herself on adhering to law and order, she would have traded her law book for a very large knife to stab that tawny-eyed devil!

"What time is it?" Tempest asked with a scowl.

Cord shrugged carelessly. "What does it matter? You have nothing better to do than wait."

Tempest bit her tongue while Miguel dealt the cards. Why she always felt the urge to know the exact hour and minute, she wasn't sure. Force of habit, she supposed. Time was of little consequence. There was naught to do but sit and wait to determine which of these foul-smelling hooligans would attempt to rape her—and what she was going to do to prevent it.

Cord scooped up his cards and gave them a quick look-see before studying the stubbled faces of his companions. Obviously, Miguel thought he was sitting pretty with his fistful of choice cards and Antonio was holding a winning hand himself. As Cord expected, Miguel had dealt him losing cards. Boldly, Cord reached over to pull the remainder of the deck toward him.

"I'll take three cards," he announced before Miguel's stubby hand folded over the deck.

"I'm dealing, *amigo,*" Miguel reminded him with a threatening growl.

One thick brow lifted in a mocking taunt. "You do not trust me when I trusted you to deal fairly? Are you suggesting that I would cheat?"

Miguel's gaze darted from Cord's deadly calm expression to the exposed pistol strapped across his broad chest. There was something unsettling about this hombre's glittering golden eyes and self-imposed reserve. It was like staring at still water, knowing a deep, forceful current swirled beneath it. Miguel also knew that he had stacked the deck so that he would receive the aces that lay in the pile. As Miguel feared, Cord dealt to himself last, leaving himself the choice cards.

When Cord turned up two aces, Miguel squirmed in his chair.

"What an honest man you are, *amigo,*" Cord said with the faintest hint of sarcasm. "Now bet your hand against my woman and don't be cheap. She's a prize and you damned well know it."

Miguel and Antonio tossed several coins in the middle of the table—a table that had so much tequila spilled on it that the sleeves of the men's shirts stuck to it. With bated breath, she waited for the gamblers to show their hands.

A quiet chuckle rippled through the air when Cord laid his cards on the table—"Aces and Kings."

"I could accuse you of cheating, hombre." Miguel flung Cord a steely glance.

Cord raked the coins into his pocket. "You could, but then I would have to kill you for insulting my integrity, *amigo.*" When Miguel's fingers curled and inched toward his pistol, Cord's hand shot across the table like a bullet. "Careful, hombre. I am not always so easy to deal with. You do not wish to see me angry, I assure you."

"You believe in living dangerously, don't you, *amigo?*" Miguel said through clenched teeth.

"Is there any other way?" Cord rose from the table and released Miguel's gun hand.

This rapscallion had incredible gall, thought Tempest. He'd sauntered in here as if he owned the place, invited himself into a poker game with crooked gamblers, and put her up as his stake. Now he intended to waltz out with the coins. She was surprised he hadn't simply robbed some defenseless victim on the street and been done with it.

"Another hand, double or nothing," Antonio baited as he leered at Tempest for the umpteenth time.

"You had your chance." Cord hoisted Tempest from her sticky chair. "You lost. She stays with me."

Lucky me, thought Tempest. There was no telling what this blackguard was planning to do next. Thus far, her attempt to second-guess him hadn't panned out.

"Now what?" she demanded to know after Cord hustled her through the back door and down the alley. "You have money, so why drag me along behind you? What time is it now? I need something to eat. I'll faint from hunger if I don't get nourishment soon. Maybe you can survive, but I need food—" Her breath came out in a whoosh when Cord stopped short, causing her to slam into his back.

"Are you always this much trouble, lady?"

"No, only when my bath has been interrupted, when I've been abducted without apparent motive, and when my life has been threatened. I've missed several meals and it spoils my disposition." She paused for a breath. "Usually, I'm in very good humor."

Cord couldn't help but be amused. Nor did he have difficulty understanding why Victor Watts had set his sights on this lively bundle of irrepressible spirit and unrivaled beauty. This female had not once reacted as Cord expected during the course of the afternoon.

Impulsively, Cord crooked his finger beneath her pert chin, tilting her face to his. "Smile for me, *chica*. I would like to see the evidence of this customary good humor you boast about."

Tempest jerked away from his touch as if she'd been snakebit and then childishly stuck out her tongue. "You'll get nothing close to pleasantries from me until I've been properly fed and released from your clutches."

He chuckled, undaunted by her tirade. Gliding his arm around her waist, he herded her through the maze of crates and trash cans to step into a shop that served chili and some other Mexican dish Tempest couldn't name. But the food did tantalize her taste buds. While she wolfed down her meal at the inconspicuous table in the corner, Tempest studied her perplexing companion. Just when she was sure she despised this handsome rake, he did something as courteous as feeding her. He could be rough and brutal one moment and generous and playful the next. He was a walking contradiction, and she couldn't quite figure him out.

"Feeling better, *chica?*" Cord questioned as he pulled the hat low on her forehead to conceal her identity from the two customers who had ambled inside.

"Much," Tempest assured him between bites. "What time is it now?"

Cord shook his head at her peculiar preoccupation with the hour of the day. After assisting her from her chair, he paused beside the proprietor of the restaurant and flashed him a shiny coin. "Will you sell your timepiece to the lady? She cannot survive without knowing the exact time every other minute."

The friendly Mexican grinned at the pretty face shadowed beneath the sombrero. With an agreeable nod he exchanged his timepiece for the money. In amazement, Tempest watched Cord drop the gold chain and timepiece into her hand. A gift? If she lived to be one hundred and ten, she would never understand this man!

While she stood there, brushing her thumb over the carved case of the watch, Cord drew the proprietor aside. He handed the Mexican another coin, and the note he'd written before he'd ventured to Victor's *hacienda.* Tempest was too preoccupied to notice the exchange. While she and Cord exited the same way they came in, the proprietor scurried off to fetch one of his sons.

Tempest followed Cord into another shop where he purchased all sorts of supplies. Then he hustled her down the alley—always through the alley—to the blacksmith's barn where he purchased a horse.

"What do you need with another horse and saddle when you already have one?" she questioned suspiciously.

"It's for you," Cord informed her as he fastened the girth strap.

"Me?" She blinked like a startled owl. "I don't ride and besides I—"

"You don't ride?" Cord jerked upright. "Good Lord, lady, where have you been all your life, trapped in an ivory tower?"

Tempest took quick offense. "Now look here, mister, I've been a reasonably good sport about this madcap escapade of yours. You haven't hurt me and I haven't tried to hurt you back, except for that slap on the cheek which you most certainly deserved. But I must admit I could have shot you for putting me up as stakes in that stupid poker game with your crooked friends—"

"They aren't friends of mine," Cord interjected.

"Of course, they aren't. You probably don't have any. And just where would I be right now if you had lost?"

"You were never in danger of being dragged off by a desperado," he assured her. "I wasn't going to lose because I can cheat as well as the next man. I can also handle myself with a pistol and knife."

"What impressive talents!" she scoffed before returning her attention to the matter at hand. "The fact remains that I do not need a horse because I've no intention of going anywhere that I can't get to by stage or buggy. Now if you'll kindly give me enough coins to hire a buckboard, I'll be on my way."

Cord stared at her outstretched hand and burst out laughing. This female was an absolute marvel! She was ordering him around as if *he* was *her* captive.

Although Tempest braced her feet, Cord hooked his arm beneath her knees, uprooted her from her spot, and deposited her none too gently on the saddle. "If I say you're going to learn to ride, then by damned you'll ride. Don't make me mad, lady. When I'm good and mad, it's not a pretty sight. I'm running things around here and you'll cooperate or you'll never see Victor Watts and his fancy hacienda again."

Tempest would have liked to protest, but that look of smoldering rage stopped her cold. Getting on this rascal's bad side was not wise. But if he thought he could buy her off with a gold timepiece and food, he was mistaken. She could be a little mean and nasty herself. And when he cooled down, she'd fire him up again, just to make sure he knew she wasn't accepting her fate without putting up a fight.

Holding her tongue, Tempest waited for her captor to regain his composure. Odd, wasn't it? she thought to herself. This rapscallion had put a stranglehold on his temper when he was dealing with the riffraff in the cantina, but he flew off the handle when she defied him. Another of his puzzling characteristics. And whatever his intentions, he was keeping his own counsel. Tempest didn't have the faintest notion what he was planning or why.

With his newly purchased supplies strapped on his horse, Cord led Tempest and her steed down the alley, past the mission, and across the river. His destination was the foothills of the Franklin Mountains and beyond to the Hueco Mountains east of El Paso.

"Where are we going now?" Tempest demanded as she squirmed uncomfortably on the saddle. "And what time is it getting to be?"

"Hell, I don't know. You're the one with the timepiece. You tell me."

Tempest parted the folds of her *sarape* to stare at the watch she had tucked in the garment. "It's three o'clock. If you don't take me back to the *hacienda,* you'll be in more trouble than you can imagine. I've got things to do and I—"

"Silence!" Cord boomed. He reined his steed to a halt and pulled her mare up beside him. "You may as well stop kidding yourself, honey. I didn't abduct you from the *hacienda* just to wager you in a card game for quick money. You aren't going to see Victor or anybody else until I say you can. And if trouble arises, you better cling tight to your horse or you'll fall off and break your lovely neck!"

"I demand to know what this is all about!" Tempest yelled at him. "And stop treating me like some witless female. I'm going back to El Paso and if you don't like it then you can just shoot me!"

When Tempest snatched the reins from Cord and steered her horse around, he pounced like a cougar. Tempest was forced off balance and the next thing she knew, Cord had her straddling his horse and facing his black scowl.

Cord didn't know why he did what he did next. Before he could control his impulsiveness, his mouth came down hard on hers. It must have been the tantalizing feel of her hips straddling his thighs, the feel of her shapely body brushing suggestively against his. His arms fastened around her, molding her soft curves into his hard contours, aching for her.

Fire raced through Tempest's bloodstream when his mouth forced her lips apart. His expertise and the sudden gentleness that replaced the first few seconds of the assault caused her resistance to waver. His tongue probed the soft recesses of her mouth and then withdrew. His teeth nipped at her bottom lip before he kissed her again—and again.

Tempest trembled at the wildly intimate gestures of his thrusting tongue. Shock waves undulated through her body when she felt those sinewy arms enfolding her, crushing her against the stone wall of his chest.

She had expected to be repulsed by his kiss, but that was not the case. Her femininity betrayed her, and sudden tingles of forbidden pleasure shot through her. It was absurd. It was outrageous . . .

When his hands migrated up her ribs to caress the curve of her breast, Tempest felt an electrifying jolt ricochet through her every nerve ending. Her breath froze in her throat when his lips skimmed over her neck to spread a row of burning kisses over the swell of her breasts. His hands and lips were teaching her startling discoveries about the art of intimacy. The newness of a man's lips on her skin left her gasping. Her unexpected reaction to this scoundrel made her feel weak and vulnerable, and Tempest valiantly mustered her defenses before she lost the will to battle the deliciously wicked pleasure of his masterful touch.

Jerking away, Tempest cocked her arm. She slapped him good and hard, not because she was offended by his kisses and caresses, but because she had *liked* it! She slapped *him* because she felt like kicking *herself*—if that made any sense. It didn't! What had come over her?

Cord didn't even flinch when she struck him soundly on the jaw. He expected as much. But what he hadn't expected was this tight coil of desire that knotted in his belly and burned through his loins. He was painfully aware of this fierce attraction he felt for this feisty firebrand. He liked kissing her, even if she didn't seem to have much experience at it. He'd wanted to take her petal-soft lips under his since the instant he'd laid eyes on her. That was a fact. But *now,* for God's sake? In the middle of a debate on the back of a horse? *Caramba!*

Tempest felt awkward and self-conscious. The plodding motion of the steed kept bringing her hips into intimate contact with his. Every movement made her starkly aware of their provocative position on the horse. His blazing kisses still burned on her lips.

"Why'd you do that?" Tempest found herself asking between gasps.

"Hell, I don't know. Why'd you kiss me back?"

"I did no such thing!" she protested hotly.

A teasing smile bordered his lips as he inspected his stinging jaw with his fingertips. "That's why you slapped me, wasn't it, princess? You were peeved because you liked kissing me and you didn't want me to know it."

Tempest gasped at his shrewd perception. He was exactly right, but she would have killed herself before she admitted it. "I hate you! The last thing I wanted was to be attacked by a lecherous scoundrel like you. I hated your kiss!"

"Then maybe you'll approve of this one," he murmured as his eyes focused on her mouth and his head moved deliberately toward hers.

Tempest, who had fended off dozens of amorous advances since the moment men had begun to notice her almost a decade earlier, found it impossible to resist the leisurely expertise of a kiss that destroyed her defenses in one second flat. Cord had lifted her to him, pulling her body down on his, making her vividly aware of the anatomical differences between a man and a woman. And when his full lips covered hers, she felt her innocent body melt against him as if she belonged there, even when she knew better!

The man was positively impossible! Half-civilized! On one hand, she despised his domineering attitude yet, on the other hand, she was unwillingly attracted to him. It was insane and she was a senseless fool. Her mind rebelled against this man who'd captured her and refused to free her without explaining himself.

She didn't even know his name! It was demoralizing to realize a man could affect her so easily, especially a rascal like this. He represented everything she disliked. He was a scoundrel, a step above an outlaw, a daredevil . . . But he could kiss a woman until her flesh practically dissolved! It was . . . scary! He had somehow tapped a hidden well of passion inside her that she never realized existed. Now she wasn't even sure she could trust herself when she reacted so explosively to his advances!

Cord was a mite rattled himself when he finally came up for air. He could have kissed her for hours on end, teaching her all sorts of techniques of which she'd obviously been deprived. Lord, he'd never tasted anything so sweet or innocent in all his life.

He couldn't imagine how this delectable imp could have stayed pure so long. And she was definitely inexperienced and ignorant of the lusty desires that could engulf a man. He could feel her naive body trembling in response to his exploring caresses and penetrating kisses. Everything he did was new to her. Somehow or another she'd managed to elude Victor's desires. Wouldn't Victor pop his cork if he discovered that Cord MacIntosh had seduced his fiancée? That would really put ole Victor in a blind rage and keep him there, wouldn't it?

Nonplussed, Tempest peered into the shimmering amber eyes that locked with hers. She felt hot and shaky, remembering the potent impact of his kiss. She trembled, feeling her legs wrapped all too suggestively around his thighs while his steed ambled down the dusty path toward the distant mountains.

Cord didn't like what he was thinking and feeling, not one whit. This gorgeous little sprite was getting to him in ways he hadn't expected. Damn, kidnapping Victor's fiancée was turning out to be a very bad idea!

Determinedly, Cord reminded himself of what Dub Wizner had said about women. Cord knew better than to become too intrigued by a female, but he had allowed himself to forget it in the heat of such a tantalizing kiss. Women were trouble. They could beguile a man and make him do crazy things. The past few years, Cord had taught himself not to care about anyone except his own family. He had refused to put his emotions in turmoil. He had shut himself off from the world until this fiasco with Victor erupted, until his father became the victim of treachery and murder. Now Cord was bitter, mistrusting, and angry. He didn't need more trouble than he already had—which was too damned much!

Caramba! This temptress was dangerous. She

could distract him without trying and she made the morning's unpleasant ordeal at the jail seem a million miles away.

"Unless you want to find yourself deflowered where you sit, princess, I suggest you climb back on your own horse," Cord muttered.

His blunt comment jarred her brain into gear. With a profuse blush and an outraged gasp, Tempest wiggled free and leaned out to crawl back onto the mare that ambled alongside them. Her fingers clenched the pommel of the saddle until her knuckles turned white. Willfully, she tried to get her chaotic emotions in hand.

This rough-edged renegade was far more dangerous than she'd ever imagined. He could seduce her and make her like it! Where was that strong thread of moral fiber that had been knitted to her composure all these years? How could such a man bring out the slumbering passion inside her when she had never been aroused by even one gentlemanly suitor who had pursued her? What horrible irony!

It won't happen again, Tempest assured herself determinedly. If he tried to kiss and caress her, she would be prepared to reject his advances. The next time, she would elude him. She would, however, allow him to believe she had accepted her captivity. And when he let his guard down, she would thunder away in a cloud of dust. And if he decided to shoot her out of the saddle . . .

Well, if he did, then he did. Tempest wondered if this peculiar relationship hadn't reached the point where she was more afraid of herself and her irrational responses than she was of him!

Five

Victor Watts sat atop his steed, surrounded by his army of *vaqueros,* staring in all directions. Curse it, where had that surly half-breed gotten to? He should have known it would be next to impossible to keep the sly renegade in jail for any length of time. As Emilio Reynosa had said, Cord had a remarkable ability to vanish into thin air. It must be the Apache in him, Victor mused. He had even paid Juan Tijerina a handsome fee to keep a watchful eye on Cord, to harass him unmercifully. Obviously, Juan had pushed that half-breed too far. That fool . . .

The clatter of hooves heralded the arrival of an unidentified rider. Victor's brows furrowed over his green eyes when a teenaged Mexican galloped toward him, waving a letter over his head.

"For you, señor," the messenger announced.

Victor snatched the note from the boy's hand and scanned its contents. He couldn't believe the ransom note he was reading! While he was searching every nook and cranny in El Paso and El Paso del Norte, Cord MacIntosh had sneaked to the hacienda to kidnap his fiancée!

A murderous curse exploded from his lips as he reread the taunting message: Cord vowed to keep Victor's fiancée captive until Victor was prepared to admit the truth about Paddy MacIntosh's mysterious death and confessed to framing Cord for cattle rustling.

"Emilio! Take half the men and trail east," Victor demanded. "Cord has kidnapped my woman."

Emilio's dark eyes popped from their sockets. "He stole your *novia?* If he totes her off to his cabin in the mountains, it will take us forever to track him through those treacherous passes!"

"Then you damned well better find him before he reaches the mountains." Victor scowled. "And kill him this time, Emilio. There's a new charge of murder against him. We have every right to dispose of that ruthless bastard. We should have done it the first time instead of hauling him to jail."

Nodding grimly, Emilio volunteered eleven of the most seasoned bravos to accompany him east. When the men thundered off, Victor and the remainder of the rescue brigade wheeled around to race back to the *hacienda* to gather more men. Once he collected provisions, he intended to contact the cavalry at Fort Davis. He would enlist the services of the scouts and the black buffalo soldiers—as they were called by Indians—many of whom had been slaves on Southern plantations. It was a damned shame the Texas Rangers had been disbanded after the Civil War and the state was now under strict military rule. The federal government had refused to allow the southern states to organize bodies of men for any purpose for fear of another revolt. Most of the western forts, like Quitman, Hancock, and Bliss, had been abandoned, and the citizens were again vulnerable to bandit, Comanche, and Apache raids. Victor needed the aid of law officials and soldiers and there were damned few of them in the area to come to his assistance.

Colorful oaths poured from Victor's lips as he raced home, envisioning the torments his dainty fiancée was enduring at Cord's hands. That bastard! Cord had found a way to infuriate and humiliate him. No doubt his future father-in-law would now question his ability to protect Annette from the constant danger that arose along the border. And there was no telling what that wild renegade would do to a defenseless woman!

Victor galloped to his ranch, mentally organizing his plans. This time he wouldn't make the crucial mistake of taking Cord MacIntosh for granted. The man had no discipline whatsoever and it would be difficult to second-guess him. There was a natural turbulence and independence about that rough-edged half-breed that made him scorn obedience and ignore threats. He was definitely a force to be reckoned with, because of his superior physical strength, agility, and quick-witted intelligence.

The fact that Cord had escaped from jail and sneaked to the hacienda to whisk Annette away wasn't surprising. The man seemed to have a complete absence of fear. He didn't buckle to threats or strong-arm tactics. Now that he thirsted for revenge, he had struck with enough force to devastate and demoralize his enemy. With his strength and endurance and knowledge of the treacherous mountains, it could take weeks to find that scoundrel. Cord had the Apache's keen knowledge of the winding trails. He knew the location of water, wild game, and grazing pasture for his horse. Now he was in his natural habitat and he would revert to his Indian ways. He would be traveling lightly with his saddle for his pillow and his feet to a small campfire. He would find his own food and seek protection in the rugged, unforgiving country where even rattlesnakes and coyotes had difficulty finding shelter.

Muttering at this stroke of rotten luck, Victor leaped from his horse, spouting orders like bullets as he scurried into the storehouse to gather supplies.

He would find a way to turn this infuriating incident to his advantage. He'd see to it that there was a high price on Cord's head. Cattle rustling was a serious offense—it could get a man hanged. But murder and kidnapping would ensure a tight noose around Cord's neck. Annette would undoubtedly suffer degrading torture at this vindictive tyrant's hands, but Victor's primary concern was what Emory Partridge would think of his future son-in-law. Victor needed the backing of Emory's vast wealth to expand his ranching operation. Annette was only a device to get him what he wanted—a pretty one, but still a device . . .

When Victor burst into the bunkhouse, he found Cord's discarded clothes—the ones he'd been wearing when the *vaqueros* had dragged him to jail. Obviously Cord had confiscated new garments to disguise his identity before packing Annette off to his sanctuary in the labyrinth of canyons to the east.

While Victor was gathering supplies, the *vaqueros* scattered to prepare for their gruelling cross-country journey. The *rancho* was bustling with activity, and Victor was in the midst of it until a quiet voice behind him stopped him dead in his tracks.

"Victor? What is going on around here?" Annette questioned. "I cannot find Miss Litchfield anywhere. Her luggage is still in her room, but she has vanished."

Victor lurched around to find Annette safe and sound. When he realized the ruthless half-breed had made a critical error, a deep skirl of laughter reverberated in his chest. Cord had managed to cut his own throat. The renegade had sneaked into the house to abduct Victor's fiancée, unaware of the woman's name or her physical appearance. But he hadn't abducted Victor's fiancée at all. Cord had kidnapped the woman who had been sent to defend him in a court of law. The man wouldn't stand a chance of being exonerated from his crimes now. He was as good as dead.

Annette lifted a delicately arched brow. "Victor? What is so amusing?"

"Nothing, my sweet," he assured her as he guided her out of the bunkhouse. "Cord MacIntosh tried to play a vile trick on me, but it seems it has backfired." He gave her a gentle nudge toward the *hacienda*. "Go back inside and help the servants prepare for the *fandango* tonight. I have to ride back to El Paso to send off a few messages. I'll make it up to you when I return this evening. I promise."

After blowing Annette a kiss, Victor swung into the saddle. Oh, this was ripe! He could turn every citizen in west Texas against Cord MacIntosh once and for all. That heathen didn't stand a chance in hell of foiling his plans now. Once Victor contacted Judge Litchfield in San Antonio, there would be hundreds of men hot on Cord's heels. The judge would he outraged by this ironic twist of fate that led to his daughter's abduction. The bounty on Cord's head would triple in less than a week!

Snickering at the trouble Cord had unknowingly brought upon himself when he kidnapped the wrong woman, Victor raced to town to send a message to the judge and to the commander of Fort Davis. Very soon, the mountains would be crawling with soldiers, scouts and bounty hunters. Cord MacIntosh wouldn't make it out of his stronghold alive!

Tempest managed her horse as well as could be expected, considering she was a novice in the saddle. The gruelling hours of traveling left her leg muscles aching and her derrière bruised. Tempest had never faced such a rugged ordeal in all her pampered life! She was being forced into situations that challenged her not only physically but emotionally as well. It left her to wonder if this was some sort of test of her endurance and character, or if she had simply awakened in hell and would be stuck here for the rest of eternity.

The sun beat down relentlessly. Tempest had depleted her supply of canteen water an hour earlier. Still, her captor showed no signs of slowing his swift pace over the arid plains. Praying for divine intervention, Tempest stared toward the looming walls of the Hueco Mountains. To the left, she could see the huge conical peak of Cerro Alto, shouldered with patches of puffy clouds that occasionally pocketed the blaring sun, bringing momentary relief from the heat.

"If I'm not permitted to rest I'll collapse," Tempest bemoaned as she mopped perspiration from her brow. She had shed the heavy poncho miles ago, but she was still as hot as dry kindling in a campfire. "I refuse to stir another step until I rest!"

Cord's arm was very nearly jerked from its socket when Tempest yanked on her horse's reins—the ones clenched in his fist. Reluctantly, he glanced over his shoulder to survey the rumpled beauty whose low-necked pink muslin gown displayed her femininity all too well. Cord had tried not to notice. Finally, he'd stopped feeling guilty and admired the tantalizing sunburned cleavage, tangled chestnut hair, and startling blue eyes. After he'd allowed his eyes to devour her, he sent her a hard glare that warned her to remember her place. It was a waste of energy. Tempest tilted her smudged chin and matched his stare.

"Look, lady, we can't stop out in the middle of nowhere. We'd be sitting ducks, vulnerable from any direction." He gestured toward the looming peaks and gigantic rocks scattered over the mountains.

"We'll stop when we reach the protection of the foothills."

Cord didn't wait for Tempest's approval. She hadn't really thought he would. He simply tugged on her reluctant steed and led her through the sand, sage, and cactus.

"Well, I should at least like to know why I'm being dragged over hill and dale," she insisted as she reached over to retrieve his canteen, helping herself to his water.

Cord smiled at her audacity. She hadn't asked permission—she merely took what she wanted. He wondered what it would take to intimidate her. Considering her plight, she was very self-assured. It still irked Cord that Victor had attracted such a lovely, spirited prize. There was no way in hell that bastard deserved a woman like this. She was gorgeous—sunburned but gorgeous—resilient and headstrong.

"I'm holding you for ransom," Cord finally admitted.

Tempest's hand stopped in midair, her cracked lips poised above the canteen. "Ransom?" she croaked.

Cord nodded. "And until your precious Victor admits the truth and drops the charges of cattle rustling against me, he won't be allowed to see you again."

Her thirst forgotten, Tempest stared frog-eyed at the sinewy man beside her. "Just who the devil are you anyway?" Tempest was afraid she already knew the answer to that question and yet she was unable to believe it.

Cord nudged his steed toward the foothills of Hueco. "The name is Cord MacIntosh, honey."

Seeing her shocked expression, Cord chuckled. He never thought he'd see Tempest at a loss for words.

"I gather Victor has told you all about me. I'm surprised he even bothered. I thought he'd be whispering sweet nothings in your ear, filling your head with ideas about a bright and sunny future after your wedding."

"Victor said you were locked in jail," Tempest squeaked and then drenched her vocal cords with much-needed water. She was shocked to learn his identity.

"I was in jail until this morning," Cord confirmed. "I'd enjoyed that rat hole as long as I could, so I left."

"You escaped?" Tempest blinked, astonished.

"Well, the jailer sure as hell didn't let me go with his blessing."

After seeing Cord MacIntosh in action, Tempest could easily believe he'd found a way to break free. He was as solid as the boulders they skirted as they ascended into the mountains.

Tempest replaced the canteen and clamped both fists around the pommel when Cord veered off on a precarious path that caused her horse to lurch and scramble to gain its footing.

Confused, she contemplated Cord's previous remarks before the truth dawned on her. He had erroneously assumed that *she* was Victor's fiancée. So that was why he had toted her away from the *rancho* and taken pains to disguise her, and himself, while they tramped through El Paso del Norte.

Tempest considered blurting out her true identity, but then she gave it a moment's consideration. If she announced that she was to be his defense attorney, sent by her father, Cord would probably treat her much differently. This way, Tempest would have the perfect opportunity to know and understand him. She could pry information about the case from him without his knowing that she was actually his lawyer. She would discover exactly what kind of man

Cord MacIntosh really was. As of yet, he had not been unnecessarily abusive, only inconsiderate. If he did become violent and excessively cruel, she would tell him the truth. That would save her from disaster. But until then, Tempest would play along with his scheme to get valuable information and background for her investigation.

At the moment, the criminal offenses against Cord MacIntosh looked exceptionally grim. She had heard Victor's side of the dispute, one which made Cord sound like a ruthless fugitive who lived a miserable life, with a disreputable character for a father and an Indian squaw for a mother. Tempest had always been curious about what made her clients tick, wanting to learn what various influences had made them become the individuals they were. She was convinced that environment had a great deal to do with the moral fiber of a man. In short, a man was what he learned to become, molded by those around him.

This rugged outlaw fascinated her. Cord didn't seem like the vicious villain Victor made him out to be. He may very well be as guilty as original sin, but in her estimation Victor Watts was no saint himself.

Cord frowned at the ponderous expression that knitted Tempest's brow. She had certainly grown quiet all of a sudden. He wasn't sure if it was because of the difficult climb or his previous remarks. Whatever the case, she said not another word as they threaded through the rocky ravines toward Hueco Tanks north of Buckhorn Draw.

Tempest peered at the rock-bound enclosure that seemed to form a natural fortress in the mountains. Wind and rain had carved several water holes in the soft stone. Shallow caves and overhanging cliffs offered protection from the blistering sun and inclement weather. Pictographs that suggested the presence of ancient Indian tribes were etched in the walls. This did indeed seem to be an Indian domain, and Cord MacIntosh didn't appear to be a stranger to this rugged terrain. He knew exactly where he was going, and Tempest no longer minded that she was traveling with him, even if she didn't possess his stamina. Before this misadventure was over, she would know if her client was guilty or innocent. If Cord was all the terrible things Victor said he was, Tempest would testify against him in court herself!

An appreciative sigh escaped Tempest's parched lips when she spied a crystal-clear spring embedded in a limestone basin. It was like a long-awaited oasis inside the perimeters of hell! With a squeal of delight, she slid off her horse and scampered toward the pool. So anxious was she to peel off her grimy gown and soak until she'd soothed her sun-baked skin that she almost forgot about her companion. With an embarrassed gasp, Tempest yanked her gown back into place and threw Cord a glance. Although she did have her back to him, the garment had slid down to her waist, baring far more flesh than she had intended. It was most fortunate that he had been behind her rather than in front. Otherwise, he would have gotten an eyeful—again!

"A little late for modesty, isn't it, princess?" Cord teased.

"It's true that you were a Peeping Tom while I was in my bath," she muttered. "But all the same, I am not about to disrobe in front of you."

That would invite trouble, Tempest assured herself. After all, this man's reputation was definitely questionable. And he was most definitely a man. Tempest had seen that for herself. She was not about to give him an opportunity to take advantage of her. He already had more opportunity than any of her male acquaintances and she wasn't making herself more vulnerable than she was.

With her cheeks ablaze with color—embarrassment and sunburn—Tempest pivoted to face Cord. "I should like my privacy for a bath," she demanded in a firm tone she hoped would squelch any argument.

Cord burst out laughing. Rarely was the precocious spitfire at a loss for words, even when she had nearly embarrassed herself by forgetting she wasn't alone before she started stripping. And even when she was stone-cold serious, she still amused him with her courage, daring, and confidence. He wondered how many other captives made such demands of their captors. Damned few, Cord reckoned. There weren't many females like this blue-eyed vixen.

Still snickering, Cord bowed down in a mocking parody of obedience. "As you wish, my lady."

When Tempest realized how pushy she must sound to a man who obviously wasn't accustomed to accepting orders from a woman—and what man was?—she smiled. "I suppose you think I'm bossy and spoiled," she speculated.

Cord rose to full stature and returned her grin. It was fascinating the way those dimples cut into her cheeks, the way her eyes sparkled like sunshine dancing on water when she smiled. "I figured there had to be some reason why you are as old as you are and still unmarried," he replied in a teasing tone. "It couldn't have been because of your looks since you are extraordinarily lovely."

Tempest could not think of one logical reason why she should be flattered by the backhanded compliment. But she was, just the same. She usually resented it when men called attention to her God-given looks, as if she had something to do with that. But a compliment, coming from this particular man, brought a flush of pleasure to her cheeks.

"And it obviously isn't because you are dirt poor and have no dowry to bring to your betrothed." One thick brow elevated to a curious angle. "Do you have any other flaws I should know about, besides being bossy and short-tempered?"

"Only one," Tempest replied. "I don't have all that much respect for men. They aren't to be trusted. Usually, when a man refers to a woman's good looks, he expects something in return. Did you want something more, Mister MacIntosh, or am I allowed to take my bath without further interruption?"

Cord stared into that enchanting face, fighting down the urge to kiss her, as he had done so impulsively the previous afternoon. Of course, that would have confirmed her theory that a man only complimented a lady when he wanted something. He did want something, he was ashamed to admit. He wanted things that he doubted she knew how to give a man.

It was truly remarkable that she could inspire his sexual fantasies at such a phenomenal rate. One look at those lips and he hungered to taste and touch her again and again.

Get hold of yourself! Cord silently scolded. He wasn't usually this distracted by females. He had damned well better concentrate on harmless conversation rather than letting his mind detour down other avenues.

"If you are wary of men, how could you have let yourself fall in love with a man like Victor Watts?" Cord asked bluntly.

"Who said I was in love with him?" Tempest countered, playing her role without actually lying about her true identity.

"You aren't?" Cord frowned dubiously.

"I *aren't,*" Tempest confirmed. "But don't think I approve of this shenanigan of yours, Cord MacIntosh, for I most certainly do not.

Breaking and entering and kidnapping are serious offenses. You should have found a better way to deal with Victor."

"What do *you* know about the law?" he scoffed. "I figured a spoiled aristocrat like you only knew about knitting, giving parties, and working your wiles to acquire a wealthy fiancé."

Tempest bit her tongue and swallowed the guilt that tapped at her conscience. Part of her wanted to confess her true identity and another part of her argued that, given the ordeal he was putting her through, she owed him absolutely nothing. True, she was virtually lowering herself to his level, but then, she wasn't sure ethics applied in this case. And if she did admit she wasn't Victor's fiancée, she might find herself abandoned; at the moment she seemed better off with this renegade than without him.

"Kindly leave for awhile. And I would like a bath and decent meal."

Cord gaped at the bossy female who had just dismissed him. "Now you wait just a damned minute, Miss God almighty—" He studied her curiously. "What the devil's your name anyway?"

It was apparent that Cord had been given only sketchy details about Victor's engagement.

"Tempest Litchfield," she replied, introducing herself and wondering if Cord might recognize her surname.

Cord frowned. Litchfield . . . Had he heard that name somewhere before? It seemed to ring a vague and distant bell.

"Now about my bath . . ."

Cord found himself ambling off in the direction Tempest had pointed. When it dawned on him that he had let her order him around he scowled in irritation. He zigzagged around the boulders to reach the cliff overlooking the sparkling spring. He would allow that female whirlwind to think he had obeyed her, but he was going to keep a watchful eye on her in case she tried to escape. She could be pretending to accept her captivity, just to throw him off guard. If she attempted to flee, he'd be on her like a wolf on a rabbit . . .

Cord sat down before he fell down and gazed toward the circular pool carved in limestone. Spellbound, he watched Tempest wade into the spring. Damnation, this was turning out to be another one of his very bad ideas. To see this lovely goddess was to want her desperately. He ached to caress her as freely as the rippling water was doing at this very moment. He longed to run his fingers through the curly strands of chestnut hair that shone in the sunlight. He could almost feel the satiny texture of her skin beneath his hands, feel those soft lips melting against his like summer rain.

If Cord hadn't been sitting down he would have kicked himself for hallucinating about seducing this gorgeous firebrand. Oh, he'd like to take her, to appease this ravenous craving, to enjoy another kind of revenge on Victor. But there would be no pleasure in forcing a woman like Tempest Litchfield. He wanted her warm and willing and without a fight. She was a bona fide lady. She probably didn't know beans about satisfying a man, even if she was willing to try. And since she didn't hold men in high esteem, she would definitely reject his amorous advances. Knowing Tempest, and Cord had come to know her quite well already, he imagined Victor had to do some fancy talking just to steal an occasional kiss. Cord had stolen one himself—it had cost him a teeth-rattling blow to the jaw, but it had definitely been worth it. She tasted every bit as good as she looked . . .

He forced himself to his feet to tread along the winding path. He couldn't sit here and lollygag, he had supper to catch. Obviously, Tempest had no motive except to enjoy a bath, and he was getting himself steamed up for nothing. If he tarried much longer, ogling her, he might succumb to his lust.

He also knew this journey to his cabin in the mountains would be much easier if he and Tempest didn't become involved. He would mind what few manners he had and keep his distance. But he would dearly love to know why she had agreed to wed Victor Watts. She must have what she considered a good reason. Perhaps she was as anxious for wealth and social position as Victor was. That would certainly explain the alliance between the families. Tempest had said that she didn't love Victor. Well, that made two of them. Cord didn't like that murdering, deceitful bastard one bit and he was *not* letting himself become distracted by that bewitching little sprite, even if her presence tempted the man in Cord to the very extreme!

Six

After Tempest had bathed and eaten her meal of roasted rabbit and wild berries, she expected to stretch out on a pallet for much-needed sleep. That, however, did not fit Cord's plan for the evening. To her utter dismay, Cord bundled her off to retrieve her horse, which seemed as thrilled by the prospect of travel as Tempest did.

"We're tramping off in the dark?" Tempest muttered. "Can't this possibly wait 'til morning?"

"If I know Victor, he'll have a pack of *vaqueros* combing the countryside in search of us," Cord predicted. "And besides, Hueco Tanks is the only dependable water source for miles. I have no wish to encounter unexpected guests. In these parts, one can't be too careful of the company he keeps."

"Amen to that," Tempest sniffed, tossing Cord a look that suggested she wasn't too pleased with the company *she* was keeping.

"I'm not the scoundrel Victor has made me out to be," Cord said in his own defense.

Why he felt compelled to explain himself to a woman he didn't know. He never had before. His previous encounters usually lasted no longer than the time it took to take care of his sexual needs. He had never been one to talk much about his life to anyone who bothered to listen. He was a private man, a loner who had difficulty fitting into the Indian or the white man's world. He'd come closer to settling in with the Apache, but there was always that strange, unexplainable restlessness gnawing at him. Cord had been born under a wandering star, ever searching for that part of himself that seemed to be missing, hunting for that certain something he'd never been able to find in all his twenty-eight years.

"Then what sort of scoundrel do you profess to be?" Tempest prodded when Cord drifted off into silent contemplation. This was her chance to gain insight into this enigmatic man and hear his version of the story.

"For starters, I'm half-Apache and half-Scottish," Cord said as he picked his way along the serpentine trail, guided by instinct and moonlight.

"Is that supposed to have some drastic influence on becoming a scoundrel?" Tempest teased good-naturedly. "I'm half-English and half-German, but I'm not a rake and a rounder."

Cord chuckled despite himself. Although Tempest could be a bossy shrew at times, she had an uncanny way of making a man put his guard down. She also had the ability to appear genuinely interested in him as a fellow human being. Although Cord had never carried on a similar conversation with anyone but his own relatives, he revealed the information Tempest seemed eager to hear. Why it mattered to her, he wasn't certain. Insatiable curiosity on her part, he supposed. For damned sure, she had the kind of inquisitiveness that had killed scores of cats.

"My father was a dreamer and a drifter," Cord explained as he wove through the maze of boulders to reach the broad valley flanked by the moonlit precipices of the Sierra Diablo Mountains to the south. "My Apache mother died when I was only ten and my father always seemed to be off in search of rainbows. It was only three years ago that he and I became close. My grandfather took a hand in raising me for a few years before my father's sister insisted that I receive proper book learning. I spent part of my time with my aunt's family, part with my grandfather, and part by myself, perfecting the skills of survival. My grandfather always said the mark of a man is his ability to survive when all his enemies want him dead."

"And what else did your wise grandfather have to say?" Tempest questioned as they trekked across the desert landscape toward the distant Guadalupe mountains to the east.

Cord flung her a sly grin. "He said inquisitive females would inevitably learn more than they could ever hope to understand."

The teasing remark hit an exposed nerve. She jerked up her head to glare at the imposing silhouette perched on the steed beside her. "I sorely resent that attitude," she snapped indignantly. "Women have minds of their own and they can and do use them."

Tempest had used her mind to acquire a law degree, but she would be damned if she would reveal her profession to a client who may or may not be allowed the expertise of her legal counsel. *Not,* if he kept blurting out such narrow-minded opinions! And furthermore, she was sick and tired of her conscience nagging at her about unethical conduct unbecoming a lawyer when Cord hadn't treated her with the courtesy and respect a person had a right to expect.

She really shouldn't be feeling the least bit guilty about not being honest with a man who'd done her wrong a dozen different ways. She may have been lying by omission, but Cord had kidnapped her for revenge. If he had no true regard for her welfare, then she owed him nothing. Laughter rumbled in Cord's chest when he saw the moonlight reflecting the hot sparks in Tempest's eyes. "Those were my grandfather's words, not mine. As for me, I never really gave women much consideration."

Tempest could guess why, too. No doubt Cord MacIntosh had but one purpose for women. When his lust was appeased, he went on his way, never looking back. He did not seem the kind of man who was influenced by emotional attachments—if she could depend on Victor as a reliable source for information. Any man who would join the Union to escape a prisoner-of-war camp, and then join the battle in the West against the Indians, had no sense of obligation or responsibility other than to himself.

"Although you don't give a flying fig about how women feel and what they think, I wish you would explain why you took to wearing the blue uniform after you'd been captured during the war," Tempest insisted.

Cord swiveled his head toward her. Now it was his turn to glare. Obviously Victor had spread rumors to every citizen west of the Pecos, up to and including his fiancée. *Caramba!* There was no telling what vicious tales were wagging on Victor's tongue. The man was a master of subterfuge, always employing deceit to twist situations to his advantage.

"In that instance I followed my conscience," Cord growled.

Tempest wasn't sure he had one.

"I didn't give a damn what everybody else thought I was doing and I never have. If a man is ruled by what he *thinks* his neighbors are thinking then he is nothing but a puppet dancing on a string."

"Another of your grandfather's famous quips, I'm sure," Tempest said.

"Yes, as a matter of fact, But the way I saw it, I wasn't doing the South any good rotting away in a prisoner-of-war camp after that idiotic commander I had the misfortune of serving under blundered into a battle we couldn't win. That was the very last time I was foolish enough to take orders from a man who didn't know his ass from—"

"You needn't be so descriptive," Tempest interrupted with a distasteful sniff. "I get the picture, Mister MacIntosh. Do go on. I'm hanging on the edge of my saddle, yearning to know how you rationalized turning traitor to the South. You do seem to have a most remarkable way of alienating your countrymen."

"I presume you think if the war had been fought by women it would have turned out better," Cord smirked.

"If women were allowed to hold political office, there would have been no war at all," Tempest assured him with great conviction. "I have always contended that men have more brawn than brains, and they are plagued with an inborn need to demonstrate their physical superiority. It is simply a flaw of your gender, I'm afraid."

"I've seen a few females engage in fisticuffs in my time," Cord insisted. "They fight dirtier than men, I can tell you that for a fact." I hate to burst your idealistic bubble, Miss *Witch*field, but there are just as many obnoxious women in this world as there are men."

"For the sake of argument—and that is the only reason I won't debate the issue, by the way," she added with a haughty sniff, "we won't quibble over the unfortunate war. So why did you change your colors from Confederate gray to Union blue?"

"It's none of your business."

"I really would like to know," Tempest assured him in all honesty. "Forgive me. I suppose I'm argumentative and confrontational by nature and by habit. Another of my defects in personality, I'm sad to admit. But I can't begin to understand your motivation if you don't explain it to me. And I truly would like to understand."

Damn it, she'd done it again. She had drawn him out with that soft, sincere tone that appealed to his emotions rather than his intellect. Cord wasn't accustomed to dealing with the likes of Tempest Litchfield, probably because she was such a rare creature.

"When a man turns to spying for the South while wearing the Union uniform, he can't very well brag about it, now can he? That would defeat the purpose," he began.

Tempest blinked in astonishment. "You were acquiring information for the Confederacy?"

He nodded positively. "At the time, the Confederate Army was marching toward New Mexico to seize Santa Fe. Although my unit had been sent west to track down Cochise, who was at the height of his towering fury against Americanos and Mexicans, I was privy to important information. Our secretive communications passed through an intricate line of Southern sympathizers to Confederate commanders. It turned out to be a hopeless cause for the South and I looked to be a traitor to my fellow Texans." His broad shoulder lifted in a lackadaisical shrug. "But then, half-breeds aren't offered much respect anyway."

Tempest fell silent, marveling at this complicated man. She was beginning to understand him and yet she wasn't sure she knew him at all. He confused her. He seemed cold and callous at times, but there was still a lot of good in him, even if very few individuals were aware of it. But was he really telling her the truth? She wondered . . .

"When my commander learned that I was part Apache, he sent me to scout Cochise's strongholds, to chart the location of Victorio's and Geronimo's villages. I scouted them, all right," Cord snorted sardonically. "But not to lead a garrison of soldiers for an attack on women and children. My grandmother had been butchered by Mexican soldiers who followed the commands of crazed colonels years ago. I warned the Apache away from disaster. When my superior officer realized I wasn't working for him but against him, he had me court-martialed."

Now Tempest knew how Cord had acquired his bad reputation. He had no need to lie to her to protect himself since he was unaware she had been sent to defend him. She was fairly certain he had spoken the truth. He *had* followed his conscience, despite what the rest of the world thought. He refused to call any man master, to answer to others. Tempest could certainly identify with that . . .

Tempest nearly shrieked when she heard an eerie rattle beside her. Her mare bolted away from the sound, leaving Tempest clutching at the reins. The jolting gait rattled her bones and jarred her teeth. She grabbed the reins in frantic desperation. Now she regretted that Cord had trusted her enough to allow her to manage her own steed. He could have kept the frightened mare under control by sheer strength alone. She, however, could not! The horse seemed to race toward the ends of the earth after being spooked by the rattlesnake.

Frantic, Tempest clamped herself to the saddle and prayed for all she was worth. Despite the fact that the pommel stabbed her repeatedly in the chest, she clung to the mare's neck. All she could hear was the clatter of hooves and the creak of leather. She could feel the massive strength and taut muscles of the terrified creature beneath her. Each time the mare swerved from a shadow or leaped over a clump of cactus, Tempest swore she was about to be thrown. But somehow she held on and even managed to pry her eyes open to stare at the ground whizzing past her at phenomenal speed.

Then she spied the ghastly white landscape in front of her, broken by shimmering waves of silver. Rings of incandescent white stretched out before her and unexplainable ripples rolled across what appeared to be some sort of lake, flickering with flame-like animation in the moonlight. The mare seemed just as startled as Tempest. Dancing moonlight was playing tricks on their eyes, and both horse and rider became lost in the effervescent glow that swallowed them alive.

"Tempest! Pull down on the bridle and bit!" Cord bellowed as he raced after the runaway mare.

Tempest couldn't hear Cord. The only sound to penetrate her brain was the pelting of hooves that caused suffocating clouds to billow around her.

Suddenly the mare skidded to a halt and stumbled forward. Tempest and the mare abruptly parted company. She was catapulted over the mare's head and she held her breath in terror of what was to come. Her eyes stung as she squinted to watch the fingers of white fire reach upward to engulf her. Tempest knew she'd break her neck the instant she hit the ground. It was inevitable, considering she had been launched through the air at the speed of light. But to her shock and relief, she landed with a splash rather than a thud. Instead of plunging into the foggy depths she merely bobbed on the surface like a buoy, which was a darned good thing since she couldn't swim a lick.

The taste of salt was on her lips. It burned like fire in her eyes. Tempest finally realized where she was. This had to be one of the salt lakes that had been discovered six years earlier. Here she was, floating on a lake where it was practically impossible to sink because the water was so saturated with salt.

Blindly, Tempest thrashed toward the whinny of her steed and the clatter of an approaching rider.

She heard a splash in the shallows and felt a lean hand hoisting her up into sturdy arms.

"You okay, Tempest?" Cord questioned before he set the salt-caked bundle on solid ground. "Why didn't you pull down on the bit like I told you? The mare would have stopped before you bruised her tender mouth."

"I didn't hear you," Tempest grumbled. "I had salt in my ears, for heaven's sake!"

Her feeble attempt at humor didn't amuse Cord. His attention was focused on the fallen mare that refused to struggle back to her feet. Reluctantly, Cord knelt beside the bay mare to inspect her leg. Broken. He was afraid that was the case. Damn, he hated to put down a good animal. He had a certain affection for horses. He'd been raising and training them since he'd been dismissed from the Union Army.

Grimly, Cord reached for the rifle he had purchased in El Paso del Norte.

"What are you doing?" Tempest demanded when she wiped the salt from her eyes to see Cord taking aim at her steed.

"Back off," Cord ordered. "I have to put her out of her misery."

Tempest stared down into those doleful black eyes. The helpless creature was begging for assistance and Tempest responded by placing herself between Cord and the injured steed.

"I won't let you do it," she said with finality.

"There's nothing I can do to save her."

"But—"

Before Tempest could voice another objection, Cord's hand snaked out to jerk her out of the way. She stumbled over the soggy hem of her gown. She had barely hit the ground when the rifle barked in the night, followed by a sickening silence. The realization of how quickly life came and went hit Tempest with vivid clarity. She blamed herself for being too inexperienced to prevent the fall. She blamed Cord for having all the sensitivity of a rock.

"You brute!" Tempest attributed the tears in her eyes to the sting of salt, though she knew better. In frustration, she muffled a sniff and scraped herself off the ground. "If you have no more regard for life than to destroy it without first attempting to save it, then you are probably guilty of every offense Victor says you've committed!"

Cord jerked her to him with his free hand and shook her good and hard. Her head snapped backward, sending a waterfall of tangled hair tumbling over her shoulders. Through misty eyes Tempest watched Cord stick his face into hers and snarl. Again she found herself confronting the dark, explosive side of this paradoxical man. It was terrifying to have him loom over her.

"Look, Miss *Witch*field, I did what I had to do, whether you and I liked it or not," he fumed. "The *crime* would have been to let the mare suffer, dragging death into torment. Sometimes life can be cruel. You've been living in your ivory tower so damned long you try to judge all the world and everybody in it by your standards."

He made a stabbing gesture toward the effervescent salt lake. "My father lost his life because of this piece of land and a fertile mountain pasture *he* laid claim to. *Your* greedy fiancé wanted it. Paddy was a man, not a horse. Now don't talk to me about what's right and wrong and who committed the unpardonable sins around here! If you want to throw stones, throw them at your precious Victor!"

"You're hurting my arm!" Tempest yelped when his lean fingers bit so deeply into her elbow that he cut off her circulation.

Cord released her abruptly and wheeled toward his steed. "Climb on behind me, Miss *Witch*field, or start walking. I don't particularly care which at the moment."

The incident at the lake caused bitter memories to surface in Cord's mind. It was like pouring salt on a festering wound. Although Paddy had never been a model father, he was still Cord's blood kin. His need to avenge the senseless death returned in full force. Damn that Victor Watts, Cord seethed. That sneaky viper would pay for what he'd done!

It was not Tempest's nature to be submissive, but with bowed head she ambled toward Cord to accept his outstretched hand of assistance. Reluctantly, she curled her arms around his waist to steady herself behind him on his horse.

The feel of his body brushing familiarly against hers set off an unexpected chain of sensations. Tempest inched away as far as the saddle would permit, allowing only minimal physical contact. But she still felt trapped in the phenomenal aura that hovered around Cord MacIntosh. Tempest felt a strange affinity toward him that defied better judgment. At times, he seemed capable of ruthless violence. He hadn't batted an eyelash at putting the mare down, even though he said he didn't like doing it. And at other times Cord could be tender and generous . . .

Tempest dug into her pocket to retrieve the timepiece Cord had given her. The watch had not suffered irreparable damage from the salt water. Luckily, it was still ticking so she pinned it on the sleeve of her gown to let it dry out.

They had ridden in silence for a quarter of an hour before Tempest cleared the salt from her vocal cords. "I'm sorry, Mister MacIntosh," she said.

"Cord," he corrected.

"I'm sorry about the mare. It was all my fault. And I'm terribly sorry about your father, too. I don't know the details surrounding his death, but—"

"Of course you don't," Cord cut in. "Victor only

tells you and everybody else his version of things. They believe what he wants them to believe. And if you marry that conniving bastard, you'll be making the biggest mistake of your life."

"And just what are you implying?" Tempest inquired as she stared at his rigid back.

"Somehow or another, Victor disposed of my father because he wanted possession of the salt lakes and the ranch in High Lonesome Valley. Victor has been slandering the MacIntosh name for two years before he became impatient enough to resort to violence. He and his associates in El Paso want the rights to the lakes so they can charge a high fee for the removal of salt. Before 1862, El Pasoans on both sides of the Rio Grande had obtained their salt supplies from the Tularosa Basin in New Mexico. When news of these Texas lakes reached the border towns, scores of wagons rolled out here. My father didn't charge fees for the salt, not to Americans or Mexicans."

Cord tossed her an accusing glance. "Your darling Victor tried to buy the rights to the lakes from my father so he could ship supplies to the interior of Mexico for huge profit. He wanted to monopolize the salt and increase the revenue by making his neighbors pay for something my father generously gave away. The only reason my father bought this land in the first place was to be sure the Indians had rights to it as well. You know how white men are. They have a natural tendency to think whatever originally belonged to the Indians is theirs for the taking."

"Victor claims your family had little or nothing," Tempest countered, eyeing Cord suspiciously. "Why wouldn't your father have seized the chance to sell the minerals on land he'd acquired? And where did he get the money to purchase it in the first place?"

"Does everything have its price to you and your precious Victor?" Cord snapped insultingly.

"You don't have to bite my head off," Tempest flung at him, along with a sizzling glare. "I was only trying to understand you and your father."

"*Caramba!* You'd make one whale of an attorney," Cord snorted. "You're relentless with your questions."

Tempest chose not to enlighten him. She had trained herself to ask leading questions that prompted voluntary information. She was learning things about Cord and Paddy MacIntosh she might never have known if Cord was aware of her identity. She was gaining a broader perspective of the man himself. Since Cord didn't know who she really was, he had no reason to play a role, as most of her clients tended to do when they offered their explanations. Cord played no charade, made no pretense. And because of her abduction she had learned to read Cord's moods. She'd seen him tired, bitter, spiteful, and even playful, but never frightened.

That facet of his personality truly fascinated her. How could a man develop such incredible courage? Undoubtedly, his vast and varied experiences had made him immune to fright. He'd seen and done all there was to do in life. Nothing surprised or scared him. He'd built a thick shell around his emotions that nothing could penetrate. He seemed to operate on the theory that if he expected nothing from anyone then he would never be disappointed.

"You'd have to live off the land, as if you were a part of nature, if you want to understand the workings of the MacIntosh mind," Cord said in belated response to her remark. "How can a man truly own something that has been here since the beginning of time? The Apache cannot fathom how white men can presume to sell off chunks of earth, as if it were theirs to dispose of and purchase on a whim. To the Apache, one could just as easily slice off a portion of the sky and put a price tag on it."

"But you mentioned earlier that your father purchased these lakes and a mountain valley," Tempest reminded him.

"Yes," Cord acknowledged. "He did so to protect it from greedy intruders like Victor."

"With what?" Tempest pried. "Victor insisted that your family lived hand-to-mouth for several years. He also speculated that—"

"Victor doesn't know all and see all," Cord muttered in interruption. "I've got everything your darling Victor has, except a pack of lies. *He* flaunts his money and *I* don't."

Cord didn't like what he was feeling when it came to the subject of Tempest Litchfield and her relationship with Victor. He was damned tired of hearing her refer to what Victor said and what Victor thought! If Cord didn't know better, he'd swear he was experiencing a twinge of jealousy. That was ridiculous! And worse, he didn't like that helpless feeling in the pit of his belly when Tempest's mare had bolted away from the rattlesnake earlier in the evening. Good God, he'd actually been frightened. Not for himself, but for her. What the hell was wrong with him? Nothing usually scared him these days. He'd stared death in the face a dozen times without batting an eyelash.

"You bought all this land with the profit you've made from training horses and selling cattle?" Tempest quizzed, refusing to drop the conversation until she satisfied her curiosity.

Absently she glanced at her watch, wondering when, where, or if Cord would see fit to pause for the night. As it was, there wasn't much left of it.

Cord twisted in the saddle to peer into her moon-drenched features. That was a mistake because he liked what he saw a lot more than he wished he did. And to make matters worse, his arm accidentally brushed against her breasts, increasing his awareness of this chestnut-haired siren.

"Don't you ever get tired of asking questions and prying into everybody's business?" he asked in his usual plainspoken manner.

"No, I'm all curiosity," Tempest assured him without daring to gaze into that chiseled face.

Their incidental body contact was quite unsettling. Tempest didn't appreciate this heightened awareness of Cord, either. The man was beginning to stir her in ways she didn't expect and that wasn't a good thing! She had strived to keep their relationship as impersonal as possible and wasn't sure she could handle emotions that leaned toward the romantic.

Cord was agog with curiosity himself. It had nothing to do with *who* this feisty lady was but rather *why* she had such an incredible effect on him. He found himself aching to retest his volatile reaction to their first kiss. The taste of this temptress was still on his lips and the presence of her body beside him was a constant lure. When he stared into those thick-lashed blue eyes, he could think of nothing but the hungry need deep inside him.

When his head moved slowly toward hers, Tempest's gaze locked with those glowing pools of amber. She had resolved never to let him kiss her. But when his sinewy arm glided around her to pull her close, her willpower melted. *Here we go again,* Tempest thought.

Warm, sensuous lips closed over hers with such gentle expertise that she lost the will to fight him almost at once. The faintly demanding pressure of his kiss allowed her to give only as much as she desired in return. The sharp contrast between the bold, ominous renegade and this tender seduction threw Tempest completely off balance. Her analytical mind failed her, leaving her innocent body vulnerable to the wild tremors that danced down her spine. Without rhyme or reason, Tempest—a dedicated spinster who had never experienced anything remotely close to love or passion—was suddenly craving all this sensuous outlaw had to offer.

Her traitorous body tingled with titillating sparks, kindling fires that burned in the core of her being. She had been kissed on several occasions, but never quite like this! This was no respectful peck, nor was it a ravenous embrace. It was as warm and compelling as their first kiss. The erotic sensations fed upon themselves until Tempest swore there were actually waves of fire undulating through her bloodstream.

As if her arms possessed a will of their own, they glided over the muscled expanse of his shoulders to toy with the wavy hair that dangled against the nape of his neck. For a moment his mouth left hers and he stared down into her passion-drugged eyes. Tempest felt as if all her body had ceased to function. Only when he kissed her could she breathe. It was as if she needed his lips on hers to survive. It was scary to be so absorbed in a kiss which shouldn't have happened at all! The first one had knocked her to her knees. This one would have knocked her feet out from under her if she had been standing!

Before Tempest could rally her defenses and pull away, his mouth moved expertly over hers. Her lips involuntarily opened when his tongue probed. A quiet moan wobbled in her chest when his hands began to wander freely over the taut peaks of her breasts and then drifted over the ultrasensitive flesh of her thighs. Suddenly Tempest was drowning in a sea of forbidden sensations. Cord had only whetted her appetite with his kisses and caresses. Despite her previous resolve, she found herself arching toward him, wanting more.

Cord felt his heart give a frantic lurch when he dared to touch Tempest so familiarly, to kiss her as if they were long-lost lovers who'd been separated for an eternity. Desire burgeoned inside him, wreaking havoc. He couldn't seem to get enough of this curvaceous beauty who tasted like fine wine and felt like heaven. He was instantly addicted to the feel of her ripe body nestled in his arms, to those honeyed lips whose only experience was what she had learned from him.

God! He wanted things this naive beauty didn't know how to give. Wasn't it enough that he was using her as a pawn in his feud with Victor? Did he have to want her so desperately as well? He hated what she did to him, hated how vulnerable she made him feel. And more than that, he despised being envious of anything a snake like Victor Watts called his own!

These traitorous feelings had been building inside him like a stockpile of explosives since the moment he'd first seen Tempest. He'd fought the lusty feelings quite admirably, if he did say so himself. He didn't remember ever wanting a woman as much as he wanted Tempest, even though she was unaware of what transpired between a man and a woman in the throes of passion. For God's sake, what a time to find himself alone with a virgin who had turned his emotions inside out!

With considerable effort, Cord pried his arms and lips away and clutched at the reins. His breathing was heavy and the ache in his loins left him on the verge of doubling over in pain.

Tempest clenched the cantle of the saddle for support, refusing to lean against Cord unless absolutely necessary. She feared she would catch fire and burn if he touched her again. Sweet merciful heavens, why did this hard-bitten renegade affect her so? They were as different as night and day. They came from contrasting backgrounds and they led very different lives. But if it were true that opposites attract, Tempest feared she was headed for disaster!

Although she had always loved a challenge and there was nothing more challenging than this dark-haired renegade, she had to keep her distance. He was both dangerous and alluring. She was intrigued, despite the fact that he could have easily been guilty of the crimes he allegedly committed. She knew for a fact that he was guilty of kidnapping, if nothing else.

It would be in her best interest to reveal her true identity and insist that Cord return her to El Paso posthaste. But that would alter everything between them. And God help her, she was beginning to like things just the way they were! Tempest tried to tamp down the lingering sensations his kisses and caresses had evoked. She wasn't quite ready to return to El Paso yet. She wanted to know where this madcap adventure would lead. And she did crave adventure. It was another of her foibles, one which would probably get her into more trouble than she could handle!

Seven

Tempest peered up at the Guadalupe Mountains that had been looming down at her for more than a day. But no matter how many hours she remained in the saddle, plodding ever eastward, she never reached the craggy peaks shouldered by dark threatening clouds. She knew something was amiss when Cord shifted uneasily in front of her on their weary steed. In wary anticipation she watched the churning clouds engulf the mountains and roll across the desert, lifting the sand into a choking fog.

As if it wasn't enough to contend with the rapidly approaching storm, Tempest heard the echo of gunfire to the west. She and Cord swiveled simultaneously to see a dozen bravos racing toward them.

"Damn, Victor's men," Cord said with a scowl. He had expected to have a rescue brigade trail him sooner or later. He'd hoped it would be later, after he reached the sanctity of the mountains. "I'm sure you're delighted to see them."

Just when Tempest was beginning to like him, Cord did something to turn her against him, leaving her to wonder if he wasn't as merciless as Victor claimed. Instead of doing the gentlemanly thing by hoisting her in front of him to protect her, Cord remained where he was, leaving her unshielded against flying bullets.

When Tempest considered letting go and tumbling off the back of the steed to be rescued by the *vaqueros,* her self-preservation instincts betrayed her. Cord gouged their mount, forcing the gelding into his swiftest pace and Tempest stuck to Cord like glue. Bullets whistled around them as Cord zigzagged from one mesquite bush to another. Tempest instinctively dug her nails into Cord's waist and clamped herself around him like Spanish moss.

With wild eyes, she watched Cord rein the steed right into the path of the churning cloud of sand. In less than a few minutes they were engulfed in the rolling storm. Sand pelted her like miniature hailstones and Tempest sputtered to catch a breath that wasn't saturated with fine granules. Although she could barely see her hand in front of her face with this dust in her eyes, she felt Cord rein sharply to the north.

He was shrewd, she'd give him that. Victor's riders would have difficulty tracking them through this driving sandstorm. The wind howled and whirled around them so fiercely that Tempest clutched the hem of her gown, drew it over her face, and pressed her cheek against Cord's back. She could feel the tautness in his body as he galloped blindly ahead, depending on pure instinct to guide him toward the protection of the mountains.

When the laboring steed stumbled, Tempest was instantly reminded of being hurled into the salt lake. Desperately, she clutched at Cord, who was propelled forward by the momentum of his steed. The only difference was that he had the good sense to fling himself backward and jerk the horse's head up with the reins. If Tempest had been the one in control of their mount, they would have been swan-diving into the shifting sand.

A muffled yelp burst from Tempest when Cord flung himself toward her, mashing her nose into his spine. But better a bent nose than a broken neck, she decided. She would have to remember that tactic if a steed ever stumbled beneath her again.

"You okay, Tempest?" Cord questioned when he heard her groan.

"You have the gall to ask me that after you were inconsiderate enough to leave me sitting behind you to catch all the bullets?" she muttered.

"A simple yes or no was all I wanted." Cord scowled as he spit sand out of his mouth.

"You were unnecessarily reckless with my life," she accused. "I'm beginning to think you're every bit the scoundrel Victor says you are!"

"When are you going to stop giving me hell, woman?" Cord growled.

"When have you deserved anything else?"

At the moment, Cord didn't give a whit what this sassy bundle thought of him, nor did he have the time for a lengthy debate about his lack of consideration. He wanted to lose himself in the labyrinth of canyons before Victor's henchmen caught up. Knowing Victor, he would order Cord brought back dead or alive—dead being the preference. That would certainly simplify Victor's problems, and Cord would be out of the way permanently.

For more than an hour Cord navigated his way through the swirling sand before he reached the foothills of the Guadalupes. The blockade of towering peaks improved visibility enough for Cord to dismount and pick his way along the familiar path he'd traveled dozens of times in the past. Cord tugged Tempest along with him, headed toward the many cave sites carved into the limestone cliffs of Madera Canyon and eastward to Forbidden Mountain.

Tempest stared curiously at the pictographs etched in the cliffs. Roasting pits and fire holes that had once been used to distill whiskey from sotol plants were in front of the shallow caves. It was obvious that Indians had also utilized this area during their treks cross-country to raid the hated white settlers and their life-long enemies in Mexico.

When Tempest dared to glance over the rim of Needle Rock Peak, around which they'd been traveling for the better part of an hour, she instinctively backed away from the ledge to cling to the jutting stone wall. A huge canyon lay beneath her at a sheer drop of one thousand feet. The steep rock gorge opened like the jaws of a prehistoric monster, waiting to swallow her up.

Tempest sucked in a breath of air and focused on the cave rather than the vast expanse of nothingness that stretched out in front of her. It was difficult to believe that a few hours earlier they had been plugging across the arid desert. Here at these higher elevations the temperature was a good twenty degrees cooler and yellow poppies, phlox, and blue flax waved in the breeze, contrasting with the cactus and scrub brush that had filled the scenery the past few days . . .

Tempest assured herself it was the change in temperature rather than her unnerving fear of height. She had damned well better get used to tiptoeing along the precarious precipices because it looked as though she would be doing plenty of it for the next few days. Every step would leave her flirting with disaster.

Her ridiculous romantic notions and her desire to understand Cord were forgotten in the face of this most recent challenge. Tempest wasn't accustomed to this rigorous pace or lifestyle. As adventurous and daring as she was, all in the name of improving the esteem of womankind in this man's world, her fortitude wavered when her eyes fell from the towering rocks to the plunging arroyos. Instinctively, she latched onto the first possible handhold and backed against solid rock. Her scalp prickled. Her nerves stood on end and so did the hair on the back of her neck.

"I want to go home!" Tempest croaked while she clung like ivy to the perpendicular rock wall behind her.

Cord glanced at the wind-blown beauty plastered against the limestone wall. "Then go ahead and jump if you're in such an all-fired rush."

It amused him to see this strong-willed woman cowering for a change. He made a mental note to threaten to throw her off a cliff the next time she sassed him. Falling seemed to be the only thing that unraveled her composure. Nothing else fazed her.

Tempest, still rooted to the spot, flashed him a glare that was hot enough to melt rock. She did not appreciate anyone seeing her weakness, especially not those of the male persuasion in general, and Cord MacIntosh in particular! Why she had the slightest need to impress him in the first place was a perplexing question she'd been unable to answer. No doubt a man like Cord would be impossible to impress. He was utterly invincible. While she was clinging to the wall for dear life, Cord was moseying along the edge like a bird that could have spread its wings and sailed off any time. Damn him for being so agile and fearless, and damn her for being such a coward!

"Come here, princess," Cord chuckled, extending his hand to her. "You should see the view from the windows of your ivory tower. It's quite spectacular."

Tempest was determined to stay where she was. "I like it where I am, thanks just the same," she chirped, her voice and her knees nowhere near as steady as she'd hoped. "I'll just—" A terrified shriek exploded from her when Cord snaked out his hand and uprooted her.

Although Tempest would have liked to strangle this ornery rascal for teasing her about her worst fear, she clamped onto him in sheer desperation. She buried her head against his chest and instinctively squeezed.

"I hate you, Cord MacIntosh," she choked out. "You're a horrible beast!"

Still chuckling, he pried her loose and turned her so her back was pressed to his chest. He forced her to stare across the panoramic valley filled with gigantic boulders, ponderosa pine, fir, and oak trees. The brisk winds that swept down the side of the mountains vibrated through the needles of the pines and every branch seemed to come to life. Her senses were so attuned to the sights and sounds and smells of nature that she marveled at the maelstrom of emotions that rippled through her.

Tempest could not make herself relax. She was battling this innate fear that left her feeling as if she was going to be drawn into the wild expanse of emptiness like metal to a powerful magnet. But she did admit there was something exhilarating about the view. When Cord gestured toward another cave at lower elevations, she spied a black bear lumbering along with its woolly cub bounding behind her. Cord called her attention to a pair of deer drinking from the silvery stream that meandered through the valley floor. She had a bird's-eye view of the world and a strange peacefulness overcame her.

As the fear subsided, Tempest drew a breath and looked out at a world unmarred by humans. There was a certain beauty, yet an untamed savagery in these mountains. She was beginning to understand why the Apache thought it ridiculous to attempt to buy and sell Mother Nature's handiwork. She could even comprehend Cord and Paddy MacIntosh's belief that the salt lakes in the desert to the west were another of God's gifts, just like these rugged peaks and spectacular canyons. Man was merely steward of this land, taking only what he needed without upsetting the balance of nature.

"Sometimes, Tempest, that which we fear most becomes as precious to us as life itself," Cord murmured as he stared at the grandeur. "My grandfather says fear is no more than a lack of understanding. We are afraid to trust what we cannot comprehend. He says we should challenge and conquer rather than retreat."

"Your grandfather certainly has a lot to say," Tempest replied. "I wonder how philosophical he'd be if you were nudging *him* toward the crumbling edge of this cliff."

"He employed this same tactic on me when I was a child."

"You were actually a child at one point in your life?" She sniffed sarcastically. "I was under the impression that you came unassembled and were put together without sympathy and consideration."

Tempest was purposely being sarcastic. It was her only defense. She was beginning to like the feel of Cord's arms around her a little too much. His touch left her body quivering like a tuning fork. Her remarks served as a barrier between them.

"I grew up just like most folks," Cord assured her. "But there's a big difference between you and me. I didn't ply my grandfather with wisecracks when he stuck me out on a ledge. I looked to see what I could learn instead of where I might fall. If you weren't so busy being defensive you might learn something by living on the edge."

She was learning something all right. Cord had slipped his arms around her waist and was resting his chin on the top of her head while she clutched at his hips for support. A few minutes earlier she would have liked to shoot him for teasing her. Now she was wishing he'd . . . Well, it was so utterly preposterous it didn't bear thinking about. She did *not* want Cord to kiss her after he'd used her as a shield and then pushed her to the edge of this cliff!

"Let me go," Tempest snapped, furious with her traitorous body. When Cord released her, she dug her nails into his hips, fearing she would plunge to her death. "Let me rephrase that." She gulped hard when she found herself pulled by the unnerving force of gravity. "Get me out of here! You're scaring the living daylights out of me."

"For a kiss I'll—" Cord tried to bargain with her but she cut him off in midsentence.

"I'd rather jump, you scoundrel."

She squawked in panic when Cord stepped back a pace, leaving her feeling alone and afraid.

"Go ahead then," he offered generously.

Tempest flew into his arms and clung to him for all she was worth, humiliating herself all the more. That scamp! He was enjoying this game of his at her expense. It was a dirty trick and she intended to tell him so as soon as her lungs and vocal cords began to function properly.

Cord would have enjoyed standing there for the remainder of the evening, feeling Tempest's shapely body against his. But they still had miles to go before he would deem it safe to stop for the night. The trail that meandered through the mountains was better traveled in daylight—too many treacherous curves. As inexperienced as Tempest was, she could find her worst nightmare a reality if she took one step in the wrong direction.

Besides the fact that they needed to make tracks to elude the *vaqueros,* Cord found himself hounded by erotic sensations. He was fascinated by this gorgeous female. He didn't want to be, not when he could almost taste revenge against Victor. For two weeks he had paced the jail, plotting to repay Victor for his lies and deceit. When he received the news of his father's death, thoughts of vindication had completely poisoned his mind. Now this woman was distracting him, making him want things that had nothing to do with retaliation.

Tempest was Cord's trump card, a means to an end. And when she stirred him physically, he should simply take her for his own pleasure—another method of tormenting Victor. And yet, bitter and spiteful though Cord most certainly was, he couldn't lower himself to subject this chestnut-haired beauty to animal lust.

Cord wondered if he was crazy as he led Tempest and the horse along the narrow path flanked by a towering limestone wall on one side and a five-hundred-foot drop on the other. Since when had a woman's feelings mattered to him? And when had his feelings mattered to the females who had come and gone from his bed? Emotion had nothing to do with sexual satisfaction, at least not the kind he'd experienced. It wasn't personal or sacred. It was merely fulfilling physical needs which, once satisfied, no longer mattered. He had never spent so many consecutive hours with a woman, learning her moods, watching her confront her fears and battling situations that tested her stamina and her spirit.

That was my mistake, Cord realized in mid-step. He had gotten to know this female who was as quick-witted as she was beautiful. He probably would have felt the same way about any other woman with whom he'd spent endless hours. It wasn't Tempest *per se.* It was only the situation. *Yes, that had to be it,* Cord assured himself confidently. He was only intrigued by what made females tick, learning how they responded to danger and difficulty.

Cord felt much better after having a heart-to-heart talk with himself. Now he could put his mission back into proper perspective and plan the next phase of his retaliation against Victor. When he'd had his long-awaited revenge, he would gladly send this hell-cat back where she belonged. He would have tired of her and be anxious to have her out of his hair.

Caramba! There for a minute Cord thought he might actually *like* this blue-eyed shrew. Luckily, he had analyzed the situation and realized his gnawing hunger was a natural male response. Cord shoved his pensive musings aside and picked his way down the winding path to the stream, convinced that nothing had changed. He still had one primary objective in life and nothing or no one would divert him, not even this shapely she-male who begrudgingly clung to his hand to keep her balance.

Tempest sucked in her breath and willed her weary legs to keep trudging along the endless path. They had reached the part of the trail where pines and fir trees lined the canyon rim. The path circled and gradually descended into the bowl-shaped valley that lay like a plush green oasis in the distance. Then they came to the treacherous stretch of the trail . . . Tempest swallowed apprehensively. The path seemed to stretch toward heaven and then drop toward the dark pits of hell. How she was going to find footing on the angled boulders Tempest didn't know. Even the horse looked as if it was wondering how to proceed when the snake-like trail barely left enough space for one foot, much less four hooves, in front of the other.

Cord drew Tempest ahead of him so that she, he, and the gelding could move single file between the wind-scoured boulders. They climbed upward at a sixty-degree pitch before being forced to descend at the same steep angle. Tempest found herself squeezing Cord's hand nearly in two when she had to inch along the face of another cliff on a narrow ledge. When they had reached a plateau of limestone that jutted out over a four-hundred-foot drop, Tempest hesitated.

"Don't stop. Keep walking and look straight ahead of you," Cord instructed. "We're doing fine."

"Speak for yourself," Tempest replied. "I'm scared stiff, if you want to know."

"We're almost there," Cord replied, trying to encourage her.

Almost there? Tempest would have burst out laughing but she feared she would hurl herself off the cliff. They would be almost there, all right, if they leaped off the stone platform and fell the rest of the way to the valley floor!

Tempest had learned a great deal about herself since this ordeal began. For one thing, she was a bigger coward than she had thought. No matter how many times she rallied her determination, this ominous fear of height came rolling back like a tidal wave, leaving her clinging to Cord in frantic desperation.

What a helpless ninny he probably thought she was! Once she had been taken out of her own element she lacked her usual self-confidence. In a courtroom or at a social gathering she could move with poise and self-assurance. But out here in the howling wilderness, civilized society and its rules did not exist. Cord was dragging her through a world that was as foreign as China and she was involuntarily balking at each new obstacle. That wasn't like her at all!

Finally, they reached the valley floor and Tempest waded into the waist-deep water. She had managed to survive, though she swore she'd been a goner at least a dozen times.

An amused smile pursed Cord's lips as he watched Tempest relax in midstream. "Don't get too comfortable, princess," he teased. "There is another valley below this one. This river pours underground just around the bend and then plunges out through a cave into a waterfall."

Tempest swiveled her head to stare at the powerfully built man standing on the creek bank. "Surely we're not going to tackle another path in the dark!"

The horrified look on her exquisite features provoked Cord to chuckle. "No, I suppose we can spend the night here, but prepare yourself for tomorrow . . ."

The sound of tumbling rocks brought Cord's head around. A scowl clouded his bronzed face when he spied movement in the underbrush. "Damn, not again!"

But sure enough, there were the *vaqueros* with Emilio Reynosa at the helm. Cord should have remembered that Reynosa had a nose like a bloodhound. It was a shame that skilled *pistolero* had to work for a bastard like Victor Watts. Emilio was a hard man to shake. He had brought his men up through Guadalupe Pass to Blue Hole and Tricky Gap to cut them off. Damn, what rotten timing! Cord and Tempest had yet to catch their breath and the chase was on again!

Tempest's heart slammed against her ribs when she heard the crack of rifles echoing around the box canyon. In the twilight, dark heads emerged from behind the looming boulders to the east. Her wild-eyed gaze swung to Cord who was the target of gunfire. While he was dashing toward her, one of the bullets caught him in the left arm. He plunged into the river, leaving a trail of blood behind him.

The cavalcade of bravos poured down from the canyon rim like swarming hornets. Rifle fire exploded around Tempest as she watched Cord cut through the water like a shark. Before she had time to catch her breath, he clutched her shoulders and dragged her beneath the rippling surface.

Tempest was not a swimmer and she had never

claimed to be. She could barely dog paddle and stay afloat and she never waded in over her head . . . until now. Cord was tugging her toward the depths of the channel where the current rushed them along the stony river bed. She was sure her lungs were about to burst. Frantic, she surged toward the surface for air. Her panicky gaze landed on the pack of *vaqueros* who had their backs to her, staring at the spot upstream where she and Cord had gone down.

"You'll have to hold your breath a good long while," Cord whispered as he rose beside her. "We've got to follow the river underground if we're going to get out of here alive."

"Underground? As in a dark sepulcher of water?" Tempest croaked like a waterlogged bullfrog. Lord help her, she was going to drown. Terror gripped her throat when Cord clutched her arm and jerked her with him toward the limestone arch where the river disappeared from sight . . . and so would she in a matter of seconds!

Despite the burning pain in his arm, Cord hoisted Tempest and himself up for one last breath before the water surged through the pitch-black tunnel. He glanced anxiously toward the *vaqueros,* who had charged off in the wrong direction, certain their prey had headed toward the reeds that skirted the northern bank of the river. While the Mexicans were thrashing through the weeds, Cord pulled Tempest's rigid body down with his to be swept along with the fierce current.

Tempest grimaced uncomfortably when her hip collided with rock. She hadn't realized she had a fear of closed spaces until she found herself swallowed in a watery grave. Her heart hammered against her ribs and her lungs ached as if they would burst any second. Horrified, she opened her eyes, hoping and praying that a light would appear in the near distance. But it was so dark in the underground river that she wouldn't have recognized her own father if he swam by.

The feel of Cord's lean fingers clamped to her elbow was the only indication that she had not gone to her grave alone. Tempest was desperate for air. She would have given away all her worldly possessions and sold her soul for a precious breath! She wouldn't make it out alive. Her lungs were on the verge of exploding!

Wildly, Tempest thrashed upward, only to clank her head on a rock. Terror riveted her when her life flashed before her eyes, assuring her that this ordeal was nearly over and she would be on her way to the pearly gates.

She would never see her beloved father again and she was going to die with a guilty conscience. She had always tried to be open and honest, until she purposely deceived Cord because of her own spiteful pettiness and her unscrupulous attempt to outsmart him. She had so many sins against her because of this complicated man.

At that instant, when time stood still and Tempest prepared to meet her destiny, a pinpoint of light appeared before her. It grew larger with each erratic beat of her pulse. But still she could find no breath of life, no salvation. The light consumed her and she felt herself falling through space, wondering if she were being transported to a lower sphere where the demons lurked. Tempest knew, without a doubt, what the resident demon looked like. He had midnight hair and tawny eyes that glittered with mocking amusement. She was going to spend eternity in hell for lying about her identity and for succumbing to a physical attraction for the kind of man she shouldn't even tolerate, much less desire! She was going to be roasting over the flames with the man who had dragged her through one life-threatening situation after another before he finally managed to kill her with this last daredevil stunt . . .

That was the last thought to skip through Tempest's dazed mind before the shimmering light lapsed into darkness and the rush of water evaporated into deafening silence . . .

Gasping for breath, Cord exploded to the surface of the deep pool that lay beneath the waterfall. His frantic gaze darted from side to side, searching for Tempest. When they had burst from the opening of the cave, he'd lost his grasp on her limp arm and now she was nowhere to be found.

Darkness had settled over the canyon and the *vaqueros* were left at higher elevations. It would take them the rest of the night to make their way around the treacherous cliffs of the box canyon unless they followed the same perilous course. Cord and Tempest would have time to pick their way along the valley . . . if only he could find her, if only she wasn't . . .

Cord refused to let himself believe that she had perished. She was a willful woman, after all. She would survive, if only to give him hell for putting her through such torture . . .

When Cord felt something float past his knee, he reached down to clutch at the object which turned out to be Tempest's soggy gown. Hurriedly, he jerked her upward and side-stroked toward shore with her lifeless body draped over his shoulder.

"Damn you, woman," Cord growled. "Don't you give out on me now."

Cord would never be able to forgive himself if he cost Tempest her life. He had made her his pawn in a vengeful game against Victor. The thought caused Cord to grimace. He had felt regret many times over the years for the things he'd had to do, but he was unaccustomed to the oppressive feelings that hounded him now. He had put Tempest's life at risk several times. He had ridiculed her, and judged her . . . And damn it, he probably killed her!

Forgetting his own wound, Cord pulled Tempest ashore and shoved the heel of his hands into her shoulder blades. Over and over again, he forced the water from her lungs, refusing to let her slip away, willing her to battle the odds and survive.

"You know you want to get back on your feet and shoot off that mouth of yours," Cord muttered at his lifeless patient. "You live to torment me, don't you, Tempest? Now don't disappoint me, woman. Live!"

Cord cursed when he received no response, no matter how hard he tried to revive her. Desperate, he rolled her to her back and put his lips over her blue-tinged mouth, giving her his own breath, his strength, his fierce determination.

When she finally sputtered and gasped, Cord turned her to her stomach, hoping to force the last of the water out. He was *not* giving up until she was breathing on her own, even if it took the whole damn night.

After what seemed like a hundred years, Tempest roused to consciousness. She felt Cord shoving her spine into her chest and mashing her face into the grass. For several minutes she sucked air like a fish out of water. With a wheeze and a cough, Tempest felt life's breath filling her saturated lungs. Although she felt like a limp jellyfish, she did manage to voice the curse Cord MacIntosh so richly deserved.

"Damn you, Cord," she choked out. "I'll never forgive you for that. I hope Victor hangs you from the tallest tree in Texas!"

Tempest would have killed him herself, tortured

him very slowly over an open fire, but she was too exhausted at the moment.

Cord's shoulders sagged in relief. Tempest had survived, if only to chew him up one side and down the other.

Mustering her energy, she rolled to her back to flash Cord a poisonous glare. When she heard a squawk overhead, she glanced up to see birds soaring in the moonlight. Tempest didn't know what variety of fowl they were, but she quickly assumed that if they were circling over her they had to be buzzards.

"Well, that wasn't so bad, was it?" Cord questioned, trying to tease her into good humor.

It was a wasted effort. Tempest refused to be amused.

"Wasn't so bad?" she spluttered. "I'm still half-dead and you say it wasn't so bad!"

"If you weren't so inconsiderate you'd be thanking me for saving your life," Cord grumbled.

Tempest braced herself up on her elbows and glared daggers at him. "Why should I thank you when you're the one who very nearly got me killed? Thanks to you, I have a few more scrapes and bruises as souvenirs of this escapade!"

"My grandfather says any man who can find a way to survive when he faces the impossible is—"

"—I'm getting sick and tired of hearing what your grandfather has to say," Tempest cut in crossly. "What time is it, anyway?"

Cord glanced at the waterlogged timepiece pinned to her sleeve and grinned. "It's time to get a new watch."

Tempest peered at the glass case filled with water. Never again was she going anywhere a watch couldn't go. Her time had almost run out in that watery tunnel, thanks to this daredevil. He could have killed them both and he'd damned near succeeded, too!

"Can you stand up?" Cord queried.

"No," Tempest insisted, and she wasn't even going to try!

Nevertheless, Cord hooked his elbows under her arms and set her upright. Her knees buckled but he slid his right arm around her waist to support her. "We have to keep moving."

"Perhaps *you* do," Tempest muttered. "But *I* don't."

Cord scowled into her pale face. "I'm not leaving you here, so forget it."

"I have no intention of going anywhere with a man who has so little respect for my safety and total disregard for my life—" Cord's hand clamped over the lower portion of her face as he propelled her around two looming boulders. "Keep quiet," he hissed as he dragged her along with his impatient stride. "If you don't, I'll stuff a rock the size of a melon down your throat."

Tempest was too exhausted to fight him. She was having enough trouble keeping her legs moving without tripping over her own feet.

Eight

Without her watch, Tempest had lost all track of time. It seemed they had trudged through the darkness, feeling their way around boulders and trees. When Cord finally decided to stop to rest, she didn't sit down; she collapsed.

Tempest was truly beginning to understand why the Apache had so little use for the materialistic things in life. Surviving in this rugged terrain was a full-time job that left little time for luxuries. Food and shelter were of utmost importance—this was definitely survival of the fittest in its purest form! She and Cord had nothing but the clothes on their backs. Their steed and their saddlebags had undoubtedly been confiscated by the *vaqueros.* Cord's pistol had been lost somewhere along the way, and they had nothing but the knife in his moccasins for protection against man and beast.

The way their luck had been running, Tempest expected to see a black bear, lobo, or mountain lion lumber toward them any second. Hadn't she heard it said that just when a person thought things were as bad as they could get, they became worse? After so much calamity the past few days, Tempest was becoming a pessimist . . .

Her thoughts trailed off when she heard Cord

groan in pain as he sank down beside her. She glanced over to see him attempting to perform primitive surgery on his left shoulder with his over-size knife. Where Tempest found the energy to crouch beside him she didn't know, but she was there, insisting on coming to his aid.

"Give me that," she demanded in a no-nonsense tone.

"Why? So you can plunge it through my heart?" Cord muttered.

"Of course not, you imbecile. You don't have a heart," Tempest assured him emphatically.

"Do you think I'm enjoying this? I found myself tossed in jail and chased by cutthroats, without the chance even to pay my last respects to my father. What little reputation I had is being ruined by that greedy bastard Victor who has forced me to kidnap you in hopes of surviving long enough to clear my name!"

With effort, she wrested the dagger away and stuffed the heel of her hand into his chest, forcing him to the ground. "Just hold still," she commanded. "I never claimed to be a physician, only a—"

Tempest snapped her jaw shut before her tongue outdistanced her brain. This was not the time to break the news to Cord that he had abducted the wrong woman. He'd be hopping up and down in frustration and she'd never get the buckshot out of his arm.

Cord would have given most anything for a pint of whiskey to numb the pain that Tempest unintentionally inflicted on him in her effort to remove the buckshot. A muted growl vibrated on his clenched lips when the point of the knife penetrated tender flesh. Fire sizzled along his nerve endings and perspiration beaded his brow.

"Damnation, you're about as gentle as a gorilla," he gritted out while he clutched his arm.

Tempest willed her hand to stop shaking. This task required deliberate precision, and she possessed no surgical skills whatsoever. The closest she'd ever come to operating on anybody was when she'd dug splinters from her fingers as a child. It wasn't helping matters that she was performing surgery by moonlight, either!

"I'm being as careful as I can," she assured him before focusing on the jagged wound. "This isn't pleasant for me, either, you know."

"Well, try a little harder to be gentle," Cord snapped in agony. "And I can guarantee you that this is hurting me a helluva lot worse than it is you . . . ouch!"

"Done!" Tempest announced proudly.

Cord half-collapsed against a rock with a long-suffering sigh. "Don't ask me for a reference should you decide to enter medical school."

"And don't ask me to testify if you wind up in court for rustling, stealing, and kidnapping," Tempest flung back. "You've committed so many crimes it would save more time to list the offenses you *haven't* committed."

She wondered if Cord had any idea how much truth could be spoken in sarcasm. She could easily be the one who made sure he hanged or spent the best years of his life in jail.

After the past few hours with this man, Tempest wouldn't put anything past him. He was barely civilized, after all. He had wandered back and forth between the white and Indian world, making up his own rules as he went along. There was no telling how many laws he'd broken in the past decade. He was spiteful and vindictive and he'd proved that when he abducted her to get even with Victor. Who was to say he hadn't stolen Victor's cattle for revenge?

Cord had said himself that he despised Victor and detested the rumors the man had spread about father and son. If Tempest were forced to decide Cord's guilt or innocence at this moment, she would have found herself leaning toward a lifetime sentence without parole . . .

"What are you thinking, princess?" Cord tilted her face to his inquisitive stare. "That you'd rather marry a man you don't love instead of being stuck out here in the middle of Nowhere, Texas, with the likes of me?"

Tempest retreated from his caress. She couldn't resist it when he plied her with that dark, sensual charm. The physical responses he evoked were certainly not logical. This amber-eyed devil was capable of anything. Why, the next thing she knew he'd be trying to charm her into standing up for him against Victor.

Nothing would please Cord more than to have Victor's fiancée fall in love with his worst enemy. That would be a demoralizing blow to the rancher. Cord MacIntosh was a man who seized every opportunity and played it to his advantage. He was as wily as a fox and as elusive as a shadow. But Tempest wasn't a witless fool and she wasn't going to fall in love with this rake, even if she wasn't really Victor's fiancée. Yes, Cord was undeniably attractive. And yes, damn it, he appealed to everything feminine in her, despite the fact that he'd come close to getting her killed more times than she cared to count!

"I prefer that you don't touch me unless absolutely necessary," Tempest insisted.

"Why? Because you like me more th an you want to admit?"

Up went her chin. "There is nothing about you that pleases me—"

Cord's moist lips feathered over hers in the slightest breath of a kiss. Tempest was utterly astounded that this man, who could be so forceful and overpowering in physical strength, could also be so tenderly persistent when the mood suited him. He touched her and her entire body glowed. He drew her down against the hard contours of his body and she melted. Cord MacIntosh, scoundrel though he was, could make a woman glad she was a woman. He could crumble her resistance and make his will her own.

Cord told himself that he was in need of compassion to soothe the nagging pain in his arm. He wanted to forget their hair-raising escape. Any woman would have satisfied him at the moment. He didn't really want to kiss Tempest. He didn't want to feel her shapely body against his. The fact that Tempest was Victor's betrothed was an extra added pleasure, another blow to his enemy's pride. Cord felt no emotional involvement, none whatsoever. This was only the sweet taste of revenge.

And if that was true, then why did that beguiling image of chestnut hair and lively blue eyes appear when he closed his eyes and drank in the sweet, compelling taste of her? He was kidding himself if he thought he wanted to hold just any woman. He wanted Tempest Litchfield . . .

Litchfield. Cord was sure he remembered hearing that name somewhere before. But now wasn't the time to pursue that nagging question. All he wanted was to enjoy this kiss, to languish in the feel of her luscious body against his.

Cord eased Tempest down beside him and peered into those innocent blue eyes and his self-control evaporated as if it never existed. To hell with being noble, Cord decided when his hungry lips feasted on hers. God, how many times had he visualized what it would be like to peel away the garments that separated them, to see this bewitching goddess as he'd seen her that first day in Victor's hacienda.

Each time he closed his eyes he could picture her lounging in her tub, her silky skin sparkling with diamond water droplets, her glorious mane of hair enshrouded by sunlight. For days, Cord had been hounded by forbidden dreams. He had imagined himself discovering the sweetest secrets about this lovely witch-angel.

It had finally reached the point that touching her and stealing an intoxicating kiss now and then was no longer enough. He wanted to feel her exquisite skin pressed to his, feel that wild, heady surge of passion that he knew would await him.

Despite the obstacles and differences between them, Cord wanted her like hell on fire. Nothing but taking absolute possession was going to make the nagging need go away. Oh, he'd fought the feelings quite admirably, if he did say so himself. But there was simply no will left to fight the long-harbored hunger that gnawed at him.

In fact, Cord wondered if his true motive for forcing Tempest to accompany him was to have her all to himself so he could satisfy this maddening craving that had finally brought him to the point of no return.

Tempest assured herself that the only reason she didn't put up a fuss when he kissed the breath out of her was because she was still riding an emotional carousel after escaping an underwater sepulcher and thoroughly losing her temper. Heightened sensations made her traitorous body far more receptive than it should have been. Her half-hearted attempt to restrain herself was just that—a token gesture to soothe her stinging conscience. No doubt she would regret her impulsiveness when she could think straight. But she had never been able to think straight when Cord plied her with those kisses and caresses.

The only thought that threaded through Cord's

mind was this desperate need to end the suspense of wondering how it would feel to make wild, sweet love to this feisty beauty. She appealed to everything in him. *Wanting* her had become his obsession. Cord was through fighting his desires; he surrendered to them . . .

Lord, how easily he could lose himself in those lips! His body surged closer to hers as he deepened the kiss to drink in the addictive taste of her. He could feel her delectable body so close and yet so unbearably far away.

Tempest marveled at the electrifying sensations that spilled through her when his seeking hands drifted across her all-too-receptive flesh. These were definitely not the feelings she wanted to experience when Cord touched her in places no other man had dared to touch. She never reacted as she thought she should have when he drew her to his virile body and let her feel the stark difference between a man and woman. Tempest knew she should have been recoiling in indignation instead of waiting to see what other deliciously wicked sensations were going to assault her naive body.

She sighed deeply as his skillful hands traced her feminine contours. Her body seemed to know what it needed far better than her mind. She could feel the heat of Cord's flesh searing through her clothes. She could taste him, touch him, absorb his strength. But nothing could compensate for the wild, breathless needs that multiplied with each scorching kiss.

Suddenly Tempest was feeding on each brazen caress that glided over her body in familiar possession. Cord's kisses breathed that vital breath of life into her and put her senses to flight. It was so irrational, and not at all like her to abandon better judgment, but Tempest surrendered mindlessly. It was as if she were silently begging for his practiced touch, as if she thrived on his delicious kisses. The limited experiences he'd given her in the art of passion were no longer enough to satisfy the hot, aching pressure that burgeoned inside her. She wanted him to teach her all the wildly intimate pleasures his touch had promised.

Tempest wished she understood why this one particular man could ignite those forbidden fires. Cord MacIntosh was not the kind of man she had ever imagined for herself, never in a million years! Her fascination defied understanding. Despite every crime he'd ever committed, she felt something for him, something that couldn't be described or explained. It just existed, a phenomenal sensation that had fed upon itself since the first time he'd dared to kiss her.

Suddenly his tongue flickered over the rapid pulsations on her throat. When he nibbled at the sensitized flesh on her collarbone, Tempest felt the tingles ricochet down her backbone. With masterful ease, Cord unhooked the stays on the back of her gown to bare her body to his eyes, hands, and lips. Tempest's breath lodged in her chest when his hands tunneled beneath the garment to cup her breasts. When his index finger encircled each rigid peak, she felt air clogging her throat and pleasure fogging her thoughts. She should have grabbed his roaming hands to discourage him, but wild longings sizzled through every fiber of her being, leaving her to burn like a human torch.

When his warm mouth drifted over the valley of her breasts to tease one taut peak and then the other, Tempest knew she was lost forever. His greedy lips suckled and aroused until Tempest swore she'd melted into a pool of liquid fire. She couldn't even form a protest to save her soul when he drew the gown away to devour her with those hypnotic golden eyes. He treated every inch of bare flesh he exposed to another round of kisses and caresses. Shamelessly, she arched toward his seeking hands and whispering lips, craving more—oh, so much more!

She never realized it was possible for a woman to want a man as much as she wanted Cord. He was leading her down a dark, sensuous corridor, introducing her to indescribable sensations of pleasure that brought sweet torture to her innocent body. Cord was so exquisitely gentle that Tempest never gave another thought to rejecting him. To deny him would have meant denying herself, and she had no will to stop what her aching body had no power to control.

Over and over again, Tempest felt his patient caresses exploring and arousing every sensitive point of her flesh. The bubbly sensations he evoked left her gasping for air. She was suffocating in the utterly masculine scent that was becoming an integral part of her. When his lips descended down the ladder of her ribs to feather over her abdomen, Tempest clutched at him for support. The world was swirling around her, leaving her mind in a dizzy whir.

"Lord, you're the loveliest creature I've ever seen," Cord whispered.

Tempest was silk and satin, all the right curves in just the right places. Cord couldn't remember enjoying the sight and feel of a woman quite so much. Perhaps it was because she had been such a challenge. For certain, he had never waited so long to satisfy his desire. She was a banquet after years of starvation.

In his previous experiences with women, he had been impatient to ease his needs and be on his way. Now he savored each new phase of passion that he alone had introduced. It gave him an odd sense of pride and pleasure to know that he was her first intimate experience, that no other man had made his way through her defenses to the hidden needs she had only begun to realize she possessed. All she knew was what he was teaching her. But with that scintillating thought came the stark awareness of a responsibility he had never before confronted with a woman.

Cord knew this crucial encounter would determine whether this blue-eyed beauty would dare to let go of her inhibitions with a man again. If he took her quickly to satisfy the monstrous craving inside him, she would experience only pain without fulfillment. He also knew that she would never have yielded to him if their difficult journey hadn't left her so vulnerable.

He knew his forbidden fantasy might never come this close to reality again. This might be his one chance, a splendorous moment that may never be repeated, especially if he left her with unpleasant pain and bitter memories.

It was with more deliberate patience than Cord even realized he possessed that he moved closer to the fire that flickered between them. He forced himself to take no more than Tempest offered him, even though it damn near killed him to progress at such a slow pace. Until now, he'd always allowed himself to be governed by savage passion, to follow the flow of desire. Now he savored each moment of pleasure as he kissed and caressed Tempest.

Cord feared he was being far too bold as he plied this naive goddess with seductive techniques that were usually reserved for far more experienced lovers. But he couldn't stop himself. He wanted all of her, in all the ways a man could hunger for a woman. He wanted to teach her everything, to savor each magical moment for as long as it would last.

Every muscle in Cord's body tensed with intense desire as his hands and lips tasted the honeyed texture of her skin. His mouth lingered on the tips of her breasts, feeling the peaks grow taut and beaded against the warm moistness of his tongue. He felt

Tempest's spontaneous response to his bold kisses when he measured the curve of her waist and the smooth plane of her belly with his lips and the pads of his fingertips. He felt her uncontrollable shudder as if it were his own, felt the heat radiating from her luscious body—a heat that burned him by maddening degrees.

When his tongue traced a teasing path down her satiny thigh, he felt Tempest go rigid, heard her broken gasp. He knew for certain that no man had been allowed the privileges he was taking now. The staggering thought that he was the first to see her reactions to a man's intimate touch sent blood hammering through his veins.

Ever so gently, his fingertips splayed across her hip, curling, swirling, reveling in her trembling responses. With the subtle guidance of his arm nudging at her thigh, he eased her legs apart, granting himself access to the hidden valley of femininity that he ached to explore, to touch the silken fire and feel the rain of sweet, innocent desire surrounding him.

Mystified, Cord watched the spasms of passion's first touch claim Tempest's exquisite face as his fingertip glided into the liquid flame. Tempest was so fragile, so warm, so utterly feminine that he wanted to taste and touch each hidden secret that she didn't even realize she possessed. As he bent his head to brush his lips across her thigh, he felt her body contract around his fingertip, felt the shock waves rippling through her, then vibrating through him like a harpstring.

Tempest couldn't bite back a gasp when Cord's seeking fingers were replaced by his lips and tongue. She found herself in the grips of something so wild and maddening that her innocent body shuddered as if it had been besieged by an earthquake.

It was frightening to feel so completely out of control, so utterly bedeviled. But in less than a heartbeat she was arching toward his hands and lips, begging him to appease the monstrous needs that exploded inside her. Tempest heard his name tumble from her tongue and echo around her. She felt the hungry cravings swell out of proportion, subside, and then burgeon again as he worked his sensual magic.

"Please . . ." Tempest choked out when another tidal wave of immeasurable pleasure crested upon her.

She was going to die. She was positively certain of it. The molten ache had spread from the core of her being and channeled through each nerve and muscle. Spasms of ecstasy drenched her body as she clutched at Cord in wild desperation.

Cord had never felt more of a man when he twisted above Tempest to peer down at her. Unappeased desire sparkled in her eyes like fiery blue crystals. He had made Tempest want him with every part of her being, despite her animosity. He had crumbled the walls of her firm resolve, made her defy her own feelings toward him. But she was no simple conquest. She was a priceless treasure. This stubborn, contrary female, who had such a penchant for knowing the time of day—every single minute—was lost to that magical dimension where time ceased to exist.

Although his passions raged inside him when he saw the unbridled hunger in her thick-lashed eyes, Cord slowly eased from his clothes to settle exactly above her. As much as Tempest thought she wanted him now, he feared he would shatter the spell when he took total possession. If he rushed her voyage from maidenhood to womanhood, she would be deprived of the ecstasy of lovemaking. He wanted to prepare her for the inevitable pain, to reassure her, but words failed him. His muscular body slid down hers, allowing her to feel his arousal, to adjust to the feel of a man's body moving familiarly against hers.

Holding her wild-eyed gaze, he bent his head to offer a kiss that bespoke of the rare gentleness he felt toward her. Cord had never kissed a woman so tenderly, but the warm, bubbling feelings he was experiencing demanded that he convey his emotions in the only way he knew how.

Tempest swore the grass beneath her had become a soft feathery cloud. She felt only the warm, hard length of Cord's muscular body blending into hers, tasted only the gentleness of a kiss that cherished and worshipped her as if she were special to him. And when Cord insinuated his masculine body upon hers and eased his knee between her thighs, guiding her legs apart, Tempest welcomed him, all of him. She longed to end this maddening torment of wanting him so desperately and being deprived of satisfaction . . .

When he took absolute possession, searing pain overshadowed the haze of rapture that enshrouded her. Tempest tensed, bracing her hands on the solid wall of his chest to push him away. Her lashes fluttered up to see those tawny eyes flickering like the golden flames of a candle. The soft expression on his rugged features testified to his sympathy and concern. It was as if he longed to absorb the pain he'd unintentionally caused her.

Tempest swore she'd never forget that tender look as long as she lived. There, beneath those chiseled features that could sometimes appear as cold and hard as granite, was a hint of emotion that he'd never before revealed. It was the look of a man who confronted his own vulnerability—a look tempered with caring and compassion. She was seeing a glimpse of the gentle giant who lived behind the stone wall that hard living had imposed.

Tempest found herself reaching up to him, drawing him closer. Her hands entangled in his wavy raven hair, bringing his lips to hers. This bold callous man, who had put her through nine kinds of hell and infuriated her to the very limits of her sanity, had somehow touched her heart in that breathless moment. Tempest had looked past the initial pain and shocking intimacy to allow his masculine body to communicate with hers in a delicious language that required no words. Suddenly, she was overwhelmed by the need to return the ineffable pleasure he had given her, to admit that he stirred her in ways no man ever had.

Then he felt Tempest's slender arms enfolding him, guiding him back to her. When her untutored body moved toward his, a shudder rocked his soul. Sweet mercy, passion wasn't supposed to be like this! So all-consuming, so wildly intimate, so emotionally engulfing! It never had been before!

Cord swore he knew all there was to know about desire, but he suddenly realized how wrong he'd been. This wasn't sex for the sake of lust. This was lovemaking in its purest, sweetest form. His entire body trembled at the thought of how far he and Tempest had come. The past didn't matter anymore. They were only a man and a woman lying heart to heart and soul to soul. They were discovering each other for the very first time, finding in each other's arms something mystically satisfying that they had never expected to experience . . .

That was the last sane thought to filter through his mind. The savage passions he had carefully restrained exploded with maddening force. His body was moving without command, seeking ultimate depths of intimacy. Cord kissed her as if they were about to plunge over a roaring waterfall and that was exactly how he felt! With a groan of unholy torment, he enveloped Tempest in his arms and surrendered to the firestorm of ecstasy that swamped him.

His body drove into hers and she answered each hard, demanding thrust. Cord likened the experience to what he supposed a man and woman would feel if they had spent years together, knowing all there was to know about each other, sacrificing their own identities, unashamed of the exquisite sensations that caught and held them together in wondrous passion. It was as if they had been soul mates forever and ever, instinctively knowing how to please, how to express the turbulent emotions they had discovered in each other.

Tempest heard Cord's name tumble from her lips as passion bubbled forth like lava from a volcano. Shudder after convulsive shudder bombarded her, rhythmically matching the spasms that besieged Cord's body. They clung to each other as if the world had exploded around them. They rode out the waves of fire that carried them along the rocky summits of rapture.

Suddenly, Tempest was free-falling through space, but without the innate fear that had once terrified her. She was gliding like a hawk on a draft of wind—soaring, diving. When she let go of her emotions she had experienced a new kind of freedom. It was as if she had pulled free of the physical restraints of life to skyrocket through eternity.

It was impossible to measure time and for once Tempest didn't care how much time had elapsed since she had plodded along the shores of reality. Being in Cord's arms was like riding the breakers of the sea, watching the waves surge forth to erase past memories and the footprints of time. She had become a maelstrom of wild passions seeking release. And this brawny giant had satisfied her every hunger. He had blown the stars around and turned her well-organized world upside down. This raven-haired wizard had brewed such a potent spell that she had become hopelessly entranced.

Tempest snuggled up against Cord as if he were a cozy blanket. His arms provided warmth and security and she was so very tired, having exhausted the full spectrum of her emotions. Tempest accepted the protective feel of Cord's muscular body curled tightly to hers and drifted into peaceful dreams.

Tempest moaned groggily when skillful hands coasted over her tingling skin, causing a warm throb of pleasure to pulsate through her loins. Her body instinctively arched toward the heated flesh that seared her, aroused her, teased her with sensations that rippled through every nerve and muscle. Slowly but surely, Cord was peeling away the garments that separated them to press his lips to each throbbing point on her quivering flesh. Her hand clutched at his forearm, wanting to push him away and yet drawing him ever closer, longing for him to appease this burgeoning need that engulfed her . . .

"Tempest?"

When the faraway voice floated through a dark, hazy tunnel, Tempest felt herself jarred abruptly. Another persistent shake brought her awake in mid-dream to find Cord propped up on an elbow, hovering above her.

"Are you okay, princess?" Cord questioned in concern. "You were moaning and squirming as if . . ." A devilish grin crinkled his shadowed features as he studied the shocked expression on her face. "You weren't dreaming about the two of us doing the same intimate—?"

"Oh, hush up, Cord MacIntosh," Tempest snapped, thoroughly humiliated that she had not only surrendered to a man who was completely wrong for her, but that she had awakened, dreaming about their lovemaking. "You conceited ogre, how you flatter yourself!"

His hand brushed lightly over the tip of her breast, causing Tempest to tremble from the familiarity of his touch. "Then suppose you tell me why you were moaning in your sleep. If you had been dreaming about our swim through the underground tunnel, you would have been screaming in terror," he reasoned.

"How do I know what I was moaning about?" Tempest was mortified that the glowing horizon betrayed the blush that stained her cheeks. "After all the torturous ordeals you've put me through, all in the name of your revenge, I'm probably having a nervous breakdown. When people suffer mental imbalance, they're prone to talk and groan in their sleep. I'm sure your grandfather has some mumbo-jumbo about that, too. He seems to have something to say about everything else . . . What time is it?"

"It's long past too late to pretend nothing happened last night and that you were dreaming about it this morning."

When her tangled lashes fluttered up to see Cord's ruggedly handsome face spotlighted by shafts of sunlight, the stark realization of what she had done hit her with full force. It made matters ten times worse when she noticed his satisfied expression. She knew that he was feeling the arrogance that only a man could feel when he'd made another conquest. The proof of her lost innocence clung to his body, reminding Tempest that he had taken what no man had ever stolen from her and could never steal again. She imagined that Cord was exceedingly pleased with himself because he thought he had deflowered Victor's fiancée. And *that* was his primary reason for seducing her. It had nothing to do with *her,* Tempest realized with a humiliated groan. It had everything to do with who Cord *thought* she was.

A hot blush stained her cheeks as Cord rolled away to fetch his clothes. What a fool she had been to let herself believe Cord had actually felt something special for her. Sex was simply second nature to him.

She was just another prize to conquer, the fulfillment of his needs, a gambit for his revenge.

The demoralizing thought made Tempest feel all the more ashamed and mortified. God, she needed to have her head examined for yielding to this seductive rake! She had soiled her reputation forever. She had given this renegade her virginity and no decent man would have her if she ever *did* decide to take a husband! Sweet mercy, she could never undo what she had done in a reckless moment. She had committed an unpardonable sin and disgraced her family name. If her father ever found out, he would be appalled that Tempest had degraded herself—in the arms of an outlaw, of all people! Dear God in heaven!

While Tempest was battling her bruised pride and guilty conscience, Cord was feeling decidedly uncomfortable himself. In the past, he had gone through the paces of passion for the sole purpose of feeding his male appetite. He had never been one for lengthy conversations after sexual encounters. That wasn't his forte. It was customary for him to simply get up and go his way. But suddenly everything had changed. He had to take this female with him! And worse, he knew that Tempest would have difficulty coping with what had transpired between them. *Caramba!* He was having trouble dealing with it himself! It may have been Tempest's first time, but it was sure as hell his first time with a woman's first time. Lord, he felt awkward!

Without another glance in Tempest's direction, Cord rose to an upright position to fasten himself into his breeches. "We better get moving. I don't want Emilio Reynosa and the other hired assassins breathing down my neck all morning."

Tempest desperately tried to get herself in hand, despite her mortification and regret. Difficult though it was, she was determined to conceal the fact that she was upset with *herself* for submitting, and with *him* for seducing her.

"What about breakfast?" Her stomach rumbled in complaint, giving her the perfect excuse for posing the question. It took her mind off the humiliation that left her wondering if she had been a harlot in another lifetime. Sweet mercy, the things she had let him do! How could she live with herself? How could she even look at him without feeling embarrassed and ashamed?

"We skipped last night's supper," Tempest continued, looking in every direction except at him. "I barely have the energy to stand up, much less walk all over creation," she added grumpily.

Cord reached up to pluck some wild chokecherries from the bush that grew from the side of the canyon. With a stabbing gesture, he offered Tempest a handful.

"Breakfast, your highness," he declared, staring at the air over her head. He couldn't face what he'd done any easier than she. Damn, he'd give most anything if he didn't have to confront his conscience, which was presently nagging the hell out of him! "What else would you like, my lady?"

"Your heart roasted golden brown," she muttered before biting into a sour cherry that made her lips pucker.

Tempest couldn't help herself. The frustration came pouring out, despite her attempt to pretend nothing had happened. Anger was the only way she had to hide her shame!

"That's not what you wanted last night," he had the gall to say and then wished he hadn't. Tempest went off like a firecracker on the Fourth of July!

"That was *not* what I wanted!" she spewed in outrage. Her cheeks blazed and her eyes sparked hot blue flames when she rounded on him. "And don't think for one minute that I would ever fall in love with someone like you, I'm not a complete idiot, you know. I am perfectly aware that all you wanted was the satisfaction of having one more revenge on Victor. Well, for your information, I'm not even his—"

Cord jerked her along behind him, causing the remainder of her sentence to burst out in an inarticulate whoosh. Before she could finish what she intended to say, Cord crammed another handful of sour cherries in her mouth to shut her up.

"I don't want to hear any more about Victor," Cord growled, his tone as bitter as the unripened fruit. "The very mention of his name spoils my good disposition in nothing flat."

"You don't have a good disposition," Tempest retorted after she'd choked down her cherries. "You're either incredibly spiteful or impossibly ornery most of the time."

"My grandfather always says—"

"Clam up, for crying out loud!" Tempest spouted. "I don't want to hear any more of your grandfather's proverbs. What time is it getting to be now?"

"Caramba! It's only ten minutes later than it was the last time you asked me," Cord snapped. "Damn it, woman, if I didn't need you to bargain with Victor, I'd hand you over to Emilio Reynosa in a minute! No wonder you were a spinster who had to settle for marrying What's-His-Name. You-Know-Who deserves to have to tolerate your temperament and your big mouth."

Tempest flashed him a furious glare. How dare he carve her into bite-size pieces! How dare he even speak to her after what he had done!

"You lout!" she spewed. "It's plain to see you're no prize yourself. You're a half-breed outlaw with the morals of a lecher and the soul of a villain. No woman in her right mind would have you. Not that it matters. You won't have any time left for women after you serve your sentence for kidnapping, rustling, thieving, and only God knows what else!"

After they had exchanged verbal blows, Cord and Tempest lapsed into silence to list mentally all the reasons why they disliked each other so much. He randomly categorized all Tempest's defects. Tempest, being analytical and organized, listed Cord's numerous flaws in alphabetical order.

It was just as Cord had predicted. He had finally reached the point that he'd tired of this fire-breathing witch. The mystical spell had been broken. He regretted stealing her virginity and he sorely regretted that he had *liked* it so much while he was doing it!

Damn, what was really getting to him was the fact that he *wasn't* smug about seducing Victor's betrothed. What bothered the hell out of him was knowing this gorgeous, passionate beauty would one day be sleeping in Victor's bed. Now *that* really got to him! *She* was getting to him, more than he wanted to admit. She was getting on his nerves and under his skin. But as alluring and attractive as she could be in her gentler moods, she was still a spoiled, waspish debutante who expected every man on the planet to bow and coddle just because she was stinking rich and a female. Hell would sooner be encased in a glacier before Cord bowed to this hot-tempered hellion! She wanted him to apologize and kiss her feet, did she? Well, she could just kiss his—

Tempest's startled yelp jolted Cord from his resentful musings. He wheeled around in time to upright Tempest after she'd caught the ripped hem of her gown and lost her footing. Her next step would have been a doozy. The ledge upon which they trekked overlooked a fifty-foot drop. The bottom of the arroyo was strewn with rocks and scrub trees that would have broken her fall *and* her neck.

Despite the fact that she was grateful Cord had

prevented her from taking a nasty fall, Tempest snatched her arm out of his grasp, squared her shoulders, and stamped off. Odd, she wasn't nearly as afraid of height when she was infuriated with this horrible excuse of a man. Hell and damnation, she couldn't even see the cursed gorge below, not when this fiery red haze glazed her eyes!

Damn the man. His sexual know-how had caused her to lose the good sense she'd been born with. Now she was a tainted woman, an outlaw's whore. Sweet merciful heavens, she was beginning to wish she had drowned in that underground river or walked off the edge of the cliff. It would have been better than dying of humiliation and being forced to go on living with her shame. Of all the men in all the world, she had to get mixed up with this social deviant who had stolen her innocence and made her like it! She would never forgive this golden-eyed devil for what he'd done and she would never *ever* forgive herself for letting him!

Nine

While Emilio Reynosa was zigzagging his way through the deep chasms and scrabbling up the towering cliffs in search of the elusive fugitive, Cord was working his way around the secluded spring. Just to the south, Soldier Lookout Point loomed in front of them. Before the Civil War, sentries had kept watch for the Butterfield stages which were often set upon by raiding Indians and gangs of outlaws. Renegades and cutthroats still terrorized the stage road and this stretch of rugged country was left unprotected. Since the fall of the South, there were no bands of Texas Rangers to protect travelers, no Army dragoons to guard the roads. Texas had always been a little wild and lawless, but conditions had deteriorated since the state had come under federal control. The carpetbaggers who called themselves politicians had overrun the government and law and order had become extinct.

Considering the general state of things and his own personal problems, Cord expected to confront a raft of thieves as well as Victor's surly henchman. But thus far, he had managed to bypass trouble. With the exception of the one hundred-ten-pound bundle of disaster, Cord amended. Tempest had given him the cold shoulder for so long that he was feeling the symptoms of frostbite. But who was he to complain? He hadn't said a civil word to her, either, not in the last six hours. They were fighting with icy glares and chilling silence, but it was time to break the silence, whether Tempest wanted to or not.

"Brace up, princess, it won't be much farther to the Pinery. You'll find yourself in the company of some very nice people," Cord assured Tempest when she sank down on a boulder to rest.

"Thank God for small favors," Tempest muttered, breaking her vow never to speak to this varmint for the rest of her life. "If I have to spend much more time alone with you, I'll be as much of a maniac as you are . . . I wonder what time it is . . ."

Cord rolled his eyes heavenward for divine patience. The woman was driving him nuts with her obsession with time. He would buy her a clock the size of Big Ben and then maybe she'd stop.

Tempest's spirits soared at the sight of Pine Springs Canyon which cut a steep-walled niche beside Guadalupe Peak. The Pinery—the terminal stage station—was a sight for sore eyes. Tempest wished there was a cavalry of soldiers on hand so she could fling herself at their feet and beg to be freed from this infuriating ordeal. She had tolerated Cord MacIntosh for as long as she could. He was guilty of every crime Victor had accused him of and she wouldn't defend him in a court of law, not for all the gold in the federal mint!

Ah, Tempest couldn't wait to see the look on this big baboon's whiskered face when she informed him that he had kidnapped the wrong woman. When he discovered her identity, he would know for certain that he had braided his own rope for his necktie party. Tempest swore she deserved the last laugh after the torment she'd lived through.

And now was the perfect time, she decided. When Cord realized his mistake, he would leave her at the

Pinery and she could take the next stage home. Cord would have such an exorbitant price on his head that every law official, bounty hunter, and soldier west of the Pecos would be on his trail. Since Cord seemed obsessed with revenge, he should appreciate her vindication. If nothing else, she now understood what motivated this Goliath of a man.

Tempest had just opened her mouth to blurt out the truth and stun Cord to the bone when she heard the click of a trigger beside her. She found herself hauled up in front of Cord's massive chest like a shield. That made her positively furious! He was forever using her body for protection against his enemies. The man had no concern for her whatsoever. He only kept her alive for his selfish purposes. She despised him, truly she did!

When a lean, rugged man who looked only a little older than she stepped from his hiding place among the boulders, Tempest flinched. The snarl on the man's face evaporated the instant his hazel eyes flooded over her body and then leaped over her head to lock with Cord's narrowed gaze.

A welcoming grin curved the corners of Jefferson Jones's lips. "Well, I'll be damned, Tosh. I was beginning to wonder if I'd ever see you again."

Tosh? Tempest frowned curiously. Obviously, Cord had a nickname, derived from his surname, one that was used by his friends. Funny, she doubted he had friends. Tempest wouldn't have thought it, knowing what a rascal he was.

"I'm damned glad to be here, cousin." Cord watched Jefferson glide his six-shooter into its holster. "This is Tempest Wi—Litchfield," he hastily corrected himself.

Jefferson tipped his hat respectfully. "I know all about her, Tosh. We've been receiving bulletins from every stage driver who passes through." He glanced solemnly at his cousin. "But no matter what, nothing has changed between us. I just want you to know that."

Before Cord had the chance to quiz Jefferson about the meaning of the last remark, his cousin wheeled around to lead the way down the rock-strewn path.

Several steps later, Cord caught up with Jefferson. "What do you mean *nothing has changed?*" he queried.

"I mean I don't blame you for escaping and taking a hostage," he replied, leaning close. "And a damned pretty hostage, too, Tosh. I knew you'd be upset when we sent the letter telling you about Uncle Paddy. I'm really sorry, Tosh."

Cord gritted his teeth at the mention of his father's name and then stopped in his tracks when a troubled thought crossed his mind. "When's the next stage due? I don't want to put you and your family in any kind of danger or let anyone know you're my kinfolk. I'll make sure we're safely tucked away when the passengers arrive."

When she overheard his comment, Tempest glared at Cord's broad back. He didn't want his relatives to suffer repercussions because of their connection with him. But never mind that he'd nearly gotten her killed a half dozen times and then used her. Damn his insensitive, uncaring hide!

Jeff waved away Cord's concern. "You're safe for the afternoon," he insisted. "The next coach won't be through here until six o'clock."

"What time is it now?" Tempest wanted to know.

"Nearly noon," Jeff informed her with a smile. "Hungry? Mama will have dinner waiting after she feeds the two passengers making stage connections to Tucson."

When Cord hesitated once again, Jeff tugged him along the path. "We'll keep the two of you out of sight. One of the passengers is a drunk who hasn't sobered up since we hauled him off the stage. The other is a merchant who clings to his satchel as if he's got a pile of money stuffed in it. They won't bother you."

Oh great, thought Tempest. What a thing to tell this renegade. Cord would steal the merchant's cash in no time.

"That lush hasn't come out of his room for more than five minutes at a time. He has Mama deliver his meals to him," Jefferson explained.

When the threesome ambled toward the adobe way station beside the corrals, barn, and a small hotel, Tempest stopped short. A man and woman who looked to be pushing hard at fifty came dashing out to hug the stuffing out of Cord. Tempest didn't know this callous scoundrel was capable of such tender emotion . . . Well, she did, but she was doing her damnedest to forget those forbidden moments. She preferred to think of Cord as a man with a heart of rock and a soul of stone. After all, she was hell-bent on hating him for a thousand reasons.

"Oh, Tosh." The red-haired woman spilled a few tears while she embraced her nephew. "We've all been so worried about you. We wanted to send Jefferson to deliver the news in person, but we've been so short-handed around here since our hired man up and left us without notice."

Tempest watched the rotund older man with a doughy face wipe the mist of tears away after he'd given his nephew an affectionate squeeze. How anybody could feel any fond attachment for this hard-hearted heathen she didn't know. Tempest had felt a brief stirring of sympathy and affection a few times the past week, but she had valiantly fought those sentiments in her saner moments.

"Come inside, Tosh," the older man invited. "We'll discuss our problems over dinner. I always did think it best to feed frustrations."

After Cord and Tempest had freshened up, they followed the mouth-watering aromas to the table, which was laden with heaping bowls of tantalizing food. A real meal! Tempest licked her parched lips in eager anticipation. It had been days since she'd tasted food that did more than provide basic nourishment.

"Tempest Litchfield, this is my Aunt Myra Jones and my Uncle Jelly Jones," Cord said.

Tempest graced her host and hostess with a polite smile before diving into her meal enthusiastically.

"I'm really sorry about all this, Tempest," Myra apologized as she sent her nephew a condescending glance. "I'm not proud of Tosh's methods, but you must understand that desperation often leads a man astray. Tosh is a good boy and we raised him to abide by the laws. But some folks like to twist the rules to suit their own purposes. Tosh just got squeezed into the middle of it."

From the look and sound of things, Tempest concluded that Cord had spent part of his formative years living with his aunt, uncle, and cousin. Even if Paddy MacIntosh had been the irresponsible drifter Victor claimed he was, Myra had opened her heart and home to her nephew. Obviously, Myra had tried to become the mother Cord had lost. But it wasn't Myra's fault Cord had turned out to be a scoundrel. She loved him blindly and she'd defend him against his every sin.

"We know Tosh only did what he felt he had to do," Jelly added between bites. "But it was most unfortunate about what happened."

Cord took a sip of the cool water Jelly had drawn from the spring below the stage station and stared somberly at his uncle. "Just exactly what did happen to my father?"

Jelly gobbled down his meal like a python before pausing to wipe his chin with his napkin. It was obvious to Tempest that Jelly's favorite pastime was eating. No doubt, jelly was one of his favorite foods—hence the nickname.

Cord saw Jelly cast Tempest a discreet glance, debating about whether to explain in front of her. "Go ahead, Uncle," he encouraged. "Tempest needs to know what kind of man she plans to marry."

A muddled frown knitted Tempest's brow. If the Joneses had heard about her captivity, why hadn't Victor made it known that she wasn't his betrothed? That was rather odd, wasn't it? What did Victor have to gain from such a ploy?

"Well . . . Paddy was up at the cabin in High Lonesome Valley," Jelly began hesitantly. "He'd come by here to mail a letter to an old friend whom he thought could help you fight the charges against you. He said some judge in San Antonio owed him a favor, but he was in such a rush to check on the cattle and horses, for fear Victor would try to steal them during his absence, that he didn't go into detail."

"Mama sent me up to check on Uncle Paddy." Jefferson took up where his father left off. "She had this odd premonition about her big brother so she wanted me to go to the cabin and make sure he was all right. Paddy had planned to visit you in the El Paso jail and he hadn't returned when he said he would."

Jefferson stared bleakly at his plate. "I found him in one of the meadows, not far from the spring. There were dead cattle strewn around the pond and . . ." He paused to inhale a deep breath before he plowed on, "Uncle Paddy was with them. I think somebody poisoned the water with strychnine. There wasn't a mark on any of them."

Cord scowled as he digested what his cousin had told him. His blazing amber eyes bore into Tempest's. "Your precious Victor," he muttered. "Or perhaps his bloodthirsty henchman, Emilio Reynosa."

"That would be difficult to prove in a court of law," Tempest countered.

Blast it, why did she feel the least bit sympathetic toward this man? She didn't want to care how he felt, but sentiment for the loss of his father kept getting in her way.

"I'm sure Victor took into account how difficult it would be to bring charges against him for murder by poisoning," Cord said. "But he got what he wanted. With me in jail and my father out of the way, he could lay claim to the salt rights, the ranch, and the—" Cord stopped short and shifted uneasily in his chair.

Tempest glanced around the table, puzzled by all the averted glances. Obviously, the Joneses knew what Cord intended to say and she was not to be privy to it. She wondered why they were being so secretive.

"Was Paddy MacIntosh's death reported and investigated?" Tempest questioned.

"It was reported in El Paso, but nothing was done about it," Jelly said. "Victor has those flimsy excuses of law officials in his hip pocket. They all want to be in on the take when he acquires the rights to the salt lakes. And despite the fact that Cord escaped from jail and made matters worse, he wouldn't have gotten a fair trial. We all know that. They would have hanged him, sure as the world."

The plump manager of the Pinery slumped back in his chair and heaved an enormous sigh. "I'm sorry, Miss Litchfield, but Victor Watts is a four-letter word around here. He's been trying to buy out my brother-in-law for two years. The Salt Ring got impatient, but Paddy refused to sell out to them, no matter what cruel lies Victor spread. And Paddy refused to tell Victor that Myra would inherit all his property if something happened to him and Tosh, for fear Victor would come after us. And I'm telling you now, missy, if he finds out about us, we'll know where Victor got the information."

My, my. It was definitely true that there were at least three sides to every issue, thought Tempest. Now she almost found herself believing Cord's claim of innocence and conspiracy against him. Almost. She wasn't prepared to forgive him *that* easily!

"But Tosh!" Myra said. "Did you have to kill that jailer when you escaped? Couldn't you have just knocked him silly for a few minutes and left a knot on his head? Now that you're wanted for murder, kidnapping, and rustling, Victor will have such a strong case against you that you'll never be acquitted."

Murder! The word exploded in Tempest's mind like a judge's gavel pounding out a sentence. *Guilty!* She'd been abducted by a thief, a rustler, *and* a murderer? Good God, how could she have yielded to this seductive devil? The very thought upset her more than she already was. She peered at Cord and felt sick all over.

"Murder?" Cord asked as his startled gaze locked with Tempest's expressive blue eyes. He could tell in one second flat that she believed him capable and guilty of the crime. But what did he care, he tried to tell himself. She was only a means to an end—a troublesome, quarrelsome one at that! Damn that shrew. She looked at him and the condemnation in her gaze cut him all the way to the bone. Cord didn't know why the hell he felt the need for this chestnut-haired witch to trust him.

So what if she didn't believe he was innocent? They meant nothing to each other, nothing at all. Hell yes, he was physically attracted to her. What man with eyes in his head wouldn't be? She was a raving beauty with a body that could stop a cavalry dead in its tracks. But there was no sentimental attachment. She was only a woman—a damnfool woman who planned to marry Victor Watts for the wealth they could provide each other. Just look who was calling whom a ruthless mercenary!

"I did not kill Juan Tijerina!" Cord proclaimed. "He damned sure deserved to die, but all I did was slam that chunk of rock he called his skull into the iron bars. When he collapsed, I took the keys and let myself out of the cell. He couldn't have been dead. It would have taken more than a couple of blows to his hard head to dispose of him."

"Blows to the head have been known to cause a man's demise on more than one occasion," Tempest argued.

Before Cord could jump down Tempest's throat, Jelly waved his stubby arms. "Hold on a minute, both of you. I read the report myself. It said Tijerina had been strangled with his own bullwhip."

Tempest's flashing eyes darted to Cord and lingered with intensity. She had the unshakable feeling she knew what had caused the crisscrossed scars on Cord's back and shoulders. Obviously, Juan Tijerina was cruel and brutal. Cord had more than enough motive to seek revenge on the jail guard. In a moment of fury and madness, Cord had struck out to get even with Juan. *Guilty as charged.*

When the entire family began talking a mile a minute, Tempest had an impossible time keeping up with the Joneses. With a flick of her wrist, she brought the congregation at the table to silence.

"One at a time, please," she requested. "For my own curiosity, I would like to know what this is all about, and it is impossible to make any sense of it when everybody is chattering at once."

Jefferson delegated himself the speaker of the household, for the moment at least. "According to the report, the jail was in chaos. The convict who was to be hanged that day was found dead in his cell, sprawled on the floor beside his overturned cot. The priest and executioner discovered the bodies of both men. When they dashed off to spread the news and request assistance, a band of outlaws took advantage of the turmoil. They broke their bandit friend out of jail, robbed the bank, and took off hell-for-leather."

"What?" Goggle-eyed, Cord slumped back in his chair to review the day of his escape. Ever so slowly, the pieces of the puzzle began to fall into place. In his mind's eye, he could see Juan sprawled in front of both cells—his and Dub Wizner's. Now that he thought about it, there had been an oddly calm and deliberate expression on Dub's face after Cord refused to shoot Juan in cold blood. The old man had bypassed the chance to gain his freedom. Dub had just stood propped against the bars, wheezing for breath and staring at the hated man who whipped them for his own fiendish pleasure . . .

"Dub Wizner . . ." Cord mused half-aloud.

"Come again?" Jefferson queried.

Cord jerked forward to rest his forearms on the table. "Dub Wizner was the convict who was about to be hanged in front of a crowd of sadistic spectators. He was already in poor health when I offered to release him. He refused because he said his weak heart wouldn't hold out. He must have picked up Juan's whip and strangled him with it."

Cord's gaze swung to Tempest. Her expression indicated she didn't believe him for a minute. In her eyes, he was guilty and nothing was going to change that intractable mind of hers. She wanted to hate him and this report offered her an excellent reason.

"Oh certainly, blame the dead man," Tempest smirked. "How very convenient. Who, I wonder, would believe such a tale as that? The jurors in a courtroom would laugh themselves sick."

"I didn't kill him!" Cord boomed in self-defense.

The words of denial reverberated around the room and came at Tempest from all directions. She, of course, deflected them.

"The penitentiary is crammed full of criminals who shout their innocence to high heaven," she said.

Cord's fist hit the table, rattling the plates and silverware. "I'm sick of listening to you rattle off all the crimes you *think* I've committed and I've had about enough of your lectures on the law. Who do you think you are? God's one-woman Supreme Court?" He scowled at her. "You'd love to pin another crime on me, wouldn't you? Then you could convince yourself that you detested me each time I dared to kiss you. But, by damned, you kissed me back because you liked—"

"I did not!" Tempest bolted to her feet and flung him a stabbing glare. "How dare you bring something like *that* up at a time like *this!*"

"Cord MacIntosh! Shame on you for taking improper liberties with this young lady," Myra scolded before she reached over to pull Tempest back into her chair and comfortingly pat her shoulder. "Anyone can tell at a glance that you're a sophisticated lady, Tempest, even in these tattered clothes. And Tosh, you shouldn't be kissing anybody's fiancée, not even Victor's. Haven't enough innocent victims suffered already?"

"Well, I can tell you which *guilty* party hasn't begun to suffer enough," Cord sneered, eyes flashing. He stalked around the table to hoist Tempest from her seat. "Uncle Jelly, I want you to marry Tempest and me this very minute."

"Are you out of your ever-loving mind?" Jefferson crowed.

At the most inarticulate moment of her entire life, Tempest stood there gaping in stupefied astonishment. But she did second the opinion that

Cord was certifiably insane, even if she couldn't muster the words.

Jelly gathered his scattered wits. It took a moment. "Now, Tosh, calm down. I understand why you want revenge on Victor Watts and Emilio Reynosa. But I think you're carrying this vindication a mite too far."

"And what of the lady's honor?" Cord questioned with a devilish smile that Tempest itched to slap off his face. "As you said, Aunt Myra, I took indecent liberties and now I'm honor bound to do the right thing by her."

Tempest gasped in offended dignity when Cord callously announced they had shared more than a kiss. That miserable, unscrupulous lout! The words *cunning* and *deceptive* had been coined to describe him. He thought he was having his revenge on Victor by marrying her. Well, the joke would be on him if he dared to follow through with such an outrageous scheme.

"Oh my . . ." Myra breathed as her hand flew to her palpitating bosom. "Oh my . . ."

"Uncle, fetch your law book," Cord ordered. "I've seen the error of my ways and I'm prepared to face the consequences. I plan to marry Tempest here and now."

The declaration momentarily robbed Tempest of speech. She stumbled back as if she'd endured a physical blow. She decided, there and then, that a strain of insanity affected one side of his family or the other. The man was obviously a maniac!

Jelly Jones, more by convenience of his position as stage station manager than by preference, had been delegated to the office of Justice of the Peace at the Pinery. There were scant few law officials scattered through the unpopulated area. Though he never claimed to know the law backward and forward, he had accepted the office to which he'd been appointed by the district court in El Paso—such as it was. Jelly had performed only two marriages in his time. This third one looked to be a disaster from the onset. His irate nephew was striking out against all the injustices that had been heaped on him. But if Cord had compromised the young lady while they trekked eastward, then there was naught else to do but rectify the situation. If Jelly didn't do as Cord demanded, his nephew would have sexual molestation added to the charges against him. My Lord, thought Jelly, things were going from bad to horrible!

"I will not consent to a wedding under any circumstances!" Tempest sputtered in outrage. "This is preposterous!"

She tried to twist herself out of Cord's restraining arms and bound out the door. But as quick as she was, she was no match for Cord's tigerish agility. Tempest had taken only one step before he hauled her against him and clamped his good arm around her.

Meanwhile, flustered though he was, Jelly was thumbing through his outdated law book which had been mailed to him a decade earlier. "With the power vested in me— No, wait, that's the last part," he grumbled as he reached for his reading glasses. "Now where does this confounded ceremony start—?"

"I do," Cord declared impatiently.

"I do *not* . . . ouch!"

Tempest wailed when Cord wrenched her arm up her back in a most agonizing manner. The man knew every pressure point. With one quick twist of his hand he had Tempest groaning in pain.

"She does," Cord answered for his belligerent bride-to-be.

"I do . . . ouch!"

This time, Cord made certain he applied pressure

at the right moment to cause Tempest to break off in protest a word too soon.

"Now read the part about the vested powers," Cord ordered his uncle. "I never was much for pomp and pageantry anyway."

"By the powers vested in me, I now pronounce you man and wife," Jelly officiated when he relocated his place in the law book. "Well, I guess that's that."

Tempest had never been more irate in all her born days. She was married to a murderer? The very idea! She? A practicing attorney? God help her. Somebody had to!

"Oh damn," Jefferson muttered when he heard the clatter of approaching riders.

He bounded from his chair and scurried to the window to see a procession of *vaqueros* trotting up the stage road. His frantic gaze swung to Cord who was having one devil of a time subduing his seething bride. If looks could kill, it was glaringly apparent that Tempest would have liked to be a wife and a widow in the short span of five minutes.

"I'd swear that's Emilio Reynosa leading his pack of wolves up the road," Jefferson said bleakly. "Go hide in the barn loft, Tosh. I'll preoccupy them while you slip out the back door."

Bodies scattered in a flurry of activity. Myra scooped up the two extra plates and glasses and plunged them into the dishwater. In record time she scrubbed the utensils clean and shoved them into a nearby cabinet. Moving with more speed than she'd employed in years, Myra repositioned the two chairs in the corner where they belonged.

Jelly gulped down several more bites of his unfinished meal to calm his nerves and then scuttled up behind his son to block the entryway.

In the meantime, Cord shoveled Tempest out the back door. He anticipated that she would scream her head off, given the chance, so he stuffed a napkin in her mouth to shut her up and tied her hands behind her back. Cord was no fool. If he had improvised by clamping his hand over the lower portion of her face, Tempest would have bitten his fingers off. Although she wiggled and squirmed and contorted her body, he snatched her up in his arms and carried her to the barn.

So furious was she that she even lowered herself to beat her fists against the wound on his arm that she herself had tended in one of her more sympathetic moments. As it turned out, Tempest wished she'd let the injury fester with infection. It would have served this rascal right. How dare he announce to his family that he had seduced her and she had liked it! How dare he marry her just to have his fiendish revenge on his arch enemy. Of all the low-down, dirty tricks! She'd kill him herself and save Victor the trouble.

"Tempest, for God's sake, you're making mincemeat of my arm," Cord said with a grimace.

That was the whole idea and Tempest would have dearly loved to tell him so if he'd have removed her gag. Instead, Cord lifted her over his shoulders as if she were a sack of oats and tiptoed up the steps to the barn loft. Although she couldn't reach his tender arm in this jackknifed position, she did kick her feet against his thighs. But the repetitive blows didn't seem to faze him. Cord was concentrating on what he was going to do with her while he kept his eyes trained on the cutthroats Victor had sent to kill him.

Cord would have delighted in getting Emilio Reynosa alone for a few minutes. He would bet his life that Emilio was teeming with valuable information. Emilio was probably the one who poisoned the spring, if Victor had been too much the coward to do it himself. Emilio and Victor were kindred spirits—ruthless, heartless, and conniving . . .

Cord's pensive gaze landed on the hook, rope, and

pulley that stretched across the rafters of the barn. A wry smile pursed his lips when an idea hatched in his mind. He knew exactly where to stash Tempest so she wouldn't cause him trouble or alert Emilio to their presence.

With quiet strides, Cord approached the dangling hook to which shocks of hay were lifted from the back of wagons to be stored in the barn for feeding the teams that pulled the coaches. Cord and his father had provided the hay from their lush mountain pastures, transported them by wagon to the stage station, and helped Jefferson stack the bundles in the loft. This, however, would be the first time the hoist would be utilized to keep an outraged someone airborne while Cord stood lookout in the barn.

Hurriedly, he constructed a makeshift halter of leather straps to restrain his fuming bride. When the harness was fastened in place, Cord released Tempest and dashed to the back of the barn to grab the rope and hoist her high in the air.

Although she had scampered forward in hopes of anchoring herself to a wooden beam, she wasn't able to clench her arms around the post before Cord lifted her. Her forward momentum left her swinging to and fro like a trapeze artist. Wild-eyed, Tempest watched the floor whiz past her while she ascended to the top of the towering rafters. Oh, she was really going to get even with that blackguard for this prank, she vowed vehemently. Cord knew she was afraid of height and he had purposely left her dangling like a bundle of straw. If she squirmed for release and met with success, she would plunge to the planked floor of the loft. Damn the man. He always seemed to know which string to pull. He was cruel and spiteful and insulting and she hated him!

After Cord had pulled Tempest to the back of the barn and left her walking on air, he crept along the wall to peer out at the scraggly looking bravos who had congregated at the front door of the way-station.

A frustrated growl rumbled in Cord's throat. Murder? He was being sought for murder, too? *Caramba!* What he didn't need was another crime against him. Absently, he glanced over his shoulder to see Tempest swinging in the distance. God, what had gotten into him? Forcing that firebrand to marry him had to be the craziest thing he'd ever done. But when he'd seen the contempt in those sapphire eyes, he wasn't sure if he'd been striking out at Tempest or at Victor. But he had needed some sort of compensation after receiving still another emotional blow. Realizing that Dub Wizner had let Cord take the blame for a murder that he didn't commit sent him right over the edge. Cord and the ailing old-timer had become friends—of sorts, at least. They had shared the company that misery loved so well. Cord wanted to believe Dub would have confessed the truth if he had lived. And yet, he knew what a murderous rage Juan Tijerina had put Dub in that fateful morning. Cord had entertained visions of killing Juan himself after being whipped and humiliated so often. But what was done was done, and Dub had found his own way to escape the hangman's noose . . .

The creak of timber jarred Cord from his musings. He half-twisted in his crouched position to see Tempest freeze in midair when one of the halter straps came loose. Now she didn't dare move a muscle for fear of falling to her death. Of course, she wasn't in danger of falling, but Cord wasn't about to tell her that. He had secured the harness in four places and purposely left one loose. Tempest could writhe and buck to her heart's content and she would still be dangling from the rafters. If there was one thing Cord knew how to do it was tie knots. He'd left one cinch just loose enough to scare the wits out of her. She couldn't have been safer if she was nestled in his arms—the last place, he imagined, she ever wanted to be . . .

Ten

Jefferson Jones ran his lean fingers through his crop of dark hair and ambled onto the stoop to greet the haggard group of *vaqueros.* "What can I do for you?" he asked.

Emilio eyed the rangy cowboy for a long moment. "We are looking for a fugitive, señor. I'm sure you have been notified that a man named Cord MacIntosh murdered his jailer and escaped from El Paso."

Jefferson nodded affirmatively. "We received the bulletin. I think maybe your fugitive paid us a call in the wee hours of the morning."

Emilio stared at the station agent from under the shadowed brim of his sombrero. *"Si?"*

"Si," Jefferson acknowledged. "This morning when I went out to the storeroom the door stood ajar and some supplies were missing—blankets, tinned foods." He gestured toward the corral where the horses and mules were munching on their daily ration of grain and hay. "Two of our best animals were missing, too—a roan and a gray gelding." He frowned, pretending to mull over a thought that had just popped to mind. "I don't know why your fugitive would need two horses, but—"

"He has a woman with him," Emilio interrupted.

"A woman?" He frowned meditatively. "Yes, that's

right. That was in the bulletin, too. I'd forgotten. Well, that does explain the need for two horses. But good God, surely you don't think that murderer would drag a female with him through this rugged country, do you?"

Jefferson was doing a dandy job of utilizing his theatrical ability. He wondered if there might be a place for him on the stage—and not the kind on which passengers commuted from one locale to another.

Emilio's thick shoulders lifted noncommittally as he glanced past Jefferson and Jelly, just to be sure Cord wasn't inside the station, forcing the agents to lie for him. Emilio wasn't taking chances. With a pistol clamped in each hand, he elbowed his way between the Joneses to inspect the station. Glancing in all directions at once, Emilio searched every nook and cranny. His probing gaze slid over Myra who was busying her nervous hands by washing dishes.

Myra's apprehensive gaze circled the room and her heart stalled in her chest. The picture of her brother Paddy MacIntosh was on the bureau, and she cringed at the thought of answering questions about that. Drying her hands as calmly as she could, she walked across the room to retrieve extra silverware and carefully stash the portrait facedown in the drawer.

"Would you like me to fix you and your men something to eat?" Myra inquired, her voice not quite as steady as she hoped.

Emilio paused to light his cigarillo as Myra turned clutching an extra supply of eating utensils.

"No, señora. We have a murderer to catch," Emilio replied, much to Myra's relief.

She hadn't wanted to cook for these scraggly ruffians. She had only needed an excuse to get to the bureau to conceal her brother's picture.

In swaggering strides, Emilio pushed his way past

Jelly and Jefferson to rejoin his men. He pivoted on the stoop to stare the stage agents down. "The hombre is dangerous," he reported grimly. "I have orders to shoot to kill. I advise you to do the same if MacIntosh shows his face."

Jefferson nodded his dark head before Emilio swung into the saddle. Pensively, he watched the *vaqueros* trot down the stage road that led southeast through the mountains.

Myra half-collapsed against the oak bureau with a gasp. "I shudder to think what would happen to Tosh if that creature got his hands on him."

"It doesn't bear thinking about," Jefferson muttered. "Tosh told me that Reynosa used to ride with a band of *Comancheros*. He related some of the atrocities Emilio had committed against the Comanche and Apache, even when he claimed to be their allies. Emilio can be ruthless when he has to be."

Jelly shook his head in dismay as he plunked down in his chair to gobble a piece of apple pie. "Lord, have mercy! Tosh has gotten himself in way too deep looking for revenge. Victor will have every able-bodied man in a saddle, scouring the countryside to find Tosh. And now that he's married Victor's fiancée . . ." His voice trailed off as he swallowed another bite of dessert.

The threesome silently speculated on what repercussions Tosh would encounter for marrying Tempest. It had been a rash decision on Tosh's part, to be sure. The Joneses felt certain he would regret it. If nothing else, Tempest would make sure that he did.

It was impossible for Tempest to calculate the amount of time she had spent dangling on the rafters like a spider. The very idea of finding herself married to a conniving felon like Cord MacIntosh was truly outrageous. When she finally got this gag out of her mouth and set her feet on solid ground, she was going to lambaste him but good! Oh, he'd be sorry, so help her he would!

Cord knew he was going to have hell to pay when he finally ambled over to work the rope and pulley that kept Tempest aloft. The blue fire in her eyes could have set the stables aflame. And sure enough, the instant her feet hit the floor, she launched herself at him like an enraged wildcat, muttering muffled oaths that were most unbecoming to a lady. Although her repertoire of salty talk wasn't extensive, she used every word she knew to describe the horrible beast of a man who had mistreated her.

With lightning agility, Cord dodged the oncoming bundle of fury. When Tempest overstretched herself to make a second attempt to run Cord into the floor and grind her feet on him, he tossed her over his shoulder and headed toward the steps. Cord was not foolish enough to remove the gag until he stashed Tempest in the stage station room that had once been his bedroom during his teen-age years. Tempest's anticipated tirade would likely bring Emilio and his cutthroats back to the way-station for an unwanted showdown.

Cord eased down the stairs while Tempest pummeled the side of his head with spiteful blows. His scheme for revenge had taken an unexpected detour. The murder charge would make his situation even more difficult. There was only one man who knew Cord hadn't strangled Juan Tijerina with his bullwhip—Ellis Flake. Where Ellis and his band of outlaws were hiding was anybody's guess.

Cord was almost tempted to deposit this hotheaded she-devil on the next stage and let her ride off into parts unknown, never to be seen or heard from again! Blast it, the harder he tried to even the score, the more entangled his life became.

Three pairs of sympathetic eyes focused on Tempest when Cord set her inside the back door. Oh, she knew his strategy as well as she knew her own name—a name she had recently acquired and abhorred! Cord presumed she was too much of a lady to throw a tantrum in front of his kinfolk. But he had underestimated her temper. The instant Cord tugged the gag from her lips, Tempest proceeded to tell him what an imbecile he was, right in front of his relatives.

"How dare you string me up like a carcass of beef and leave me hanging there!" she raged, her face purple. "I have never in my life been treated so inhumanely! You despicable cur! You vicious heathen. You—"

"Keep your voice down," Cord growled, casting apprehensive glances at the door. "The hotel guests might hear you. And worse, Emilio might come roaring back here if you're screeching like a banshee. He's likely to slaughter us all!"

The Joneses shifted uncomfortably while Tempest and Cord squared off toe-to-toe and eye-to-eye, sneering disrespectfully at one another. Aware of the uneasiness he was causing his kinfolk, Cord latched onto Tempest's arm and herded her into his room. When he had kicked the door shut with his heel, he turned a glare on her that was as cold as the Klondike.

Tempest shoved her palms against his broad chest, pushing him back into his own space, and tried to keep her voice down to a low roar. "You think yourself so clever, Cord MacIntosh?" She raked him with scornful mockery. "Well, I'll tell you what a bungling idiot you are. And I'll also tell you what was in the letter your father mailed to San Antonio." Her chest heaving, she took a furious breath and plunged on. "I know what was in that letter because *I* read it!"

A muddled frown creased Cord's brow as he sank down on the edge of the bed to watch Tempest stomp from wall to wall in an effort to relieve her pent-up frustration. It obviously didn't help. She was boiling.

"That letter was a request for legal counsel, sent to my father in San Antonio," she informed Cord through clenched teeth.

It gave her immense pleasure to see this brawny giant sitting on the edge of his seat, trying to comprehend what she was telling him. Just wait, she thought spitefully. She hadn't even gotten to the good part yet!

"*My* father is the man who owed his life to *your* father—a debt incurred almost twelve years ago when the stage on which Abraham Litchfield was riding was set upon by Mexican *banditos*. My father was a circuit judge at the time. Now he is a district court judge and you have just cinched the noose around your throat."

Cord looked as if he'd swallowed a pumpkin. His eyes bulged in amazement as he peered up at the tangle-haired hellion who was at the height of her towering rage.

"I happen to be the lawyer who was sent to defend you in your case against Victor," she shouted with immense satisfaction. A wicked smile pursed her lips and her eyes twinkled with spiteful menace. "Would you like to guess whether I find you guilty or innocent of the various and sundry crimes against *you*, plus the offenses I know for a fact you have imposed on *me?*"

Cord stared at her in mute astonishment. He opened his mouth to speak, but his vocal cords had collapsed. Not one sound came from his throat.

"After I heard the news of your father's death, I sought out the man who had filed the complaints, hoping to understand what was going on. Your father was not specific in his request, and I was left to piece together what I could from every available source," Tempest explained as she wore a path on the carpet. "I am not Victor's fiancée. I was only at his ranch looking for information." She paused to glare at the bug-eyed giant who had yet to find his tongue. "You are an imbecile, Cord MacIntosh. You kidnapped the wrong woman and you also wed her in a moment of vengeful madness. The joke isn't on *Victor.* It's on *you!*"

Gasps erupted from the dining room where the Joneses stood with their ears plastered to the door.

Cord was on his feet in a single bound, jerking Tempest to him with a back-wrenching jolt. He'd never been so furious or felt so betrayed—and that was saying a lot because he'd been good and mad and ruthlessly mistreated often! But *Tempest* had lied to him, misled him, deceived him. *He* had been feeling guilty as hell for putting her through one life-threatening ordeal after another? What a waste of perfectly good emotion! Damn it, he couldn't trust her any more than he could trust Victor. She had never even tried to be honest with him.

"Why didn't you tell me the truth in the beginning, you little witch?" he seethed.

Tempest wormed loose from his painful grasp and winced at the stab of guilt provoked by the look in his eyes. She told herself she had every right to keep silent after he'd dragged her all over creation. But her conscience had never quite accepted that as an honorable excuse.

"I was taking the opportunity to glean information from my would-be client, to determine just what kind of man he really was, what he was capable of doing," she told him. "I knew perfectly well that you would change your attitude in a hurry if you knew my true identity. Over and over again, you showed your true colors, my dear husband." She made the endearing title sound like a curse. In fact, it was a curse—the curse of *her* life!

"You used me as a shield when your life was threatened. You heartlessly dragged me through difficult terrain where a horse could barely survive. You taunted me and humiliated me, after you purposely murdered the jailer to ensure your escape! You are beneath contempt and I wouldn't defend you! Never in a zillion years!"

Cord scowled at her. "That's a damned lie."

"What is?" she smirked, enjoying her advantage over this mountain of a man. For once in their exasperating acquaintance she was in command of the situation and she enjoyed it with relish. "Are you referring to your behavior toward me? You seem to forget that I was there. I was the one you inflicted your cruelties upon—the one who will be filing another battery of charges against you. You can damned well bet your miserable life on that and I'm the one who can make it stick in a court of law!"

"I did not kill Juan Tijerina," Cord declared.

Tempest's gaze flickered over his broad chest in disdain. "After what you've put me through, surely you don't expect me to believe that. You have proved yourself capable of anything."

Cord was consumed with so much frustration that he feared he was about to explode. For the life of him, he didn't know why he cared what this firebrand thought of him. But damn it, he did care. Too much, in fact. He was going to prove to her that he had been framed. And by God, one day he'd hear Tempest Litchfield admit she had been wrong!

"Jefferson! Get in here pronto!" Cord bellowed.

Since Jefferson and his parents still had their ears pasted to the door, it only took a second for him to make his entrance. The bleak expression on Jeff's face indicated that he'd heard every word and that he and his parents were worried as hell.

"Tosh, I think you better give up and throw yourself on the mercy of the court," Jefferson advised before Cord could squeeze a word in edgewise.

"Hell, Jeff, she *is* the court!" Cord scowled as his arm shot toward Tempest. "As if I would have stood a chance anyway, with a lady lawyer to defend me!"

That remark earned him another dose of Tempest's ferocity. It reminded her of all the disrespectful comments uttered by many a narrow-minded man.

"I'll have you know I'm a qualified attorney," Tempest blared. "And I could have proved your innocence, if you weren't so guilty!"

"Like hell!" Cord snorted. "You already admitted you had consorted with my enemy. The two of you were probably preparing your case against me so I wouldn't have a prayer. He bribed you, didn't he?"

"He most certainly did not," she protested self-righteously. "I cannot be corrupted. I have sworn to uphold the law."

"How? By lying when it suits your devious purpose, proving you can't be trusted to speak the truth when you had every chance to be honest with me?"

Tempest hated it when he was right, but she was angry enough to ignore the prick of regret inflicted by his scathing accusation.

"And what about that noble decree that a man is innocent until *proven* guilty?" Cord continued caustically.

"You have proven your guilt to me a dozen times over," Tempest snapped.

Cord opened his mouth to fling a suitably nasty rejoinder, thought better of it, and then wheeled on his cousin. "Fetch me two of your best mules and some provisions," he ordered abruptly.

"No need to fetch one for me," Tempest inserted, flinging Cord a contemptuous glare. "I'm planning on taking the stage to El Paso."

A thin smile bracketed Cord's lips. "You're going with me, my beloved wife. And that's that."

"You're on your way to hell," Tempest smirked.

"You won't be needing my company with all those demons in your head."

Cord silently gestured for Jefferson to do as he was told. When they were alone, Cord clutched Tempest's forearms, holding her firmly in place while he stuck his face into hers.

"You're coming with me, like it or not," he assured her crossly.

"I don't like it one bit."

Tempest felt frustrated and helpless. His family would stand by him, but her father wasn't around to protect her by annulling this ridiculous marriage. And furthermore, Cord was big enough and strong enough to make her go *when* he wanted and *where* he wanted. *She was trapped* . . .

"If you cause me the slightest trouble, you'll know just how nice I've been thus far," Cord warned with deadly menace.

"Nice?" Tempest smarted off, despite his threatening glower. "Never will that word be used to describe you. You can count on that. I think—"

The instant he moved deliberately toward her, Tempest flinched. She was not going to be influenced by the strange physical attraction she experienced when he came within three feet of her. She despised this golden-eyed devil. His touch was repulsive . . .

Tempest braced herself when his mouth swooped down on hers, stealing the breath out of her lungs and smothering her. In an instant she was fighting him, determined to break the spell this blackhearted wizard held over her. She would not succumb to him ever again . . .

Her resistance dropped considerably when his fierce hold became a tender embrace that encircled rather than restrained. Desire and denial warred inside her when the wildly sensual side of his nature preyed on her. She fought the warm tingles with every bit of willpower she could muster, but her defenses began to melt. When his lips whispered over hers, Tempest was swamped with those traitorous stirrings of pleasure that she had resented since the first time he'd dared to touch her. His hands drifted over her hips, bending her against him. It incensed Tempest that she could still find this raven-haired rascal's touch stimulating after all the anguish he'd put her through.

Why him? Why this rough-edged outlaw who had married her to play a cruel trick on his archrival? Why a man without a conscience or scruples? He was public enemy number one and she was a lawyer. What an unlikely pair! But this strong attraction proved beyond all doubt that physical desire knew no rhyme or reason.

A quiet moan escaped Tempest's lips when his skillful hands moved over her sensitive flesh, taking the kind of privileges that no other man had been allowed. This renegade's potential danger also seemed to be his hypnotic lure. He was daring and reckless and those qualities should never have appealed to her. She was too organized, sophisticated, and analytical . . . or at least she had been until Cord kissed her senseless and taught her how it felt to be a woman.

When his hands and lips teased her with erotic promises, Tempest forgot why she disliked him so much. Suddenly she was only a woman responding to a darkly sensual man. Cord knew instinctively how to arouse her slumbering passions, bringing them to life and leaving her craving every deliciously wicked pleasure.

To Tempest's disbelief, she found her anger turning to desire. Her arms involuntarily curled around his neck. Instead of strangling him she kissed him back! Her heart was fluttering in her chest like a wild bird in captivity and that peculiar ache that unfurled inside her in that dark hour before dawn began to invade her senses again. Her betraying body arched toward him as he guided her hips toward his in a wildly intimate gesture he had taught her. His tongue probed into her mouth and Tempest was shocked to find herself employing the same technique on him. She felt the compelling need to repay him for all the pleasure he had given her. And when his mouth came down on hers once again, savoring and devouring the taste of her, Tempest's chaotic senses absorbed the scent and feel of him. She clung to him shamelessly as the world faded into oblivion. Uncontrollable desire raised its unruly head and demanded more . . .

When Jefferson cleared his throat to announce his return, Tempest leapt out of Cord's arms. Her face flushed cherry red and she scolded herself fiercely for being such a helpless victim of his skillful seduction. It was certain that this ornery devil could rattle the most dedicated of souls. Damn it, how did he do that? And curse it, why did she let him? She seemed to have less willpower than he did!

Jefferson tried to bite back an amused smile. But it was difficult. When he'd left, his cousin and this feisty female looked as if they'd been on the verge of killing each other. Now they were suffocating each other with steamy kisses.

What an interesting development, thought Jefferson. He wondered if Tosh was using his charm to convince the lady lawyer that he did have a few *appealing* qualities. And yet, when his cousin turned away, Jefferson wondered if Tosh wasn't feeling the physical effects of the kiss. Just exactly what was going on here? And *who,* he wondered, was having the most dramatic effect on *whom?* It was too close to call.

One look at the chestnut-haired beauty and Jefferson knew how easily a man could lose sight of his objectives. No matter how mad this spitfire made Tosh, he was still drastically affected by her. What man wouldn't be? She was intelligent, gorgeous, high-spirited, and she had the kind of body that could leave a man lost in fantasy.

"I loaded your supplies on an extra mule," Jefferson said, shoving his musings aside. "Tosh, you can ride Flattery. He can get you everywhere," he added with a teasing grin. "And Tempest can ride Lady. But you better shake a leg if you want to be long gone before the cavalry tramps up here or Emilio realizes he's been hoodwinked."

That said, Jefferson turned on his heels and sauntered away while his lips twitched in barely concealed amusement. Tempest muttered under her breath, knowing full well that Jefferson thought she was a hypocrite. And what really annoyed her was that he was right!

"I hate you for a hundred good reasons," she hissed at Cord. "But I hate you most for that."

"You hate me because you find me sexually attractive?" he said with a snort. "I hardly think that's *my* fault, honey."

"I certainly didn't invite that mauling," Tempest huffed, highly offended. "And don't call me honey!"

"Forgive me," he said in a tone that was nowhere near apologetic. "My mistake. You aren't the least bit sweet. I should have called you *lemon.*" With an ornery grin he extended his hand to escort her out the door. "Shall we go, lemon?"

Tempest glared at his hand and then at him. Making a spectacular display of ignoring him, she veered around him and stamped into the kitchen where the Joneses waited in apprehensive silence.

Myra peered sympathetically at her nephew. She started to offer advice, hesitated, and then sighed audibly. "Be careful, Tosh. I know better than to try to tell you what to do. You've always been your own man, even when you were just a child. My prayers will be with you. And if there is anything we can do, anything at all, just let us know. We'll always be here. You know that."

When Myra's arms held him in a sentimental hug, Cord pressed a fond kiss to her worried brow. "I'll take care of myself and my new bride," he added, just to aggravate Tempest. She glared poison arrows at him.

Cord dug into his pocket to pay his uncle for the mules and supplies, but Jelly waved his arm in a deterring gesture. "I'm not taking your money after all the good deeds you and Paddy have done for us," Jelly insisted. "Now get on your way before that drunkard stumbles in here or that shifty-eyed merchant comes trotting over from the hotel with his precious satchel."

Although Tempest would have preferred to be going anywhere except with this maniac, she didn't slap Jefferson's hand away when he assisted her onto her burro. It was useless to appeal to the Joneses for assistance when they were so hopelessly devoted to Cord. And an escape attempt at present would be a waste of energy. But when Cord turned his back, she intended to take flight.

This was going to be the shortest marriage in history. She'd have this preposterous mummery of a wedding annulled the second she returned to civilization, and Cord MacIntosh would find so many criminal charges against him he'd never dare show his face in Texas again. She'd make him sorry he'd ever got on her bad side, just see if she didn't. Imagine going off on one's honeymoon—God forbid—on the back of a mule, married to a jacka—

"That isn't a nice thought to be thinking about your lawfully wedded husband." Cord clucked his tongue when he saw Tempest's resentful gaze dart from the mule to him. "Making comparisons, are we, my love?"

Tempest tilted her chin so she could look down her nose at him. "I find it ironic that the two stubbornest creatures God placed on this earth now find themselves joined at the saddle."

With laughing amber eyes, Cord stared first at Tempest and then at the mule named Lady. "I couldn't have put it better myself."

Tempest tossed her head and looked the other way as they aimed themselves toward the rocky precipices to the southeast. "I would prefer you don't speak to me again for the rest of my life."

"No, you don't," Cord said. "That's not what that body of yours was saying to me a few minutes earlier. You were all too eager to communicate with me and you know it."

Tempest swiveled her head around to glare into Cord's eyes. Oh, how she hated that mischievous smile that reeked of male arrogance. For a moment, she was hard pressed to break the vow she had made never to acknowledge his presence or engage him in any type of conversation. But she remembered herself in the nick of time. She would not dignify that comment with a response.

Her body spoke to him? Indeed! He would be in his grave long before she found herself in his bed again, allowing him his husbandly rights. If Cord MacIntosh thought for one minute she would appease his lust each time the mood struck him then he was crazier than she thought. He could get down on his knees and beg, for all the good it would do him. She was never giving in to wanton desire again. Once had been too much and this was one promise she was going to keep!

Eleven

Judge Abraham Litchfield sat down before he fell down. Although he stood six feet tall and considered himself stout and robust, the message he'd just read knocked his legs out from under him. A muted growl tumbled from his lips as his blue eyes raced over the letter a second time, but it was no easier to accept than it had been the first.

"Herbert!" Abraham roared in frustration. The butler's name ricocheted off the oak-paneled walls and vibrated down the tiled foyer like the crack of thunder.

Within a matter of seconds, a stoic, gray-haired servant appeared at the door of the resplendent study. "Yes, Judge?"

"Have my brougham brought around immediately," Abraham commanded.

"Trouble, sir?" Herbert watched the judge bound to his feet to pace—an unconscious habit Tempest had picked up from her father.

"Tempest has been kidnapped by the very man she traveled to El Paso to defend!" Abe boomed. "Damnation, I should have sent someone else out there!"

Herbert, who prided himself in his ability to remain calm and impassive, staggered back against the doorjamb as if he'd received a doubled fist to the stomach. "What kind of horrible heathen would dare to take Tempest hostage?" he croaked, aghast.

"A guilty one, obviously," Abe muttered.

Composing himself as best he could, Herbert did an about-face and scurried out the back door to send the judge's order to the groom.

"Curse it!" Abe stalked over to pour himself a brandy. His mind raced, mentally organizing his plan. Although Victor Watts hadn't gone into extensive detail about the incident that left Tempest in the hands of a murdering thief, Abe's imagination was running rampant. He had heard enough descriptions of similar incidents in court to worry himself sick. God, the torment Tempest must be enduring! Although his daughter was fiery and determined, she would be no match for a desperado.

Abraham took another drink and willed himself to calm down. It didn't help. How could this have happened? And where was Paddy MacIntosh? He should have been protecting Tempest from foul play. What kind of son did the man have?

Paddy had saved Abe's life those long years ago, just a month after Jerelyn Litchfield had died of pneumonia. If not for Paddy's skill with weapons, Abe would have perished and Tempest would have been all alone in this world. She was all Abe had left and losing her was unthinkable.

"Your carriage is waiting," Herbert announced.

After downing the remainder of his brandy, Abe surged out the door. He would see to it that every bounty hunter, law official, and soldier in the western half of Texas was notified of this vile crime against his only child. And when he caught up with that ungrateful scoundrel, Abe vowed to show Cord MacIntosh no mercy, even if Paddy *had* saved him from disaster in years past!

* * *

Tempest had developed a strong dislike of mules. She had nothing but bad experiences with Lady, the contrary critter that carried her along the treacherous trails that meandered through the rugged Delaware Mountains south of the Guadalupes. The burro behaved like no lady Tempest had ever met! Although the creature had performed admirably during their perilous trek along lofty precipices, Lady had purposely bitten Tempest once and thrown her twice. The ornery animal seemed to delight in causing trouble every chance she got.

A rumble of thunder echoed through the tree-choked canyon below them. Tempest clamped a tight grip on Lady. "I cannot imagine why you're dragging me with you," she muttered, casting Cord a mutinous glance. "If I wasn't slowing you down, you could have been long gone. You'd be far away from the crimes you've committed in Texas."

Tempest had already broken her vow of silence. She was sorry to say that no matter how hard she tried she couldn't keep her mouth shut. Another of her character flaws, she supposed.

Cord wasn't sure why he'd become so testy of late. He had tried to attribute his foul mood to the fact that he'd been unjustly accused of murder and that he had kidnapped the wrong woman. But it was more than that. For a man who prided himself in being confident, capable, and self-reliant, it amazed him that he needed this she-male's acceptance, approval, and trust. Her opinion mattered, but damned if he knew why! He was incensed that this blue-eyed hellcat believed the worst about him. Since Tempest refused to believe him, Cord was bound and determined to find the one man who could attest to his innocence. He wanted this sassy shrew to hear the explanation with her own ears.

And for better or worse, he'd married her in a spiteful, impulsive moment and they were stuck with each other . . .

"Well?" Tempest prompted when Cord didn't reply as quickly as she thought he should. "Just what is the point of this rigorous—?"

Her question transformed into a startled squawk when Lady decided it was time to unseat Tempest again. The ornery mule took three wild leaps, ducked her head, and launched Tempest through the air. She landed with a thud and a groan. The unladylike curse that burst from Tempest's lips was drowned out by another fierce clap of thunder.

When Cord swung to the ground to pick Tempest up and dust her off, she slapped his hands away as if he were a pesky mosquito. "Don't touch me," she railed, unable to bite back the tears that clouded her eyes. The fall had dented more than her pride. Her entire body was still vibrating from her crash landing. "Just go away and leave me alone, damn you."

Tempest chastised herself for displaying a weakness she abhorred. She was as frustrated as one woman could get, extremely weary, in considerable pain, and exasperated by the intolerable situation she found herself in. The events of the past few days had piled upon her like the thunderstorm that swallowed the sun. First, she had surrendered to Cord's considerable charm. Then she had been forced into a marriage neither of them wanted, only to discover her new husband was a murderer. Now she was being dragged off on another wild-paced trek through difficult terrain.

Despite her determination, the floodtide of emotions came pouring out in huge sobs. Tears streaked down her cheeks. She wanted to go where she belonged, back to the safe, secure, predictable world she'd known in her father's home. She wanted to hear Abraham's comforting voice reassuring her, just as it had when she was a child, battling the tragic loss of her mother. Where were her father's protective arms and tender whispers when she needed them? All she had was a fugitive for a husband and a mule that had a personal vendetta against her . . . and buckets of drenching rain.

When the sky opened up, Tempest lost the last of her crumbling composure. This latest escapade had been one long exercise in frustration. She was ready to give up. She had reached a point where she didn't even protest when Cord scooped her up in his arms and cradled her close. She was long past caring. The feel of his sinewy arms was the only available consolation. Truly, he was the last person she wanted to turn to. But he was all she had, depressing though the fact was.

"I hate you, Cord MacIntosh," Tempest blubbered, saturating the only dry spot on his shirt.

"I know. I hate you, too, Tempest," Cord grumbled when he felt himself responding to this impossible female. Problem was, hatred couldn't overcome desire. She was in his blood and he could never seem to get enough of her.

Watching such a proud, stubborn woman in tears touched Cord in an unfamiliar way. He had taught himself to bury all his tender feelings under armor, but when those big shiny tears trickled from Tempest's eyes to mingle with the rain that soaked her to the bone, he felt the ice around his heart begin to melt.

He had been inconsiderate and cruel, and she had every right to hate him. He was putting her through a dozen kinds of hell. Tempest had come to El Paso in response to his father's request, and he had destroyed what should have been a friendship, an alliance. In the beginning she might have defended him against Victor's accusations. But not now. He had spoiled any chance of that.

Blinding flashes of silver streaked across the gray

sky. Lightning struck a tree deep in the canyon. The booming echoed and re-echoed for several minutes. The smell of burning wood mingled with the scent of rain. A curl of smoke drifted up to the ledge where Cord stood.

Heaving a sigh, he surveyed their surroundings. The late afternoon thunderstorm had made travel inadvisable. There was naught to do but make the climb to one of the caves etched in the cliffs and seek refuge from the inclement weather.

"You're going to have to walk a ways," Cord announced as he set Tempest to her feet.

"I'd prefer to simply sit down and die," she sobbed. "I just don't care anymore."

Cord jerked her to him. "You'll do what I tell you, damn you," he snapped brusquely. "Now grab Lady's reins and follow me. I don't have time for a typical bawling female."

He knew there were times when a man had to be cruel in order to be kind, as ironic as it was. But the path to the caves was treacherous and he couldn't carry Tempest and manage all three sets of reins. If he ignited Tempest's volatile side, she would survive on her hatred until they reached the cavern.

When Cord slapped the reins into her hand and tipped the brim of his sombrero to the driving rain, Tempest felt a surge of fury replace the fog of depression that had closed in around her.

Cord bit back a wry grin when he glanced over his shoulder to see Tempest draw herself up and head defiantly into the rain and wind. He'd made her mad enough to fight back, if only to prove to him that she wasn't the weak creature he thought she was. And it was damned important that she grit her teeth and plow on. They were about to reach one of the most precarious sections of the trail where they had to step up three feet and then inch along the path under a limestone cliff. If Tempest was preoccupied with her fear of height rather than concentrating on the narrow path . . . Well, Cord didn't even want to consider what could happen.

Tempest gulped apprehensively when she realized where Cord was leading her. Her footsteps faltered as she clutched Lady's reins. Her gaze wandered helplessly over the sheer cliff covered by rivulets of water rushing toward the valley below. The sweeping wind billowed around her, threatening to tug her off the ledge and send her plummeting to her death.

Cord glanced down to see the terrified expression that claimed Tempest's delicate features. "Keep moving," he barked. "Now's not the time for another one of your lapses."

The insult served its purpose. Tempest's head snapped up with a glower as hot as the hinges on hell's door. Courageously, she clawed her way up to the higher ledge, just to show him she could go anywhere he could go and do anything he could do, only better! Curse his hide! She'd prove she was made of sturdy stuff . . . or die trying!

Lady became a credit to her name. She scrabbled up the boulder to the stony ledge, behaving splendidly, as mules could do when danger was near.

Things were going as well as could be expected until the low ceiling beneath the overhanging cliff forced them to walk in a stooped position. There was no head room and the only way to proceed was in a crouch. Tempest inched beneath the limestone ceiling, avoiding jutting rocks. All of a sudden disaster struck. Lady's saddle horn scraped against the underside of the ledge, startling her. Instinctively, Lady brayed and bucked, accidentally throwing herself off balance on the narrow trail.

Frantically, Tempest clutched at the reins, trying to hold the burro upright until she gained her balance.

"Let her go!" Cord bellowed when he wheeled to

see what had caused the commotion. "She'll pull you over the edge with her!"

The blaring command contradicted everything inside Tempest. Although she had cursed Lady several times for her mischievousness, Tempest didn't have the heart to let the mule plunge to what had to be instant death. When the momentum of the falling mule tugged at her, causing her to stumble all too near the perilous edge, Tempest screamed.

"I said let her go, you little fool!" Cord bellowed.

Tempest didn't realize how fierce her self-preservation instinct was until that horrifying moment. Her fingers released the reins and they slid across her palms, leaving nothing to which Lady could anchor herself. Terrified, Tempest watched her beast of burden topple into the vast expanse of wind-blown rain to drop into the tangle of brush fifty feet below.

"*Caramba!* I swear you have the worst luck with horses and mules," Cord croaked after his vocal cords began to function again.

Tempest had practically scared the pants off him when she waited until the last possible second to release the reins. He'd very nearly suffered a heart seizure at the prospect of watching Tempest being pulled off the ledge by the falling burro. She was excavating feelings that he didn't know he still had—stark, paralyzing fear, for instance! When this blue-eyed horror was hurting he bled. When she found herself facing life-and-death situations he wound up suffering the tortures of hell. Since when had he become so aware of Tempest's feelings, needs, and concerns? He wasn't accustomed to worrying about anyone but himself and he felt uncomfortable fretting himself sick over a woman. Curse it, he had even begun to think of *them* instead of just *him!*

"Hurry up," Cord demanded as he led his mule and the pack mule under the ledge. "Water will roar down the sides of this mountain any second."

Squeezing back more tears, Tempest felt her way under the limestone wall that overlooked the ravine. She couldn't see Lady among the brush and boulders, but she knew the poor critter's dismal fate. What little determination Tempest had mustered to meet the perils of this journey disintegrated.

She was humiliated to find herself crying all over again, hysterically so. It upset her terribly that she had killed her mare and now her mule.

Tempest didn't see the firm hand that gripped her elbow to hoist her up onto the higher ledge. Fear of falling consumed her when she was left dangling in midair for a horrifying second. When her body finally brushed against Cord's, Tempest clamped onto him like a barnacle to a ship, buckling beneath her panic. Although Cord's shirt couldn't have been wetter, Tempest cried her eyes out on his collar. Her cheek was nestled against the warmth of his neck, and she didn't care if he made fun of her. He was her port in the storm, and she wasn't letting go of him until the turmoil inside her subsided. Her emotions had taken a beating the past week, and she couldn't keep the frustration bottled up a second longer. It exploded, leaving her a shambles. Huge sobs wracked her body, and she collapsed before Cord's very eyes.

"Sh . . . sh . . . !" Cord whispered against her forehead. "You're safe, love. It's all right now . . ."

Cord almost laughed out loud at his own voice. He had never been one to offer consolation, especially to a woman. And he sure as hell wasn't any better at it than he was when he'd made love to Tempest the first time, feeling guilty and ashamed. But seeing Tempest fall to pieces got to him, and he was murmuring comforting words as if he were an old hand at it.

In four lithe strides, Cord ducked into the cavern that opened onto the cliff. The howling gale swirled around the cave entrance, but the dark recesses offered protection from the raging storm. Now that the worst was over, he found himself trembling from the aftereffects of what could have been catastrophe. He held Tempest's shuddering body close, providing the security and warmth she so desperately needed.

When she tipped her face to his, Cord drowned in the blue of her eyes—they were alive with emotion and he knew he was lost. His head dipped toward hers, taking her trembling lips beneath his. That was all it took to ignite the banked fires inside him. He could only remember one other time when he had been so aware of the woman in his arms. It was the first time he'd made love to Tempest. The mere thought of that splendor was enough to leave him burning like a bonfire. The feel of her body was enough to drive all other thoughts from his mind. Their wet garments left him feeling as if they were already flesh to flesh, but it wasn't enough to satisfy this burgeoning need that uncoiled inside him.

One kiss, and passion was eating him alive. This unexplainable chemistry between a certain man and woman baffled the mind. All the ingredients could lie dormant until just the right someone came along. When he looked at Tempest he went hot all over. He wanted her, just as he had the first time—wildly, urgently, desperately. And nothing else would make this maddening ache go away.

Suddenly their perilous trek in the rain was forgotten. Cord could think of nothing but his need for this female who could so easily tie his emotions in knots. Tenderly, his hands framed her tear-stained cheeks.

"Tempest, I need you," he rasped before his lips feathered over her quivering mouth. "I want you the way I've never wanted another woman in all my life . . . And yet, I can't trust you with my life because I know you'll eventually crucify me. Every time I kiss those lips I taste the lingering poison I can't get out of my system. What is the cure for this curse?"

Tempest made the mistake of returning his gaze. She was all too vulnerable, all too aware of the feel of his masculine body fitted to hers. His words echoed around the dark cavern, tormenting and yet hypnotizing her.

Ah, how she wished she knew how to cure this mutual craving that vibrated from his muscular body into hers until her nerves hummed and her muscles trembled with anticipation. Almost immediately, she lost the will to fight the traitorous sensations that spilled through her. She needed Cord to help her forget how close she'd come to death, to dissolve the inner turmoil that pulled on her from two directions at once—*away* from him and *toward* him.

Cord was a wizard who weaved a potent spell. It had done no good whatsoever to promise herself that she would never let him come this close again. That was one promise Tempest was afraid she couldn't keep, not when Cord's masterful kiss tempted her with wild, sweet promises.

Twelve

The sound of pounding rain and howling wind faded into oblivion as Cord's sensuous lips rolled over Tempest's. All she could hear was the thunder of her own accelerated heartbeat in her ears. When his caresses glided down her back and hips, bringing her full length against him, the need to appease the hunger inside suddenly became as important as her need for survival had been a few minutes earlier. Her mind and body were totally immersed in one compelling thought—satisfying the white-hot ache.

In her own way, she needed Cord, too. He had the power to send the world away, to make her forget the terrors she had endured. When she was in the protective circle of his arms everything seemed right, even when it was all wrong. No matter how hard she tried to deny this attraction, it tugged at her like a kite battling the wind. She had always wanted him, even when she *hadn't wanted* to want him. He was the only man alive who could make her defy her own will and yield to the mysterious pleasures of passion.

Tempest's harrowing experiences had scattered her wits and uprooted every deep-seated inhibition. Cord had kept her living on the edge so long that she had come to expect danger. And there was nothing more dangerous than this tawny-eyed rake who aroused her most wanton desires. Tempest felt the wild urge to caress him as familiarly as he was caressing her, to explore his magnificence. She longed to discover what there was about this complex man that had bedeviled her so. Her hands moved experimentally over his muscles, wondering how difficult it would be to arouse and satisfy him.

Cord's knees very nearly buckled when Tempest's inquiring fingertips drifted over the buttons of his shirt, baring his bronzed flesh. When her hands coasted over the darkness of the hair on his chest he swore his oxygen had been cut off. Her touch wove a tapestry of pleasure around him, and he was instantly lost to overwhelming desire. Her lips skimmed his skin—tasting him, igniting fires that burned on top of each other until his nerve endings sizzled. The pressure of her shapely body brushing against his drove him wild with a wanting so fierce and intense that it shattered his self-control. Cord had never allowed a woman to take the initiative in lovemaking, but he granted this enchanting siren unprecedented privileges with his body.

When Tempest pushed the damp shirt from his shoulders to gaze at him in unguarded appreciation, Cord experienced an odd sense of pride. She may have despised him, but deep down inside she was stirred by the sight of him. There was that, at least, he thought shakily. If nothing else, they both shared this unexplainable fascination that bound them together when so many obstacles tried to force them apart.

Tempest marveled at the indescribable satisfaction she received from merely touching this incredible man. He was earthy sensuality, formidable power, and immense strength in repose. He was warmth and whipcord muscle. Touching him was like limning the rugged contours and sleek planes of a Roman statue, the epitome of masculine perfection. But Cord wasn't chiseled from stone, though he liked her to think so. He was filled with potential and vitality. She could feel his tendons contract beneath her hand. She could feel his heart leapfrogging around his chest as she caressed him. In her own way, she had the power to move this mountain of a man. She marveled at the influence she seemed to have over him. It made her bolder in her explorations.

"You have made me want you when I have tried not to," Tempest murmured as her fingertips drifted over his nipples, making him flinch and groan. "And now, my lusty dragon, I will *make* you want me the way you have wanted no other woman." She took the words he had spoken a few minutes earlier and turned them around. "For once, *you* will be the one possessed . . ."

Cord knew for certain that he was possessed the instant her lips fluttered over his flesh like velvety butterfly wings. He was possessed by a blue-eyed witch who had all too quickly learned to twist his words and turn his own brand of seduction back on him, leaving him seething in a caldron of fiery desire.

"From your strength I will draw strength," Tempest assured him as her adventurous hands swirled across his ribs to trace the band of his breeches.

Cord swallowed air and braced himself when his knees began to wobble. Any second now, he was going to wilt into a heap. His heart was beating him to death and this ornery imp was killing him with her tender touch! The ache inside him was so pronounced that it burned like a hot branding iron. This was the torment, but where, oh, where was the cure?

"What was once yours will become mine," she promised wickedly as her hands glided slowly down his lean hips, giving him another jolt that very nearly stopped his frantic heartbeat. "A witch, you say?" Her throaty laughter resounded around the shadowed stone chamber. "Perhaps. But only because that is what *you* have made of me with your wizardry. I'll use what you have taught me. But this time, I'll make you *like* the feel of sweet surrender."

A mischievous smile pursed her lips when she heard Cord groan and watched him stagger back as if she had delivered a forceful blow. "You teased me for shedding tears and being afraid of heights. But when I'm finished with you, my demon lover, you'll be afraid of me, afraid of the power I have over you . . ."

He already was! *Caramba!* How could such an inexperienced female turn him every way but loose so quickly? When she practiced her exquisite torture on him, he felt like a two-hundred-pound weakling. He supposed he deserved this unbearably delicious torment after he'd ridiculed Tempest to keep her moving while they struggled over the rocky summits. She had created an inventive way to get even and she was a little too damned good at it!

When her hands and lips skimmed over his chest and belly, he felt goose bumps across his skin and bullet-like sensations shoot down his spine. And when she drew him down to the cavern floor, Cord still couldn't muster the strength to protest. He had reached the point of no return. He was willing to submit to anything, if only this lovely nymph would appease this craving that burned him to a crisp. But she only intensified the desire until he groaned for mercy. Yet, no mercy was forthcoming, only killing pleasure that multiplied until it exploded through his body and mind.

Tempest didn't know what devil had taken control of her tongue, making her say and do erotic things. And although she had always been far better at repelling amorous advances than instigating them, she had become mesmerized by the feel of Cord's flesh beneath her inquiring hands. She adored touching him. She reveled in each rock-hard plane and muscular contour, learning each place he liked to be touched.

She had hoped that by taking command of this romantic interlude she could remain untouched by passion. For once, she wanted to walk away without being so affected by his phenomenal spell. But she could never humble this brawny giant when she was as caught up in the pleasure as he was. It was such an odd paradox, Tempest thought as her restless caresses drifted lower and lower still. Making him want her in the wildest ways only made her want *him* more!

Her hands enfolded the hard warmth of him, stroking him where he was most a man, teasing him until her name tumbled from his lips in a hoarse whisper. Her feathery kisses hovered over his pulsating flesh, fanning the flames ignited by her drifting fingertips. Her tongue flicked out to taste him, intrigued by yet another paradox—the essence of man himself. He, who was the epitome of overwhelming power, was sheathed in unbelievable tenderness. He was satin steel . . . sensitive strength . . .

Tempest could feel Cord's entire body flex and then tremble as her lips closed around him, gently suckling until she had drawn this imposing giant onto a sensual torture rack, transforming his superior strength into helpless surrender. Passion, she realized, created the ultimate contradiction: the world ceased revolving on its axis and the laws of nature reversed themselves. It was that moment when the invincible became most vulnerable and the gentlest became omnipotent. The very thought fascinated Tempest, luring her deeper into that dark dimension where mindless desire reigned supreme.

Cord felt himself unraveling like a spool of thread. Tempest's brazen touch was like silk and fire, sensitizing every fiber of his being until he was living through her tender kisses and caresses, aware of nothing else. Just as the first time, when he and Tempest had fallen into passion's lure, Cord found himself exploring the furthermost reaches of desire, expanding and then transcending limits that he had never experienced before. And now he understood why! Not only had Tempest dared to unleash the kind of passion that Cord had never known, but her gentleness challenged him to surpass the previous limits of his self-control. With Tempest he was constantly being forced to redefine the boundaries of his willpower, his stamina. And when he stretched his control as far as he swore it would reach, this female exploded every concept of his own limitations to the ends of the earth and challenged him to reach deeper yet—and conquer the enemy within: unbridled desire.

He gasped when her gliding fingertips and dewy lips measured the rigid staff of his manhood, arousing him to the breaking edge of newly established restraint. Another overwhelming challenge and another round of heat-drenched pleasure filled him, demanding even more, lest he explode with this scintillating hunger that was killing him inch by inch.

"God . . ." Cord gasped at her intimate caresses, scrambling to contain the throbbing needs that raged like a flood against the crumbling dam of his restraint. Cord hissed through his clenched teeth when Tempest invented new ways to torment him and then challenged him to extend another of his limits that had just fallen by the wayside. His body quavered in response to the feel of silken hands and honeyed lips encircling, engulfing, tasting him. Frantically, Cord wondered how many men had died from sexual torment. He had the inescapable feeling he was about to be the first. "God . . . !"

Watching Cord succumb to deep waves of pleasure inflamed her own longings. Suddenly Tempest's aching body was inching toward his. With a breathless sigh, she bent over him. Her tangled hair formed a dark cloak around them, shutting out the world. This lithe, panther-like man was all she could see, taste, and feel—all she wanted and needed.

When Tempest's soft lips melted upon his, Cord could taste his own desire, inhale the scent of masculine need that she had called from him. Mindlessly, he clutched at her, shaken by the desperate desire to touch as he had been touched, to taste the feminine essence of this woman who had driven him so wild with longing.

Tempest lost herself in Cord's kiss, surrendering to the turbulent sensations that assaulted her. He held her in desperation, drawing her body down upon his. When Cord roughly yanked her gown away to ply her with intimate caresses, she could hear his ragged breath against her flesh as he lifted her to nip at the taut buds of her breasts. Her moan broke the electrified silence when his wandering hands glided between her legs to the satin heat of her need for him. Over and over, he touched and tasted her while he guided her trembling body over his, creating a wildly erotic kind of kiss and caress that drove her over the brink into total abandon.

The need to prove her power over this golden-eyed rogue was the farthest thing from Tempest's mind when the gnawing ache swallowed her alive. And when he settled her hips exactly over the pulsating length of him and his greedy lips made a meal of her, Tempest lost the ability to form rational thought. She was like a wild thing in his arms, sharing his savage impatience. She was desperate to end this maddening torment and find the quintessence of satisfaction.

It was a fierce, urgent coming together—the hungry blending of silky feminine flesh and unleashed masculinity. She clung to Cord as if she were going down with a sinking ship, tugged into a whirlpool of swirling desire. Tempest felt as helpless as she had the day Cord had pulled her down into the swift-flowing current of the underground river. She was swept through another dark abyss, but there was no fear when she was in the magical circle of his arms, only breathless pleasure. She was living and dying in the heady rapture of his muscular body moving in perfect harmony with hers. It was as if she could hear a timeless melody somewhere in the distance. And when the crescendo intensified to a maddening pitch, Tempest cried out in the wondrous rapture of it all. Sensation after indescribable sensation undulated through her as she matched the urgent insistence of each powerful thrust. When the world collapsed around her, Tempest clutched at Cord and yielded to the convulsive spasms that shattered her composure and left her drifting in a kind of luxurious contentment that defied description.

After what seemed forever and a day, Tempest regained enough strength to prop herself up on Cord's chest. She found herself staring into those amber eyes that flickered with wry amusement. Lord, it had been such an emotionally draining day already. And now this! Had she really said and done all those outrageous things? What had gotten into her? She had played the seductress as if she had been born to it.

Tempest was the first to admit she had very little control of her emotions after the events leading up to this ardent interlude. Although she hadn't fallen earlier in the afternoon when her mule plunged over the ledge, she had definitely jumped off the deep end with Cord. Heaven help her! She betrayed her morals and beliefs just to satisfy the physical cravings that he aroused. She wasn't just a hypocrite, she realized. She was also a lunatic!

A crimson blush worked its way up from the base of her throat to the roots of her hair with that thought. With a choked sob she realized what a fool she had made of herself—again! It would have been easier on her conscience if Cord had forced her into submission. At least she could have blamed him instead of herself. She would have had another reason to detest him. But *she* had seduced *him* and had taken free license with his body, as if they truly were husband and wife and she was very much in love with him.

When Tempest tried to lever herself off of him, a position that only served to remind her once again of *who* had coerced *whom,* Cord hooked his arm around her waist and held her in place.

"Let me up this instant," Tempest cried, fighting her shame and mortification. "And don't ever touch me again, you beast!"

"Beast?" Cord would have been insulted if he hadn't been so amused at the conflicting emotions that chased each other across her exquisite features. "If memory serves, and it serves me very well, thank you, you're the one who got us where we are now. I only said I wanted you. You did the rest, and quite superbly, may I add," he said with a rakish chuckle.

Damn him, did he have to put it that way? She had been thinking the same thing and she did not need to hear *him* say it!

"Don't speak to me again," Tempest demanded as she bit back tears. She refused to give him yet another weapon to use against her.

She hated allowing Cord to know how rattled she really was. It infuriated her to see him lying there looking as smug as a lion with his paw resting triumphantly on a mouse. But in this instance the foolish mouse was on top!

When Tempest reached over to snatch up her ripped gown and place it between them, Cord burst out laughing. "Why must you keep making a big production of modesty?" He shouldn't have teased her so, but she always seemed to invite it with her stubborn attempts to deny the powerful attraction between them. "We've already been as close as two people can possibly get—twice."

He lay there, totally unashamed of his nudity, staring roguishly at her tattered gown, waggling his eyebrows suggestively. Tempest cursed under her breath, pried his arm loose from her waist, and rolled away to wiggle into her dress.

"I specifically remember asking you not to speak to me," she muttered, flashing a smoldering glare.

"You always say that, minx, and you're always the first one to break the silence," he reminded her with a scampish grin. "Not only do you have to have the *last* word, but you want the *first* word, too."

When she tried to scoot farther away, Cord rolled to his side and propped himself up on an elbow. His hand rose to plunge into the shiny mass of hair that billowed around her face like a dark cloud. "Don't try to spoil something so rare and beautiful," he murmured, all teasing aside. "Is it such a crime that you and I can give each other such splendor? Must you always be ashamed of it?"

Tempest withdrew, at the risk of having her hair pulled out by the roots. "Rare? Indeed! But only in the sense that it is never going to happen again. It wasn't enough that you took what all men want from women once before. But you had to rub in the fact that I was the one who started it this time! Must you always humiliate me so?"

He leaned closer and his forefinger trailed over

her pouting lips. "It shames you that you want me every bit as much as I want you? Why?"

"Because of who you *are,*" Tempest replied with a muffled sniff. "Because of who I'm *supposed* to be!"

One thick brow elevated. "And just who am I, my fairy princess, if not your enchanted prince?"

"As if you don't know."

Tempest refused to look at him. Her eyes kept sliding over the thick hair that covered his chest and the lean muscles of his belly. He was a virile specimen who was all too easy on the feminine eye and all too hard on her blood pressure. She kept remembering every delicious caress that had taught her the most intimate things about his body. Touching him had been new and exciting and she hadn't been able to stop herself.

Cord gazed at her for a long, quiet moment. He was determined to get through the awkward aftermath better than he had the first time. He had botched up royally then. He was making a conscious effort to deal with this magic between them. But it was damned difficult when it was obvious that Tempest didn't approve of the spontaneous attraction between them anymore now than she had the first time.

"Did you learn nothing about me after everything we shared, little witch?" he queried softly.

"I learned plenty," Tempest grumbled. "I learned things I shouldn't have, and didn't want to know at all—things that change nothing between us."

Cord couldn't control his amusement. Damn, she was stubborn! "I'd say *everything* changed between us the first time we made love. But as usual, you're too contrary to admit it. Why can't you simply enjoy it for what it is—wild, sweet, and fulfilling. Women have sexual needs, just as men do. It's no crime, is it, my lovely lady lawyer?"

Tempest was accustomed to asking questions and

offering advice. Now she was forced to see things from a different angle and she was having difficulty coping. And to make matters worse, Cord had sprung the trap on her temper, even with all this patience he was suddenly displaying toward her. That made her highly suspicious. Until this point, she hadn't thought he had had any patience with her at all. She didn't know how to react to her own sense of guilt because she had never purposely set out to seduce a man. And it wasn't helping one whit that Cord was heckling her. What was she supposed to say in the aftermath of such an experience. *Thank you very much for letting me learn all there is to know about a man's anatomy, for becoming so intrigued that I would forget who I am . . .*

A suspicious thought struck Tempest and she quickly realized where this line of questioning was leading. "Ah, so that's it," she sniffed, as if she had him all figured out. "You let me seduce you so I would forget what kind of man you really are, so I would have to admit that I am here by my own choice. Well, it won't work! You may have had your way with me twice, Cord MacIntosh, but you have not influenced me to such an extent that I will swear under oath that you are innocent!"

Cord wished he understood the workings of the female mind—this complicated woman's in particular! How Tempest could leap from one conjecture to another and then stumble to such a ridiculous conclusion was something he'd probably never figure out.

Well hell, so much for gently coaxing this firebrand through the "aftermath" of lovemaking. She thought he had devised a way to make her seduce him in hopes of winning her over? She thought he wanted nothing more than sexual satisfaction, just so he could hold it over her head? Damn, and *she* thought *he* was cynical? That was a laugh.

Cord threw up his hands in resignation. *Caramba!* He may as well debate the mountains. They would be as receptive as she. Scowling, he grabbed his breeches and stuffed his legs into the wet garment.

"You are one impossible woman, Tempest MacIntosh," he muttered grouchily.

"Litchfield," she corrected in a scornful tone.

Cord jerked up his head and glared at her while he hastily fastened himself into his breeches. "You're my wife," he reminded her gruffly. "You may not like it, but you'll learn to live with it until I decide to let you go . . . which I won't until you believe I'm innocent of every charge."

"Despite the fact that you employed fiendish methods to convince me otherwise, I am still here against my will!" she flung at him. "And you're still guilty of kidnapping."

"Yeah, except for that," he amended sourly. "And you can drag me to court on that count if it will please your muleheaded pride. But I committed no murder and I certainly didn't steal Victor's cattle. They were planted in our herd." His eyes glittered as he towered over her, eclipsing what little sunlight had filtered into the cavern after the storm. "And by damn, I'll live long enough to hear you admit you were wrong about me, Tempest *MacIntosh.* That in itself will be my inspiration while I'm dodging bullets with my name on them. And *then,* when all is said and done, I'm going to say I told you so!"

On the wings of that remark, Cord scooped up his shirt and stalked outside to see the glorious rainbow that arched over the mountain peaks. Spectacular though the scenery was, it didn't make him feel a damned bit better. That blue-eyed terror was making him crazy. He wanted her respect and her trust and he sure as hell wasn't getting it. He didn't know why that feisty spitfire mattered to him and why he wanted to matter to her. He certainly wasn't in love with that vixen, even though he delighted in making love to her.

"Damned impossible woman," Cord growled.

"Infuriating man . . ." came the resounding echo from the inky darkness of the cave. "And you can go straight to hell, Cord MacIntosh."

Cord lifted his arms and eyes toward heaven. "And just where, I wonder, does she think I am now?"

Thirteen

For several minutes, Tempest sat in the dark cave, trying to corral a riptide of emotion. She honestly wanted to believe Cord was innocent of the charges against him. She didn't want to feel the way she did in the arms of a man who could be a dangerous criminal!

She rose and began pacing the cavern, trying to sort out her emotions. She supposed she had snapped at Cord to salvage her bruised pride. She wanted to hurt him, to salve her guilty conscience. But insulting and condemning him only made her feel worse. And now that he had walked out, she felt cold, empty, and alone.

Perhaps she had been too cruel in trying to protect her wary heart. In retrospect, Tempest was willing to give Cord the benefit of the doubt by asking herself if she had been too critical and suspicious. He had made a stab at being patient and gentle with her when he wouldn't have had to he. He certainly hadn't done that the first time they made love. He had simply put the incident behind him once he was satisfied and then he took up where he left off on his mission of revenge. But it was difficult for Tempest to accept this . . . this *thing* between them. Cord made her feel things that were foreign and a little frightening. She never felt so out of control, so intrigued by any other man.

Remembering the rapture caused her body to tingle, just as surely as if Cord had been kissing and caressing her. Sweet merciful heavens, what had that man done to her? My God, she wasn't actually falling in love with him, was she? Was that why she felt so threatened, so vulnerable, so tormented? He hadn't given her any reason to love him, and yet she was afraid she was beginning to anyway!

Inhaling a steadying breath, Tempest stared at the cave entrance. Pensively, she watched the sunlight peek through the clouds before the shadows engulfed her. Risky though it would probably be, she was going to . . .

Well, Tempest didn't really know what she was going to do except march herself outside, swallow this damnable pride of hers, and call Cord back from hell—where she had wished him a few minutes earlier. It wasn't his fault, after all, that she was having such difficulty dealing with her new-found feelings. He wasn't any more to blame that she was physically attracted to him than she was because he was attracted to her. It was his ulterior motives and calculated seduction that kept agitating her, she supposed. Put quite simply, Tempest was afraid to trust her own emotions for fear of getting hurt.

When Tempest stepped outside to call some sort of truce, Cord was nowhere to be found. Her heart contracted at the thought of being left alone with not the slightest idea how to return to civilization. Had she annoyed Cord to the point that he had finally, and spitefully, abandoned her?

Muttering at her inability to cope with Cord and the feelings he continued to arouse in her, Tempest ambled over to fetch the supplies from the pack mule. Well, if he did come back from wherever he went, she mused, she would have a peace-treaty meal awaiting him. And if he didn't come back . . .

Tempest scooped up the saddlebags and noticed the plain but clean gown that Myra Jones had stashed in with the supplies. Bless the dear woman! At least now Tempest would have something to wear besides her battered dress.

Her gaze darted from the calico gown, which was a few sizes too big, to the sprawling canyon and towering peaks. But still she saw no sign of Cord.

If he really did leave her out here all alone, she knew she would have just cause to hate him all over again. In fact, it was easier for her to dislike him than to adjust to the tender emotions that had put her, and kept her, in such turmoil!

It took Cord fifteen minutes to inch his way down the face of the cliff beneath the cave. He had presumed Tempest's unfortunate burro had landed in a broken heap, but since the animal belonged to Jefferson, Cord thought it best to confirm his suspicion. To his surprise and relief, Lady was peacefully grazing on the clump of grass. Cord carefully checked the mule over, only to find two scratches where her hide had been scraped when she fell into the mesquite bushes.

"You're a tough lady, Lady," Cord chuckled as he stroked her muzzle. His gaze rose to the overhanging ledge where another very tough lady awaited him.

Clutching the reins, Cord led—*dragged* was nearer the mark—Lady along the steep path. Like her contrary mistress, Lady was stubborn about following Cord anywhere. Lady balked; she had nothing on Tempest MacIntosh.

Cord wasn't certain what kind of reception to expect when he returned to the cave. Having been told to take a hike to Hades, he rather suspected he wouldn't be welcomed. But to his disbelief, Tempest sat cross-legged on her pallet in the middle of the cavern, placing tin plates on a makeshift table of quilts. She had unpacked the canned peaches, tomatoes, and milk that Aunt Myra had packed for them. The food was neatly arranged beside the cornbread and beef jerky she had also sent along.

It only took Cord a moment to notice that Tempest wasn't wearing the ragged gown that had suffered even more damage when he'd lost control and ripped it away. In place of the battered gown was a green calico dress that had belonged to Aunt Myra. Although the oversize dress didn't cling to Tempest's curves the way her tailored gown did, she still looked breathtaking in the filtered sunlight and shadows.

Tempest glanced up when Cord's muscular frame filled the entrance to the cave. Her heart gave a sudden lurch at the mere sight of him. She tamped down the memories that had hounded her after they had made love almost an hour earlier. She thought she would relish her solitude, but she had been wrong. For a woman who swore she had no fond feelings for this bold renegade, she had certainly missed him.

"I was beginning to think you weren't coming back at all," Tempest murmured, unable to meet his perceptive eyes that seemed to look right into her soul

Cord's thick brows rose at the subdued tone of her voice. Why, if he didn't know better, he'd swear she had missed him and was afraid he had abandoned her. Tempest? Not damn likely.

Pivoting, Cord stepped back outside to lead Lady forward. The instant Tempest spied the lost mule she bounded to her feet to give the critter a hug.

"I thought you had nothing kind to say about this contrary little burro." Cord chuckled, amused by the affectionate display.

Tempest retreated a step and shrugged noncommittally. "It seems one doesn't appreciate what one has until one comes close to losing it," she murmured as she stared at the scuffed tips of her shoes.

"No, one doesn't, does one?" Cord agreed with a faint smile. Impulsively, his hand moved to close the small space that separated them. His fingers curled beneath her delicate chin, lifting her reluctant gaze to his. "I know you have just cause to hate and mistrust me, princess," Cord whispered. "But know this and believe it. I have not, nor will I ever, intentionally hurt you." He paused, waiting for her darting blue eyes to meet his somber expression. "I could have hurt you both times we made love by taking my pleasure without considering yours. We didn't just have sex, Tempest. We made love, though you haven't been around enough to know the difference . . ."

Tempest stepped back a pace, willing her hammering heart to slow its rapid rate. This magnetic attraction could be triggered by the slightest touch or word.

"Tempest, do you understand what I'm trying to tell you?" Cord questioned softly.

She nodded before she resumed her place beside the improvised table. This conversation caused her suspicions and deep-seated skepticism to rise all over again. Tempest wasn't accustomed to such talk and she cautioned herself against reading more into Cord's words than was there.

"You're saying that you tried to be gentle with me because I'm the only female within a hundred miles. You don't want to damage the only merchandise at your disposal," she speculated.

Cord sighed heavily as he sank down beside her. She always looked for the worst in him, and he had never bothered to explain himself or his actions to anyone before. Now it seemed important that he did. Although Tempest had adjusted to the intimacies they had shared, she refused to let herself believe he was capable of feeling anything except lust. It was dangerous to let her know how human he really was, but the fragile bond between them would shatter if he let her think the very worst about him. Cord didn't need that when Tempest was laboring under so many misconceptions already.

Ever so gently, he slipped his arm around Tempest's trim waist, feeling her tense in wary trepidation. She studied him as if he were a dangerous animal, alert for the slightest threatening movement. The fact that she didn't immediately pull away indicated that she was willing to reserve judgment until he'd stuck his foot in his mouth, roughly embraced her—or both. Without frightening her away, Cord reached down to flick open the buttons of his shirt. His hand closed around hers, drawing it over his chest.

"I'm just a man, princess, not a beast," he whispered. He pressed her hand over the methodical beat of his heart. "You touched me earlier. Do you still think me such a monster that I react without provocation or that I wish to humiliate you for my own amusement?

"Can't you feel what you do to me when all I've done is look at you and remember the way we were. Even after the pleasure we shared, which should have been more than enough to satisfy the lustiest of men, I still want to strip you down to your silky skin and lose myself in your body again." He wondered if he had been too reckless in admitting how much she moved him. "You intrigue me, Tempest. Too much. My grandfather would say I am my own worst enemy when it comes to you."

A mischievous smile played about Tempest's lips, making her eyes sparkle. "Not as long as *I'm* alive, you aren't."

His rumbling laughter broke the tension. Tempest felt the vibrations beneath her hand. Absently, her fingertips drifted over his sleek, bronzed flesh, just as they had an hour earlier. Something very peculiar happened to her when Cord playfully grabbed her to him and pressed her down beside their waiting dinner. When she peered up into those laughing amber eyes, the smile faded from her lips. She reached up toward his rugged features and then trailed her index finger over the scars that curved over his broad shoulder.

Tempest was stung by that outrageous urge to caress Cord as familiarly as she had done earlier, to retest his reaction to her untutored touch. Did she really have the ability to make this worldly rogue tingle with the same shuddering excitement? Or would he have reacted the same way to any woman? And why did she always have such difficulty remembering what Cord was when she dared to set her hands upon him, or when he set his hands upon her?

Cord rather thought he deserved a medal for lying so still while this curious nymph rediscovered the feel of his flesh.

Taming a wild-hearted lass like Tempest would take patience and self-control. A man could never overpower her or demand her trust and affection. He had to earn it one small step at a time, day by day . . .

Her petal-soft lips drifted over his mouth and her fingertips glided over his ribs to track along the band of his breeches. Cord could feel himself teetering on the edge again, just as he had earlier. He was being a very good sport to permit Tempest to explore his body without allowing her to believe he was planning to lure her into another seduction. But Lord, at what cost! He had but to close his eyes and he could envision them as they had been earlier, lying flesh to flesh and heart to heart, discovering all the wondrously intimate things a man and woman could learn about each other.

"I think you are far more than just a man," Tempest admitted as her lips feathered over the lean muscles of his belly. "Indeed, you're a devil, Cord MacIntosh. You cast wicked spells on your female victims."

Her lips skittered over his throat to kiss his cheeks, his eyelids, and at long last his lips. "You have beguiled me," she confessed, though there was still a hint of resentment in her voice. "Is that what you want to hear? That I always end up wanting you, too? God help me for telling you that, but I do . . ."

His arms fastened around her as he rolled sideways, leaving her glorious mane of hair trailing over his shoulder in disarray. "I want to hear you say it doesn't matter who either of us is. That nothing matters, nothing but this raging fire. Feed the flames, Tempest. You're a fire in my blood, and know this," he breathed against the velvety swell of her breasts. "Having you twice still isn't enough to satisfy me, not when I know that heaven is just a touch away. I have no wish to conquer, only to enjoy . . ."

Tempest didn't even take time to scold herself. Cord had become a habit she couldn't break. He defied all her common sense. She could insist that he never speak or touch her again, but her body was always far more demanding than her brain. He could make her arch shamelessly toward his skillful caresses, as if she couldn't get close enough. She was obsessed, addicted until the maddening cravings he stirred in her found satisfaction. And surely this time the seductive devil's spell would be broken. The third time was supposed to be the charm, wasn't it?

When his lips closed over hers, Tempest gave herself up to the wild, hypnotic pleasure Cord instilled in her . . .

The howl of a lone coyote shattered the silence. Tempest blinked owlishly when Cord levered himself above her to stare toward the cave entrance. She could see the hunger in his eyes, mirroring her own needs. Grumbling, Cord pressed a hasty kiss to her lips and rolled to his feet. He muttered something about lousy timing as he tucked his shirt into his breeches and stalked outside.

Still breathing heavily, Tempest rearranged her calico gown and drew her feet beneath her. It was several minutes before she heard the crunch of rocks outside the cave. In this wild, unforgiving country there was no telling what was going to happen next, but something always did.

Tempest retreated into the shadowed recesses of the cave when she heard two sets of footsteps echoing in the corridor. Relief washed over her features when she recognized Cord's muscular frame, but the tension returned when she spied a leathery-skinned Indian who looked older than Methuselah. He hobbled along behind Cord, favoring his left leg. Tempest peered curiously at the aged warrior. His sharp, angular features were etched with wrinkles, and his long gray braids indicated years of hard living. He wore protective leather *botas* over his moccasins, just as Cord did. A colorful *rebozo* encircled his head and the fringe of his doeskin shirt and breeches rippled as he walked. Rows of shiny white elk's teeth and tiny painted shells ornamented his strange-looking necklace. His dark, perceptive eyes sought her out in the shadows, boring solemnly into her like a termite into wood.

"Tempest, this is Yellowfish," Cord announced.

It was plain to see that Tempest was leery of their unexpected guest and that she had no previous experiences with Apache. All she knew was what she had heard, and read, about the atrocities the Indians inflicted on the *Americanos.* White men never got around to publicizing the hideous crimes they had committed against the Indians.

"Yellowfish is my grandfather," he informed her.

Tempest relaxed slightly as she surveyed the old warrior in a new light. She wasn't quite certain how to react to him, not when the wild, warlike Apache had earned such a bad reputation in Texas, New Mexico, and Arizona.

Awkwardly, Tempest rose to her feet and lifted her hand in a gesture of peace and good will. "How . . . do you do . . ." she began, feeling quite uncomfortable about how to greet the old Apache.

Yellowfish's opaque eyes glinted with offended dignity as he regarded the white woman. "How do I do what?" he questioned in halting English.

It was obvious there was a language barrier in which Tempest's pat phrases were misunderstood. "What I mean is . . . How are you, sir?" she replied, shifting self-consciously from one foot to the other. Her eyes darted to the tin plates on the makeshift table. "Will you join us for supper, sir?"

With an arrogant nod, Yellowfish limped forward and plunked down on the pallet. He plucked up a piece of jerky and chewed thoughtfully upon it.

"You are Lobo Plano's woman." He scrutinized Tempest for a moment and nodded. "You will bear him many sons and live with us in these mountains."

Well, so much for social amenities and idle conversation, thought Tempest. Yellowfish certainly got right to the point. The next thing she knew, words of wisdom would be popping from his mouth. According to Cord, his grandfather was teeming with proverbs.

"It is good and right for a man to have his woman with him. She is his strength. You will adjust, even if you are white." Yellowfish made the comment sound more like a command than a statement.

Tempest shot Cord a hasty glance. In her opinion, this towering giant needed no additional strength. He was a walking source of potential energy.

"A strength of spirit," Yellowfish added when he noticed the puzzled expression on Tempest's features. "You will give him all your love and devotion and keep his bed warm with your—"

"Grandfather!" Cord interrupted.

Cord bit back an amused grin when Tempest flinched as if she were sitting on a scorpion. Yellowfish was pushing hard and he had yet to realize he wasn't dealing with a common, ordinary female.

The old man frowned curiously as he surveyed the chestnut-haired beauty who had begun to look indignant. "You do not love my grandson?" he questioned point-blank.

"Well, I—" she fumbled, her face coloring profusely.

"What is there not to love, white woman?" Yellowfish questioned, highly affronted. "Among the Apache, he has earned the name of Lobo Plano—the silver wolf who stalks in silence and strikes like lightning. He knows no fear, and has great courage. You could not find a better man, even if he is half-white."

"Grandfather—" Cord was cut off by Yellowfish's abrupt hand gesture.

"If you are his woman then you will love and obey him," he commanded. His coal-pit eyes were riveted on Tempest. "There can be no communion of souls if there is no love for him in your heart. Tell Lobo Plano you love him. I will hear it now, white woman."

Tempest had never met such a blunt, overbearing man—except perhaps for Cord. It was obvious where Cord had inherited his plainspoken manner and uncivilized nature.

Cord's mouth twitched in a wry smile while he watched the silent clash of wills. Yellowfish glared at Tempest, and not to be outdone, she glared right back. Cord was willing to bet wild horses couldn't drag any such words of affection from Tempest. She wasn't about to admit to anything when she had such difficulty even accepting the fact that she found him physically desirable. With Tempest, it was necessary to climb over one hurdle at a time—slowly and carefully. Cord and this wildcat had just passed an important milestone in their relationship a few minutes earlier. Yellowfish was rushing her to give voice to emotions she didn't feel, and Tempest had plowed into a head-on cultural collision that offended her independent nature.

Cord reached for his plate, anxious to break the tension. "I didn't realize how hungry I was. Would you like some more beef jerky, Grandfather?"

Yellowfish sat there like the proud, unapproachable war chief he was, bristling with bad temper. Huffily, he popped a chunk of food in his mouth. His ebony eyes never wavered as he matched Tempest stare for unrelenting stare. "I am still waiting, white woman."

"My name is Tempest," she informed him tartly. Why, that old buzzard! How dare he waltz in here and start ordering her around!

The old curmudgeon's sober expression never wavered as he nodded perceptively. "Storm-child—like the fierce gale that howls in these mountains. This does not surprise me." His gaze narrowed. "Tell him, Storm-child. You are to be Lobo Plano's eyes if he cannot see, his ears when he cannot hear. You will be his truth in the lies. It is your love that will sustain him like a hawk on the wind. You must begin by letting go so the love inside you, like the thunderstorm, will rain down on him like a shower to the parched mountains."

That antiquated barbarian wasn't forcing her to say anything to anybody! The very idea! Perhaps he could boss Cord around, but not her! She had been taught to respect her elders and she could be polite and tactful when she felt like it. At the moment she didn't feel like it. She was unaccustomed to dealing with overbearing old men who marched in, took over lock, stock, and barrel, and made preposterous demands to a total stranger. Yellowfish brought out the worst in her, provoking her contrariness to rise like cream on fresh milk. Just who the devil did this hide-bound old warrior think he was anyway? Tempest felt no obligation to this crusty Apache who was a living testimony to his vagabond lifestyle. He was also a monument to outdated beliefs about the role of women.

Tempest had just met the old coot, for heaven's sake, and this whirlwind marriage certainly wasn't *her* idea. It seemed that Cord should have explained the situation surrounding their rash wedding. Then Yellowfish would understand there wasn't the usual sacrificing of the soul and the unconditional giving of the heart that he expected for his grandson.

"You do not act like a proper Apache woman," Yellowfish snorted when Tempest ignored his command. "You do not know when to speak and when to keep your mouth shut. You do not know how to make your man happy."

That did it! Yellowfish's high-handed rebuke set fire to Tempest's short fuse. "Now you listen here, you brittle bag of bones, I have no desire to act like a *proper* Apache squaw," she spewed, her eyes blazing like hot blue flames. "I shall speak when and where and how I wish and I will remain silent when I choose to do so. There is not a man alive who is ever going to stop me!"

Tempest bounded to her feet, infuriated that the old geezer had driven her to such an outburst. But damn it all, Yellowfish had asked for it. The very idea of being commanded to love, honor, and obey like chattel!

"I apologize for being too easily provoked into rudeness. And now if you gentlemen will excuse me, I need a breath of fresh air." With that she stamped outside, with her back as stiff as a ramrod.

Yellowfish glared after her with disapproval. Angrily, he turned glittering black eyes on his grandson. "The white woman is not right for you," he said flat-out. "I am not wrong in this matter. Take an Apache maiden and leave the stubborn white woman with her own people. She does not fit into our world or into these mountains."

Cord hadn't realized how stubborn he was when it came to Tempest. His grandfather was probably right about that she-cat, but Cord found himself loyal to her just the same. His grandfather was wise, but he wasn't always right about everything *all* the time!

"You were wrong once before," Cord reminded Yellowfish with a wry grin that softened the blow of contradiction. "My mother often told me the story of the day you had been severely wounded in a battle with the Mexicans. When the rest of our clan decided to trek northwest, you remained behind in these mountains because you were certain it was your day to die. She stayed to attend to you. But even after you chanted your death songs to the Great Spirit, he did not come to take you up the Hanging Road to the Sky. And here you have remained for more than thirty summers."

Yellowfish snorted. "I was prepared to die from my battle wounds," he defended himself. "It was your meddling father who found me and nursed me back to health when I had already made my peace with this world and called to Holos to deliver me." He flashed Cord a condescending glance. "Your father was like you—stubborn and determined. It was the Scottish in him, Paddy MacIntosh always said. This Scottish flows in your veins as well." He cast his dark eyes toward the cave entrance. "Is it the Scottish that makes your woman contrary, too?"

Cord had never been able to sufficiently explain that Scottish was not some sort of poison that invaded a person's bloodstream and caused personality defects. Yellowfish had his own deeply-ingrained beliefs about evil spirits consuming human bodies and several misconceptions about the *Americanos*. No amount of explaining had ever changed the old man's mind. To Yellowfish, *Americanos* were *Americanos*. He didn't understand what he knew of their ancestry far across the sea. Mexicans and mixed breeds he could comprehend and that was the extent of it because he closed his mind when Cord tried to explain the history of the white man who had invaded lands that had once belonged to all Indians.

"Tempest has *English* in her," Cord declared with a chuckle. "But it is not the English in her that makes her refuse your commands. She simply doesn't love me and she will not speak what she does not feel. She has not been trained like an Apache woman, and I don't believe she has taken to the training of white women, either. Tempest is a new breed of female."

"Then it is settled," the old Apache announced with firm conviction. "I will escort her to the *Americanos* I saw riding through our mountains. They will take her back to where she belongs, and you will find a devoted Apache wife to give you strength and many fine sons."

With an anxious frown, Cord asked, "What white men are these, Grandfather?"

"The handful of men who raced through the valleys below, as if they were chased by demon spirits. They dug their graves and rode to the abandoned stone trading post that was once the camp of the dog soldiers at San Solomon Springs."

Cord grew pensive while he mulled over what Yellowfish had told him. Unless he missed his guess, Yellowfish had seen the outlaw band that had freed Ellis Flake from jail. Without Ellis's confession, Cord would never earn Tempest's trust or exonerate himself.

"Can you lead me to the graves?" Cord queried.

Yellowfish nodded. "I will even lead you to the

Americanos if you will give Storm-child back to her own people. I think the *English* is a much worse affliction than the *Scottish!*"

Odd, the thought of letting Tempest go had no appeal whatsoever. Cord had grown accustomed to her sharp wit, her testy temper, the feel of her ripe body blending intimately with his . . . He shook himself loose from that tantalizing thought. Cord didn't have time to become sidetracked by his insatiable need for her. He was running short of time. By now, he speculated that every available law official and soldier in the area would be tracking him. If the bounty hunters and dragoons got to him first, he would never be able to prove his innocence.

"Besides being plagued with the English, she is too skinny," Yellowfish grunted, shaking Cord from his silent reverie. "I may have been wrong once, my son, but I am not wrong about this. If Storm-child does not love you now, she never will. Send her away before she causes you too much trouble."

Cord's gaze shifted to the curvaceous silhouette on the ledge—but at a safe distance from the edge of the cliff—admiring the rugged beauty of the mountains. The wind caught in that wild tangle of hair that glowed like tarnished sunshine. His eyes scrutinized her luscious—certainly not skinny, as Yellowfish seemed to think!—figure in a visual caress, remembering the pleasures she had given him in her gentler moments.

"Is it so bad, Grandfather, to want a lovely creature who does not love you?" he murmured absently. "Can a man not enjoy its wild beauty and cherish it for only what it can give?"

Yellowfish half-twisted in his sitting position to follow Cord's appreciative gaze. Tempest *was* an awe-inspiring vision, Yellowfish reluctantly admitted, even if she was too skinny for his tastes. She possessed a rare natural beauty and an iron spirit. But without love as the mortar to bind stone to stone, there could be no foundation. And Yellowfish wasn't all that sure he wanted there to be a foundation. The white woman looked like trouble to him.

"A man can hold a wild bird in the palm of his hand, my son, admiring it for its beauty and the pleasure brought by gazing upon it," Yellowfish prophesied. "But the Great Spirit created the bird to soar on outstretched wings. Would you force a hawk to perch forever when it was born to fly? Would you restrain a wild creature that knows unlimited freedom and defies its imprisonment?" He gave his gray-haired braids a negative shake. "No, my son, I am not wrong in this matter. You cannot keep what will never be yours. If you try to defy the very nature of the Earth Mother, you will be doomed to disappointment. Let go before you cannot find the ability to do so."

Although Cord pondered Yellowfish's wisdom, he couldn't quite make that part of him that reached out to Tempest let go. She was a habit he didn't want to break, despite the folly of it. But perhaps when this ordeal was over, he could release this wild bird, as his grandfather insisted on referring to her. Perhaps later, Cord mused as he munched on his peaches. But not now.

His phenomenal attraction to that sapphire-eyed beauty was still too new and intriguing. When his fascination ebbed, he would send Tempest back to her father, back to a world that was far removed from the life he had known. These rugged mountains were his home, just as they were home to Yellowfish. To Tempest, these jagged summits pitted her against her worst fears.

Deep down inside, Cord knew Yellowfish was right about their star-crossed attraction. And eventually, he would release Tempest from captivity. If she spread her wings and took flight, he would do nothing to restrain her. This was his world, not hers. And as Yellowfish often said, wishing did not make dreams come true. A man had to learn to accept what he couldn't change, and nothing would change that chestnut-haired nymph. She was out of her element with Cord. She could never thrive here; she could merely survive, living for tomorrow and the freedom it would bring.

Cord knew he owed Tempest a world of tomorrows after all the terror and torment he'd put her through. In time he would have to give Tempest her rightful due. As his grandfather was so fond of reminding him—That was the way of things. Life did not change for a man, and time waited for no one . . .

Fourteen

After a full day of Yellowfish underfoot, Tempest was ready to climb the sheer canyon walls. She made the mistake of asking what time it was, and Yellowfish had proceeded to divide up the sky like an overhead clock. In a lengthy dissertation, the old Apache demanded that she learn how to gauge the hours by the course of the sun, how to determine time by the shifting stars. All this Yellowfish had spouted off in that pompous, aloof manner of his—so the "white woman," as he insisted on calling her, wouldn't have to bother him with silly questions.

At midday, the threesome paused at Yellowfish's home to take their meal. The old warrior's home was a spacious cave, a rather remarkable one at that. In fact, it was like three caverns that opened into each other from three different elevations that emitted a great deal of light—like overhead windows. Although Tempest couldn't imagine making a permanent home in a cave, this particular one would have been her choice since it resembled a stone castle built into the mountains. However, it would not have been her choice to share it with this old coot!

Before Tempest had stepped into the spacious cavern, Yellowfish had grabbed her arm and frowned in disapproval. At that point, she was given a stern lecture on Apache etiquette. According to Yellowfish, a woman entered a man's house *after* him, never before. A warrior moved to the right side of the abode and a woman to the left. Tempest was also told that it was the older man's place to initiate conversation and for the young ones to remain silent until they were invited to speak. Women, of course, were expected to hold their tongues until they were with their own kind.

With his customary aplomb, Yellowfish continued to rattle off the rules and regulations he expected Tempest to follow. She found herself on the verge of another disrespectful outburst. With extreme effort, Tempest managed to tolerate the proud old chief who was wearing out his windpipes, trying to force her to conform to his outdated standards.

"I have decided to take you under my wing like the hawk with its nest of chicks," Yellowfish announced at five o'clock that afternoon.

Tempest knew the time because she had checked the location of the sun, just as the Apache chief had instructed her to do.

"Since you were not born Apache, I will do what I can to counter the English poison in you."

Tempest cast Cord a muddled glance, wondering why Yellowfish considered her English ancestry a dreaded disease. Cord bit back a grin and wisely glanced the other way.

"While you're giving Tempest lessons on survival, I'll see if I can rustle up something for supper besides trail rations," Cord volunteered.

With that, he disappeared among the boulders. It amazed Tempest that he could appear and evaporate at will like a phantom. An inbred Apache trait, she supposed. She'd often heard it said that Comanche and Apache had the knack of materializing out of nowhere and vanishing into nothingness. Cord certainly exemplified that statement!

Yellowfish grabbed Tempest's hand and drew her down beside him. He gestured toward the variety of weeds, cacti, and bushes that skirted the trail. "The sotol plant is used by The People to distill an alcoholic drink used in rituals and ceremonies. The cabbage-like base is baked and eaten," he informed Tempest before gesturing toward another clump of vegetation. "The century plant is used for soap and medicine. The stalk is cut and the juices can be rubbed on festering wounds."

The Apache struggled to his feet, literally dragging Tempest to see strange varieties of cacti clustered around them. The Spanish dagger, rattail cactus, devil's pincushion, and yucca were only a few of the varieties he pointed out, expecting Tempest to learn them by name and appearance at first sight.

Yellowfish drew the dagger from his moccasin to slash off a spiny leaf. "Any cactus with milky sap is poison to man," he reported. "It is well that you avoid such plants since you have a strong potion of English in you already. The combination might prove fatal."

Tempest rolled her eyes and forcefully restrained herself from correcting Yellowfish on his ridiculous misconceptions. He seemed to think he knew it all and, since she had the English in her, she was assumed to be stupid.

Leaning out, Yellowfish inserted his knife into the top side of a round species of cacti, making a horizontal cut. Carefully, he removed the upper portion and cut a chunk from the center. When he handed Tempest a slice of cactus, she stared at him as if he were offering her a morsel of fried rat.

"Chew it," he commanded with his customary high-handed tone. "The juice quenches the thirst, but do not—" When Tempest choked and sputtered, Yellowfish whacked her soundly between the shoulder blades. "But do not swallow it," he finished a second too late.

Tempest wondered if she would have the slightest desire for normal food by the time Cord returned from hunting. Yellowfish had dragged her hither and yon, plucking the fruit from prickly pears, yuccas, and strawberry cacti, forcing her to sample them. If she dared to balk, he became more persistent and did not hesitate to fling insults about her contrariness and the dreaded English poison.

"Forgive me," Tempest muttered after another round of harsh ridicule. "But I hardly think it necessary to crucify me simply because I don't find cactus appealing to the palate."

"Better to be criticized by a wise man than to be praised by a fool," Yellowfish declared as only the snide old codger could.

Another of his witticisms, thought Tempest. She almost felt sorry for Cord, who'd been subjected to this barrage of philosophical flapdoodle all his life.

"Sometimes it takes much thought, determination, and concentrated effort to be agreeable with one's companions," Tempest tossed back at him before popping a chunk of cactus in her mouth.

The semblance of a smile twitched Yellowfish's lips as he watched her do as he demanded, while flashing her irritation at him with those lively blue eyes. "I can see why Lobo Plano is intrigued by you," he mused aloud. "You challenge a man at every fork of the road."

"Not for long," Tempest replied after swallowing her between-meal snack.

"That is best," Yellowfish said with a nod of conviction. "I can teach you to survive, but a white woman with a strong potion of the English in her cannot flourish out here. This land belongs to The People. We understand it and we thrive. It will always be so."

"I cannot imagine any white man in his right mind trying to take this place away from you," Tempest sniffed as she stared across the sprawling rock gorge to the V-shaped valley below.

Yellowfish instinctively felt rather than heard Cord's silent approach. He peered at his grandson over Tempest's head and nodded mutely. The old Apache knew Cord had overheard Tempest's remark. Yellowfish's unspoken message to Cord was to heed what Tempest had said without trying to change her. In the old warrior's opinion, Tempest needed to be removed from their lives—the quicker the better.

Cord scowled to himself. He knew his grandfather was right. Tempest was not the woman for him. She could not see life through his eyes and she could not appreciate the ever-constant challenge and beauty of this rugged terrain. To her, it was an inconvenience. To him, it was a way of life. But reality warred with Cord's instincts. He had only just begun to unveil the fascinating mysteries of this blue-eyed sprite. She was still a hunger he couldn't appease. The passion they had shared seemed only a foretaste of many pleasures awaiting him. Tempest had gone to his head like peyote. And when she was warm and willing in his arms, he could fly higher than this towering mountain.

When Tempest realized where Yellowfish's gaze had strayed, she lurched around to see Cord staring at her with an odd flicker in his tawny eyes. Before she could interpret the expression it was gone, replaced by a well-disciplined stare that revealed nothing of his thoughts.

"It is a woman's place to prepare the meal," Yellowfish declared as he limped over to retrieve the jackrabbits from Cord. He turned back to present them to Tempest. "You will cook while my grandson and I speak of things women do not understand."

Damn the man for trying to foist his beliefs and opinions off on her! When Tempest opened her mouth to tell that overbearing old geezer what he could do with the rabbits and what she thought of his antiquated notions about the female gender, Cord closed the space between them. His mouth swooped down, silencing her with a breath-stealing kiss.

"Grandfather has been the way he is for seventy years," he murmured. "Don't try to change him in one day's time. He may be cantankerous but he means well."

"So does a snarling dog protecting its territory," Tempest muttered resentfully. "And I don't have the foggiest notion how to go about skinning a rabbit."

Cord generously offered her the dagger. When she stared first at the knife and then at him, Cord cocked a dark brow, daring her to do her worst and see where it got her.

"Oh very well, I'll do it," she grumbled. "But you'll have to start the campfire. It will take me all night to wrestle these hares from their fur coats and gather wood. But if that old curmudgeon makes one snide remark about my cooking, I'll—"

"You'll bite your tongue and keep silent out of respect for your elders," Cord insisted as he absently caressed her satiny cheek. "You can give me hell all you want, but you'll tolerate my grandfather."

The look Tempest flashed Cord, before she turned around and stamped off to find a flat-topped boulder to serve as a table, indicated that she intended to give him plenty of hell indeed when she had the chance. Tempest was attacking the rabbits with vengeful disgust, wishing she was skinning Cord and Yellowfish alive.

With a lordly air, the old Apache plunked down on the ground. Although he did not approve of Cord building the fire when the task should have fallen to the white woman, he watched in silence. He did, however, toss a few instructions to Tempest at irregular intervals so she wouldn't damage the meat. Tempest held her tongue, vowing to take out her frustrations on Cord—later.

Curse that old Indian's hide! He delighted in making her feel subservient, incompetent, and totally out of her element. How that aging warrior could traipse around these towering summits and plunging valleys without wearing himself out mystified Tempest. Yellowfish had the stamina of a man half his age, even if he did look a few years older than God. She found herself yearning to match him stride for stride, just to prove that women were not weaklings!

Ah, she'd never outgrow her desire to establish herself in this man's world. She had tried to become her father's equal, achieving high marks in law school to prove her worth to her skeptical male colleagues. Now she was out to show Yellowfish that the female of the species was a match for any man. Of course, Yellowfish would kill himself before he admitted anything of the kind.

While the threesome was munching on their meal an hour later, Cord focused his attention on Yellowfish. "How much farther must we travel before we reach the graves?"

Tempest frowned at the odd inquiry, but she didn't interrupt. Yellowfish didn't approve of that, especially from a woman. That, she had been told several times, was taboo in the Apache world.

"We will reach the valley before sunset," he promised, taking another bite of roasted rabbit. He flung Tempest a critical glance. "The meat is too tough. You should not have kept it over the fire so long, white woman."

Tempest bit into her meat, wishing she could do likewise to the old Apache, as he gestured to the south. "The graves set in the shadow of High Lonesome Peak. It is two canyons beyond the craggy peaks where you and your father built your cabin. Why are the graves important to you?"

"It's not the graves so much as the men who dug them." Cord set his plate aside, silently requesting Tempest to cleanse it before Yellowfish made a big production of her chores and she got hot under the collar again. "The El Pasoans believe I killed a man when I escaped from jail. She thinks I killed him, too," he added, staring deliberately at Tempest.

"This does not surprise me," Yellowfish sniffed. "The white woman is stubborn and mistrusting."

Tempest gripped the plates to refrain from hitting Cord and Yellowfish over the head. These two were rubbing her nerves raw!

"One of the grave diggers was also in jail before his companions freed him," Cord continued.

He smiled inwardly, certain he was as close as he ever wanted to come to having Tempest vent her frustration on him. She looked as if she was itching to put a few dents in his skull with her dirty dishes. He was right.

"The escaped bandit is the only one who can corroborate my story," Cord added, still watching Tempest fume.

"And I am supposed to take the word of a criminal?" Tempest scoffed, unable to hold her tongue a second longer. "You do recall hearing the adage about 'thicker than thieves,' don't you?"

Yellowfish half-twisted to glare at the insolent woman who refused to stay in her place, even after he had harped on the subject for more than a day. "My grandson does not lie, white woman. He is an Apache warrior. If he says he did not kill, then he did not kill!"

"Well, ask him how he feels about kidnapping white women," Tempest sassed in an uncontrollable fit of temper. She had reached her flash point and she wasn't keeping quiet a second longer.

Yellowfish shrugged indifferently. "Captive women are all the spoils of war. It is the natural way of things."

"Not where I come from, it isn't!" Tempest declared, highly offended.

"And my grandson will take you *back* to where you came from," Yellowfish confirmed. "I have decided it will be so."

When the demigod spoke, the whole world was supposed to listen, Tempest thought sourly. Her flashing blue eyes shifted to Cord, whose gaze had wandered to the purple shadows that had begun to slip down the rocky ledges of the canyon. For the life of her, she didn't know why she was so peeved. She should have been relieved to know she would be granted her freedom. And yet, it cut her to the quick to realize Cord had simply used her before tossing her aside when she no longer amused him. All his words about wanting and needing were just another part of his seduction.

"We must leave now if we are to reach the graves before dark," Yellowfish announced, drawing his legs beneath him. "Come, white woman."

"Come, white woman," Tempest mimicked bitterly. "Stand here, white woman. Do not speak out of turn, white woman. Well, damn it, you can kiss—"

Tempest slammed her mouth shut like a flap on a picnic basket when Yellowfish lurched around. Who would have thought the old coot still had ears like a fox?

There was a dangerous sparkle in the old Apache's obsidian eyes as he watched the sunlight catch in the glorious tangle of chestnut hair and reflect the indomitable spirit that glistened in those sapphire pools. "White woman, you—"

Whatever Yellowfish intended to say was lost forever. Cord stepped between them to steer his grandfather down the steep path. "Show me the way, Grandfather. We're losing daylight."

Pensively, Tempest stared after them while she collected the supplies and the reins to the pack mule. For a moment, she thought Yellowfish was considering stabbing her with his blade. She had irritated him to the extreme. Well, good. Now they were even.

Shrugging her conflicts with Yellowfish aside, Tempest tramped off with the pack mule clomping behind her. Curiosity was getting the best of her. All this talk of gravediggers and witnesses to murder left her wondering if perhaps she really had misjudged Cord MacIntosh, at least when it came to his alleged crimes. She also wondered if she had managed to fall a little bit in love with him somewhere along the way—incredible as it seemed. Why else would she be hoping for his innocence when he seemed so guilty? Lord, the man had plenty of motive. Considering his ongoing feud with his archrival, Cord would have a difficult time convincing a jury that he deserved to walk away scot-free.

Exasperated by this constant tug-of-war between her logic and her emotions, Tempest quickened her step. When they reached another precarious cliff that veered down at a forty-degree angle toward another pile of rocks, Tempest concentrated solely on negotiating the winding path. The scrabbling sound below put her senses on immediate alert. She glanced down to see Yellowfish clawing air to maintain his balance after his foot had slipped on loose pebbles. Instinctively, she released her grasp on the pack mule and lunged forward to clutch at the fringe on Yellowfish's doehide shirt. Tempest flung herself back against the boulders, jerking the Apache back with her before he cartwheeled over the ledge. Her breath came out in a whoosh when Yellowfish ker-plopped on top of her, grinding her backbone into the boulder.

It was with stupefied astonishment that Yellowfish stirred like an overturned beetle to peer down at Tempest. "You came to my rescue when I have scorned and criticized you? Why, white woman?"

Tempest wriggled free and dusted off the back of her skirt. She couldn't imagine why Yellowfish was making such a big to-do about the incident. She would have done the same thing for any other hapless victim who was about to plunge into infinity.

"Who would teach me which cactus to chew on and which to spit out, and which ones to eat, if not for you?"

Yellowfish refused to be sidetracked. "Answer me, white woman. Why?"

"Well, just because you needed to be saved," she muttered as she reached for the pack mule's reins. "You would have done the same for me, wouldn't you?"

Yellowfish snorted gruffly. "Perhaps. Perhaps not. The last time my life was saved by the White Eyes I was obliged to give my only daughter to Lobo Plano's father."

Tempest blinked in disbelief. "You *gave* your daughter . . . ?"

Lord-a-mercy. Tempest swore she would never understand the workings of the Apache mind. No wonder it was so difficult for whites to coexist with them. Their cultures and beliefs were as different as dawn and midnight. But she was beginning to understand how Cord's father and mother had come to be man and wife . . . if indeed there had been a formal ceremony. It certainly didn't sound like a love match. Of course, knowing Yellowfish's staunch beliefs, he had simply ordered his daughter to love and obey Paddy MacIntosh because he had proclaimed it would be so. He had demanded love as if it were his daughter's duty in life. And in the old Apache's opinion, that was that. Yellowfish wanted to sit atop his mountain, magically waving his arms, watching all his wishes carried out to the letter.

Cord chuckled inwardly while he watched Tempest brood. The old warrior gave her no satisfaction and even less gratitude because she was a woman, and a white one to boot. Yellowfish had decided Tempest was not a match for Cord and he constantly heckled her. Cord almost felt sorry for her now. This strenuous expedition was an exercise in stamina, patience, and verbal restraint. She had to tolerate two men who were obviously nothing like the ones whom she had known back in civilization. And yet, despite the obvious friction between Yellowfish and Tempest, she had saved him. Deep down inside, beneath that stubborn pride and contrariness there was a heart of gold. This hellion wasn't as cold and unfeeling as she wanted him to believe . . .

"What are you grinning about?" Tempest demanded to know when she caught Cord staring amusedly at her.

"I was just thinking," he replied with an enigmatic shrug.

"I *thought* I smelled wood burning," she sniped. "You might set fire to that chunk of wood you call a skull and that could be disastrous."

"Will you permit this white woman to speak so disrespectfully to you?" Yellowfish gasped in outrage.

Cord's broad shoulders lifted in another careless shrug. "I haven't figured out how to break her of it yet."

"Torture would cure her," Yellowfish assured him.

When Cord glanced at his grandfather, he detected the slightest hint of humor in those ebony eyes. The old man would die before he admitted it, but Cord had the feeling Yellowfish liked this firebrand a wee bit more than he would have liked to. In fact, Yellowfish and Tempest were a great deal alike in some ways. Their barks weren't nearly as bad as their bites, despite all that snapping and growling for appearance's sake.

Instinctively, Cord's gaze drifted back to the fiery beauty whose soiled gown and beads of perspiration on her sunburned face testified to the grueling journey she had endured. No doubt, Tempest looked nothing like the prim sophisticate who was accustomed to the elite circle of society. But even her plain garb couldn't conceal her loveliness, nor her unflagging inner spirit.

Oh yes, Cord mumbled and grumbled about her when she burned the wick off his temper, but he couldn't help but admire her resilience. It was going to be difficult to give her up. He had grown accustomed to the sultry sound of her voice, the intoxicating taste of her kisses, and the tantalizing feel of her flesh beneath his caresses . . .

Get hold of yourself, Cord whispered to himself when the warm throb of desire assaulted him. He had an important mission to accomplish and this was not the time to be sidetracked by fantasies. Besides, Tempest had promised to give him hell for forcing her to endure Yellowfish's insults. When they were alone, he wouldn't be treated to kisses, but to a vicious tirade. No doubt that high-strung harridan would be more than anxious to chew him up and spit him out. And he'd probably let her get away with it because she deserved to let off steam.

Yellowfish would swear Cord had turned soft if he could overhear the inevitable confrontation. Maybe he had. Day by day, it was becoming increasingly difficult to remain emotionally detached. Tempest had burrowed beneath his outer shell. Cord honestly wondered how she'd done it when no other female had. It was a shame they hadn't met at another time and place, under more conducive conditions.

Cord scolded himself for wishing to tamper with fate. His primary goal was justice and his secondary one was revenge. His ill-fated feelings for this dark-haired female would only complicate matters. He would be wise not to let himself forget that.

Fifteen

Tempest stared at Cord as if he'd sprouted devil's horns when he plucked up a flat rock, employing it as a shovel to unearth the grave that had been dug in the plush valley. "Are you insane?" she gasped. "Have you no respect? When a man winds up six feet underground he's supposed to be left in peace! What in heaven's name do you think R.I.P. stands for?"

Cord ignored Tempest's vehement protests until she stalked over to grind her heel into his rock of a shovel.

"I won't let you do this!" she declared, loud and clear. "It's sacrilegious."

"There she goes again," Yellowfish grumbled. "Lobo Plano, if you do not get control of this white woman now, you never will."

"Tempest, stand back," Cord growled in his most ominous tone.

Her chin tilted to a belligerent angle, despite the dangerous glint in Cord's eyes. "I most certainly will not. Whose grave is this anyway? That of the man you intended to call as witness to your sterling character?"

Despite Tempest's attempt to prevent grave-robbing, Cord scooped her off the ground and deposited her on a chair-size rock.

Completely repulsed by the goings-on, Tempest crossed her arms over her bosom and hurled a stabbing glare at Cord's back. After he'd tossed the stone aside and begun digging with his hands like a dog uncovering a bone, Tempest peered bemusedly at the grave site.

Cord dug up the canvas sack that had been buried two feet underground and held it up for her inspection. "Here lies the money that was stolen from the El Paso bank the day I escaped," he informed her before he tossed the pouch at her feet. "It isn't unusual for bandits to bury their loot in cemeteries. They assume most decent folks will take a wide berth around the burial ground and their booty will be safe. The stolen money will be returned when you tramp back to civilization. All I want is the details from Ellis Flake, who was in jail at the same time I was. It was he and his cohorts who stole the cash on their way out of town."

Tempest peered at the pouch containing several stacks of bank notes and coins. Although she didn't apologize for criticizing Cord, there was a hint of regret in her eyes.

"Say it," Yellowfish demanded. "You were wrong about my grandson."

What was it about her, Tempest wondered, that made her balk at expressing her feelings verbally toward Cord MacIntosh? Of course, it wasn't helping matters that Yellowfish was bullying her. That old Apache brought out the worst in her and made her even more contrary than she was by nature.

"You will not tell my grandson you love him or that you are sorry you misjudged him?" Yellowfish snorted in annoyance. "I have never met such a contrary woman!"

"I will be only too happy to apologize to Cord after

you kindly thank me for saving you from a disastrous fall," she bargained, just for spite.

"Thank a white woman?" Yellowfish scoffed at the absurdity as he sank down Indian-style in the grass. "I will not do it!"

"Then neither will I," Tempest said just as stubbornly.

"You are a hard woman whose spirit is difficult to break," the old warrior grunted.

Tempest smiled as if Yellowfish had paid her the highest possible compliment. "Thank you, sir. That is even better than your gratitude."

"One of us must go," Yellowfish announced to his grandson. "These mountains are not big enough for me and this fire-tongued white woman."

Cord shifted uneasily from one foot to the other. He had no wish to insult his grandfather, but he needed Tempest to help him stay alive long enough to disprove all the false charges against him.

With monumental pride bursting at the seams of his buckskin clothes, Yellowfish rose to face Cord with a disgruntled glare. "You will come to me after you set the white woman free," he commanded. "If it means so much that you be considered an honest man in the *Americanos'* world, then do what you feel you must do." His gimlet-eyed gaze glanced off Tempest and riveted on Cord. "But you will never be a man in the Apache world again until you bring this white woman in hand. It looks to be a difficult task, my son. May the Great Spirit give you the strength and the will to succeed."

After that parting remark, Yellowfish lurched around and limped off in the direction he'd come, but not without a bone-chilling glare at Tempest. The look indicated that he wasn't admitting defeat, not by any means. He was merely retreating to regroup. Judging by his theatrical departure, he preferred this to be the last time he laid eyes on the white woman who had too much of the English in her ever to be compatible with Cord *or* him.

A mischievous smile pursed Tempest's lips as she watched the old chief weave around the strewn boulders. She was actually going to miss that old coot. She had enjoyed their confrontations and verbal swordplay. It had definitely made the time pass quickly.

Now, Tempest wasn't about to admit she *liked* the hidebound old warrior. But she did *admire* him. How could she not? He had survived in this howling wilderness for seventy years. Some folks couldn't last that long lounging in the lap of luxury. She may not have agreed with his theories and superstitions, but he was still an interesting character. There hadn't been a dull moment while he was underfoot. He had also acted as a buffer, preventing Tempest from dwelling on her feelings for Cord. Now she would be forced to face her vulnerabilities all over again. Damn, maybe she should call Yellowfish back!

Restless, Tempest hopped down from her boulder, busying herself by collecting kindling from the clump of pine and cedar trees that flanked the rocky walls of the chasm. The sun had dipped behind the horizon, casting deep crimson and purple shadows on the lofty summits above, swallowing the trees in inky shades of black. In the near distance Tempest heard the gurgling of a spring and she impulsively followed the sound to its source. She spied the sparkling water that cascaded over the rocks to form an inviting pool. It was no wonder the canopy of trees had grown tall and green in this corner of the canyon. This secluded spot was like an oasis and Tempest was instinctively lured to it.

She peeled off her gown as she walked toward the glistening spring. After draping her dress over a nearby cedar limb, she shed her scuffed shoes and stood staring at the water. Without a thought about what Cord was doing, Tempest doffed her chemise and sank down in the spring.

Ah, this was heaven, she decided as she glided across the rippling waves. Overhead, the stars began to burst into view, twinkling like diamonds that seemed so close she could reach up and pluck them from the sky. Entranced by this glittering wonderland, Tempest waded over to the miniature waterfall that tumbled from the granite boulders embedded in the side of the mountain. She sat there for the longest time, letting the water spill over her, finding an unexpected inner peace in this wild and rugged wilderness that Yellowfish called his kingdom.

Cord hunkered down on the boulder to peer at the mermaid who half-reclined beside the waterfall. Since Tempest hadn't returned to the grave site after several minutes, Cord had gone in search of her. He had wondered if she had decided to attempt an escape while he was making camp for the night. They had reached the lower elevations where the terrain wasn't so treacherous. She could have taken flight without having to cope with her fear of height. But to his surprise, Tempest had located the spring and was contentedly lounging in it.

Suddenly Tempest disappeared behind the curtain of water that cascaded into the pool. She reminded him of a playful child, frolicking in her water wonderland. Gone was the shell of sophistication and pride that usually surrounded her while Cord was underfoot. When she emerged from the waterfall, Cord's unwavering gaze flooded over her silky flesh. God, how he longed to caress her as freely as the silvery fingers of water that trickled over her skin. She was down below, leisurely enjoying her bath, and he was up above, burning into a pile of ashes!

Well, that did it, Cord decided as he rose to full stature. Why should he sit here and crave what he wanted instead of marching himself down there and doing something about it? This bewitching sprite was his wife, after all. He had his husbandly rights. Yellowfish had been nagging him the better part of the day about taking this white woman in hand. And Cord would have liked nothing better than to get his *hands* on her! The tantalizing memories they had created hounded him. He looked at her and wanted her in the worst possible way. In fact, his desires had taken him far past wanting. He *needed* her to appease this gigantic craving that had swelled completely out of proportion.

Determined of purpose, Cord picked his way down the maze of boulders and threaded through the trees. He stalked Tempest with the silence of a cougar, slowly erasing the distance between them. When he emerged from the shadows of the trees, he heard Tempest gasp in alarm. Her wide blue eyes riveted on him while she attempted to cover herself as best she could.

"You're intruding," Tempest bleated, her heart pounding like a tom-tom after being startled half to death. "I'm bathing."

"So I see." With cavalier devilment, Cord shucked his shirt.

Her gaze wandered over the utterly masculine terrain of his body, watching his sleek muscles contract and relax as he hooked his thumbs in the band of his breeches. Tempest swallowed with a gulp as she stared at the magnificent figure of the man who had no regard whatsoever for modesty. She could never be that uninhibited, never in a hundred years! She was already self-conscious about being caught naked, and Cord was stripping away his garments right in front of her, without batting an eyelash.

Her face flushed beet red, even while her gaze

roamed over the hair-roughened columns of his thighs. His state of arousal was more than obvious, and Tempest shrank back into the frothy waterfall. She had already humiliated herself twice by submitting to this brawny giant's lusts. But she wasn't going to fall for this devil's charms again. She wasn't becoming his willing harlot, married or not!

Cord made no overt move toward her; he simply waded into the pool, sighed, and sank into the chest-deep water. He then proceeded to dip and dive like a porpoise, puzzling Tempest all the more. It was as if she had been momentarily forgotten, and she found herself silently assessing this fascinating creature who was as agile in the water as he was on land. It was a shame she'd never learned to swim. She would have delighted in gliding and diving the way Cord did. Unfortunately, she had to limit herself to the shallows where she could keep her footing.

Each time Cord burst to the surface, Tempest was granted an unhindered view of his muscular physique. She found herself unwillingly admiring this Goliath of a man who had already proved he could turn her wrong side out in a dozen different ways. For that space in time she simply sat there, watching him, attempting to curb the hungry longings that seemed to crop up at the mere sight of him. And the more she saw of him, the more she . . .

Stop that! Tempest lectured herself fiercely. If Cord had resigned himself to nothing more than a swim after she'd flung him a keep-your-distance glare, she certainly shouldn't have been the one sitting there fantasizing. She had just vowed to avoid all further intimacy with the man! Land of Goshen, considering these outrageous hallucinations, one would have thought she really was a floozie in another lifetime.

When Cord burst to the surface beside her, Tempest involuntarily retreated. A firm hand clamped around her elbow, tugging her off balance. A frightened shriek erupted from her lips before she was dragged beneath the surface. Tempest was instantly reminded of that terrifying ordeal in the underground river. The fears came back in frantic force and she clawed her way up Cord's body as if he were her ladder to salvation.

Cord laughed aloud when Tempest wrapped herself around him like an octopus. "I'm not going to drown you, princess. But it's high time you learned to swim."

"That was a rotten trick," she gurgled, attempting to catch her breath and force her heartbeat to a normal rate.

It was a rotten trick, all right. Cord had done it deliberately, just to get this wary nymph in his arms. He had allowed her to believe he was more interested in a bath than in her. And as naive as she still was, she'd fallen for the ploy. But all the while he'd been swimming, he'd been biding his time, planning his scheme to get this shapely beauty where he wanted her. Hell, he'd even flounder through a swimming lesson if he had to, if it eventually led to more interesting activities.

"Now quit trying to strangle me and put your arms on the surface of the water," Cord instructed.

Tempest refused to release her vise-grip on his neck. "I can't touch the bottom of the pool," she protested.

While Cord continued to paddle with his legs, he pried Tempest's arms loose and turned her so she was floating on the water. When he had drawn her across the pool so that he could find his own footing, he slid his arm beneath her belly, leaving her to bob on the surface. Of course, he took time to grin rakishly when he was granted a tempting view of her curvaceous derrière. Mmm . . . teaching this imp to swim was going to be more fun that he thought!

"Now keep your legs—" And *Caramba!* What gorgeous legs they were, too! "—straight and paddle hard," he commanded.

Tempest did as she was told. The way she had it figured, it was better to concentrate on the lesson than on the feel of Cord's sinewy arm curled around her waist and his rock-hard chest against her ribs.

"Like this?"

"Exactly like that," Cord assured her, all eyes and roguish smiles. "Now cup your hands and pull the water toward you . . . No, not like that. You can't get anywhere by slapping the water."

He drew Tempest down in front of him so that her lovely backside was plastered against his frontside. He placed his hands over hers, demonstrating the stroking motion of one arm alternatively complementing the other.

Tempest's heart accelerated a quick ten beats when she came into familiar contact with Cord's body. She could feel him behind her, beside her, while he instructed her on the skills of swimming, just as he had instructed her in the techniques of lovemaking . . . Tempest gulped and tried to concentrate, but it was damned near impossible when her mind had detoured down such sordid avenues, taking her eager body with it.

When his hands gradually slid up her arms, allowing her to perform the motion on her own, goose bumps covered her flesh. Tempest trembled, not from the water's chill but rather from the heat of pleasure that his light touch aroused. When his hands swirled around her ribs to caress the peaks of her breasts, Tempest felt as if she were going to drown. Shock waves crested on her body, causing wild tingles to channel through every fiber of her being. His sensuous lips drifted down the swanlike column of her throat and a quiet moan betrayed her. Sweet mercy, how could this man do such incredible things to her mind and body? One minute she was concentrating on learning to swim and the next second she was craving wildly intimate pleasures.

This walking paradox of formidable strength and unrivaled gentleness could cripple her mind and paralyze her body. She hated the power he had over her. She resented him . . . and she wanted him to distraction. How could he have so much influence over her when she had once been so independent-minded and strong-willed? When he plied her with soul-shattering tenderness, it was as if she had never learned the meaning of willpower. He could make her a slave to her own passions so quickly it was scary!

Another helpless moan escaped her lips when Cord turned her in his arms. Effortlessly, he lifted her from the water so that his tongue could flick at the throbbing peaks of her breasts. Fire sizzled through the core of her being, and Tempest instinctively arched toward his greedy mouth, reveling in the feel of his lips on her skin. Ever so slowly and suggestively, he drew her quaking body down his, spreading a path of tantalizing kisses from her breasts, across her collarbone and throat, until his lips found hers to feed the flames that already raged out of control.

Her arms involuntarily slid over his powerful shoulders and her body moved instinctively toward his, feeling the full extent of his arousal. Tempest kissed him violently forgetting her previous vows of restraint, needing him more than she needed air to breathe. With each passing moment the craving intensified until it consumed all rational thought.

Exploring hands cruised over her skin, erotically guiding her hips to his and then gently pushing her a few inches away. Cord peered into those wide, luminous eyes that glowed in the moonlight and his body shuddered in visible restraint. Never in his life had he been so totally absorbed in a woman. Never had he wanted a female as much as he wanted this one. And just as before, he found himself vividly aware of her needs. Pleasing her had become tantamount. He wanted her to respond to him with abandon, to touch him, caress him as eagerly and freely as he caressed her. He wanted them to share a mutual passion that blotted out reality and sent them skyrocketing into oblivion.

When his mouth descended on hers, he spoke to her in a language that communicated with the heart, body, and soul. Tempest could no more resist that exquisitely tender kiss than she could have swum the breadth of the ocean. She could feel the need whispering through his body and echoing into hers. She answered each reverent caress, learning new ways to arouse him, inventing new techniques to return the pleasure he bestowed on her. She marveled at the warm stirrings that assaulted her when she set her hands upon him, reacquainting herself with each sensitive point on his flesh.

While Cord drew her with him to the water's edge, Tempest found it impossible to take her eyes and hands off him. He was such an incredible sight to behold, so powerfully structured, so utterly masculine. Mesmerized, she outstretched her hand to trace the scars that marred his bronzed flesh. But that was nowhere near enough to satisfy her fascination. Her fingertips set out on a bold journey of discovery, memorizing every muscle-honed inch of him.

Cord resigned himself to death by wondrous torment when Tempest plied him with evocative caresses and kisses. Her hands and lips were never still for a moment, wandering everywhere at once, turning him into a quivering mass of desire. He had never given another woman such privileges. But then, he reminded himself, he'd already broken every hard and fast rule with Tempest because she was unlike any other woman in his past. She was a lady through and through, with a pedigree as long as his leg. But beneath that veneer of sophistication and proper breeding she was a dynamic woman with a dozen kinds of passion seeking release. When he and Tempest shed the confines of pride and stubbornness, baring those carefully guarded emotions, the world dissolved around them. Despite her cynical mistrust and his obsession with revenge, there was a unique magic between them that cast its mystical spell. They set all sorts of sparks in each other, and these sparks were the best of all . . .

Cord groaned in torment when Tempest's whispering kisses moved over the taut muscles of his belly and her gentle hands explored the curve of his hips. The pleasure she offered him was beyond bearing. Streams of rapture drenched him as her touch became bolder and bolder still.

Tempest was hypnotized by the sound of Cord's deep, resonant voice rasping her name. She couldn't get enough of the taste of him, the feel of his whipcord muscles beneath her hands. Each time he gasped for air, it encouraged her to create even more ways to excite him. She constantly found herself experimenting with the stimulating techniques he had employed on her, altering them to suit her own leisurely seduction.

For more than two weeks she had been his captive, but once again he had become her slave, a prisoner of this wild dimension of passion he had introduced to her. She would make him want her as desperately as she wanted him, make him plead with her to fulfill the maddening longings she had instilled.

Cord felt the flick of Tempest's tongue and the warm draft of her breath gliding over the throbbing length of him. Clawing talons of desire sank into his body and he responded as he always did to her brazen touch. She had learned far too well how to bring him to his knees, how to leave him trembling in her hands and on her lips. And when her gentle assault receded to begin all over again, Cord felt himself stumbling along the edge of self-control, feeling the ultimate challenge rise again, knowing he would lose another skirmish to a woman who had learned to devastate him with her wildly intimate touch.

While Cord gasped for breath, Tempest twisted around to glide above him. She used her body to caress him. Her lips hovered just above his—teasing him, luring him deeper into the erotic spell.

"You really are a sorceress," Cord breathed shakily. "Do you know that? Come here, damn you . . ."

When his arms fastened around her waist to press her to him, Tempest shifted her weight, denying him ultimate satisfaction. "Do you want me, Cord?" she questioned before her lips drifted over his.

"You know I do."

"Then say it," she requested in a throaty purr. Suddenly it seemed as though she had become as demanding as Yellowfish.

Who was seducing whom here? That's what Cord wanted to know! He'd schemed to get this leery beauty into his arms and somehow their roles had been reversed. She was making him beg for love and that was the exact opposite of what he'd intended. Well hell, a man's pride could bend just so far before it broke. And Cord's male pride had just snapped in two. Nothing was more important at this moment than feeling Tempest's delectable body molded intimately to his.

"I want you like crazy," he whispered hoarsely. "Now come here before I die of torment!"

Tempest went to him then, but the victory of this tender battle was not hers alone. Instantly, she was caught up in the holocaust of fiery passion. Cord had rolled sideways to draw her body beneath his in one fluid motion. Her body melted like wax on a flaming candle. She could feel the burning inside her as he took absolute possession, setting the driving cadence of love that swept her away like smoke spiraling up from a wildfire. Tempest clung to him. Her nails dug into the scars on his back. Her body moved in perfect rhythm with his, with a need so fierce and wild that she wondered if anything could ever appease it.

Spasms of ecstasy riveted her. She was like a wild creature in his arms, shamelessly arching and writhing beneath him, unable to get close enough to the white-hot fire that burned inside and out. Tempest was terrified by her complete loss of control. This monstrous craving seemed to engulf her again and again, like the turbulent aftershocks of an earthquake. It frightened her to know she had responded even more desperately to him than she had each time before. This couldn't be happening! Tempest tried to assure herself as wave upon wave of delirious rapture buffeted her. This wasn't natural, was it? Sweet mercy, she felt as if she were splitting apart at the seams, shattering in a zillion pieces. How could she ever navigate her way back to reality when she couldn't even find herself in this star-spangled universe that had exploded around her?

Cord feared he would squeeze the stuffing out of this angel in his arms when the last breathless surge of passion hit him like a tidal wave, hurtling him into infinity. His body trembled convulsively, tearing thought from his mind and zapping his last ounce of energy. His brain and body were so numb with immeasurable pleasure that he couldn't move a muscle, much less breathe normally. *Caramba!* He couldn't breathe at all! And if he could find the strength to drag himself to his feet and walk away it would be a miracle!

Damnation, his total absorption in this blue-eyed leprechaun wasn't getting better after making love to her thrice. If anything, it was getting worse! The first two times had been incredible. This time it was . . . Hell, there weren't enough words in the Spanish, Apache, and English languages to describe these feelings that engulfed him. The sensations transcended the normal realm of physical experience, and it was impossible to make comparisons. He was breaking new ground here, if there was even ground beneath him to break.

While Cord was battling to explain this phenomenon, Tempest was fighting a slightly different battle. Her analytical mind was struggling with the dilemma Cord had caused for well over two weeks. She was afraid she knew why he had the ability to infuriate her so thoroughly and yet satisfy her so completely. And here she'd been worried about falling from towering heights while they were teetering on rock ledges! The fall she'd taken when she was in Cord's arms hadn't been fatal, but it was no less disastrous. How was it, Tempest wondered, that the man she swore she despised had become the man she loved?

Curse that ornery Yellowfish for putting these outrageous notions in her head! It was that old codger's fault. He and his demands that she love this man who was her husband! Well damn it, she did love him and she hoped Yellowfish was immensely happy because she wasn't. She was frustrated. She wasn't sure loving a man like Cord was such a good thing and she certainly wasn't enjoying it very much. It contradicted her better judgment.

Tempest had been a woman of vision and purpose until this amber-eyed rake burst into her well-organized life. She had refused to be dominated by the male of the species and now she had fallen in love with a fugitive—a vindictive criminal who saw her as a necessary means to an end. Ah, what bitter irony!

When Cord finally found the strength to move away, he eased down beside Tempest, who lay so still that he felt compelled to make sure she was still alive. "Tempest? I have a confession to make," he murmured as he monitored the pulsations in her neck with gentle kisses. "When I came to the spring, I didn't want to swim nearly as bad as I wanted to make love to you."

Her dark lashes fluttered as she stared into the shadowed features of a face that tormented her thoughts and filled her forbidden dreams. She supposed the closest a man like Cord could come to really loving a woman was wanting her body. Ah, what a cruel twist of fate, thought Tempest. She had never been interested in well-mannered gentlemen who were safe and predictable. Oh no, not her. She had to go and fall in love with her captor. Cord was daring and dangerous and impossible to second-guess. He also had a long list of offenses that would stand as an insurmountable barrier between them, even if he did have the capacity to love her back—which he probably didn't.

What kind of future could they have together? She would be destined to follow him, surviving on the few scraps of affection he might occasionally toss her. What sort of life would that be? An utterly hopeless one that would eventually end in disaster, she predicted. And what would happen when Cord tired of her, when he found another woman to give him all he really needed from a female? It was true that some love affairs—especially one-sided ones—were doomed from the beginning. This was a perfect example of a love that wasn't meant to be . . .

"Tempest?" A muddled frown clouded Cord's brow when he deciphered the remorseful expression that captured her elegant features. "What's wrong? Did I hurt you?"

Hurt her? Most definitely, but not in the ways he suspected. "No," she lied as she propped herself up on her elbow. "I'm fine."

His hand cupped her chin, holding her misty gaze. "No, you aren't. Tell me what's the matter."

"Don't pry, Cord," Tempest demanded. "You got what you wanted so be content with it."

When Tempest tried to elude him, he latched onto her arm and held her fast. The aftermath of their lovemaking was always awkward. Tempest had one devil of a time dealing with her own passionate desires because she felt it necessary to analyze everything to death. She responded eagerly to him and then regretted each intimate encounter. Well, it was high time she accepted the fact that she had desperately wanted him, too! And by damned, he was going to hear her admit it, even if he had to reach down her throat and drag out the words! This was one repetitious hurdle they were going to overcome here and now, once and for all!

"Don't try to deny that you didn't enjoy what we shared," he dared her, his voice rumbling with frustration. "I pleasure you and you pleasure me. For once just admit it."

"All right," Tempest replied begrudgingly. "You please me very much."

Finally! She had said it, even though it had nearly killed her. "So what the hell's the problem?"

"*I'm* the lawyer around here," she snapped, eyes flashing. "Don't give me the third degree!"

"So *that's* the problem," Cord scowled as he released her and began gathering his scattered clothes. "You can't tolerate the fact that a prim, highfalutin lady lawyer bedded a supposed criminal. Not a very satisfactory match for someone with your proper breeding and impressive credentials, is it, princess?"

He glared at her as he stabbed his leg into his breeches. It was the wrong leg. Growling, he began the process again. "You can't accept the fact that you have been intimate with a half-breed who doesn't fit into your world. You're ashamed of what we have because I'm not good enough for you."

He stuffed his arms into his shirt—backward. With a muffled curse, he yanked off the garment and started over.

Muttering several unladylike curses, Tempest grabbed her clothes. Why should she bother to explain what she really felt? Let Cord think what he wanted. It was much safer than offering her heart to a man who wouldn't know love if it jumped up and bit him. To Yellowfish, the love of a woman was a prize to be taken for granted. Undoubtedly, Cord shared his grandfather's outlandish view that the devotion of a woman ranked right beside the loyalty of a well-trained horse or an obedient guard dog. Love? Bah! It wasn't triumph; it was torment.

Grappling with that depressing thought, Tempest beat a hasty retreat from the spring to gather her composure. And considering the state she was in, it was going to take a good long while!

Sixteen

Miserably, Tempest flounced toward camp. So frustrated was she that she didn't realize she had stumbled onto a family of peccaries until she trounced on the runt of the bunch. The hairy pigs had settled down in the mud holes formed from the overflowing spring, wallowing as all hogs love to do. Tempest's unexpected intrusion was not appreciated by the parents and other relatives of the pint-size pig squealing in pain.

Tempest supposed it could have been worse if she had blundered into a nest of vipers, but at the moment, she doubted it. In her estimation, there was nothing worse than an angry drift of hogs that found one of its members threatened. The snorts and grunts that erupted from the wallows caused Tempest to take flight. Yellowfish had warned her that peccaries had deadly sharp teeth that could rip their prey to shreds. Tempest found a pack of two-foot-tall, furious monsters tearing after her. She shrieked and took off like a blazing bullet.

The rending of cloth warned Tempest that the little beasts that had been snapping at her ankles had caught hold of the hem of her gown. Better the fabric than her flesh, she reckoned. Frantic, she bounded off the ground as if propelled by a spring.

She grasped the overhanging limb of a pine tree, uncaring that the needles stabbed into her. She hung there while the peccaries circled and snapped. It seemed forever before she heard Cord's voice and the sound of crackling twigs behind her. Tempest swiveled her head while she hung there like laundry on a clothesline.

With a stick in each hand, Cord forged through the underbrush, bellowing and popping his makeshift whips, discouraging the peccaries from ripping Tempest to shreds. Amid the snorts and squeals, the wild pigs scattered, leaving Tempest to breathe a sigh of relief and drop to the ground.

"Next time, watch where you're going," Cord growled. He flung aside his improvised weapons and stalked off. "Peccaries aren't particular if they chew up snobs or plain folks, you know. Your pedigree doesn't mean a damn to them. Snobs and simpletons all taste the same to a pig."

"I am not a snob!" Tempest hurled at him. But of course, the lethal glower didn't faze this rock of a man one whit.

"Oh yes, you are," Cord contradicted without a second glance. He just kept right on walking.

Nothing made Tempest madder than to have a man tromp way from her in the middle of an argument. Incensed, she stalked after him. So mad was she, in fact, that her tongue outdistanced her brain, putting words on her lips that shouldn't have been there at all.

"I wanted you, damn you, not because you are a known criminal, but because you are the man who makes me feel things I've never felt with any other—" Tempest slammed her mouth shut and silently cursed herself up one side and down the other.

A rakish grin quirked Cord's lips as he pivoted to stare at the dazzling beauty who stood shimmering in the moonlight. "Do my ears deceive me, fair princess? I swore you just paid me a compliment."

Flustered, Tempest stamped her foot and clenched her fists in the folds of her gown. "I cannot imagine that you care what I think and feel," she wailed. "Does your pride demand constant feeding, just like your lust? If it does, then YES!" she all but yelled at him. "You arouse me. I love you, you big ox. Is that what you want to hear? Now I hope you and your pesky grandfather are satisfied. He wanted me to say the words the whole live-long day. Well fine, I've said it. Love and obey and all that rubbish until they hang you high for your various and sundry crimes!"

She wasn't hysterical. She was not going to *become* hysterical just because she was frustrated out of her mind. The turmoil of emotions that boiled inside her were simply bursting out because they had been too long contained while Yellowfish was underfoot. Tempest choked on a sob and wiped the exasperating tears from her eyes with the back of her hands. She marched past Cord, who stood gaping at her.

When she buzzed by, sobbing in great humiliating gulps, Cord clutched her arm to detain her. "Did you mean that, Tempest?" he questioned seriously.

"How do I know what I mean?" she wailed, worming free. "I cannot think of one good reason why I should love you. It's illogical. You and this journey are making me crazy. I just want to be left alone. And don't you dare call me a snob, ever again, curse your hide. If I was *then*, I'm certainly not *now*. In fact, I don't even know who I am these days. Thanks to you, I don't even recognize myself!"

When Tempest stumbled blindly away, Cord watched her go with a mixture of sympathy, confusion, and regret. God, what had he done to that proud beauty? He had meant to get revenge on Victor Watts. Instead, he had abducted the woman who might have helped him plead his case. He had dragged her from one terrifying ordeal to another and reduced her to tears.

In a burst of temper and exasperation, she had declared that she loved him, just to pacify him and his grandfather, who wasn't even here to gloat. But Cord was no fool. He knew perfectly well that this high-strung hellion hadn't meant what she said about love. Women like Tempest didn't fall in love with men like him. She was only trying to fool him, hoping he would stop pestering her. To Tempest, he was just a step above a savage and she was a notch below royalty. They didn't fit into each other's lives and they never would. Yellowfish had been adamant in making that point.

Heaving a sigh, Cord ambled back to camp to find Tempest cuddled into her bedroll as if it were her protective cocoon. Muffled sniffs broke the silence. Cord stood there, staring down at the shadowed bundle for the longest time.

"There will be rewards for your troubles, princess. I promise you," he said quietly. "When this is over, all that I have will be yours."

"Thank you so much," Tempest grumbled sarcastically. "I only wish I knew where I'm going to stash this pile of rocks when I return to San Antonio. I don't think the rugged decor will match the furnishings in the parlor. And I'm positively certain your herd of cattle and horses will ruin the carpet." She poked her head out to make a sweeping gesture which encompassed the world at large. "You keep your treasures, Cord. I'll muddle by on what I've got."

Of course, Cord didn't expect her to know what he meant. But one day she would understand well enough. "All the same, you'll have my treasures as your own."

Tempest wanted to tell him that loving her back

would have gone a long way toward mending her bruised heart. But Cord had no love to give. And even if he did, where would they find common ground? They couldn't, she realized bleakly. This doomed love affair was built on quicksand and she was sinking fast!

Cord swore he had just dozed off when he heard Tempest's squawks and shouts. Instinctively, he grabbed his pistol, aiming it in every direction at once. But all he could see when his senses cleared was a commotion inside Tempest's bedroll. The first thing that popped into Cord's mind was that a rattler had crawled into her quilts and attacked. Cord's heart hammered against his ribs as he leaped up like a mountain goat to come to her rescue. By the time he reached Tempest she had thrashed loose from the confining blankets and was dancing around as if someone were firing buckshot at her feet. To Cord's bemusement, Tempest, still yelping and emitting a jumble of curse words, began peeling off her gown with fiendish haste. And when she stood there bone-naked, still hissing like a disturbed cat, she snatched up one of the quilts and beat it against the ground with a vengeance.

A chuckle burst from Cord's lips while he watched the unusual carryings-on. "If you don't mind my asking, do you have these fits very often?"

Tempest flashed him a scathing glance as she slammed the blanket against the ground once again for good measure. "Ants," she snapped at him, as if the incident were his fault.

Sure enough, when Cord strode over to inspect her bed site, there was an ant colony beneath it. In the darkness, Tempest had bedded down in the worst of all possible places.

Once Tempest was satisfied that she had removed

the stinging pests from her blanket, she clenched it in her hands and wrapped it around her like a toga. And then, calling upon the information Yellowfish had given her, she went in search of the century plant that supposedly produced a natural salve for insect bites. When she squatted down to pluck up what she thought was the medicinal plant, Cord's hands folded over hers.

"That's the wrong one," he told her. "The century is over here. These two plants are similar in appearance, especially in the moonlight. You have to check the coloring on the underside of the leaves. They're like mushrooms and toadstools. Some are poisonous while others are beneficial."

Tempest was in no condition to voice complaints when Cord whacked off the stem of the plant and led her back to his bedroll. The ant bites stung like fire and she wanted immediate relief.

"Shed your quilt and lie down," Cord ordered in a no-nonsense tone.

Tempest didn't even protest, as she normally would have done when Cord ordered her around. She simply lay down without a stitch of clothing. Modesty was no match for the multiple welts that rose on her flesh like a mountain range.

Cord was doing his damnedest to concentrate on locating the affected areas of her body. He truly was. But it was hard to remember his purpose while his hands splayed over her satiny flesh. With dedicated effort, Cord dripped the juice on her skin and gently rubbed it in.

Tempest sighed in relief as Cord's experienced hands massaged the cool liquid over her burning flesh. The century plant's juices had a numbing effect that brought comfort where there had been pain seconds before. That, combined with the feel of Cord's skillful caress, worked like magic.

"Better, princess?" Cord murmured as he focused

his attention on another ant bite. Damn, he swore he deserved a medal for sitting here providing medical attention while his body was demanding something far more stimulating than first aid treatment.

"Much better." Tempest sighed, her voice wobbling from the side effects of Cord's touch. "I seem to be jinxed when it comes to offending the creatures that inhabit these mountains. I've encountered a rattlesnake and gone several rounds with my contrary mule. I put a pack of peccaries in arms and prompted the battle instincts of an infantry of red ants."

"Turn over," Cord requested.

"What else can possibly go wrong?" Tempest mused as she rolled over on her stomach and propped her chin on her hands. "Mmm . . . that feels good."

Did it ever! thought Cord. His hands were wandering over the gentle hills of her hips, lingering to dab the ointment here and there. But he was beginning to think his overheated condition was every bit as bad as Tempest's insect bites. He could simply apply lotion to the places Tempest hurt the worst. As for himself, he was beginning to hurt all over and it sure as hell wasn't from doing hand-to-hand combat with an army of ants!

Tempest flinched when she felt Cord's moist lips drifting over her shoulder in the slightest whisper of a kiss. But by the time his practiced hands reinforced the tantalizing effects of his lips, Tempest had lost all will to resist. Her body reacted instinctively to his tender seduction, just as it had since the very first time he'd touched her. It was hopeless to fight the longings that bubbled in her bloodstream and spun her nerves into tangled webs. She loved this infuriating renegade as she'd loved no other man. He touched her and her skin melted off her bones.

He kissed her and he brought her to life and made her breathe.

When Cord's masculine body slid down beside hers and he turned her in his arms, Tempest forgot her frustrations. She offered herself to him without the usual battle that pride demanded she fight. If this was to be her place in the sun—or in moonlight, as the case happened to be—then she was going to cherish each magical moment for as long as it lasted. If there was one thing Tempest had learned about life in this perilous wilderness, it was that a woman had to reap each pleasure when it came, in between the unforeseen dangers.

Instead of battling the inevitable attraction that grew stronger with each intimate encounter, Tempest vowed to leave a lasting impression on this mountain of a man. It seemed only right that he should think of her now and then in the years to come. She certainly wouldn't forget him anytime soon, that was for sure! If she couldn't earn his love, she would at least leave him with a memory that was slow to fade. Perhaps she would never be anything but a smile that twitched those sensuous lips when he remembered this wild episode in his life. But at least she would be a smile. That was better than nothing at all, she supposed.

Cord went up in a puff of smoke when Tempest's luscious body moved toward his and she offered him a sizzling kiss that left the moon dripping in the evening sky. His blood raced as her nimble fingers tracked over the buttons of his shirt and her hands roamed over the hair-covered flesh of his chest. His lungs felt as if they were filled with rocks when her soft lips skimmed over his ultrasensitive skin. He was lost—totally and completely lost—in a matter of seconds. His gentleness evaporated, replaced by a wild, savage hunger that demanded quick satisfaction.

Caramba! He'd never known another woman who

could set him ablaze so quickly and keep him smoldering like coals, even when the loving was over. But Tempest could. She was as devastating as the wild Apache wind.

It was with urgent desperation that Cord's hands and lips moved over her satiny flesh. He savored and devoured her all in the same breathless moment. His lips skimmed the beaded crests of her breasts, nipping gently, tugging until she involuntarily arched toward him. His hand coasted down her lush body, gliding over the sensitive points of her thighs. His fingertip flicked at the velvet folds, seeking entrance to the moist heat that whispered her response. He felt her need enfold his fingertip and he called forth another shuddering response that sent hot chills through his own body. Cord burned with the pleasure of her need for him.

As if she were a delicious feast, he eased downward, tasting her silky skin, inhaling the scent that had become a part of him. He longed to lose himself in the liquid fire pulsating in the very core of her being. But as intimate as his caresses and kisses had become, they were not enough to satisfy his craving. He wanted to feel himself buried within her, feel the white-hot blaze of passion contracting around him until it was impossible to tell where her desire ended and his began.

When Cord shifted to bring her quavering body beneath his, her lips brushed against the velvet tip of his manhood, threatening his control, leaving him weak and trembling as he tried to brace himself above her, fighting the turbulent passions engulfing both of them.

"Tempest . . ." Cord groaned hoarsely when her hand stroked him and then drew him to her. His gaze dipped down to those glowing blue eyes that reflected the moonlight—eyes that appeared the color of mercury in their intensity. "God, how I need you . . . Make the burning ache go away . . ."

When his muscular body settled over hers, Tempest sighed in joyful abandon. His hard, penetrating thrust sent her spiraling through a universe of glittering rainbows and warm sunshine. It was such a satisfying paradox to be held in his arms and yet experience a unique sense of freedom to soar like a wild, free bird. And when the world opened to swallow her, Tempest clutched Cord to her as if he were her only salvation—the one precious treasure that made her life worth living.

Odd, Tempest thought as she was consumed by an incredible rapture. There had been a time when her profession had been enough, giving her life purpose. But this love had strengthened and multiplied by leaps and bounds. Lord-a-mercy, how could she live without this man now that she'd come to love him? And yet, how could she live *with* him? He was a renegade who would spend his life on the run, forever looking over his shoulder as he wandered like a restless tumbleweed . . .

That thought, and the futility of this love, caused Tempest to cling to Cord in desperation. It wasn't fair, her tortured mind screamed. It just wasn't fair to love so much and receive so little in return!

Cord was startled by the zealous hug Tempest bestowed on him while he lay satiated and fulfilled. Never had she tried to squeeze him in two, not in anger or in splendorous passion.

Levering up on an elbow, Cord stared down into her haunted features. "What's the matter, princess?" he questioned softly.

Adoringly, Tempest reached up to limn the sensuous curve of his lips and trace the smile lines that bracketed his mouth. Everything was wrong, but she couldn't tell him that without confessing she loved him. She had admitted to that already, but in such a way that he had doubted her sincerity. No, she would have to find a way to explain her impulsive hug in a manner a man like Cord could understand.

"Is it so surprising to you that I have come to accept the pleasure you bring me?" she questioned his question. "You have badgered me into admitting that you arouse me. Now would you prefer that I feel nothing at all?"

"No, I much prefer a woman who can match me stride for stride. And you do it extremely well."

"As well as your other lovers?" she probed, holding his tawny gaze.

"What other lovers? I remember no one but you, princess."

"Don't you just!" she sniffed in contradiction. "How naive do you think I am? You've turned lovemaking into an art form, and nobody can become that skillful without years of practice. I doubt I'll forget my first time with you since it came so late in my life. But you probably don't even remember where, when, or with whom."

Cord's gaze rose toward the shadowed shoulders of the towering mountains and he expelled a quiet sigh. He had the feeling this saucy sprite was about to drag him into an argument. She was exceptionally good at that. Half the time he didn't realize he had fallen into the trap until he was already there. Well, that's what he got for finding himself so intrigued by this lady lawyer, he reckoned. With her impressive command of the English language, she could talk circles around him. God, he'd hate to have to confront her in court . . . which he probably would before this was all over! What an unnerving thought. She would truly and surely crucify him.

Gently, Cord shifted to curl his hand beneath her chin, tilting her face to his. The tendrils of her hair caught in the light like a halo surrounding her exquisite face. A fierce blow slammed into his heart as he memorized every delicate detail. God, she was lovely. He couldn't seem to recall a single woman who compared to this enchanting goddess. Hell, he couldn't even remember what it was like to be with another woman!

"Do you know, princess, when I'm with you, I feel as if I had only been born a fortnight ago."

My, wasn't this rake the eloquent one? Tempest was willing to bet her law practice that he'd made similar remarks to a dozen "somebody elses" before she came along. She had allowed herself to believe she was special to him while they were making love. But when reality returned, so did common sense.

"And I, of course, feel as if I'd been born yesterday," she parried.

"My grandfather would say—"

"I've heard enough of Yellowfish's wise proverbs to last me a lifetime," Tempest interrupted with an explosive sniff. "The man has a philosophical quotation for each and every one of life's crises."

Cord snickered at the irritable expression that captured her features. "The fact is you're jealous," he speculated.

"Of Yellowfish?" Tempest squirmed away and turned her back. "Not hardly!"

"No," he corrected. "Of me. You resent the fact that I've known other women before you." The thought pleased him immensely.

Tempest glanced over her shoulder at the lean, muscular giant who lounged on the bedroll beside her. It was on the tip of her tongue to deny the comment. After a moment's consideration, she decided to switch tactics.

"Jealous? No, Cord," she told him quietly. "Offended? Perhaps. I have known no other man. You have taught me all I know. But when the next man comes along, I won't be quite as wary. I only hope I can become as masterful as you are in the art of seduction. My future lovers will benefit from your teaching."

Cord jerked himself upright and glared at her. "Now wait just a damned minute, woman. You're my wife!"

"That can easily be remedied," Tempest assured him with a mischievous smile. She derived tremendous pleasure in pricking his male pride. Her pride had certainly suffered noticeable damage since she'd met him. "Our signatures on an annulment document will erase this so-called marriage from the chronicles of history as if it never existed."

His hand gripped her elbow as he pushed her to the quilts and loomed over her. The black scowl that puckered his face reminded Tempest of those first days when he had seemed so cold and ruthless. "You can write me out of your life—legally," he growled down at her. "But you can't erase the feel of my caresses nor the taste of my kisses, damn you. Those memories don't die so easily."

Tempest didn't realize how ornery she was at heart. She was sorry to report that she dearly loved to rile Cord. She was never happier than when he was frying in his own grease. Well, except when she was sailing in ecstasy in his arms, she hurriedly amended.

"You just got through telling me that you remembered no woman but me," she countered, biting back a giggle when he puffed up like a bagpipe.

"That was different!" Cord exploded. "*We* are different. Those other women meant nothing to me."

"And just exactly what does that make me?" Tempest queried, arching a curious brow.

Cord expelled his breath like a deflating balloon and reached for his breeches. "That makes you my five-foot-two-inch headache," he muttered, frustrated by the upheaval swirling inside him. "I want no more talk of future men and past women. There's only you and me—husband and wife. And as Yellowfish would say, that is that!"

Muffling another giggle, Tempest confiscated one of Cord's quilts to cover herself. If nothing else, she had set Cord to thinking about their relationship. Maybe he would never truly love her the way she longed to be loved. But he wasn't going to forget her so easily, she promised herself. She would see to that, even if she had to give him hell once a day until they parted company. He had to care just a little, didn't he? He wouldn't have his feathers ruffled now if he didn't feel something for her, would he? Perhaps it was only an overactive sense of possession that needled him. But by damned, she was not going to be the only one who walked away from this affair, changed for life! She'd chisel her initials on that chunk of rock he called his heart. Somehow or other she was going to leave her mark on his life. *Her* pride demanded that much. It was small compensation for having Cord MacIntosh tear her heart out by the taproot.

Tempest wasn't foolish enough to try to love again because she had the inescapable feeling that she would only find herself making comparisons. When a woman came to love a man like this, all other members of the male species would be nothing but poor substitutes for this magnificent creature who matched these rugged, untamed mountains.

Seventeen

Cord cursed himself but good when he awakened in the dawn's early light to feel a rifle barrel jabbing him in the shoulder. Despite his irritation over his conversation with Tempest the previous night, they had both cuddled up in the warmth of his bedroll, arms and legs entangled. He'd slept like a baby without a care in the world. That had been marvelous for sleeping, but it wasn't good for waking up to unwanted guests carrying loaded rifles. Damnation, he'd felt so content and secure with Tempest in his arms that even his senses had taken the night off!

While Cord was scowling at the predicament he found himself in, Tempest roused from slumber to blush crimson red. She was without a stitch of clothing and Cord was holding her protectively to him beneath their quilts. Two scraggly scalawags towered over them, holding the reins to two mules laden with supplies. Who were these men? And why couldn't they go away and bother somebody else!

"I think that's him, don't you, Bones?" Ricochet Wilson said. "He sure 'nuff matches the description I got from Fort Davis."

Bones Henderson's thin eyebrows puckered in a thoughtful frown. He stared down the barrel of his Winchester. "Yep, I'd say it's him, all right, Ricochet.

'Specially since he's got the lady with him. He fits the WANTED poster." He glanced curiously at the stout, bandy-legged older man. "Where'd you put the poster, Ricochet?"

Tempest peered at the man called Ricochet. He was round as a barrel and his paunch avalanched over his belt buckle. He had a crop of wiry red hair that obviously defied a brush and seemed to go wherever it pleased. His bushy brows hung over his close-set eyes like fuzzy caterpillars and a ring of carrot-colored whiskers lined his jaw. A corncob pipe was clamped between his teeth and being downwind, Tempest swore neither Bones nor Ricochet ever bathed of their own free will. She'd smelled skunks that were more appealing!

Ricochet began digging through the various pockets on his shirt and breeches in response to Bones's question. "Well, hell, I dunno where I put the damned thing. Maybe you've got it."

"I don't have it," Bones snorted. "I gave it to you since I can't read."

Ricochet came up empty-handed and shrugged his buffalo-size shoulders. "Well, hell—'scuse me, ma'am—I dunno where that dadblamed paper is. But it don't matter. We got him, don't we?"

"Reckon so," Bones agreed. He broke into a triumphant smile that displayed the wide gap between his buck teeth. "Guess yer mighty relieved to see us, ain't ya, ma'am?"

Actually no, thought Tempest as she wormed deeper into the quilt. These two dim-witted imbeciles were hardly what she called her salvation. No doubt, it was a severe blow to Cord's self-esteem to be taken unaware by these bungling buffoons. After eluding Emilio Reynosa, it was an ironic twist of fate for Cord to be apprehended by Ricochet and Bones!

"Yer Cord MacIntosh, ain't ya?" Ricochet interrogated.

"Never heard of him," Cord muttered.

Bones brandished a doubled fist in Cord's face. "Now don't get smart with us, half-breed. You may be a sly one, but caught is caught. We're takin' ya back to Fort Davis. This gal's pa is waitin' there, ready to hold court. I ain't never seen a mad judge afore, but Litchfield is fit to be roped and tied, if ever a judge was. He's already picked out a sturdy tree where he plans to hang ya high."

"You've got the wrong man," Cord insisted, watching both men like a hawk, awaiting the opportunity to pounce. The only problem was that if he pounced, Tempest would be exposed to those stranger's leering gazes. Cord didn't relish the thought of having another man feast on her beauty.

"Wrong man, hell! . . . Pardon, ma'am," Bones added apologetically. "We've got ya dead to rights and ya know it."

A curious frown plowed Cord's brow as he inched his hand down his leg to retrieve the pistol which these two morons hadn't bothered to check to see if he had. "Just who the devil are you anyway?" he demanded to know.

"Ricochet Wilson is my name. I'm a bounty hunter," he replied. "This is Bones Henderson. He's a prospector. Me and him teamed up a few days ago while he was lookin' for that legendary gold mine that's s'posed to be 'round here somewhere. Since you got such a fat reward on yer head, sonny, it looks like we both struck it rich after all, even if there ain't no gold in these here hills."

Ricochet gave Cord a nudge with the muzzle of his rifle. "Now git on up, MacIntosh."

Tempest blanched at the thought of Cord untangling himself from the quilts and leaving her to scramble to cover herself. Blast those pesky ants! They had left her stark naked and in a most embarassing predicament when these intruders showed up.

Cord was in one helluva spot. If he tried to escape, Tempest could be caught in the crossfire. And if he didn't, Judge Litchfield would be itching to make him the honoree at a necktie party. From the sound of things, Tempest's father planned to proclaim Cord guilty with only the token formality of a trial. Litchfield was ready to get on with the hanging.

A few weeks ago, Cord hadn't given a second thought to using Tempest as a shield. But now he hesitated. She had become more than a means to an end, and he felt a fierce need to protect her.

His gaze swung to Tempest who was huddled beside his shoulder. "Do you want me to get up, princess?" he questioned quietly.

Tempest's blue eyes widened in alarm. She knew perfectly well what Cord was trying not to say. It was as if she could read his mind. Somebody could wind up dead—these two woolly baboons, for instance, or maybe even her—if he came up fighting. But not likely Cord, she thought to herself. The man seemed to have as many lives as a cat. The El Paso jail couldn't hold him and Emilio Reynosa couldn't track him down.

"Now hold on here, MacIntosh," Bones snorted. "We ain't takin' a survey to see if yer gonna git up or not. Just crawl outta there nice and easy so me and Ricochet don't have to take ya back dead instead of alive."

"I'd rather you find another way," Tempest murmured confidentially.

When Ricochet opened his mouth with more of his dull-witted remarks, Cord found another way to solve his problem. He fired two quick shots through the quilt that covered him, causing lead to zing off the barrels of both rifles. He very nearly squashed

Tempest flat when he shifted above her to protect her with his own body.

Ricochet and Bones were so startled by the barking pistol that it took their slow-acting brains several seconds to respond. But it wasn't the bounty hunter and prospector who saved the day. It was the prospector's mule. The bullets bounced off the pots and pans that dangled on the critter's flanks. With a loud bray, the startled mule wheeled to kick up his heels, catching Bones in the seat of his breeches. Bones came stumbling forward, tripping over the downcast barrel of his rifle. His fingers gripped the weapon and the rifle exploded in the dirt, sending a spray of dust around him.

Before Cord could react to the unexpected kick, Bones sprawled on top of him, squashing Tempest flat beneath him. Her yelp of pain mingled with Bones's squawk and Ricochet's growl. Cord didn't have the chance to hammer Bones over the head with the butt of his pistol and he had no intention of killing either man if he didn't have to. That would give Tempest one more reason to despise him. Damn it to hell, Cord was spending too much time fretting over what Tempest thought of him and it was getting him into too much trouble!

"Gotcha!" Ricochet bugled victoriously as he stabbed his rifle into Cord's cheek. "If you blast Bones to smithereens, you'll be dead and gone, same as him. Now gimme that pistol!"

While Bones scrambled to his feet, Cord reluctantly relinquished his pistol and eased down beside Tempest. Obeying orders, Cord wiggled out of the blankets, carefully shielding Tempest as best he could. But try as he may, her bare shoulder protruded from the edge of the quilt and both men scowled at him.

"I was afraid of that," Ricochet grumbled disdainfully. "Ya couldn't be satisfied with murder, theft, and kidnappin', could ya, MacIntosh? No, ya had to go and abuse this poor gal while ya was at it. Her pa is sure 'nuff gonna have ya shot and stabbed afore he strings ya up and leaves ya for the buzzards. I'm glad I ain't in yer boots!"

Suddenly both men were overwhelmed with sympathy for Tempest's plight. Bones pulled the quilt protectively around her and assisted her to her feet. When he spied her gown lying a good distance away, he scurried over to retrieve it.

"You just hurry over there behind them rocks, honey, and make yerself decent," Bones instructed. "Ya have nothin' more to fear from this rascal. We'll tie him up good an' tight and he won't hurt ya again."

Tempest did as she was told. When she reappeared, Cord was tied with so much rope he looked like a mummy. His eyes fastened unblinkingly on her as she approached. Tempest could see the question in those golden pools just as surely as if he'd voiced it. The time of reckoning had come. She could find a way to free Cord while the bounty hunters were unaware or she could help them transport him to Fort Davis to meet his dismal destiny. Tempest struggled with the inner turmoil while Bones and Ricochet rummaged through their supplies to provide her with a meager morning meal.

While the barely civilized twosome smacked their lips and talked with their mouths full, Tempest ate in silence. She spared Cord an occasional glance, only to find his eyes boring into her, willing her to come to his assistance. Tempest squirmed uneasily, wrestling with her dilemma.

"Aren't you going to feed him?" she questioned the duo.

Ricochet sighed in admiration. "You've got too generous a heart, ma'am. After all this half-breed heaped on ya, it's amazin' that yer thinkin' of him. Yer a true saint."

That's what Ricochet thought, Cord mused bitterly. If the man got to know Tempest better, he wouldn't think so! Damn her. She was probably enjoying this. Now she was having her revenge for what she'd been through. There would be no assistance from Tempest. In her opinion, he was probably getting exactly what he deserved. She was convinced he was guilty.

"I've got a proposition for you, boys," Cord ventured.

"All yer gettin' from us is a stick of pemmican," Bones declared as he shoved the rations in Cord's mouth. "Now don't try to outsmart us with some wily scheme. We ain't lettin' ya loose fer nothin' so you can just git that notion outta yer head right now."

Cord choked down the pemmican, but he wasn't giving up. "I can lead you to the band of outlaws who robbed the El Paso bank. Not only will you receive compensation for returning the money, but you can have the reward for every bandit you capture."

Ricochet snorted. "Sure we can. Yer probably a good friend of theirs and ya think ya can set us up. We ain't fallin' for that trick."

"It's true," Tempest interjected, unable to keep silent a moment longer.

In spite of all she'd been through, she couldn't betray Cord. If there was any opportunity for him to escape, she wanted him to take it. When it came right down to it, Tempest preferred to see Cord alive and well and living in some remote location in the mountains rather than hanged. Guilty or innocent, she loved him, despite her better judgment. Love, it seemed, knew no rules, and she couldn't bring herself to adhere to the law in this particular case.

"Cord found the money those desperados buried." She gestured toward the saddlebag that lay beside her ant-infested quilts. "It's all there, just as he says it is. He knows where the bandits are holed up. You could find wealth beyond your dreams if you capture those thieves."

Ricochet and Bones put their heads together for a powwow. At irregular intervals, they cast Cord wary glances. Finally, they nodded agreeably. Greed had a way of affecting a man's logic.

"Okay, MacIntosh," Bones announced. "We'll follow yer directions to the hideout. And what is it ya want in return for the information?"

"My freedom," Cord said simply and directly. "If I help you capture the desperadoes, you can take the lady back to her father. But I go my own way."

"That's what I figured you'd say," Ricochet mumbled as he puffed on his pipe. "But how do we know ya won't feed us to them sharks?"

Cord never blinked. "You're going to have to trust me."

"Trust ya?" Bones scoffed. "Hell, mister, ya got a list of offenses against ya a mile long. I reckon lyin' would be the least of them."

"Apaches do not lie," Cord assured them stonily.

"Well, yer just half-Apache, so that means yer word ain't but half-good," Ricochet snorted.

"Oh, for heaven's sake," Tempest grumbled, finding herself at the end of her patience. "If he is lying you can simply shoot him and be done with it. You'll still receive your bounty one way or another. And if those bandits get away, you'll still have the bank's money safely hidden. You could even use it to barter with the outlaws, if things don't turn out as you anticipate. But decide, here and now. I'm baking in this sun!"

Bones rubbed his bristled jaw. "Yer sure a smart one, ma'am. I'd never have puzzled out all them options."

"Thank you, sir," Tempest replied with an amused smile. "Now shall we get on with this? As much as I relish seeing my father again, I feel I owe both of you every opportunity to cash in along the way. Why, if things work out, you could become local heroes."

"I reckon we could at that," Ricochet chuckled and then frowned. "But what about you, ma'am? Don't ya want yer revenge? If MacIntosh walks away, you won't see him pay for what he did."

"My freedom is all I desire," Tempest assured them, refusing to meet Cord's probing stare. "Revenge can poison the mind and corrupt the soul. I want no more than to return to civilization to begin my life again."

"A veritable saint with a heart of gold!" Bones praised. "It takes a God-fearin' woman like you to remind us of the truth and goodness of our fellow man. But if we was all as forgivin' as you, I s'pose we'd all pack up and part company, here and now. I'm afraid I'm a mite greedy. I wouldn't mind handin' them bandits over to the judge and takin' my reward."

"Then it's settled," Bones proclaimed. "You point us in the right direction, MacIntosh, and we'll go bandit-huntin'. Just don't git sneaky or that'll be the end of ya." He pantomimed having one's throat slit.

Tempest breathed a sigh of relief when they finally got underway. She didn't glance in Cord's direction while he led them through the valley and back into the rugged mountains to the south. It seemed the man knew every nook and cranny of this rugged terrain. Cord never lost his sense of direction, even when Tempest got so turned around she could barely tell up from down. They had wound around a jagged peak that set north of Arabella Mountain before he finally called a halt to the expedition. He suggested camping in a rocky ravine that provided a fresh-water spring and then he led the bounty hunters to the lookout point that towered over an abandoned trading post nestled in a clump of trees. With his hands still tied behind him and his arms bound to his ribs, Cord gestured his head toward the shadowed forms of two men who paced back and forth in front of the log cabin.

"Well, I guess this ain't no wild-goose chase after all," Ricochet murmured. "But I ain't figured out how to surprise them just yet. It'll take some serious ponderin' . . ."

Cord rolled his eyes skyward. "How many men have you taken back for bounty?"

"Countin' you?" Ricochet inquired.

"Yeah, counting me," Cord grumbled impatiently.

Ricochet shifted his weight from one foot to the other. "You was gonna be the first," he admitted rather sheepishly. "I just got into the business."

Tempest bit back a laugh, knowing that it rankled Cord to have the distinction of being this bungling bounty hunter's first prize. If not for her, Cord would have been long gone. He may not have loved her, but he had come to care enough about her to consider her safety as well as his own. For that, Tempest could have flung her arms around his neck and kissed him soundly. He resented the fact that he was up to his eyebrows in hot water because of her, but she loved him all the more because of it.

"If the odds are four against six, we should surprise them in the cover of darkness," Tempest suggested.

"Can you handle a rifle?" Bones asked.

"I can certainly shoot one if it's loaded," Tempest said with firm conviction. "At least I can look as if I can. Those bandits will hardly have time to ask me."

Ricochet eyed Cord with wary consternation. "I still don't know if I like this idea of givin' yer pistol back to ya."

"Oh, for pity's sake," Tempest sniffed in annoyance. "If you're going to be in the bounty hunting business, you should know you'll have to take a few risks. If Cord turns on either of you, I'll shoot him myself. Then I'll have the revenge you thought I should want. Now, are you satisfied?"

"I reckon so," Bones mumbled. "I just want to make sure I'm around to spend all the money." He handed Tempest his rifle. "You keep yer eyes on the renegade while me and Ricochet stash the bank's cash in a safe place."

When the two men lumbered off to bury the booty, Cord grinned wryly. "You're probably having the time of your life now that I'm tied in Gordian knots and you can boss those two clowns around."

"And you'll have the opportunity to prove your innocence in the murder charge," Tempest countered.

Cord cocked a dark brow and studied her for a moment. "Why did you talk those men into this, princess? You're only prolonging being reunited with your father."

An impish smile claimed her lips as she peered into his craggy features. "Because I'm a veritable saint, of course. Bones and Ricochet said so."

"They don't know you as well as I do. Now why'd you do it?"

Her shoulder lifted in a noncommittal shrug. "I was caught in a weak moment. You did your good deed for the day by saving me from a misdirected bullet this morning. I'm extending the same courtesy."

"Come here and kiss me, Tempest," Cord whispered huskily. "I haven't had the chance to thank you properly for *your* good deed for the day . . ."

Before Tempest could accept or reject the command, the sound of falling rock heralded Bones and Ricochet's approach. Tempest sorely wished she could have enjoyed one tantalizing kiss before pandemonium broke loose in the valley below. It could very well be the last time she saw Cord alone. After they laid siege to the cabin, he would disappear like a specter in the night.

Tempest resigned herself to the fact that she would never see Cord again. Impatiently, she waited for darkness to cloak the mountains. If Cord had spoken the truth about his jailbreak, it would be up to her to ensure that the murder charge was dropped when she reached Fort Davis. And if time proved Cord right, Tempest wondered if there was also truth in his claim that Victor Watts had framed him for rustling, then conveniently disposed of Paddy MacIntosh. Tempest intended to do a little investigating of her own when she returned to civilization. As far as she was concerned, Cord was still her client, even while he eluded the law. The least she could do for the man she loved was search for clues about Paddy's death.

Her gaze swung to Cord, who was still tightly bound. The mere sight of this man always had the power to stir her. It would certainly go easier on her tormented conscience if the man she loved was innocent. But of one thing she was certain: Cord was guilty of abduction. He definitely wasn't a saint, she mused as she memorized each rugged feature on his chiseled face. Oh well, she probably wouldn't have loved him if he were. She'd never been attracted to perfect gentlemen who handled her with kid gloves but never considered her their equal. Cord MacIntosh could never be accused of being a gentleman who put a woman on a pedestal. Tempest would have laughed out loud at the thought if it wouldn't have left Bones and Ricochet wondering if she were losing her sanity.

Tempest struggled for composure and stared toward the shack that was bathed in shadows. She wondered how she would hold up if this attack involved a real-life gun battle. Well, she supposed she would know the answer soon enough. She only hoped she lived to tell about it. At this point, she wasn't sure of anything except the fact that she had granted Cord a sporting chance, whether he deserved it or not. No doubt, she'd be kicking herself all the way to Fort Davis if he didn't!

Eighteen

Cord had resigned himself to the fact that he was virtually on his own when it came to corralling the bandits in the abandoned trading post. Those two ignoramuses who fancied themselves bounty hunters would only be a hindrance. And Tempest, quick-witted though she was, had no experience in gunfights.

When Bones and Ricochet finally turned Cord loose, he took instant command of the field. "I'll take care of the two posted guards," he volunteered as he stretched out his hand for his pistol. "You'll provide reinforcements, but don't get trigger-happy. Don't fire unless I tell you to."

"Just exactly what does *taking care* of the guards entail?" Tempest questioned warily.

Although the desperadoes had prices on their heads that legally permitted them to be brought in dead or alive—whichever was easiest—Tempest cringed at the thought of Cord murdering a man in cold blood.

Tawny eyes glittered down at Tempest, cold and unrelenting. "Sometimes, a man has to do what he has to do," he told her grimly.

Tempest gulped apprehensively and stared at the pistol Ricochet handed her. If she found herself faced with killing another human being to protect herself, could she pull the trigger? Perhaps it was best to react to the situation when the time came, she decided. Either way, the results would not be pleasant.

"Follow me down the trail," Cord instructed Bones and Ricochet. "Keep quiet and, for God's sake, stay out of sight. We're not sending out invitations to announce our arrival. If you make a racket you may as well sign your own death certificates."

Mulling over that bleak prospect, the bounty hunters followed obediently along in Cord's footsteps while Tempest brought up the rear. Like snakes, they slithered down the meandering, moonlit path until they reached the valley. With the silence of a panther, Cord crept toward the lone tree where one of the guards had propped himself up with his rifle cradled in his arms.

Cord hardly dared to breathe as he inched toward the bandit's blind side. When the guard yawned and shifted his weight from one foot to the other, Cord pounced with lightning-quick agility. He raised the butt of his pistol and brought it down with a hard thud. The makeshift club, applied to just the right location on the man's skull, put him out like a snuffed lantern. When the guard collapsed at the knees and his arms dropped limply to his sides, Cord snaked around the tree. He caught the unconscious body in one arm and retrieved the rifle with his free hand, easing the bandit to the ground. Then he motioned for Tempest and the bounty hunters to bind and gag the incapacitated guard.

Relieved that Cord had opted not to use the dagger in his moccasin, Tempest scurried from the underbrush to watch them tie the guard good and tight with the leather strips Cord had given them.

Cord stared at the second lookout who was lounging in a crudely built chair on the porch. The second sentinel posed more of a problem than the first because of his close proximity to the four men sleeping inside the cabin. If the bandits held true to their customary behavior, they would have passed several whiskey bottles around the table while playing cards to wile away the hours. With any luck at all, they would all be well into their cups by this late hour, snoring up a storm, making themselves easy prey to a surprise attack. But if they had been plotting their next raid and were stone-cold sober . . . Cord prepared himself for the worst and concentrated on removing the second human obstacle from his path.

His gaze focused on the lean, scruffy man draped sideways in his chair. It was obvious the guard was having difficulty staying awake. His head nodded against his shoulder and he stirred slightly before slumping again. With extreme caution, Cord eased a hip over the railing and inched along the porch. He ducked beneath the window and struck out at the drowsy sentinel in one fluid motion, employing the same tactic he'd used on the first guard. The thump of his pistol butt, however, was followed by a dull groan. Cord hurriedly clamped his hand over the lower portion of the man's whiskered face, then cursed silently as he watched the barrel of the rifle arc toward the planked porch. It was obvious this thick-headed galoot would require a second smack on the skull. Cord desperately needed an extra hand to catch the falling rifle before it clanked on the porch like a warning bell. Damn!!

Cord flinched when he felt the brush of flesh against his back. He hadn't realized Tempest had followed so closely until her arm shot past him to grab the rifle before it fell to the floor.

Although Tempest's hands were shaking, she recoiled with the rifle clutched to her bosom. She watched Cord thump the guard a second time. When their eyes met, she thought she saw appreciation and admiration in Cord's eyes. He was silently thanking her for helping him through what could have become a disastrous situation. He took the rifle from her arms and gestured for her to tie the guard to his chair while Cord stuffed a gag in the man's mouth.

Cord glanced over his shoulder to see the two silhouetted figures of the bounty hunters frozen to their spots. He motioned for Bones and Ricochet to circle behind the shack. But when Cord gestured for Tempest to follow the bounty hunters to a safer location, she refused.

Blast it, this was no time for an argument. And damn her, if she got herself shot, he was never going to forgive her! This was his quest for information, not hers. Cord had bargained with those bounty hunters for the express purpose of finding Ellis Flake, but not by placing Tempest's life in jeopardy. *Caramba!* Why'd she have to be so confounded bullheaded at a time like this!

With a wordless scowl, Cord made a stabbing gesture toward the side of the cabin, but Tempest refused to budge. Muttering under his breath, Cord hooked his arm around her waist, drawing her protectively behind him since she refused to leave. He thrust the rifle back into her arms and nodded in silent command for her to use it if her life was threatened.

Ever so gently, Cord twisted the door latch. All five of his senses sprang to life as the door eased open without so much as a squeak—thanks to its leather hinges. His discerning gaze swept the shadowy room to see four men sprawled on their cots. And sure enough, two empty whiskey bottles were on the table with a strewn deck of cards.

Things seemed to be going superbly until Cord heard a "thunk" against the outer wall of the shack. Suddenly the drowsy desperadoes stirred on their cots. Cord cursed furiously at Bones and Ricochet who couldn't even circle around the back of the cabin without tripping over each other. It was a wonder he hadn't heard those two imbeciles coming when they sneaked up on him. Hell, they may as well have marched in like an army on parade, beating a damned drum!

Like a speed bullet, Cord shot into the cabin to scoop up the four gunbelts draped over the chairs. But he wasn't foolish enough to think these *pistoleros* weren't armed to the teeth, even in their sleep. Somewhere in the shack was undoubtedly another stockpile of pistols, rifles, and ammunition. He only hoped he found it before they did!

Panic gripped Tempest when Cord launched his one-man attack. Because of Bones's and Ricochet's clumsiness, their plan had to be discarded for a far more daring option that endangered Cord's life. Tempest felt a surge of adrenaline through her blood, putting her feet into motion. The need to come to Cord's rescue prompted her to plunge into the room frantically.

Tempest went head hunting with a vengeance. She swung the rifle around backwards and hammered the first head that popped up from the nearby cot. Since she didn't have time to deliver two blows she made the first one count double. Like a cobra, she recoiled to strike at the man on the second cot. The desperado slumped back on his bed, oblivious. With rifle poised to level another brain-scrambling blow, Tempest shot toward the next cot, but she collided with an unidentified body. Her goggle-eyed gaze froze on the shadowed form beside her.

Prepared to strike, Cord wheeled around to determine who had backended him. Tempest and Cord stood face-to-face, intent on attack until they recognized each other. Those valuable seconds cost them dearly because they had neglected to fell the last member of the gang.

An enraged snarl erupted from the darkest corner

of the room. Tempest pivoted the instant before a bulky body plowed into her. The momentum caused Tempest to slam into Cord, knocking both of them off balance. Cord collided with a chair that crashed into the table, sending him sprawling backward. The outlaw had shoved Tempest on top of Cord, leaving her feet dangling off the table. With another outraged sneer, the bandit rammed the heel of his left hand into Tempest's belly, holding her and her rifle in place so she couldn't take aim.

Moonlight shone through the open door, gleaming off the dagger the desperado held poised in his upraised hand. A face as hard as granite and menacing eyes burned down on her, and Tempest knew she was staring death in the face—a sinister face that offered no mercy.

Tempest could feel Cord squirming beneath her, but she had been pinned down so effectively that she could do nothing to release him. They were trapped and catastrophe loomed only a few horrifying inches away!

When the snarling bandit uncoiled to plunge the knife into Tempest, she screamed. A shot hissed past her hip and exploded in the terror-filled silence that followed. With a guttural growl, the bandit clutched at his chest with his free hand as he collapsed on Tempest. The knife he intended to stab into her heart veered toward her shoulder. Tempest had the presence of mind to throw up a hand to deflect it, but she couldn't prevent his massive body from crashing down upon her.

She tried to push the dead man aside, impossible though it proved to be. It occurred to her, once the moment of impending disaster had passed, that Cord had swiveled his pistol—still in its holster—to shoot around her hip. There hadn't been time for Cord to wrestle his Colt loose or move Tempest out of his way. There had only been time to shoot the bandit before he buried his blade in Tempest's chest. Good Lord, if Cord had reacted a half-second later she would have been lying there dead instead.

Still thunderstruck, Tempest watched Cord reach around her to grab the desperado by the hair and send him tumbling to the floor. Swiftly, Cord levered himself off the table and set Tempest on her feet. A mutinous sneer thinned Cord's lips when he glanced down at the outlaw whose life blood had spilled out of him.

"Bones, Ricochet! Get in here pronto!" Cord bellowed as he stamped out the front door, cursing the air blue.

Bones and Ricochet wormed through the back window and stumbled into the darkened room to find three unconscious desperadoes slumped on their cots and one dead man sprawled on the floor.

"My God . . ." Bones croaked after he lit the lantern to survey the room. "Did MacIntosh do this all by hisself?"

"Mostly," Tempest mumbled. Her gaze was riveted on Cord's shadowed form looming outside the door.

"Get these men tied up before they regain consciousness," she ordered, venturing outside.

"Cord, what's wrong?" she asked. "You got what you wanted. When the thieves wake, you can interrogate the one locked in jail with you. If he says you're innocent, I'll believe him."

Cord rounded on her, his eyes flashing. "Ellis Flake isn't going to wake up," he growled. "I had to kill *him* to protect *you*. You were in the way. It was either you or Ellis and I chose to save you."

His words dropped like stones in the silence. Tempest felt as if she'd suffered a devastating blow to the midsection. Stunned, she wobbled back to brace herself against the outer wall of the cabin.

Cord glared at her in frustration. "And what gripes the hell out of me is that *you* graciously decided to believe Ellis Flake, *if* he corroborated my story. But you refused to believe *me* when I told you I did nothing more than pound some manners into my jailer after he'd whipped me bloody once a day." His breath came out in furious gasps. "I just killed *my* only witness in order to spare *your* life, princess," he repeated emphatically. "It was *my* proof of innocence against *your* life. You're alive, but now I have nothing but my word against the law officials in El Paso—men whom Victor Watts has in the palm of his hand. That—" he added bitterly, "—and my freedom, for what it will be worth if Victor and Emilio Reynosa ever get their hands on me."

Tempest reached out for Cord's arm, but he jerked away as if her physical contact repulsed him. With the swiftness of a fleeting shadow, Cord hopped over the railing and disappeared into the darkness. When she darted around the side of the cabin, he was nowhere to be seen.

"Cord MacIntosh, you come back here this very second or I'll never speak to you again! Blast it, where are you going?"

She was met with silence. Only the call of a distant coyote echoed in the night. Her shoulders slumped, Tempest reversed direction to oversee Bones and Ricochet as they secured their prisoners.

A pain the size of Texas cut through her heart when she realized this was the beginning of her life without Cord. He wouldn't be back. He was still out for vengeance. He wanted to find his father's killer and make sure Victor Watts paid retribution. Cord had kept his part of the bargain to Bones and Ricochet. And he had granted Tempest her freedom, but he had neglected to give her back her heart before he vanished into the night. When he left, he had taken her soul with him as well. Guilty or innocent, Tempest loved him—and she owed him her life.

Tempest had admitted her feelings to Cord the previous day, but she had done it in such a way that he hadn't dared believe her. Now she wished Cord *did* know the truth. It probably wouldn't come as much consolation on the wings of this latest disappointment, but Cord would have known she did care for him and that she always would. Loving Cord didn't come to an abrupt halt just because he had walked out of her life. It only made matters worse. The cavity that had once been her heart ached with an emptiness nothing could fill.

Tempest brushed away the tears that trickled down her cheeks and concentrated on binding one of the men she had hammered over the head with the butt of her rifle.

"Where's MacIntosh?" Ricochet asked after he lashed one prisoner's hands and feet together.

"Gone," Tempest murmured, willing her trembling voice not to crack.

"Well, I guess I shoulda figured that," Ricochet declared as he waddled over to grab Ellis Flake by the boots and drag him outside. "We made a deal and he delivered a handful of desperadoes, just like he said he would. It seems MacIntosh was right. Apaches don't lie."

"Yeah, they may be as deadly as rattlesnakes and as mean as grizzlies, but if they give their word they stick by it," Bones added.

"Too bad MacIntosh is an outlaw hisself," Ricochet remarked. "I kinda liked him, in spite of everythin' I've heard."

"So did I," Tempest murmured ever so softly. "So did I . . ."

Nineteen

Cord plopped down on a boulder and watched the pearly glow of dawn brighten the horizon. Gloomily, he stared down at Dead Man's Hole—the steep-walled chasm draped with shadows and slashes of sunlight. At the moment Cord was as angry and frustrated as one man could get. He had detoured from the route to his cabin beneath High Lonesome Peak, just to prove to that stubborn woman that he hadn't murdered Juan Tijerina. But ironically, Cord had been forced to kill the one man who could testify on his behalf. Yet, what really made Cord's blood boil was that Tempest would believe Ellis Flake when she had refused to accept his own word. In essence, she considered his credibility less than Ellis's!

Even now, Cord could remember the torment he'd experienced in the bandit's hideout while he lay sprawled on the table beneath Tempest. When he recognized Ellis looming above them with murder on his mind, Cord had been faced with a difficult choice. He knew Ellis hadn't recognized him and there hadn't been time to blurt out his identity. Cord's face had been partially camouflaged by Tempest's hair, and Ellis had been acting out of desperation, determined to save himself at all cost. That was just like Ellis. Cord hadn't had the chance to reason with him—there had only been time to save Tempest from instant death. The entire incident had scared the living hell out of Cord. He hadn't been able to tolerate the thought of watching Tempest die before his very eyes.

When the unnerving encounter ended and Cord was trying to cope with the hasty decision he'd been forced to make, along came Tempest. Her supposedly generous offer to believe Ellis's testimony had set Cord off and he had exploded. He had been cruel and cutting and he hadn't even bothered to tell Tempest good-bye. Which was probably just as well, Cord mused reflectively. What was there to say to that gorgeous female who had whizzed into the cabin, prepared to defy death, and come dangerously close to disaster?

Caramba! What could she have been thinking? Cord asked himself crossly. He swore he'd never understand that crazy female. She had always been high-spirited and unpredictable, but that surge of blind courage and foolhardiness was uncalled-for! She'd had nothing to gain and had forced Cord to shoot the one man he needed to take alive!

A stab of loneliness, sharp and agonizing, sliced through Cord like the knife that had very nearly ended Tempest's life. He could still see her standing there in her ragged gown with that glorious mane cascading over her shoulders. He could still hear her sultry voice whispering to him in the wind. Another ache throbbed through his body, and he scowled at the tangled emotions that boiled inside him.

Tempest was going back home where she belonged. It was for the best, Cord reassured himself. Those two clumsy clowns weren't the world's best protectors, but they could lead Tempest to Fort Davis. They could surely navigate their way through Sheep Pen Canyon and around Scobee Mountain to reach the garrison where Tempest's father anxiously awaited.

Besides, Cord didn't want that female with him when he confronted Emilio Reynosa. The outlaw gang hadn't been expecting Cord, but Reynosa certainly would be. No doubt the skilled *vaquero*, who worked for Victor Watts, would be lying in wait near Cord's remote ranch cabin by High Lonesome Peak. Victor had probably put a price on Cord's head and had sent Emilio to see the deed done . . .

The lone howl of a coyote resounded around the stony escarpment and Cord instantly flung his bitter thoughts aside. With the experienced skills of an Apache warrior, he cupped his hands around his mouth and returned the signal—the same one he'd heard the previous night when he had walked away from Tempest.

Agilely, he jumped down from his boulder, scooped up his rifle, and followed the narrow trail toward the sound that called to him a second time. Cord knew who summoned him. Yellowfish had tracked him, watching over him from a distance. Old Yellowfish prided himself in being everywhere and knowing everything, just like the Great Spirit of the Apache. He was too old and crippled to engage in battles these days, but he was the self-appointed overseer of these rugged mountains.

Cord nodded a solemn greeting when he spied Yellowfish sitting Indian-style on a huge rock surrounded on three sides by junipers and mesquite.

"You got rid of the sassy white woman. Good. It is best," Yellowfish grunted with his customary blunt candor.

Cord's eyes widened in surprise when Jefferson Jones stepped from the underbrush to grace him with a grin.

"What are you doing here?" Cord asked incredulously.

Jeff shrugged a broad shoulder as he sauntered past the old warrior. "Ma thought I'd better come check on you. You know how she frets."

"You left your parents short-handed?" Cord questioned in a critical tone.

"No, actually we hired another man," Jeff explained with another good-natured smile. "Remember the drunkard I told you about?"

Cord nodded.

"Well, he ran out of cash for meals and liquor and Ma let him eat without paying. Then she went on a crusade to sober the lush up and put him to work in the stables so I could take time off to check on you." Jeff reached inside the pouch strapped to his back to produce three pints of whiskey. "I confiscated his stock of liquor prematurely so he'd be indebted to my folks," he admitted unrepentantly. "By the time I get back, Ma will have delivered her sermon on temperance and filled him with the fear of God so many times that the old coot will be a converted Christian."

Cord snatched the bottle from his cousin and popped the cork. He guzzled an early morning drink, but it didn't numb him to the agonizing loss of leaving Tempest. He took another swallow . . . or four.

"Slow down, cuz." Jeff chuckled. "I know you're anxious to celebrate the departure of your new bride, but you'll fall off this mountain if you get too sauced."

Curse it, Cord thought. He wasn't drinking to celebrate Tempest's absence; he was drinking to forget that he missed her like hell. And damn it, she hadn't even been gone two days!

"We have business at your ranch," Yellowfish announced somberly. "Jefferson told me of the gunman your enemy has sent to destroy you. I have seen the Mexican. He hides in the edge of the forest in the valley like a hungry lion waiting to pounce. He has almost a dozen men with him. They have enough supplies to wait forever, Lobo Plano." The old Apache eased to the ground. "Come. I will show you where they are."

While the aging chief led the way, Cord explained that he had been captured by the two bounty hunters and had offered his life in exchange for the reward on the outlaw gang. Then at the abandoned trading post he reported the incident that had forced him to take a man's life to save Tempest's.

"Did you question this man for whom you searched?" Yellowfish inquired.

"I didn't have the chance," Cord muttered without going into further detail.

Yellowfish wasn't satisfied. "Why not? The whole point of your search was to find your witness to the murder in El Paso."

"Ellis Flake didn't give me a chance to ask him any questions," Cord scowled sourly. "He's the man I had to shoot before he could stab Tempest."

Yellowfish gasped. "You made the wrong choice, Lobo Plano."

Jefferson bit back a grin. "Your grandfather hasn't had one kind word to say about Tempest," he confided to Cord. "He told me she had the tongue of a viper and the bite of a wolverine. I take it she stood up to Yellowfish as zealously as she defied you at the Pinery."

Remembering the series of amusing clashes between the proud chief and Tempest put a faint smile on Cord's lips. "No, they didn't appreciate each other very much," he admitted.

"That's too bad," Jeff said with a forlorn sigh. "She sure was pretty, even if she did have the temperament of a wounded tigress. I liked her spunk, even if Yellowfish insists she wasn't good marriage material. You married the wrong woman by mistake to have your revenge on Victor, but I suppose things worked out for the best."

Not the *wrong woman,* Cord mused sullenly. Just the wrong place and the wrong time for what might have been the *right woman.* If ever there was a female who could have become the special treasure in his life, it was that keen-witted, high-strung temptress . . .

"I just hope Tempest doesn't decide to have her revenge on you," Jefferson murmured uneasily. "Since her father is a judge and she's a lawyer, you could find yourself in one helluva spot!"

Cord fell silent, wondering to what extremes Tempest would go. There were times when he could have sworn she really did like him. However, those times had been few and far between. But when they were in each other's arms, gliding toward paradise, she didn't despise him quite so much, even if she did resent the fierce physical attraction between them. Yet, pride would never permit a woman like Tempest to use her femininity to pass judgment on a man. Her analytical mind would refuse to allow her to take that fragile bond between them into consideration.

Cord didn't know what to expect from Tempest or how she truly felt. He would never return to her good graces, even if he *had* saved her life. *Caramba!* What was he thinking? He'd never been in Tempest's good graces.

In spite of everything, Cord made a vow to make up for the misery he'd caused Tempest the past three weeks. Even if she saw to it that the price on his head increased another few thousand dollars, he would repay her for her trouble.

Cord discarded the thought and forced himself to concentrate on the problem at hand. He had to put Tempest out of his mind and focus on Emilio Reynosa. For certain, Reynosa would not be sidetracked when the two of them clashed. Cord promised to wring the truth about Paddy's death from that *vaquero* if it was the last thing he did. He may never have the chance to prove himself innocent of murder, but he would damned sure find out what had happened to Paddy!

Victor Watts smiled triumphantly as he stared at the documents he had procured in El Paso. He had persuaded his colleagues to forge ahead with their plans to obtain the salt rights and land deeds, despite MacIntosh's claims. Victor had argued that the man who had inherited Paddy's holdings could not file for possession of the property when he was wanted for murder and various other offenses that would demand the death penalty once he was apprehended. It was inevitable that Cord's property and livestock would be on the auction block, but Victor wanted it *now*.

The magistrates in El Paso were itching to make a tidy profit off the Salt Lakes as well. They had rushed through the formalities of ownership and signed over the deeds to Victor, assured that Cord was as good as dead. When Emilio Reynosa finished the task he'd been sent to accomplish, the matter would be quickly concluded. The legal rights were already in Victor's hands and all he had to do was await word from Emilio.

The *vaquero* had sent a message the previous week to Victor that Cord had yet to arrive at his cabin. But Victor was far from discouraged; he had returned the dispatcher, ordering Emilio to hold his position. Sooner or later Cord would return to his stomping ground to check on his livestock. Even if Cord was dragging that female lawyer with him, he still wouldn't stand a chance. And if the chit had perished, Cord wouldn't have a prayer. Her death would only be added to Cord's growing list of transgressions . . .

"Victor?" Annette Partridge hovered in the doorway of the parlor. "Have you heard any news about Tempest Litchfield?" She shuddered repulsively at the thought of being abducted by that vicious half-breed Victor had described on numerous occasions. "When I think that I could have been the one in his clutches—"

Her voice broke and Victor set his documents aside to console his fiancée. "You mustn't dwell on such grim thoughts, my love," he crooned as he cuddled Annette in his arms. "We can only hope my men will hunt that scoundrel down and rescue Miss Litchfield. Her father arrived at Fort Davis to enlist the assistance of the buffalo soldiers stationed there. MacIntosh can't remain free much longer while so many men are searching for him from all directions."

"I feel so sorry for Tempest," Annette murmured against the collar of Victor's jacket. "She was such a strong-willed and dignified lady. How horrible to be dragged off by that vile barbarian!"

"We must hope for the best and prepare ourselves for the worst," Victor whispered, giving her another sympathetic squeeze. "Let's focus our attention on our upcoming wedding and let my *vaqueros* and the soldiers do what they do best." He bent to press a kiss to Annette's puckered brow. "My foremost concern is ensuring that you are safe and happy, my darling. I will protect you from all harm and you will want for nothing."

When a rap resounded on the door, Victor excused himself. While he was conversing with one of his associates from El Paso, Annette wandered around the room. A curious frown knitted her delicate features when she spied the legal documents Victor had left on the desk. Although she never claimed to have a head for business, having been groomed and trained to become a proper hostess and a wealthy man's wife, Annette wondered at the propriety of assuming control of property belonging to a man who was still alive somewhere in the mountains. Was it legal to strip a criminal of his holdings before he had been tried, sentenced, and hanged? And if it wasn't, why had Victor assumed control of the Salt Lakes and the ranch valleys stocked with horses and cattle?

Her gaze narrowed on the carefully worded insertion on the document pertaining to any mineral rights that might be located on the property or in the vicinity of Paddy MacIntosh's ranch. That was a rather odd amendment to a deed, Annette thought. Did Victor actually believe there was a hidden gold mine in that region, even though he had scoffed at the prospect in Tempest's presence? Victor had claimed Paddy had *stolen* the gold nuggets that had been used to acquire his land investments. But perhaps Victor hadn't been perfectly honest when he conveyed his version of the story to Tempest on that fateful day . . .

The sound of approaching footsteps and the drone of voices wafted out of the office. Hurriedly, Annette bounded to her feet and returned to the spot Victor had left her a few minutes earlier.

"I have to make another trip into El Paso," Victor informed her. "I won't be gone too long. Amuse yourself, my dear, and I will compensate for abandoning you when I return."

Annette watched Victor cross the room to retrieve his documents. After he had locked them in the bottom drawer of his desk, he sailed off, pausing only long enough to press a hasty peck to her cheek.

Sighing dismally at the thought of being left to twiddle her thumbs again, Annette wandered to the kitchen to visit with the cook. It worried her that

Victor was so secretive about his business endeavors, but Annette reminded herself that it was not a woman's place to involve herself in a man's affairs unless he asked her to take part.

Her mother hadn't been privy to family finances and Annette had been told that was the way of things. But she wished she could have pursued a career, just as Tempest had done. And yet, that might not be such a good thing, Annette mused as she poured another cup of tea. She was safe and sound at Victor's *rancho* while Tempest was being forced to endure only God knew what kind of hideous atrocities. No, she would remain in her place as she had been instructed to do by her parents who believed that young ladies were not meant to be independent-minded or assertive. She wouldn't have traded places with Tempest for all the gold that Victor obviously suspected could be found in Paddy MacIntosh's lost mine!

"Can I git ya anythin' to make ya more comfortable, Miz Litchfield?" Ricochet asked as he tucked another blanket around her to ward off the night's chill.

"I'm fine, thank you," Tempest insisted. "But I would like to know when you expect to arrive at the fort."

Ricochet rubbed his bushy jaw in thought. "Well, if we don't have no trouble with them prisoners or rovin' bands of Apache or Comanche, I s'pect we oughta be there by this time tomorrow."

Tempest savored the thought. She couldn't wait to be reunited with her father. The past few days without Cord had been unbearably lonely.

Wistfully, her gaze drifted toward the precipice to the northwest—the one Yellowfish had called High Lonesome Peak. Somewhere in those timbered ridges on the far side of the mountain was the place Cord called home. But why should she care where he lived or what he was doing, she asked herself dispiritedly. He hadn't even bothered to tell her goodbye before he slipped out of her life like a disembodied spirit vanishing into the night.

Determinedly, Tempest shoved all thoughts of Cord aside. In one day's time, she would see a familiar face that could pull her out of this pit of depression. She wanted to fly into her father's arms and put the past behind her . . . and yet, she couldn't stop thinking about how frustrated Cord had been when his only witness had perished before being interrogated. She knew how much it had meant to Cord to be exonerated from that murder charge. Tempest had refused to believe him when she was bitter, upset, and fighting this love she felt for him. But she had begun to think Cord wouldn't have detoured to that cabin if he hadn't told her the truth. He would have had nothing to gain unless he could have gotten Ellis alone and persuaded the outlaw to lie for him.

A frown furrowed Tempest's brow as she glanced toward the five men bound to trees like tethered horses. Perhaps Ellis Flake had never mentioned the jailer's death to his companions. And then again, maybe he had. There was only one way to find out if anyone knew what had happened during that jailbreak in El Paso.

Tempest flung the quilts aside and rose to her feet. Surely one of these men knew about the incident at the jail. And if none of them did, Tempest had nothing to lose by asking. She would even be willing to do a little legal bargaining if one of these desperados had information about Juan Tijerina's death. Her father probably wouldn't approve of her aiding Cord since he was still considered a ruthless criminal, but Tempest had to know the truth for her own peace of mind. Her curiosity wouldn't let her rest until she had interrogated each and every outlaw.

"There." Yellowfish gestured a bony finger toward a clump of cedars and pines that flanked one side of the grassy valley. "The Mexicans have made camp and refuse to budge." His arm swept to the south and then to the east. "I have seen guards posted on those points. Now they are hidden in the shadows. But they are there . . . waiting like vultures."

Cord studied the spacious cabin he and his father had built after he'd returned from the war—a war that had brought him nothing but unpleasant memories and a bad reputation as a traitor to Texas and to the cause of the South. Until now, this peaceful valley was the only place where he could escape the world and do what he loved best—train his horses to sell to travelers who stopped at El Paso, the Pinery, and other way stations along the Butterfield Trail. But now he was faced with nothing but more trouble. His father had perished. Tempest was on her way to Fort Davis, and Emilio Reynosa undoubtedly had been given orders to bring Cord back riddled with bullets.

"Any suggestions, Tosh?" Jefferson queried as his gaze swept what should have been a serene valley dotted with cattle and horses.

"Only one," Cord stared at the tower of rock that served as one of two lookout points.

"Oh, no you don't," Jefferson blustered. "I know what you're thinking and you're not going to do it. I won't let you and neither will Yellowfish. It's too damned risky. I came here to help you and by damn, that's exactly what I intend to do!"

Yellowfish guessed his grandson's strategy just as

quickly. It was a favorite Apache technique that earned a warrior praise around the campfire when he returned from raiding. But Cord wasn't going up against a bunch of incompetent ranch hands or Mexican soldiers who'd had too much whiskey. He was pitting himself against twelve of the best-trained *buscaderos* west of the Pecos.

"We do not count coup, Lobo Plano," Yellowfish muttered. "We count only your life."

"And I have no life up here in the mountains or down below until I learn the truth from Emilio Reynosa," Cord declared, wheeling to face his grandfather and cousin.

"Then take the gold I gave your father and leave here," Yellowfish demanded. "Let the Texans believe the lies. They have scorned you since you were but a young man trying to fight their war battles for them. I would rather go to meet the Great Spirit knowing you are alive than to have my only living seed perish before me." He clutched Cord's arm, his dark eyes beseeching. "Go, Lobo Plano. Those of us who know you for the man you are know the truth. Geronimo and Victorio will accept you into their bands. You favored them by steering them away from a massacre when Father Washington tried to destroy them with his army. They will give you refuge. Go to them with my blessing."

"No," Cord's brisk tone discouraged further debate.

"It is because of that crazy white woman," Yellowfish grumbled contemptuously. "Before you found her, you did not care what the White Eyes thought of you. You were much more Apache then. Do you wish to prove the truth to *her* more than you wish to avenge Paddy's death, even if it means sacrificing your life?"

Cord snatched up his rifle and stared grimly at his grandfather. "If I don't survive, I want your promise that you will lead Jefferson to the gold. It is to be my wife's treasure in compensation for all that she endured. I want your promise, Grandfather."

Yellowfish stuck out a defiant chin. "I will give the white woman nothing."

"You owe her your life," Cord reminded him.

The old Apache scowled in disgust. "I knew you would throw that in my face. She has bewitched you and now you have become as stubborn as she is. The *English* poison is far worse than the *Scottish* because it spreads and contaminates."

"Promise me," Cord demanded, his unrelenting gaze fixed on his grandfather. "It will be my last wish if I don't return."

Yellowfish's shoulders sagged in defeat. "It will be done, but I will not like it."

"Jefferson?" Cord arched a dark brow, demanding his cousin's promise as well.

"Whatever you say, Tosh," he grumbled begrudgingly. "Just make sure you come back. I don't relish toting a pot of gold to San Antonio, especially when I'll be bearing bad news."

Yellowfish drew the magical necklace over his head and placed it on Cord's neck. "This will ward away evil spirits."

When Cord disappeared into the rocks and scrub brush, Jefferson sank down to wait. "I don't like this, Yellowfish. Not one bit. That cousin of mine is going to wear the wings off two good guardian angels!"

"Do you see what the wiles of a woman can do to a man?" the old Apache muttered disgustedly. "That white woman has become Lobo Plano's curse, not his blessing. She does not give him a second pair of eyes for him to see. She blinds him! He does things for *her* more than he does for *himself!*"

Jefferson would have debated the issue that Tempest was poison, but he didn't dare to rile Yellowfish any further. Jefferson knew Cord had sworn to avenge Paddy's death. But true, Tempest did seem to be a determining factor in Cord's actions. Jefferson suspected it was a combination of Tempest's influence and long-awaited revenge that motivated his cousin. It seemed to Jefferson that Cord was behaving like a man who had nothing to lose. Cord had always been daring and competent. Perhaps that would give him the winning edge. One could only hope!

"I will find you a docile, obedient Apache woman," Yellowfish said out of the blue. "You will not make the same mistake Lobo Plano has made. No man needs a woman's approval and you will not be bothered with such trouble if you take a loyal Apache wife."

Jefferson grimaced. The old man had taken him under his wing ten years earlier when Cord had brought him along for visits in the mountains. Jefferson had been allowed to learn many of the Apache ways because of his family ties to Cord. Yellowfish had accepted Jefferson as an adopted grandson. Now he was trying to rule Jefferson's life the same way he tried to rule Cord's. Jefferson wondered if Yellowfish was making such preparations because he doubted Cord's return.

The thought hit Jefferson in the belly. He didn't mind the responsibility of looking after Yellowfish, but he cringed at the prospect of losing his only cousin who was more like a brother. Damn it, he shouldn't have sat still for this! But Cord was a man accustomed to doing things his own way. He would never change. Jefferson sure hoped the Apache necklace contained powerful magic and good luck. Cord was going to need all the spiritual assistance he could get!

Twenty

Cord crammed the sombrero down on his forehead to conceal his identity. He had been waiting at High Lonesome Peak for almost an hour for another guard to relieve the lookout. It had been a simple matter for Cord to surprise the first sentinel, who had been doing more sleeping than watching. During the late afternoon, with the bright sun to blind his prey, Cord had struck with swift efficiency. In a matter of minutes, he had left his unsuspecting enemy bound and gagged, wedged between two boulders.

The methodical crunch on the rocks below assured Cord that the second sentinel was about to arrive to take his shift. When the *vaquero* reached up for a helping hand to assist him onto the ledge, Cord accommodated him. One hand clamped onto the *vaquero*'s wrist while the other struck with the butt of his pistol. When his victim teetered on noodly legs, Cord yanked him onto the bluff. Repeating the same procedure, Cord tied the *vaquero* with leather straps and stashed him alongside his cohort.

Satisfied that the first phase of his plan had come off without a hitch, Cord eased off the ledge and ambled toward the bravos' campsite, garbed in the *sarape,* hat, and breeches he had confiscated from his first victim. The sun had ducked behind the mountains as Cord followed the winding trail into the valley overlooking his ranch house. With two of the *vaqueros* out of the way, he had left himself with ten-to-one odds. Not the kind of odds a betting man would eagerly take, but under these circumstances, Cord couldn't afford to be choosy.

This was *his* battle, not Yellowfish's or Jefferson's, and Cord was determined to exclude his grandfather and cousin. Once he got his hands on Emilio Reynosa, the other *vaqueros* would back away for fear of their leader's life—he hoped.

Cord's attention shifted to the second lookout point that stood between him and the camp. Singing a Spanish ballad, he ambled toward the guard who monitored his approach. Thinking Cord was the man who had just been relieved from his watch, the sentinel called to Cord as he ambled down the slope.

"How much longer do you think we'll have to wait on that half-breed?"

"Not long at all, *amigo*—"

Cord came uncoiled like a human spring. The oncoming blow to the jaw took the guard by complete surprise, his head whiplashing from the powerful right-cross. As he staggered back to gain his balance, Cord snatched the rifle from him and swung it like a club. The guard wilted on the spot.

"Nine-to-one odds," Cord declared as he reached into his pocket to fish out another set of leather straps to bind his third victim.

The closer Cord came to the camp, the more intense was his concentration. Now that he had assumed the identity of the most recently relieved guard, he felt certain his appearance would invite no suspicion. He could have a knife at Emilio's throat before the former *Comanchero* knew what had happened. While Cord ambled through the pines toward the clump of men, he heard the drone of voices.

Cord flinched when four seasoned *buscaderos* rushed toward him. But to his relief, the men seemed intent on some other purpose. They darted from one tree to another, remaining within the shelter of the timber as they made their way down the slope.

Cord was grateful for whatever distraction had sent the men scrambling out of camp just before dusk. That narrowed the odds considerably—now it was only five-to-one. Cord couldn't help wondering if Yellowfish and Jefferson had been monitoring his progress and had devised a scheme to distract the men while he pounced on Emilio Reynosa. He had insisted on capturing Emilio alone, but he didn't really mind the distraction, as long as his grandfather and cousin didn't jeopardize their own lives.

Since the horses had been left unattended, Cord detoured away from camp to find them grazing near a thick clump of cedars. If the *vaqueros* tried to give chase after Cord abducted Emilio, they would damn well have to hunt for their steeds or chase down the horses from Cord's roaming herd. That would give Cord valuable time to spirit Emilio away for questioning.

Cord only hoped nothing unforeseeable happened to foil his plans. When he had laid siege to the bandit's hideout near San Solomon Springs, he had been forced to shoot Ellis Flake. He intended to take Emilio alive! The man was a fount of valuable information pertaining to Victor Watts's sinister activities. Cord wanted answers. And by God, this time he'd have them!

Jefferson squinted into the late-evening sunlight from his position in the rocks above the *vaquero*'s camp. "Damn it, who the hell could be riding toward Cord's cabin?"

"I do not know." Yellowfish stared at the lone rider

in the distance. His gaze lingered on the shabbily dressed man on the mule. "Whoever the man is, he is about to meet disaster." He gestured toward the *vaqueros* who had begun to move in from all sides to surround the unsuspecting rider. "He may be seeking refuge at the cabin, but he will not be met by friendly faces."

And sure enough, Yellowfish was right. The man had no sooner swung from his mule than the crack of a rifle shattered the silence of the peaceful valley, echoing around the chasm walls. Yellowfish watched the man bend at the knees and fall facedown in the grass before the four *vaqueros* swarmed around him.

Jefferson glanced grimly at Yellowfish. "The poor bastard never even knew what hit him." His solemn gaze circled back to the *vaquero* camp. "If I know my cousin, he'll be making his move right about now. Although Tosh didn't ask for my assistance, he's getting it nonetheless."

As Jefferson stood up, Yellowfish clutched the younger man's arm, using it as support to gain his own feet. He indicated the clump of brush to the south. "I will take cover in the bushes. You can work your way closer to camp from the north."

Jefferson gave his dark head a shake. "Tosh wouldn't want you to endanger your life for him."

Yellowfish clutched his rifle and drew himself up to proud stature. "My grandson does not grant me all my wishes. Nor will I grant him all of his." Having delivered his parting remark, the old Apache hobbled into the underbrush, ready and willing to protect Cord from whatever danger might arise.

While Jefferson and Yellowfish were silently making their way into position behind the *vaquero* camp, Cord was closing in on his prey. Emilio was far too preoccupied with the commotion near the cabin to notice the disguised man lingering beside him.

"The intruder has been shot," one of the *buscaderos* reported.

"MacIntosh?" Emilio questioned hopefully.

The man shrugged his shoulder. "I do not know yet. I only saw the hombre fall. He is too far away to tell."

When the five men, including Emilio, pivoted, anxiously awaiting their cohorts' return to camp, Cord attacked. His arm shot around Emilio's broad chest, grabbing the pistol on his bandoleer. By the time Emilio could react, Cord's dagger was pricking his throat, warning him not to move a muscle or dare to speak.

Emilio's dark eyes widened in disbelief when he glanced sideways to see the chiseled features of the man who held him at knifepoint. When Emilio daringly opened his mouth to mutter a vulgar curse, Cord drew a drop of blood. He had expected this ruthless cutthroat to bleed ice water, but that was not the case. And although Emilio had no particular concern for the lives of others, he was very partial to his own. He didn't struggle when Cord slowly retreated from the camp, propelling his captive with him.

Cord breathed a sigh of relief as he pulled Emilio back behind the protection of a tree. He shielded himself and his captive from the other *vaqueros* whose backs were turned while they whispered among themselves. Cord could not believe his luck. He had waltzed into camp and abducted Emilio without incident. He was chagrined that some poor fool had ridden to his cabin while the *vaqueros* were waiting like a pack of starved wolves. Cord hadn't seen the rider coming before he inched down from the lookout point. His foremost concern had been disposing of the last guard and dragging Emilio away to answer questions. The sooner he whisked the *vaquero* away, the better. And if his luck held, he and Emilio would be crouched behind a huge boulder before the other men realized they were gone.

Cord tensed when he caught the darting movement out of the corner of his eye, but he relaxed when he saw Jefferson inching forward. Within a few seconds, Jefferson was beside him. He removed the bandoleer from Emilio's chest, leaving the man with no weapons, not even the knife in his boot.

While Jefferson and Cord herded their captive out of the trees and up the slope, Yellowfish held his position in the underbrush. Dark, curious eyes fastened on the unconscious body slung over one of the *vaquero*'s shoulders. Yellowfish frowned pensively when the body was dropped in an unconscious heap. When the *vaqueros* removed the wounded man's hat, murmurs surged through the crowd of men and they hurriedly encircled their victim. Yellowfish scowled. Before the startled group could wheel around to consult their missing leader, Yellowfish backed from the underbrush and hurried toward the boulders where Jefferson and Cord waited with Emilio.

"We must move quickly," Yellowfish urged. "Soon the *vaqueros* will come in search of Reynosa."

Hastily, Cord and Jefferson bound, gagged, and blindfolded Emilio. While the *vaqueros* scattered in all directions, calling Emilio's name, Cord led the way up the steep slope, cautiously remaining within the cover of the trees that jutted out of the cracks in the boulders. He didn't notice the ponderous expression that claimed his grandfather's features until they were safely tucked beneath an overhanging granite ledge. But there was no time to question Yellowfish. Shouts resounded through the grove and silhouettes scattered in the fading twilight.

"Where are we taking Emilio?" Jefferson questioned quietly.

With a wry smile Cord glanced at his cousin.

Jefferson grinned. He knew Cord didn't wish to

divulge their destination, but Jefferson had the feeling he knew where they were going. Although he was aware there was a gold mine somewhere in these rocky summits, he had never been allowed to know the exact location. As a child, he had heard his uncle Paddy relate the tale of how Yellowfish had led him through the winding chasms to the remote cave he had discovered years earlier. It had been the old Apache's gift of continued friendship to his son-in-law.

In turn, Paddy had shared his good fortune with his sister and her family. Paddy's generous donation had gotten the Joneses through rough times and had enabled them to make several improvements at the way station. There were those who believed Paddy had stolen the gold nuggets he traded for livestock, land deeds, and supplies over the years. And there were those who claimed he had discovered the booty buried by Indians or bandits and kept it for himself. Others simply scoffed at those speculations, claiming the old prospector had never found any riches at all, that he had simply earned his wages from travelers who required his assistance as a jack of all trades.

Although Jefferson was itching to know where the fabled cave was, he was still just as curious when he arrived at the site in the cover of darkness. Of course, he had no intention of sneaking back to mine the gold nuggets for himself since the old Apache chief had permitted Paddy and Cord to share the wealth with their family. But all the same, for the sake of curiosity, Jefferson would have liked to say he knew the location.

After Cord had bound Emilio's legs, leaving no possible hope of escape—with the exception of inching across the rocks like a worm—he glanced at his unusually quiet grandfather. Yellowfish was sitting cross-legged at the entrance of the cave, staring into the distance. It had taken only twenty minutes to reach the mine and the old Apache had breathed not one word. Now he sat like a human statue, gazing into the night.

"Is something troubling you, Grandfather?" Cord questioned as he hunkered down beside the aging chief.

Yellowfish was battling his conflicting emotions. He had seen the wild tangle of chestnut hair tumble from beneath the hat when the *vaqueros* unceremoniously dumped their victim in camp. He didn't know where Tempest had acquired the breeches and shirt or why she had trekked toward High Lonesome Peak. For all he knew, she may have been setting a trap, leading the cavalry of buffalo soldiers to Cord. Yellowfish couldn't say for certain if Tempest was dead or alive. To venture back to the camp again would invite more danger. Perhaps it would be best if Cord didn't know. The white woman seemed to have a magical hold on him already.

"Grandfather? I asked you a question and I demand an answer," Cord said impatiently. "I know you too well. There is something on your mind. Now what is it?"

For a full minute, Yellowfish sat immobilized, wrestling with his dilemma. It was true that he owed the feisty white woman his life, though he detested the very thought. She was still trouble. Cord could bring the wrath of the *buscaderos* down upon himself if he dared to return to camp. And what if the white woman had already perished? What purpose would rescuing her serve?

"We have no secrets from each other," Cord murmured. "Tell me what is wrong."

"Keeping silent is wisdom, my son, and speaking is often folly," Yellowfish replied without glancing in Cord's direction. "Your most crucial moments in your enemy's camp were without words. Is that not so?"

"And there are also times, Grandfather, when silence does not save a man from being wrong, but rather from being right. It is wrong for you not to confide in me when I know something is haunting you."

Yellowfish sighed. Cord had hit an exposed nerve. Although the old chief would have preferred to cut out his tongue he knew he would be tormented by the silence. Honesty had always been an Apache tradition, even if it was often painful.

After agonizing deliberation, Yellowfish threw his grandson a glance. "I know the identity of the lone rider who fell beneath the *vaquero*'s rifle."

"You have met him before?" Cord queried, meeting Yellowfish's somber gaze.

Yellowfish nodded his gray head. "It was not a he, as the clothes suggested. It was your white woman."

The quietly spoken words hit Cord like a sledgehammer. "What!" he croaked as he staggered to his feet. Icy terror froze in his chest, sending fingers of aching cold pulsating through his arms and legs. "But how—?" The horrifying thought caused his mind to reel, robbing him of speech.

"I do not know if she survived the rifle shot," Yellowfish continued grimly. "But I think she is where she should remain—for better or worse."

Something inside Cord snapped. His frantic gaze swung across the jagged peaks that separated him from the trees where the *vaqueros* camped. "I've got to go back for her."

Yellowfish clutched Cord's arm before he could pull away. "No, my son. Twice you have walked into the valley of death and twice you have returned unharmed. The Great Spirit has been generous. Do not become reckless in thinking your good fortune will hold. If the white woman did survive her wound, the *vaqueros* will return her to her own people where she belongs. And if she did not—"

Cord flashed his grandfather a look that branded him a traitor. "You should have told me about Tempest long before now." Scowling, he shook his hand loose and dashed back into the cave. The empty ache in the pit of his belly was about to swallow him alive. He couldn't leave Tempest behind, not without knowing what had become of her. Damn it, why had she ventured off alone? What the hell was she doing in men's clothes? And how was he going to live with himself if she died? It was his fault. *His* fault! He had dragged her away, forced her through an ordeal, and brought her to this lowly end. God in heaven! If that blue-eyed beauty perished it would lie on Cord's conscience like a festering boil.

"What's the matter with you?" Jefferson quizzed when Cord dashed into the dark cave. Cord's very stance, framed in the pale light, was cause for alarm. Jefferson swore his cousin was about to come apart at the seams.

"The man the *vaqueros* shot wasn't a man at all," Cord growled in frustration. "It was Tempest."

Jefferson gasped in disbelief. He had seen the lone rider fall and he well remembered thinking the unsuspecting victim hadn't stood a chance. "Oh God . . ."

"I need a horse," Cord growled as he stalked over to yank Emilio to his feet. "I hid the *vaqueros'* mounts in the cedars to the north. Fetch me one."

Jefferson rolled to his feet to stare at his cousin. "What if she's—?"

"Damn it, I have to know," Cord exploded. "I have to try!"

Even the darkness couldn't disguise the frustration that simmered inside Cord. It was in his voice, in the reflection of his eyes, in his rigid stance.

"Yellowfish will lead you back to camp," Cord added after he'd regained a small degree of composure. Cord was so worried about Tempest that he could barely think straight. All he knew was that he had to reach her and every second was critical. "Reynosa got me out of camp and he'll get me back into it. He's my insurance."

Jefferson decided his cousin needed plenty of insurance. There was no way to predict how the other *vaqueros* would react. If they had accidentally killed Tempest, they would lay the blame on Cord, that was for certain. And who could know how loyal those cutthroats would be to their leader? They could easily shoot through Emilio to dispose of Cord, who would probably be blamed for Emilio's death as well. Cord had walked into a death trap once already. Now he was planning to do it again—twice in the same damned day, in fact!

Cord showed no mercy as he dragged the handcuffed and blindfolded Mexican down the treacherous path, not caring how many scrapes and bruises Emilio sustained en route. He couldn't top the rugged peak and scale the boulders quickly enough.

"You better hope Tempest is still alive," Cord sneered at Emilio. "You gave the order to have her shot, and if she dies you will bear the blame, just as surely as if you had squeezed the trigger." His bone-crushing grasp bit into Emilio's arm. "I promise you, Reynosa, if she dies you will know every method of Apache torture. I'll hear you beg me to kill you before I'm through with you."

By the time Cord had descended the perilous slopes, he had worked himself into a crazed fury. He was annoyed with Yellowfish for delaying telling him the truth and vindictive toward Reynosa, who had given the order to shoot to kill without even knowing the identity of his victim. He was also exasperated that it was taking Jefferson so damned long to return with a horse! He'd better not have run into complications. That's the last thing they needed right now!

"Don't you dare die, Tempest," Cord muttered as

her face rose in his mind to torment him. He squeezed his eyes shut and prayed to the white man's God and to the Apache's Great Spirit. Tempest had to be alive, because if she wasn't . . .

The plodding of hooves heralded Jefferson and Yellowfish's approach. Cord's head swiveled to see two riders zigzagging through the brush.

"Curse it, I said *one* horse," Cord scowled when his grandfather reined the steed to a halt.

"I will come with you," Yellowfish declared in a tone that brooked no argument. "You will need me to carry the white woman out of camp."

"I'll go in his place," Jefferson volunteered.

"No," Yellowfish insisted. "You will wait with your rifle ready if the Mexicans decide to open fire." He made a stabbing gesture into Emilio's chest. "And he will be your first target. If we do not come out alive, this man will not, either."

Cord opened his mouth to object to Yellowfish's demand, but the words died on his lips when he met the old chief's stony expression. The moonlight shone across Yellowfish's wrinkled features, which looked as if they were carved from rock. It had taken great courage for the old Apache to reveal the truth about Tempest since he had no wish for her to be part of Cord's destiny again. But now Yellowfish felt obligated to repay his debt—one life for another. The Apache code of honor was strong, even when a man didn't necessarily like what he felt he must do.

"Do not expect too much," Yellowfish cautioned while Cord forced Emilio into the saddle and swung up behind him. "Sometimes hope is not enough."

Cord grimaced at the words. He couldn't bring himself to consider the possibility that Tempest had died. And although hope wasn't always enough, as Yellowfish warned, it was still all Cord had. He wasn't abandoning that, even when Tempest's future—or lack thereof—looked pitch-black . . .

Twenty-one

Difficult though it was, Cord schooled his face into an impassive expression, revealing none of the turmoil that raged in him. He rode toward the *vaquero* camp, using Emilio as his shield. The dagger pressed against the Mexican's throat, just as it had earlier. Behind Cord, tall and proud in the saddle, rode Yellowfish. The old Apache had flatly refused to exchange places with Cord. In Yellowfish's estimation, Cord would be the primary target of gunfire. As long as Cord was protected by Emilio's bulky frame, he would be reasonably safe . . . or at least as safe as a man could get riding straight into the jaws of hell!

A flood of muffled Spanish broke the silence as the small procession rode boldly into camp. Cord's gaze was riveted on the wan features of the woman who lay beside the campfire. Fresh bloodstains saturated her clothing, which she had obviously confiscated from Bones Henderson. The homespun garments looked like those the older man had worn. A noticeable bump marred Tempest's forehead, suggesting she had struck a rock when she had fallen forward after being bushwhacked.

Cord had to force himself to concentrate on the congregation gathered in front of him. The sight of Tempest lying so motionless, so deathly pale, knocked him for a loop. She looked as if she were barely alive. Cord soundly cursed these bastards who had done nothing to save her. It was as if they were waiting for her to breathe her last so they could dispose of her . . .

The torment put a murderous scowl on Cord's face and he held his agony in check by pricking Emilio's throat with the dagger, just so the vicious Mexican would have some idea of the misery Cord was experiencing.

"We have come for the woman," Cord growled in fluent Spanish. "If you dare to make one move to stop us, Reynosa will die." Flickering golden eyes circled the grim-faced group. "Take a message to Victor Watts. Tell him I will come for him, but I will not abide by the white man's laws that he has twisted to suit his purposes. I will come as an Apache. Watts will understand what I mean."

Boldly, Yellowfish swung from the saddle and limped directly toward the cluster of men who formed a semicircle around Tempest. Cord tensed. He could see the darting glances of the *vaqueros* who were trying to decide whether to open fire or hold their position. Cord had purposely left Emilio blindfolded and gagged so the leader couldn't send any signals to his men . . .

Cord caught the slight movement of Rafael Sandoval, who was partially concealed by the men on either side of him. Rafael was inching his hand toward his holster. The glint of the pistol's silver barrel sent adrenaline pumping through Cord's veins. With lightning speed, Cord hurled his dagger, catching Rafael in his shooting arm. The pistol exploded, sending dirt splattering at the horse's hooves, forcing Cord to wrestle with the startled animal to hold his position. But even as the steed shifted in alarm, Cord reined him back and retrieved his Colt. Emilio tried to hurl himself off the horse, but Cord gave him a quick thump on the head. With a dull groan, Emilio slumped against Cord's chest.

In those crucial seconds while Cord was trying to keep a tight grasp on Emilio and provide cover for Yellowfish, another bold *vaquero* tried to pick Cord off his horse. Two pistols exploded and Cord instinctively ducked away from the whistling bullet that missed his shoulder by mere inches. Cord's shot, however, hit its mark. The daring *vaquero* staggered back, clutching his chest.

When Cord tried to steady Emilio, whose limp body had rolled sideways during the gunplay, the blast of a rifle exploded in the air. Cord flinched when he spied the gleaming pistol that belonged to another *vaquero*. But the hombre dropped to his knees, unable to fire because Jefferson's aim was as good as his eyesight.

Cord didn't know where the hell Jefferson was, but his marksmanship had come in handy. He had moved into position to scatter buckshot at the daring *buscaderos*. Thanks to Jefferson, no one else dared to confront Cord.

Cord was amazed by his grandfather's unwavering courage in the face of adversity. The old chief had moved ahead, despite the blazing bullets. He knelt beside Tempest to ascertain her condition. When the gunfire ended, he scooped up the lifeless form and wobbled to his feet.

Cord glanced from Tempest's pale features to his grandfather's bleak expression. A coil of terror constricted Cord's chest when the old Apache shook his head sadly and stared down at the limp body in his arms. With considerable effort, Yellowfish lifted Tempest over his horse into a jackknifed position. When he had seated himself, he reined the horse away, leaving Cord to back out of camp with his prisoner lying over his arm.

The instant they reached the giant boulders that

rimmed the edge of the canyon, Cord shoved Emilio to the ground and leapt from the horse to pull Tempest into his arms. He could barely feel the pulse in her throat, and the thought of losing her forever terrified him. She looked as if she were dead to the world—literally—and that scared the hell out of him. Like a small child clinging to security, Cord clutched Tempest to him, willing her to live.

"It will require strong medicine to revive her," Yellowfish murmured. "Already, she communicates with the spirits." He slid to the ground and handed his reins to Jefferson. "I will collect the ingredients for a potion while you remove the bullet."

When Yellowfish disappeared into the night, Cord followed the narrow path to the cave. Jefferson trailed along behind him, leading Emilio who had roused to consciousness when Cord let him drop to the ground like a rock.

"Tempest?" Cord whispered against her waxen cheek. "Can you hear me?"

He was met with a silence that tore his heart in two.

When Cord reached the cave, he gently laid Tempest on the floor and sat there shaking while Jefferson tied Emilio to a tree outside and then gathered firewood. Although Cord held Tempest's hand, she gave no indication that she knew he was beside her. She simply lay there, hovering on the border between life and death, leaving Cord to bemoan his inability to reach out and bring her back from the cold darkness that engulfed her.

Once Jefferson had set the small fire ablaze near the entrance of the cave, Cord reflexively reached for his dagger and cursed the fact that he'd been forced to use it against the trigger-happy Rafael Sandoval.

"Here, Tosh," Jefferson murmured, offering his cousin his own knife. "What do you want me to do?"

Cord passed the blade over the curling flames of the fire before he glanced at his cousin. "Fetch the canteen, your stock of whiskey, and pray . . .

"I've been doing that since you rode into camp," Jefferson answered. "I hadn't planned on stopping yet."

While Jefferson bustled around, boiling water and tearing strips from his extra clothes to serve as bandages, Cord unbuttoned Tempest's shirt. A grimace tightened his lips when he spied the oozing wound that lay dangerously close to her heart. Tempest had barely missed death. Cord wanted to scream in frustration and grief, but he feared the sound would divulge their location to the *vaqueros.*

With his jaw clenched, he dripped whiskey over the wound. The fact that Tempest didn't wince was less than encouraging. She was so oblivious that even the burning pain of the whiskey didn't faze her.

Beads of perspiration popped out on Cord's brow as he began to use the knife as a scalpel. During the war, he had been forced to employ his meager surgical techniques for the other prisoners of war who had been neglected, and later, on the Union soldiers with whom he rode. He found himself far more emotionally involved now than he had been then. In Spanish and Apache, Cord soundly cursed the man who had fired the shot that had entered Tempest's flesh.

It seemed to take hours to dig out the bullet and Cord swore colorfully when the probing blade struck a second pellet of buckshot. The fact that there was more than one slug forced him to probe even deeper to be sure he hadn't overlooked another fragment. God, if Tempest did manage to survive, she would be unbearably sore, Cord predicted. He hadn't had time to be gentle since she had already lost so much blood.

Damn those *vaqueros!* How could they let her lie

there for over an hour without making an effort to save her? Their lack of concern could easily cost Tempest her life. He should have shot every last one of them!

"I hope Aunt Myra thought to stash thread in that first aid kit of yours," Cord grumbled to Jefferson.

Jefferson placed the needle and thread in Cord's trembling hand and glanced down at the ragged wound just below Tempest's left shoulder. "You know Ma. She's very organized and thorough," he replied for lack of much else to say.

Gritting his teeth, Cord performed his last surgical duty and cursed his lack of ability. When he had made the stitches and dressed the wound, he slumped back to guzzle the whiskey Jefferson offered him.

In gloomy silence, Yellowfish hobbled into the cave with his supply of roots, berries, leaves, and cactus. One glance at Tempest's death-like mask spurred Yellowfish to action. Hurriedly, he ground the ingredients together and set them above the fire to brew. While he waited, he limped over to remove the magical pouch from Cord's neck. After Yellowfish sprinkled the spirit magic in the bubbling poultice, Cord retrieved the necklace and laid it around Tempest's throat.

Several minutes later, Yellowfish stirred the potion and removed the dressing from the wound. Once he had applied the healing salve he propped himself against the stone wall. His gaze lingered on the leaping fingers of the fire, remembering the day he had prepared himself to meet the Great Spirit after he had suffered serious battle wounds.

"Now we must wait," he murmured. "The Great Spirit will decide if the white woman will live or die."

Cord hated the thought of having no control over the situation. He detested not being able to do anything more to help Tempest. To sit there and wait was pure and simple hell. He couldn't do it; he *refused* to do it. If Tempest was to perish, even after his attempt at primitive surgery, then she would die secure and protected in his arms.

Consumed by that thought, Cord stretched out beside her, cradling her against him. He wanted to relieve her pain and provide comfort. He longed to offer his strength when she had none left to battle the dark angel of death.

Yellowfish peered at his grandson who was whispering quiet consolation in feathery kisses. He almost wished he had spared Cord the torment of watching the white woman die in his arms. There were times when a man was better off not knowing what fate had in store. If Yellowfish had kept silent, Cord would never have known Tempest lay unconscious in the *vaqueros'* camp. Now Cord was forced to suffer right along with her.

Gesturing for Jefferson to double-check their hostage, Yellowfish limped outside to sleep beside the cave. Cord needed no companionship while he was completely absorbed in the woman who lay lifelessly in his arms. There were some things a man had to face alone. This ordeal was one that Cord had undertaken—now he had to face the consequences of bringing Tempest with him.

Cord was certainly enduring all the torments of hell as he cuddled Tempest's body against him for added warmth and support. The sight of her released invisible tentacles that wrapped around his bleeding heart, squeezing the life out of him. It hounded him to see this vivacious, high-spirited beauty lying so still. One moment he cursed her for daring to venture to his cabin; the next second he was cursing *himself* for cursing *her* when she was so dangerously close to death.

He couldn't help but wonder what brought Tempest back. Had the outlaw gang escaped? Had something happened to Bones Henderson and Ricochet Wilson? Those clowns were supposed to be carting Tempest to Fort Davis, for God's sake! The fact that this novice trailblazer had even found his cabin beneath High Lonesome Peak was no small feat. Just her luck she had reached her destination, only to be cut down by an assassin's bullet that was meant for him!

Cord inched far enough away to stare into Tempest's beautiful but frail-looking features. His index finger trailed over her blue-tinged lips, remembering the way she had been, rather than dwelling on the way she was now. A chain of burning memories encircled him and he hoarded them, as if each were priceless. He could almost see those lively blue eyes flashing with temper, her chest heaving with indignation when he taunted her. And even more vividly did he recall those moments of terror that claimed her features when she was left to balance upon some lofty perch, fighting her fear of falling. She was falling now—falling into a deep, dark, silent chasm where she could find no direction or purpose . . .

Reverently, Cord bent to graze her unresponsive lips in a kiss that offered her the breath of life and the will to survive against all odds. His hand absently flowed over her hip, bringing her full length against him. Ah, of all the things he remembered about this feisty nymph, the spark of passion they ignited in each other was foremost. They had always made love as if each splendorous moment would be their last . . .

The haunting thought brought a mist of tears. He couldn't remember feeling quite so desolate since his mother's death those long years ago. He had suffered another emotional blow when he learned that he'd lost his father. But the threat of losing this sassy goddess was killing him, bit by excruciating bit. Cord could barely tolerate the thought of never again gazing into those captivating blue eyes. It left him feeling empty inside, as if he were watching part of himself hang on by a single thread.

"Don't leave me, princess," he whispered before his mouth descended upon hers. "You'll take the sun and moon if you go. My world will be as black as this cave. Ah, Tempest, why prove my innocence if I must forfeit your life? Come back to me, Tempest. I need you with me . . .

The quiet sounds that wafted from the cavern caused Yellowfish to shift uneasily on his pallet. He could feel Cord's pain pricking his own heart like cactus needles, and yet Yellowfish was torn by his own feelings about Tempest.

"I know you don't have much regard for the woman," Jefferson whispered to Yellowfish. "But I think Tosh truly loves her. You should have seen him while he was operating, wishing for medical skills he didn't possess, feeling her pain, stricken with sorrow and regret. I've never seen him like that before, and never with a woman."

"He shoulders all the blame," Yellowfish observed. "He is only bedeviled by her beauty and fiery spirit. She could have been setting a trap for him, awaiting the buffalo soldiers from the fort. You are too much like him, Jefferson. You do not look beneath her beauty to see the poison, either."

Jefferson snorted at the stubborn Apache. Yellowfish had decided not to like Tempest for whatever reason and so he didn't. "It is her spirited nature that offends you then? Just because she is not easily subdued is no cause for contempt. If she wasn't married to Tosh, I'd be fiercely attracted to her myself. She is a rare breed, Yellowfish."

"And if she lives she will be your woman," Yellowfish grunted. "She is *your* breed, not my grandson's. He is too much Apache to be white."

"And what if Tosh really loves her?" Jefferson countered.

"He does not. He wants only the pleasure a woman's body can offer a man," the old Apache insisted adamantly. "Now he feels regret and responsibility for her plight. That is all, Jefferson. That is all it will ever be. I know my grandson. He will never be a slave to any woman."

Jefferson reckoned he could argue until he was blue in the face and it wouldn't change Yellowfish's mind. The old chief and Tempest had clashed a number of times. Yellowfish had said so himself. His Indian beliefs had been entrenched for seventy years. He had forced himself to accept Paddy MacIntosh as his son-in-law, most reluctantly at first, or so the story went. But in time Yellowfish had come to like the Scotsman. Unfortunately, the old Apache may never have the chance to appreciate Tempest if she didn't live . . .

Scowling at the thought, Jefferson tucked himself into his bedroll and begged for sleep. He almost hated to see dawn come sliding over the ridges, clearing away its deep purple shadows. He feared it would bring with it the worst possible news. Jefferson had seen Tempest's wound. In his estimation, it would take a miracle for her to survive.

"What the devil do you mean you lost my daughter?" Abraham Litchfield raged as he paced back and forth across the commander's quarters at Fort Davis.

Bones scratched his head and frowned, trying to explain himself as best he could. "Well, judge, I woke up this mornin' and she just wasn't where we put her the night before."

Abraham lurched around to glare at the unkempt prospector-turned-bounty-hunter. Damn, this ordeal was destined to turn his hair white. "Do you mean to say you think that renegade sneaked back into camp and abducted her again?"

"We don't mean to say nothin' of the kind," Ricochet piped up when Bones wilted beneath Abraham's ferocious glare. "Last night yer daughter was itchin' to know how far it was to the garrison. We just s'posed she was so eager to see ya that she took her mule and trotted off, hopin' to be intercepted by the soldiers that have been searchin' for her. Maybe the Comanche found her. Them and the Apache got trails all over these here mountains. So do them renegade Mexican outlaws. They ransacked this very fort when it was abandoned durin' the war, ya know. Yer daughter coulda met up with just about anybody 'round here."

Abraham broke into muted curses while he wore ruts in the braided rug. He was ready to tear out his hair. After wandering around the fort beside Limpia Creek for more than a week, he felt the need to go . . . somewhere . . . anywhere!

"Commander, I want some of your guards to accompany me to El Paso," Abraham demanded of the pudgy officer lounging at his desk, puffing on his cigar.

"Whatever you say, judge." The commander levered himself out of his chair. "What do you want me to do with these bandits the bounty hunters brought in? Or are you taking them with you?"

"Stash them in the stockade for safekeeping," Abraham instructed as he dug into his wallet. "We'll pay these bounty hunters off now and I'll let the state reimburse me later." He flung Bones and Ricochet a dour look. "I shudder at the thought of leaving these outlaws in their custody. They'll probably lose them the same way they lost my daughter!"

After delivering the parting insult, Abraham stalked toward his quarters to gather his gear. A more unlikely pair of bounty hunters Abraham had never seen. And if a man was no good at bounty hunting then what the devil was he good for? Damn it, how could they have lost Tempest? Or had she simply tromped off on her own, just to rid herself of those two buffoons? Tempest had never been particularly tolerant of men. As companions and guides, Bones and Ricochet left a lot to be desired. Poor Tempest. What a horrible ordeal. There was no telling what had become of her now. She could have traded one unbearable situation for another simply because of her impatience.

Abraham prayed his daughter was safe from harm. If she wasn't, he didn't know what the hell he was going to do. This *not knowing* was driving him mad!

Twenty-two

With extreme reluctance, Cord roused from slumber and opened his eyes to stare into the ashen face that had haunted his dreams. It had been two days since his meager attempt at surgery. Each day that dawned found Cord thanking his lucky stars that Tempest was still alive. He had lain beside her, keeping constant vigil, bathing her in cool water when her fever raged, and speaking to her when she was as still and silent as the grave. But nothing changed her critical condition. Cord was filled with so much despair that he was on the verge of giving up hope . . .

"I prepared us some breakfast." Jefferson ambled into the cave, carrying two tin plates. "Yellowfish chose to fix his own meal and eat outside. He says this white man's cooking doesn't agree with him." He glanced down at Tempest. "Any change, Tosh?"

Cord sat up cross-legged and accepted the plate. "She's the same," he reported dully.

"So is Emilio," Jefferson snorted. "I've been pumping him with questions for two days and he's spit in my face four times. That Mexican has no inclination whatsoever to admit he had anything to do with Paddy's death."

"Maybe you aren't using the right methods of

persuasion," Cord grumbled between bites. "Emilio is an ex-*Comanchero*. He's lived hard. Questions won't loose his tongue."

"That's what Yellowfish said, but I refused to let him have a go at Emilio. Considering the mood Yellowfish has been in the past few days, I'm afraid he'll cut the Mexican into bite-size pieces before we get a confession out of him. And yet, starving Emilio into submission didn't work, either. He just fainted from lack of water and nourishment so I'd have to feed him to keep him alive."

Jefferson shook his head, sighed, and went on. "I'm not getting anywhere with that tough Mexican. And when Yellowfish spied the buffalo soldiers swarming around your cabin. I had to gag Emilio before he yelled his head off. We have to get moving, Tosh. This place is jumping with cavalry, bounty hunters, and *vaqueros.* We can't stay here much longer. They might spot us."

Cord arched a thick brow and grinned for the first time in days. "Would you have found this cave if we hadn't led you to it?"

"Well, no, but somebody might accidentally stumble onto it," Jefferson argued.

"I wouldn't be so sure, cuz," Cord parried. "The angles and shadows in these mountains vary continuously during the day. These peaks look essentially the same with their piles of rocks and dark, hollowed-out niches. Even if one of the soldiers spotted us, he'd have one helluva time retracing his steps with reinforcements. A man has to feel his way to this cave to locate the small opening. I lost the direction a half-dozen times myself in early years, even when my grandfather had brought me here a score of times."

"Yellowfish wants to leave," Jefferson declared, glancing in Tempest's direction. "And I don't think it's because of the buffalo soldiers in the valley. He's had a difficult time accepting the fact that you have devoted the past two days to the *white woman,* as he insists on calling her. He thinks you care too much and that rankles the Apache in him."

Yellowfish was one hundred percent Apache, to be sure. That was the problem. Cord found himself in a mental conflict, torn between his desire to keep Tempest alive and his respect for his grandfather. But this bullheaded stubbornness had to stop! Yellowfish was purposely keeping his distance to emphasize the point that he didn't particularly like Tempest. Neither did the old Apache approve of the fact that they had tarried so long at the mine.

When an Apache was crippled or severely wounded, it was understood that the feeble would remain behind for the good of the tribe, never slowing the others down and endangering their lives. When Yellowfish was critically wounded, he had remained behind to die, as was the custom. His daughter had dutifully stayed to tend him. In time he would have died, if Paddy MacIntosh hadn't come along to nurse the ailing chief back to health. Now it was the white woman who impeded progress. Yellowfish had made only a token effort to help Tempest by preparing a poultice for her wound. But he had made no attempt to try any of his other healing ointments on her. It was high time Cord confronted his grandfather, as distasteful as that would probably be. But damn it, Cord wasn't leaving Tempest to die—as was the Apache custom—and that was all there was to it!

Cord handed Jefferson the smelly potion. "Change the bandage and put fresh salve on the wound while I speak to my grandfather," he requested.

"I'd rather not," Jefferson said with a grimace. "I can barely stand to see her like this!"

Cord turned and glared at his suddenly squeamish

cousin. His hard expression didn't invite translation in English, Spanish, or Apache.

"Oh, all right," Jefferson muttered. "And while you're out there, try your hand with Emilio. He certainly won't confess a damned thing to me."

When Cord emerged from the cave and squinted to adjust to the bright light, he found Yellowfish sitting Indian-style on a boulder. He was hurling marble-size pebbles at Emilio, who was tethered to a juniper tree, cursing under his gag.

"I would like a word with you," Cord demanded.

Yellowfish continued launching his missiles at their captive. "Then speak."

"I prefer privacy," Cord insisted. "Will you walk with me, Grandfather?"

Disgruntled, Yellowfish tossed one last pebble at Emilio and eased off his rock. In silence, he led Cord around the sheer face of the limestone mountain to the lofty point overlooking the fertile valley. Riders dotted the distant countryside like a colony of ants trailing out of their hill.

"I want you to work your Apache magic on Tempest," Cord demanded as he stepped in front of his grandfather.

"She is white," Yellowfish reminded him. "You used the white man's medicine on her and I gave you the Apache poultice. I have done all I can do."

"No, you haven't," Cord contradicted. "You don't like Tempest and that is as bad as casting an evil spell. I want her to live."

Yellowfish crossed his arms over his chest and stood with his feet apart, refusing to budge. "She has brought you nothing but trouble."

Cord shook his raven head. "*I* brought *her* trouble. She brings *me* happiness."

"An Apache wife would bring you far more pleasure," Yellowfish said with a snort. "You have risked your life time and again for this white woman, attempting to win her approval and her trust. Even if she survives she will never be one of us, and you can never be one of them, even with the Scottish in you. You are Apache, Lobo Plano. She is white. I will take her to the buffalo soldiers and they will tend her."

"No!" Cord replied disrespectfully, causing his grandfather to jerk up his head in offended dignity. "You came to accept my father and he was white. Now you will accept Tempest."

Yellowfish's obsidian eyes glittered in ill-disguised annoyance. "I accepted Paddy MacIntosh because he was much like the Apache who respects the Earth Mother and gives to her without demanding so much in return. And he was also a man—a man who understood and accepted the way of The People. But I will not accept this white woman—ever!"

Cord took a threatening step forward and spoke with a stern tone that he had never dared to use with his grandfather. "We are coming to an understanding once and for all about Tempest. She is my wife. Her misery is mine and so is her pain. I brought her with me to the mountains against her will and she has suffered too many hardships already because of me. I want her to live and I will not leave the cave without her. And just as my mother remained behind the tribe to watch over you, then so shall I attend her. *I* will be her eyes when *she* cannot see, her strength when *she* cannot move."

"That is a woman's duty, not a man's," Yellowfish scoffed. "Will you become a squaw just because of this white woman? Will you no longer be a man?"

"Will you refuse to help Tempest when you know that in essence it is *I* whom you are refusing to help? *I*—your own flesh and blood?" He met his grandfather's infuriated glare. "Do not make me choose between the two of you. I know in time I will have to send her back to her own world. But for now I want her with me. I want her to know that I am a man of

Apache honor, that I am innocent of the crimes against me. What she thinks matters to me and it always will, even when she returns to her people. Do you understand me?"

Yellowfish tilted his chin a notch higher and looked away—stubborn to the end.

"She matters to me—white and Apache," Cord emphasized. "It's the woman she *is* that lures me, not her race or creed. What good will it be if I am exonerated if sacrificing *her* life is the price I have to pay? If she dies because of what I've put her through, I will only be half a man, plagued by my conscience, my sense of what's right, my sense of honor!"

Yellowfish lurched around and stalked back toward the cave. "If you insist on prolonging the pain, then so be it," he said over his shoulder with a disgruntled glare. "But do not expect pity from me when the time comes to release her—*if* she survives at all. You will regret your decision either way, Lobo Plano."

Cord rolled his eyes skyward after his grandfather disappeared. For the life of him, he couldn't figure out why Yellowfish was being so damned contrary. But at least the old chief had finally consented to try his hand at reviving Tempest, begrudging though he most certainly was.

Caramba! Sometimes Yellowfish acted so much like Tempest it was uncanny. Of course, Cord wouldn't dare voice that observation to Yellowfish. The old Apache would throw a ring-tailed fit and never forgive Cord for what he would see as the ultimate insult.

One day soon, Cord intended to sit Yellowfish down and try to get to the bottom of this animosity toward Tempest. He couldn't tell what was really troubling the old man. Why had he refused to open his heart and give Tempest a chance? Cord would dearly like to know what terrible secret the old chief harbored in his soul. It must be so deeply embedded that Yellowfish refused to speak of it. From the look of things, the old Apache was talking circles around his emotions, and sooner or later they would push their way to the surface, Cord assured himself. He would just have to have a little patience. A little patience was about all he had left! And curse it, Tempest's desperate condition wasn't doing *his* disposition one damned bit of good, either!

Yellowfish stalked into the cave, flapping his arms like a crow. "Leave, Jefferson," he ordered brusquely. "I will tend the white woman." He glanced at the leftovers on the tin plates. "And take the white man's scraps with you."

He limped around the cave, making expansive gestures with his arms, as if to shoo the evil spirits away. "Bring me the sap from a strong, healthy mesquite tree. And I need hot coals from the juniper tree, roots from the bittersweet vine. Cactus thorns and roots—and willow leaves," he added in afterthought.

Smothering an amused grin, Jefferson rose to his feet and strode outside to fetch the ingredients. It was obvious that Yellowfish had come to the cave under protest. He didn't want to help Tempest any more now than he had that first night she'd been wounded.

Within a half hour, Jefferson returned with the supplies. Although some white folks scoffed at Indian remedies, Jefferson and Cord did not. In fact, they knew perfectly well that some of the white man's medicine was derived from ancient Indian remedies. They had seen the results of nature's cures and had occasionally become the beneficiaries of Yellowfish's ministrations. To the Apache's way of thinking, the Great Spirit had provided all things for The People.

Cactus roots were prepared for treatment against gangrene. Willow leaves could be brewed into tea to help reduce fever. Bittersweet roots, added to willow leaves for tea, helped restore bodily functions after illnesses. Mesquite sap was boiled to form a healing balm that cleansed open wounds. Juniper coals were used to cauterize infected wounds . . .

Jefferson grimaced at the thought of having Tempest undergo that painful process. No doubt Cord would refuse to be on hand during that phase, too. He'd had enough difficulty performing the surgery. Jefferson swore his cousin had suffered right alongside Tempest. It hadn't been a pleasant experience for Jefferson, either!

While Yellowfish was preparing his potions, teas, and salves, Jefferson frowned curiously. "I know what you plan to do with all your ingredients except the cactus needles. What purpose do they serve, Yellowfish?"

Irritably, Yellowfish brushed Jefferson aside since he was standing in the light, directing Jefferson's attention toward the swollen knot on Tempest's forehead. "The thorns are used to prick her head, leaving her to bleed and relieve the pressure. Her head wound prevents her from rousing to consciousness. My grandson should have known that, but he has been too absorbed in his own feelings to think like an Apache medicine man."

"Prick her head?" Jefferson choked before turning away. "Dear God!" On that frightening thought, Jefferson scurried outside to see Cord employ some of his most persuasive tactics to loosen Emilio's tongue.

The blow Cord had leveled to Emilio's belly forced most of the air from his lungs. He had just enough energy left to hiss an insult.

"Half-breed bastard," Emilio seethed, sucking in a ragged breath.

Cord came unwound like a striking snake with another body-jarring blow to Emilio's underbelly. If nothing else, Cord was exacting his own revenge. Emilio had tied him up and beat him to a pulp before carting him to the El Paso jail. But Cord had a long way to go before he got close to even—Emilio was still conscious. Cord hadn't been when he was dropped in the foul-smelling cell and left to endure Juan Tijerina's vicious lashes.

With a menacing snarl, Cord yanked Emilio up by the lapels and breathed down his neck. "Who gave the order to have me framed? And who killed my father and the livestock?"

Emilio skewed up his mouth to spit in Cord's face. That was a mistake. Cord responded with a meaty fist to the jaw, sending stars circling around Emilio's dizzy brain. Then Cord spit in *his* face.

"Answer me, Mexican swine!" Cord snarled, giving the dazed Emilio a fierce shake that sent his throbbing head snapping backward.

"Go to hell, half-breed," Emilio spat out, only to be backhanded and left to fall backward, tripping over his own rope-bound feet.

Like an enraged grizzly, Cord loomed over his fallen prey. There were times Cord could show a casual brand of menace, but this wasn't one of them. He was deadly when his fury was aroused to such an intense degree. His tawny eyes glittered with loathing and his chiseled features were frozen in a dangerous expression that caused Jefferson to retreat a pace, even though he wasn't on the receiving end of that killing glare.

"Mexican bastard," Cord spat back, his massive chest heaving with barely controlled rage. "You scorned the Indians and yet you made your living off them as a *Comanchero*. You raped their women and offered them bad whiskey so you could steal back the supplies and rifles you sold them."

Mercilessly, Cord stuffed his moccasined foot in Emilio's belly, causing his enemy to scream in misery. "And then you signed on with Victor Watts to do his dirty work," Cord muttered contemptuously. "You helped spread rumors about me and my father, and when we wouldn't sell out to Victor and move to a place where no one knew us, you set out to destroy us any way you could, didn't you?" The question was punctuated with a jab of the heel to Emilio's already-bruised chin.

"You son of a bitch," Emilio ground out from the side of his mouth that wasn't quite so swollen.

"I've been called worse by better men than you," Cord scoffed.

"Apache pig!" Emilio snarled hatefully.

To that, Cord replied with a doubled fist to Emilio's left eye. The same eye, in fact, that Emilio had blackened for Cord during their last confrontation before reaching El Paso's jail. Of course, Emilio still looked and felt ten times better than Cord had when he'd been tossed in his cell. His own father had barely recognized him when he'd come for his first and only visit.

When Cord had been forced to endure similar beatings, he hadn't succumbed easily. He didn't expect Emilio to, either. This was only the beginning for the ex-*Comanchero*. Emilio had meted out far worse punishment. Now the time had come for the Mexican to taste his own medicine *and* his own blood.

With the swiftness of a tiger, Cord latched onto Emilio and jerked him up on noodly legs. "This one's for Tempest," he jeered as he reared back a meaty fist, allowing Emilio to see exactly what was coming. "You better pray she lives. She will be the only one in this camp who'd ever try to stop me from killing you."

Cord directed a blow to Emilio's cheek with

enough wallop to fell a polar bear. Emilio dropped to his knees and fell onto his belly, gasping for breath.

"Breakfast, Emilio?" Cord taunted as he set a plate of scraps just out of his reach, forcing him to crawl like a worm if he wanted to eat. "You can expect to be treated in the same manner you and Juan Tijerina treated me . . ."

Cord's frosty voice trailed off when he heard an eardrum-shattering scream echoing around the cavern. The haunting sound almost knocked Cord to *his* knees. For a moment he stood immobilized, feeling icicles forming on his spine. Even Emilio blanched at the bloodcurdling screech that never seemed to end. Jefferson paled considerably as his gaze darted to the dark entrance of the cave.

But things got worse instead of better. Another howling cry split the air and Cord felt as if a knife had been twisted in his gut. All he could think of was that Yellowfish was applying Apache torture rather than medical treatment. The terrible sound of Tempest's torment went right through him, leaving his nerves jangling like high-pitched bells.

Cord swung about and charged toward the cavern with frantic haste. The sight of Yellowfish bending over Tempest with flaming coals lashed to a green willow branch stopped him dead in his tracks. The smell of seared flesh permeated the air and Cord's haunted gaze landed on the blackened wound before darting to the trickles of blood streaming over Tempest's eyes and cheeks.

Like a madman he launched himself forward, practically shoving his grandfather out of the way to enfold Tempest protectively in his arms. "I asked you to save her, not torture her!" Cord growled disdainfully.

Shock registered on Yellowfish's wrinkled features when his grandson stared at him with such blatant disgust. Cord had coiled up with Tempest's limp body clutched to his chest, as if protecting her from an evil spirit.

"I had to sear the wound against infection," Yellowfish said as he pulled himself into a standing position.

"Was that before or after you decided to scalp her?" Cord muttered sarcastically. His hand absently drifted over Tempest's face, wiping away the blood that stained her brow and cheeks.

Yellowfish muttered several rude remarks in Apache before switching back to English. "I had to lance the goose egg on her head. If you had not been so overwrought with sympathy for the white woman you would have remembered to do so yourself."

Still grumbling at his grandson's total lack of respect, Yellowfish dipped up the bittersweet tea and pressed it to Tempest's trembling lips. "You have walked with the White Eyes too long, Lobo Plano. You are beginning to act like one. I did what had to be done. It was *your* request."

Straightening up, Yellowfish loomed over Cord who was still huddled in the corner like a child clutching his most cherished possession. The sight sent a stab of frustration into Yellowfish's heart. With a grunt, he turned around and limped out of the cave.

When Cord was left alone, he grabbed a cloth to cleanse Tempest's face. He constantly whispered words of consolation. She was weak and trembly and every bit as pale as she had been that first night. But her breathing was stronger, though still erratic. He could feel her flinch involuntarily, as if she were reliving the painful ordeal Yellowfish had put her through. Ever so gently, Cord applied the poultice his grandfather had concocted.

Cord froze when Tempest winced. He knew the salve burned through her semiconscious mind like the fires of hell—which was exactly where Cord felt he was at the moment. He'd have ten times rather tolerated another of Emilio's beatings or Juan Tijerina's floggings than watch Tempest suffer. And she *was* suffering, even if she hadn't roused enough to realize how much pain she was in.

"Tempest . . ." Cord murmured against her clammy cheek. His hand closed around hers, giving it a gentle squeeze. "Open your eyes, princess. Look at me."

Cord heard a yelp and glanced toward the mouth of the cave.

A few seconds later, Jefferson poked his head inside. "That was Yellowfish giving Emilio a swift kick in the most sensitive part of his anatomy," he explained and then grinned wryly. "I think he would have liked to kick you for lashing out at him, but he let Emilio have it instead." His smile evaporated when he saw Tempest's pallid face. "Has she awakened yet?"

When Tempest moaned weakly and her lashes fluttered up, Cord forgot about Jefferson, Yellowfish, and Emilio. He gave Tempest his absolute attention, even though she was peering up at him with a blank stare that went right through him. But at that moment, it was as if he himself had come back to life, as if the sun had emerged from a great gray cloud.

Cord looked down into those sapphire pools and felt his heart begin to beat again after it had languished in his chest like a ton of lead for more than three days. The mere sight of those eyes smoothed every last wrinkle from his soul. His head dipped with a tender kiss that conveyed his pleasure and relief in a way that words could never express.

She had survived! Cord wanted to shout his joy to high heaven!

Twenty-three

Through a blur of pulsating pain, Tempest opened her eyes after what seemed a century-long nap. Her gaze struggled to focus on the incongruous shape that drifted across her line of vision. Her brain felt as if it were filled with wool. She still seemed to be hovering on the fringes of reality, unable to navigate her way back from the hazy darkness.

Tempest hurt all over. Her head throbbed in rhythm with the beat of her heart and her shoulder felt as if it were on fire. Dear God, it seemed forever since she had been in the bounty hunters' camp, an eternity since she'd heard the crack of a rifle and felt the burning sensation in her chest. And then the world turned black and she was left in a jungle of confusion.

Tempest didn't have the faintest idea where she was or who was huddled beside her. Despite her atrocious headache, she squinted to bring the face into focus. Ever so gradually, her vision cleared and familiar features materialized through the gray haze.

"Cord . . . ?" Tempest rasped weakly. "Is that you?"

Sweet mercy, she thought, it required tremendous energy just to speak. Her voice sounded as if it had rusted. When her hand instinctively rose to limn the smile lines that bracketed Cord's lips, Tempest felt her arm tremble from exhaustion. She had no strength and she was racked with such unbearable pain that she couldn't think straight.

"Hello, princess," Cord murmured as he held her quaking hand against his cheek. He turned his head to press a kiss to her palm. "Welcome back from the living dead. For awhile there I thought I'd lost you."

There was a strange inflection in Cord's voice that Tempest didn't recognize. She wondered if the foggy image above her was who she thought it was. It was so difficult to tell when she was afraid to trust her eyes or her thoughts. Had she almost died? She couldn't remember.

When Cord shifted to offer the cup of bittersweet tea, Tempest sipped it as he requested. Her mouth was so dry she could have spit cotton and every gulp seemed precious.

"Slow down, princess," Cord said with a chuckle. "You can't compensate for three days of food and drink in one minute."

Tempest slumped back. Spasms of pain covered her face and she winced at the ache hammering at her shoulder and pulsating through her chest. "Three days?" she parroted in a gravelly voice.

Cord nodded. "And I'd dearly like to know how you came to be in High Lonesome Valley. I thought you were on your way to Fort Davis."

Tempest drew a shallow breath, struggling to keep up with the rapid flow of words that seemed a foreign language to her sluggish brain. "I borrowed a set of Bone's clothes and washed them as best I could so I could come back to tell you that I—"

A frown knitted her brow. Lord, not only couldn't she concentrate on what Cord had said, but she had trouble following her own train of thought.

"Why did you come back?" Cord prompted

when she looked utterly confused and was barely coherent.

"I came back to tell your I believe you," she finished with a tremulous sigh.

"You came through this harsh terrain, fumbled your way to my cabin when you weren't even sure where it was, just to tell me you believe in me?" Cord's brow jackknifed and he laughed softly. "Lady, you really are something." His gentle kiss skimmed her bone-dry lips. "If you waded through that kind of hell just to tell me that message, I suppose I ought to thank you, good and proper."

And he did. The kiss numbed the throb in her head and chest. Warm tingles fanned through every nerve and muscle in her body. Mmm . . . Tempest swore she'd be up on her feet in no time just because of Cord's kisses. They not only filled her with desire but also served a phenomenal medicinal purpose as well. She only wished she could muster the strength to arch forward and absorb him!

When Cord broke the kiss, Tempest sighed disappointedly. Her head and shoulder were aching again and the gray haze began to cloud her vision.

Concern filled Cord's expression. "What's wrong, princess?"

"I felt considerably better when you were kissing me," she admitted in a hoarse whisper. Tempest managed a feeble smile that put a touch of the old sparkle in her eyes. "It was powerful medicine, Mister Apache. Would you mind very much doing it again?"

What man could possibly refuse? Certainly not Cord! He'd prayed non-stop for three days that Tempest would survive. Now that she had, her every wish was his command. He'd shower her with kisses night and day if it would help, if it would return her to that sassy, high-spirited nymph he'd come to know. He'd missed this hellion in ways he'd never dreamed possible. He hadn't even realized how much he enjoyed arguing with her until his long hours were filled with deafening silence. His eyes had ached to gaze at her. His ears had yearned for the sound of her voice. His hands longed to caress her and his body craved the passion he feared was lost and gone forever.

Like a honeybee drawn to nectar, Cord gave Tempest a kiss to end all kisses. He secretly wished he could be the fabled prince whom Aunt Myra had told him about during his childhood—the one who awakened the sleeping beauty from her death-like trance.

Odd, Cord thought to himself. He had been no more than a shell of a man these past few days. Now that shell housed a hungry craving that multiplied with each delicious taste of her. Suddenly Cord felt whole and alive again, as if *he* was the one who had returned from the dead. He was like a spring flower unfurling its petals to the sun, bursting with new life.

Tempest found herself falling through time and space as Cord's lips moved expertly over hers and his darting tongue explored the recesses of her mouth. She wanted to curl her arms over his massive shoulders and hold him close, but she couldn't find the strength. The world was slipping into inky shadows again, and she felt herself losing what little grasp she'd had on reality. She was so incredibly weary . . .

Cord flinched when he felt Tempest lapse into a deep sleep in mid-kiss. He reached to check her pulse, reassuring himself that she was still among the living, that she hadn't roused for those last few minutes just to say goodbye forever.

He soon realized Tempest had just expended what little energy she had before drifting off into slumber. He wondered if she would even remember their brief conversation or their kiss. She seemed to have so little command of her body and her senses. She reminded Cord of a rag doll with whom he had played make-believe, imagining she had responded to him.

Adoringly, he traced the delicate arch of her eyebrows and the elegant curve of her cheeks. A smile spread across his lips, remembering Tempest's words—words that had touched him so deeply. She had risked life and limb, just to tell him that she believed in him. Damn, who would have thought those few words could make him feel so good. Perhaps Yellowfish was right. Maybe he did feel a fierce need for this woman's approval when he had never given a jot or a tittle what the rest of the world thought of him . . .

"You have lingered long enough, Lobo Plano," Yellowfish remarked as he hobbled into the cavern, looking as sour as curdled milk.

The old Apache had been eavesdropping at the entrance, watching Cord and Tempest. He didn't like the expression on Cord's face or the reverent way he touched this storm-child. Yellowfish could see what was happening and he felt an urgent need to stop it, just as he had from the start. This white woman was a threat that could cause serious conflict between grandfather and grandson.

"The white woman requires more spirit magic if she is to recuperate," Yellowfish proclaimed. "You are disturbing the process. Keep your distance so the potion can work its powers on her."

Cord could not understand the bitterness in the old chief's voice or his belligerent manner. To Cord's way of thinking, Yellowfish was being unnecessarily stubborn. What had she done to offend the old Apache so deeply? True, she had always stood up to men, refusing to be dominated. She wasn't the last of a dying breed, but rather the revolutionary type of female determined to make her own place in this man's world. She and Yellowfish seemed to have deeper problems than the mere clash of two cultures. But what was the source of this animosity? Just what the devil made Yellowfish so antagonistic toward Tempest? Cord still had no idea and Yellowfish refused to enlighten him!

"Grandfather, I have asked you this before," Cord began as he jumped to his feet. "But you have refused to tell me why you—"

Yellowfish's arm shot toward the exit like a bullet. "Leave us alone," he commanded gruffly. "If I am to bring the white woman back to health it will require more medicine magic. This is your request and I have granted it. Do not badger me with foolish questions."

Cord was getting nowhere fast with his grandfather. With a shrug, he ambled outside to see Emilio glaring daggers at him. Now here was a man Cord could sink his teeth into. It was time for another round of intense interrogation—Apache-style. Every time Cord stared at that vicious *vaquero* he remembered Emilio had given the order to shoot to kill. Tempest was paying for this brutish Mexican's lack of mercy. His own father had paid the ultimate price, and Cord had suffered greatly because of Emilio's brutality.

"What are you going to do?" Jefferson asked when Cord stalked purposefully toward Emilio to untie him from the tree.

"This time I'm getting some answers," Cord assured his cousin in a deadly calm voice.

Jefferson wasn't so sure he wanted to be around to witness tactics severe enough to provoke a confession from this tight-lipped Mexican. Cord had that ominous look about him—a look that seethed with vengeance and barely-subdued fury. Odd, how tender and gentle Cord could be with Tempest and how ferocious he could become with his foe. Jefferson had always admired his cousin and strived to emulate him. But there was something innately dangerous about Cord that couldn't be imitated or duplicated. Jefferson was damned glad he called MacIntosh his friend. He'd hate like hell to be his enemy!

Victor Watts frowned as he spied the rag-tag riders approaching his *rancho*. His concern multiplied when he counted the men to find their numbers considerably fewer since the day, almost a month ago, that he had sent Reynosa and the hard-bitten *vaqueros* to dispose of Cord MacIntosh. He was alarmed to realize Emilio wasn't leading the dwindled pack and Cord wasn't with them.

Rafael Sandoval swung to the ground to face his employer. He wiped the dust and perspiration from his brow with the sleeve of his soiled jacket. "I bring bad news, señor."

Victor studied Rafael's bandaged arm and bleak expression. "What is it? And where the blazes is Emilio?"

"MacIntosh took him hostage," Rafael reported. "It appears he is well deserving of his Apache name. Silver Wolf is swift and as destructive as lightning. He eluded us a dozen times in the mountains before we staked out his *rancho* in High Lonesome Valley. But somehow, he sneaked into camp and abducted Emilio right out from under our noses. One minute Emilio was there, and in an instant he had vanished into thin air."

Victor exploded in frustration. "Damn it, the man is not immortal, nor is he blessed with the ability to become invisible! You blundering fools! We'll all hang if that bastard returns to El Paso with Emilio."

"There is more, *amigo*," Rafael said with a weary sigh. "We thought we had spotted Lobo Plano riding to his cabin. We ambushed him. But it was the woman who was with him instead."

Victor wobbled back as if he'd received a staggering blow to the jaw. "What?" he crowed in disbelief.

"*Si,*" Rafael confirmed gloomily. "I do not know if she lived or died. The wound was serious. We held little hope for her. But while we searched for Emilio, who had disappeared during the commotion, Lobo Plano returned to camp. He was atop one of our missing horses, holding Emilio in front of him like a shield. There was an old Indian with him. He strode into our midst like an invincible warrior, as if he knew no bullet could touch him. They took the woman away with them."

"And you stood there like a bunch of lily-livered cowards!" Victor raged.

"No, señor." Rafael lifted his blood-stained arm to expose a festering knife wound. Then he pulled out the dagger that had caused his injury and slapped it into Victor's hand. "Lobo Plano is deadly with a blade and even more dangerous with a pistol. We tried to capture him, but before we knew what happened, buckshot was exploding around us. I don't even know where the other bullets came from. And when we searched the valley for Emilio we could find no tracks."

"Well, I'll just have to turn this incident to my advantage somehow or other," Victor said. "We'll let it be known that MacIntosh murdered Tempest Litchfield, as well as Emilio and some of our men. As soon as you have rested, eaten, and restocked supplies, I want you to go out again. MacIntosh has to be somewhere in that godforsaken pile of rocks. And next time—"

Rafael cut him off with a gesture of his good arm. "There will not be a next time, señor. We will not ride against Lobo Plano again. He has the stealth and cunning of a handful of Apache warriors. We lost too many *vaqueros* in the hunt of one man."

"You will do as I say, you superstitious imbecile!

MacIntosh has to be killed, whether you think him legendary or not!" Victor bellowed. "If he is allowed to return to speak the truth we will be ruined!"

"Not even all the gold in that mine MacIntosh is rumored to have in those mountains could lure us back into the jaws of hell," Rafael growled. "We will not ride against Lobo Plano." Dark eyes glistened like black steel. "We returned only to deliver Lobo Plano's message. He is coming for you, but not as a white man. He will come as an Apache. And *Dios* help you, señor. In this, it will require far more than the devil's luck." With that, Rafael turned and walked away.

"Damn it, come back here!" Victor roared, but to no avail.

The trail-weary *vaqueros* headed toward the bunkhouse to recuperate. Although they had arrogantly considered themselves hardened mercenaries after their years of riding with the *Comancheros,* they refused to pit themselves against Silver Wolf again. They had watched him cheat death too many times not to believe he was charmed. And they had lost too many friends trying to capture the half-man, half-beast who could materialize out of nowhere and vanish into nothingness!

With a growl and a curse, Victor stamped toward the stables. He intended to report the incident to law officials in El Paso posthaste. By the time he had twisted the story, Cord MacIntosh would definitely be public enemy number one. He would be accused of multiple murders—if that damned Emilio could keep his mouth shut. That half-breed wasn't going to best Victor Watts! And Judge Litchfield would ensure that Cord MacIntosh paid for his sins with his life!

Legendary indeed! Before long, Cord MacIntosh would be the deadest man who ever lived! If he dared to attack Victor while an army of *pistoleros* surrounded the *hacienda,* Cord would be every kind of fool. That half-breed didn't stand a chance!

While Victor was dashing off to El Paso, Annette Partridge slumped back against the doorjamb, stunned by what she had overheard. While she was in Victor's presence, he had been the epitome of gentlemanly manners and loving devotion. But today she had seen a side of Victor that terrified her. Victor was not at all as he had appeared when he had come courting!

Annette turned to gather part of her belongings—as much as she could carry without slowing her down. She would gladly pay a king's ransom if one of the hired men would escort her to the nearest stage station. She was going home to her family. Her father would be outraged that she had taken it upon herself to break the engagement, but he would change his tune when he learned what the real Victor Watts was like. This betrothal that was contracted for the benefit of two wealthy families would be dissolved. Annette wanted no part of such a life and she was going to assert herself the way Tempest Litchfield always had. There had to be more to life than being a subservient wife and Annette was determined to follow in Tempest's footsteps.

Oh, how she hoped Tempest had survived the bushwhacking! It would be such a waste! Annette had admired Tempest's poise and intelligence from the moment they'd met. She'd strived to become like her—Tempest was an inspiration to womankind!

Tempest drifted in and out of consciousness. In the distance she swore she heard screams and muted curses before she was engulfed in silence. She was unaware that it had been Emilio's voice that penetrated her dreams, Emilio who was feeling the effects of Cord's forceful persuasion.

Occasionally Tempest experienced an agonizing pain in her shoulder, as if unseen hands were pouring liquid flame on her flesh. But she could never be sure if the screams that reached her ears were her own or someone else's. She faintly remembered swallowing some sort of foul-tasting substance and hearing a gruff, persistent voice demanding that she eat and drink. And now, as she shifted to a new position to rest, it didn't seem to deplete every ounce of her strength.

Tempest couldn't be certain, but she thought she recalled being carried into the sunlight by a pair of strong arms. She had instinctively cuddled closer to the warmth. And there were times when she had suddenly awakened, thinking there was a muscular body beside hers. But all the dim memories and fuzzy images seemed to come from a befuddled dream. Her body was so sluggish she had very little control over it. It was as if . . . as if she had awakened from one hallucinatory dream after another, wandering along a shadowed boundary without being able to distinguish reality from fantasy . . .

Cord sat outside the cavern at twilight with Tempest propped beside him. He had brought her out for fresh air an hour earlier and she had been mumbling between lapses of silence and intermittent giggles.

Cord knew Yellowfish had been giving Tempest potions of mescal and peyote the past few days. The old Apache had insisted that Tempest needed to move about without feeling unnecessary pain, in order to circulate her blood and exercise her limbs. It had seemed logical to Cord, too, but he hadn't expected her to be quite so outrageous while under the influence of Indian medicine.

She had whispered every possible version of his name in the past few minutes. Her roaming hands had drifted over him with a familiarity that had Yellowfish scowling in disgust and Jefferson coughing to camouflage his laughter. When her adventurous hand landed on his lap, Cord had promptly removed it. Tempest's carryings-on were tempting to be sure, but hardly permissible with an audience. The only one who wasn't complaining or snickering was Emilio Reynosa. The man had proved himself to be as tough as leather, but Cord had begun to make headway after several tactics which had finally loosened his tongue . . .

Cord's thoughts dissolved instantly when Tempest curled up beside him to place a row of kisses along his neck. Her hand glided inside the buttons of his shirt to caress the breadth of his chest and Yellowfish erupted in another disgusted snort.

"It is time to put her back to bed," he announced with his customary authority. "She is not a toy you bring out to play with at your leisure. An Apache woman would be disgraced if she behaved so wantonly under the peyote!"

"So would a white woman, I'll wager," Jefferson sniggered when Tempest's hand trailed along the band of Cord's breeches as if it had been there a few times before.

"I think perhaps it's time to take Tempest to the spring to bathe," Cord decided as he guided her hand to his chest and held it firmly in place.

Yellowfish's eyes narrowed at the suggestion. "The cool water will help bring her up from the depths of the potion, it is true, but I think Jefferson should be the one to take her to the spring."

Cord glared at his cousin who looked a mite too eager to assume the task. It seemed Yellowfish was anxious to foist Tempest off on Jefferson. He'd tried that tactic several times in the past few days. Once Cord had entered the cave to find Tempest caressing Jefferson in a most disconcerting manner to which

Jefferson—rake that he was and always would be—had responded with a grin and a wink. The incident hadn't set well with Cord. He didn't appreciate his own cousin enjoying such familiarity with Tempest. She belonged to Cord, in body at least, and he found himself fiercely possessive.

"She is still my wife and I will be the only man to bathe her," Cord insisted.

He rose to his feet and scooped Tempest's body into his arms. She instinctively sidled closer, her restless hands trailing over the collar of his shirt and up his chin to his lips. Without giving it a thought, Cord kissed her fingertips. The reflexive gesture provoked his grandfather for the umpteenth time.

When Cord strode off with Tempest, Emilio glanced up from beneath puffy eyelids. The glower he directed at Cord was meant to maim and mutilate.

"Half-breed bastard," Emilio hissed through swollen lips.

"Mexican swine," Cord automatically flung back. They had been flinging insults at each other for so long that it had become second nature.

By the time Cord reached the bubbly spring, he had forgotten about everybody and everything except the delicate woman in his arms. Gently, he eased Tempest down to remove her stained garments. Undressing her was sheer pleasure. It seemed a decade since he'd been allowed to feast on her exquisite beauty. Cord regretted the scar just below the curve of her shoulder, but that couldn't diminish his appreciation of her silky curves. Tempest had regained the color in her cheeks and the frailty that consumed her a few days earlier wasn't quite so noticeable.

Thanks to Yellowfish's tireless but begrudging efforts, she was on the road to recovery. The old Apache had put Tempest on her feet that morning, forcing her to walk, even while she was heavily drugged with peyote. Cord had objected that it was too soon, but Yellowfish had been adamant, insisting that they had tarried too long with the white woman already. Obviously the physical therapy had been beneficial because Tempest looked far better this evening than she had the previous night.

In silent appreciation, Cord's eyes gazed lovingly at her voluptuous figure, fantasizing about what he would prefer to be doing at the moment. He ached for this lovely nymph. There wasn't a helluva lot he could do about it, except take a cold bath . . . which he proceeded to do. If he didn't get control of his urges—and quickly—he would be of no help to this groggy sprite.

Damn, Cord thought as he waded into the water. Why was it so difficult to control his reactions when Tempest needed a compassionate companion, not a lover? His eager gaze drifted back to the blanket where he had left her while he got himself under control.

A sigh of defeat tumbled from Cord when he realized a cold bath wasn't going to cure what ailed him. All he had to do was glance in Tempest's direction and he grew more and more aroused.

Caramba! There was no reason why he couldn't combine her bath with his own ravenous need to kiss and caress her. He would simply be gentle and considerate. A little loving, Cord decided, would be better than none at all.

Bearing that in mind, Cord waded ashore. His eyes feasted on Tempest as if she were a meal he longed to devour. Just a few kisses and caresses, Cord promised himself. Just enough to curb his appetite and ward off this coil of gnawing hunger that was eating him alive!

Twenty-four

Tempest found herself drifting through another erotic dream. A sigh escaped her lips when she felt tender caresses and kisses cruising over her flesh. Her body tingled with sensation as skillful hands glided over every inch of her. Reflexively, she arched toward those hands, craving more.

Suddenly Tempest felt the refreshing sensation of water rushing over her, jolting her from the fuzzy depths of slumber. Her lashes fluttered up to see what appeared to be Cord's shadowed face surrounded by streams of pastel sunlight. With a faint smile, she looped her arm over his sturdy shoulder.

"Mmm . . . this must be heaven," Tempest murmured half aloud. "I wondered what it would be like . . ."

"It certainly feels like heaven to me," Cord agreed as his eyes and hands savored the sight and feel of her body in his arms. "But if this isn't paradise, it's as close as I ever care to get."

Tempest stared dazedly at the dark hair that covered Cord's chest before her attention shifted to the knotted muscles that wrapped around the wide expanse of his shoulders. "Such a gorgeous man," she breathed as her fingers drew lazy patterns around his nipples. "I wonder why the Lord didn't see His way clear to make more of you?"

Cord chuckled at Tempest's slurred words and her giddy mood. He'd never seen her like this. She could be a sassy firebrand when she wanted to, but now she was saying the damnedest things. The peyote was clouding her thinking, putting ridiculous words on her tongue.

"Men aren't gorgeous," Cord corrected her.

"Says who?" Tempest gurgled as she arched back to drift on the water. "I think you're a gorgeous hunk of man and I shall write a law to present to the governor to make it so. I can do that. I'm a lawyer, you know."

"Oh really?" Cord snickered. "I hadn't heard."

"The men of this world don't like to think so," Tempest babbled, "They resent me because I'm a woman with intelligence. They think that's a dangerous combination, a threat to their malehood . . ." Tempest frowned ponderously. "Is that a word? I can't seem to remember." With a limp shrug she tossed the thought aside. "Yellowfish thinks I'm a misfit and a witch."

"You're definitely a witch," Cord confirmed with a grin. "Witches weave magic spells and they cast no shadows, only haunting images."

Tempest curled into a cuddly ball in Cord's arms, still giggling. Cord didn't know why and he wasn't sure Tempest did, either.

She was quiet for a long moment, dozing off and then stirring from drug-induced slumber.

"You should meet him," she said out of the blue.

Cord froze to the spot, motionless in the waist-deep water. Tempest was leaping from one topic of conversation to another and he couldn't keep up with her.

"Meet who?" he prodded.

"Silver Wolf, of course," she replied thickly, as if everybody ought to recognize the name.

It dawned on Cord that Tempest had drifted into a dream and she didn't have the foggiest notion whom she was talking to. She was simply chattering like a magpie while her dazed thoughts dashed to the tip of her tongue and leaped off.

"Now there's a man who can make a lady feel like a woman, even after she swore no man on the planet could please her," Tempest confided as she paddled her arms and then winced when a sharp pain registered in her sluggish mind. "Damn, that hurts. I wish I could figure out where that pain comes from."

"And what has this Silver Wolf got that other men supposedly don't have?" Cord persisted.

"He's got everything," Tempest slurred. "He's no gentleman, of course. I detest stuffed shirts with all those proper manners and all that proper flattery that's flung out to snag unsuspecting women. He's his own man, this Silver Wolf. He's wild and free, bound by no restrictions."

If Cord listened to much more of this praise his head would surely swell and burst. Tempest had never been one to lavish praise on any man. And since it was a rare occasion, Cord had gobbled up the compliment like a starving dog.

"And when Silver Wolf seduces a woman, she knows she's been seduced," Tempest rambled on.

Cord grinned roguishly. "He's that good, is he?"

"Even better," Tempest said with absolute assurance. "Do you know how it feels to fly, to spread your wings and soar like a bird? Have you ever felt as if you were standing apart from yourself, feeling and yet watching? Have you felt as if you'd reached up and grasped the stars and glided over rainbows?"

"Rainbows?" Cord shifted uncomfortably. These were intimate confidences. Tempest would probably die of embarrassment if she knew she'd shared such comments with anyone, especially him.

Tempest gave her head a nod and rolled onto her belly, letting Cord support her while she paddled her feet. "He taught me to swim, too," she added groggily. "But it wasn't near as much fun as flying."

Cord could have kicked himself for posing the next question. It was a dirty trick to get information from anyone who was not in complete command of her senses—which Tempest obviously wasn't. "So you're saying you have a great respect for Silver Wolf, are you?"

Tempest rolled over again to peer up at the fuzzy image floating before her glazed eyes. "Respect him? Why, of course. How could I not? You cannot know a man like that without being affected by him. I love him, but I don't dare tell him so. He hardly needs the likes of me when there are scores of somebody elses to take my place and bring him pleasure. That's all he really wants from a woman."

Cord gaped at Tempest. "You *really love* him?" he croaked.

She couldn't love him. How could she? Why would she? What had he ever done except give her grief, frustration, and pain? Why, just look at her now! She was as far away from her world as any woman could get! She was drugged half out of her mind with peyote to numb the pain from a near-fatal bullet that had *his* name on it. Not only did he not deserve her love, but he hadn't even expected it. Her approval and acceptance? Yes. But love? He had wanted her desperately for the time and space they had shared together. He'd known since the beginning that he'd have to send her back where she belonged. Yellowfish had harped on the subject so often that Cord had accepted it without trying to change it.

And what about him? How did he truly feel, deep down inside in that previously untouched region of his soul? This feisty woman certainly aroused him. There was no denying that. She was courageous, beautiful, and spirited. He admired everything about her. She distracted him and amused him. She also infuriated him beyond words—it *infuriated* him that she had the ability to *infuriate* him when no other woman ever could.

But love? It was completely out of the question. Cord knew his limitation with Tempest and with life itself. He had tried to settle into the Apache's world and then into the white man's. He was uncomfortable in both. He was a loner by nature, by instinct, and by experiments with two worlds that didn't suit the man he was . . .

His thoughts disappeared when a choked sob burst from Tempest. Moments before she had been giggling and babbling like a child. Now she was crying and cuddling up to him for consolation.

"I didn't want to love him," she sobbed against his shoulder. "I tried not to, I truly did. I refused to believe him because I felt myself falling in love with him. In order to prevent that I had to reject everything about him. I had to! It was the only way to protect myself." A muffled sniff interrupted her tearful soliloquy. "But he's like a legend no one can touch, one who must be adored from afar. There's no future in it . . ."

When Tempest broke off with huge sobs, followed by body-wracking hiccups that had her wincing in pain, Cord moaned in frustration. They had been better off when they had simply wanted each other physically. He had married her, not only for revenge but because the wanting had reached an unbearable point and he was obsessed with claiming her as his own, physically and legally.

Cord hadn't meant to hurt Tempest, but the man in him desired her beyond reason. She had begun to matter too much, even though he'd fought it every step of the way. In his saner moments, he had tried to remember their vast differences and all the obstacles that stood between them like the rugged Guadalupe Mountains. Yellowfish had constantly objected to this ill-starred affair, and Judge Litchfield would have a conniption fit if he learned his daughter had married a half-breed renegade. Hell, the judge wanted Cord crucified today. Yesterday would have pleased him even more.

He and Tempest had no future together and she knew that as well as he did. Cord couldn't survive in her world and she couldn't fit into his wild life that hovered between two conflicting cultures. Damn it, a man might just as well try to hammer a square peg into a round hole or mix oil with water. It was futile and he and this lovely lass would only torture each other if they tried their hand at love.

By the time Cord waded ashore with Tempest in his arms, she had lapsed into a fitful sleep, sobbing and murmuring. But while he washed her soiled clothes and waited for them to dry, she roused from slumber. For the first time in a long while she actually seemed coherent, aware of her surroundings and aware of the pain beneath the joint of her left shoulder. When she glanced down at the wound and gasped, Cord hurriedly tossed his shirt over her.

"It doesn't matter," he told her as he hunkered down beside her.

"No?" Tempest grimaced as she levered into a sitting position and then braced her right arm when the world careened around her. "And what man would want a scarred woman when there are plenty around who aren't?" God, the very sight of burned flesh, bruised skin, and jagged stitches was enough to nauseate her!

Cord half-twisted to call her attention to the unsightly scars on his back. "You wanted me, didn't you, even after Emilio Reynosa and Juan Tijerina did this to me?"

"It's not the same for a man as a woman," Tempest burst out, unable to control the tears. Lord, why did she suddenly feel so depressed and ill? What was the matter with her? One minute she swore she was as high as the towering mountain peaks and then she had nose-dived into despair.

"Oh, never mind." She muffled a sniff. "I don't know what I'm fussing about. I wasn't even sure I was alive, to tell you the truth. I've been having the strangest dreams . . ." Tempest wiped her tears and studied her surroundings. "What time is it anyway? And where the blazes are we? And where are my clothes and how did you find me?"

She was fully awake all right, Cord noted. It was certain that this was the first conversation she would remember having with anyone. The world had suddenly converged on her from all directions and Tempest was feeling the aftereffects of peyote. All the symptoms were there—mood swings, frustration, panic, and nausea that caused her complexion to flush crimson red.

Cord retrieved her garments and helped her into them. "After you had been shot by the *vaqueros*, I took you from the camp. You have been in a cave recovering for the past six days," he told her. "We took Emilio captive and Yellowfish has been filling you full of Indian potions. That's why you don't recall much about the past and feel as if you have been hallucinating."

"Did Emilio tell you what you wanted to know?" Tempest asked as Cord helped her to her feet.

When she swayed dizzily, Cord held her arm while he shrugged into his shirt. "He told me plenty."

"Then I'm taking your case," Tempest declared.

"No, you're going to find your father," Cord

insisted. "He's probably worried out of his mind by now."

Tempest peered up into that chiseled face that was suddenly as hard and unyielding as stone. "Just like that?" she queried, tormented by this one-sided love that refused to die a graceful death, even when Cord was doing his best to kill it with his impersonal tone of voice.

"Just like that, princess," he said firmly. "This long ordeal is over. You can send the annulment papers to me at the Pinery and I'll sign it. I have all the information I need to confront Victor. I don't need a court of law—Victor knows I'm coming. I sent his *vaqueros* back with fair warning."

Cord was behaving exactly the way he had the night he had stalked off from the bandits' hideout to disappear into the darkness. That was the last conversation she remembered having with him. The past week was still a confused blur. Bits and pieces of memory seemed to bob across her mind like driftwood, floating away before she could grasp them and put them in proper sequence.

Obviously nothing had changed since Cord left her with the bounty hunters. He had wanted her out of his life to do what he felt compelled to do—avenge his father's death. For a time she had been his pawn, a gambit to be played to his advantage. Now she was only slowing Cord down and he was impatient to get on with his crusade.

Tempest had known it would end like this. She had even tried to prepare herself. But after she had questioned the bandits and learned that Ellis Flake had told them about the incident in the El Paso jail, she had seized that insane excuse to go after Cord. She had wanted to assure him that there were men who could corroborate his story, even if it was second-hand.

"You will be pleased to know that I interrogated

Ellis Flake's bandit friends. I heard the real story of your jailbreak," she announced, attempting to appear unruffled after Cord had crushed her with his impassive tone. "Ellis described the incident to the other outlaws when they questioned him about the change in their original plans. They had intended to free Ellis while Dub Wizner was marching to the gallows. Ellis saw you escape before he heard Juan Tijerina gasping for breath. Ellis also heard the commotion in Dub's cell when he collapsed. You were telling the truth, Cord. Dub Wizner strangled Tijerina as his last act of vengeance and he died before anyone could find out what happened."

Cord jerked up his head and looked at Tempest's pale features. So that's why she had come to believe him. Even though she had admitted to loving him while she was under the influence of peyote, she hadn't really believed him until she heard the story from a gang of thieves. That was hardly what Cord called unconditional love! And what the hell did Tempest know about love anyway, he asked himself. And why did he think he could believe her when she didn't even know what she'd said? Maybe he hadn't heard her secret confessions at all, but rather tangled thoughts that he presumed were intimate truths. If anything, Tempest had mistaken passion for love.

After all, he was her first experience with desire. She had even said that she had little use for other men. She happened to like his body, but it was only a physical attraction, and her confused mind had attempted to label it love because of her guilt and sense of propriety. If Tempest had more experience with men she would have known the difference. Or perhaps she only thought she should love him because she had allowed him to seduce her and had enjoyed it. No doubt that noble conscience of hers required that she love the man who had made love to her.

As he shepherded Tempest up the path to the cave, Cord realized he'd become so distracted by all her accolades that he hadn't taken time to properly analyze Tempest's motivation or her true feelings. Hell, he knew her better than she knew herself! No matter what she said while in a stupor, she didn't really care for him. She hated him and she'd said that more often than she'd said she loved him, that was for damned sure!

Not that it mattered, Cord reminded himself. Nothing had changed and nothing was going to change. Tempest was returning to her father as fast as he could get her there.

Cord had become so immersed in his guilt and regret that he had allowed his emotions to control him while Tempest recovered from her near-fatal brush with catastrophe. But she had survived, just as he prayed she would. Now they were going their separate ways—once and for all. Yellowfish would be hopping up and down with delight when he found that out. The old Apache's nose had been out of joint for a month. The conflict between grandfather and grandson would disappear the moment Tempest was out of sight—forever. It was for the best, Cord tried to convince himself.

When Cord returned to the cave, he was not only upset with himself, but with Tempest and with Emilio, who had given him weeks of grief. Cord felt the sudden need to relieve his pent-up frustration on the man who definitely deserved more punishment. Emilio hadn't suffered nearly enough to compensate for the hell he'd put Cord through. With a rough jerk, Cord yanked Emilio to his feet and shoved him forward.

"Tell Tempest what you told me," Cord demanded, startling her with his vicious snarl and brutish temper.

"I said Lobo Plano was a half-breed bastard," Emilio muttered in defiance.

Cord's steely arm closed around the bandit's throat. He grabbed Emilio's tangled hair and jerked his head back to a painful angle that stretched his neck out like a giraffe's. There was a menacing threat in those ice-like amber eyes, and Tempest winced as if she were the one being attacked.

"Unless you want another dose of torture, you damned well better tell her the truth! You'll find yourself hanging upside down with your head dangling over a fire."

Tempest braced herself against the boulder behind her, stunned by the malicious sneer on Cord's craggy features. He had become a vicious savage before her very eyes. Why? Why was he so intent on reminding her of what he could be like when he was vindictive? Lord, sometimes Cord could be so devoid of warmth and compassion that she wondered if he truly possessed any tenderness. Perhaps he had only pretended gentleness when he wanted her as a woman. The unnerving display left Tempest with serious doubts about Cord—again!

And why was he still tormenting Emilio, who looked as if he had been physically abused enough? She had told Cord that she believed his story. She didn't have to hear it from this ruthless *vaquero*. Why had Cord beaten Emilio to a pulp? Just for vengeance? Was he really a barbarian? How could she ever have fancied herself in love with this brute? She must have been mad. This was obviously the real Cord MacIntosh—Silver Wolf—the barely civilized beast. His true nature had come pouring out and Tempest didn't like what she saw!

"Tell her, you stinking son-of-a-bitch," Cord growled. "Tell her all of it!"

While Yellowfish stood aside, watching the distasteful scene with an expression that gave none of his thoughts away, Jefferson frowned disapprovingly. In his opinion, Tempest didn't need to see Cord like this, especially in her condition. She could easily suffer a relapse after seeing such a cruel interrogation.

A howl erupted from Emilio's puffy lips when a fierce yank left him swearing his scalp was being torn off. His entire body was already one huge, purple bruise. The fight had almost gone out of him—*almost.*

When Emilio clamped his mouth shut in defiance, Cord exploded in a malicious sneer and slammed his victim with a well-aimed knee to the spine. "Tell her, bastard."

Emilio's knees dropped out from under him and he landed so close to the campfire that he could feel, and vividly remember, the intense heat that had come close to frying him alive the previous day. "Watts sent me to brand his cattle with MacIntosh's irons so it would look like rustling," he ground out before Cord shoved his face into the flames. "We took Cord captive. We beat him, whipped him, and yet he survived the trip to jail. Watts sent me back to dispose of his father before Cord was hanged for rustling. We poisoned the cattle and then tied the old man up to force poison down his throat. We freed him when the poison took effect so it would look like an accident. When Cord escaped from jail, Watts sent me to kill him."

Tempest was feeling more nauseated by the second. Not only was the confession disgusting but Cord's brutality was revolting. In her weakened condition, it didn't take much to put her brittle emotions in a tailspin. Tears clouded her eyes as she stared at Emilio's battered features and then at Cord's icy glower. He had repaid Emilio for the abuse he'd received and for the murder of his father. But enough was enough.

She and Cord had finally come the full circle—

back to where they had been at the beginning. What they had was over, she realized despairingly. That was obviously the way Cord wanted it. He had allowed her to see the vicious side of him again, to remind her of what he really was and what he would always be. His actions were even more devastating than his moodiness and the words he'd spoken at the spring. Now he was making certain Tempest knew that she wasn't a part of his harsh life. She had been living on hopes and dreams. She had only seen in Cord what she had wanted to see, but after this eye-opening incident she could see clearly.

With a muffled sob, Tempest scurried into the cave to collapse on the pallet. But she didn't cry for long—exhaustion overtook her almost immediately. She wanted to forget this past month and go home to her father and take up where her life had left off. This had been nothing but a ghoulish nightmare and she longed to forget it had ever happened—all of it. But most of all she wanted to forget the cruel, vicious man who had only played at tenderness. God, she hated Cord for that most of all! Even after all they had been through together, she was still just appeasement for his lusts. He would have played out this spiteful game, even if it had been Annette Partridge whom he had kidnapped.

Tempest could have been Annette and the end result would have been the same. Damn him. She cursed herself for ever trying to love a man like Cord. It had been a foolish romantic illusion and she didn't care if she saw him again—ever! In fact, it would have been a blessing if she didn't, and it was all the same to her if she awoke to find that golden-eyed demon gone!

Twenty-five

After Tempest had dashed into the cave, Jefferson threw down his coffee cup and stamped toward Cord. His hazel eyes burned into Cord like pinpoints of flame. "Damn it, Tosh, did you have to expose Tempest to this? You've suddenly become abusive to everyone who comes within snarling distance. My God, don't you have an ounce of sympathy in you anymore?" He stared at his cousin with disdain. "You know perfectly well that poor woman has just barely gotten back on her feet. In her frail condition she hardly needed to see you threaten to burn off Emilio's face! She was staring at you as if you were a monster, and damned if I don't agree!"

"What I do and how I do it is none of your concern," Cord snapped. "Little miss lady lawyer wanted to know the details of this case. Now she knows them."

"Why the hell didn't you just tell her yourself after you dragged the confession out of Emilio yesterday?" Jefferson fired. "Hell, that little scene even upset *me!* What the devil's gotten into you? First you sit out here with Tempest, playing with her as if she were a kitten. Then you come stomping back and light into Emilio like a mountain lion and—"

"Shut up, Jeff," Cord growled ominously.

"And what if I don't?" Jefferson hurled with a militant glare. "Are you going to drag Tempest out here to watch you beat your own cousin black and blue?"

"I said—"

"I don't give a bloody damn what you said," Jefferson interrupted. "I'll say what I have to say and I'll shut up when I'm good and ready!" He took an angry breath and plunged on. "I overlooked the fact that you strung Tempest up on a hook in the barn loft to keep her quiet at the Pinery. I even held my tongue when you married her to retaliate against Victor—even though you abducted the wrong woman by mistake. Then I admired you for going back to retrieve Tempest when she was dying in the *vaquero* camp. But for chrissake! That little episode with Emilio was uncalled-for. If I were Tempest—which I'm damned glad I'm not—I'd never speak to you again—which I may not, even if you *are* my own flesh and blood!"

Jefferson wheeled around, as if the sight of Cord repulsed him. "If you need me, I'll be wandering around in the rocks. I'm not too fond of the company I'm keeping."

When Jefferson disappeared, Cord sank down cross-legged beside Yellowfish who hadn't moved a muscle since the heated conversation began. "Well? Don't you want to rake me over the coals, too?" Cord asked sourly.

A wry smile crinkled Yellowfish's weather-beaten features. "No, my son. I knew what you were doing and why. Sometimes it is hard to be cruel in order to be kind. I know the tactic very well."

Cord reached out to pour himself a cup of coffee and stared up at the darkened sky, watching the sentinels of the night twinkle into view. "I wanted her to hear the truth from Emilio. She seems to find it easier to believe everyone but me."

Yellowfish nodded slightly. "You wanted her acceptance of the truth. But there was more to this than that," he added perceptively. "I am not blind, Lobo Plano, only old. Jefferson could not see the point because he is too moved to emotion by the white woman. He thinks of *her* instead of what is best."

"She said she loved me," Cord burst out, sipping his coffee.

"As well she should, even from the beginning when I demanded it of her and she refused to admit that you are a man to be admired. There is much about you for a woman to love—Apache or white," the old chief calmly replied. "But in the end, I knew you would do what must be done. What you did for the white woman took great courage. You showed her the side of you that cannot fit into her civilization. The Apache was born to wander under the Great Spirit's sea of stars. We were not meant to be confined as the army wishes so they can take our lands and claim our hunting grounds. This land is of the Great Spirit, Holos, and the Earth Mother. It cannot be taken or given, only used and then returned."

"So you don't condemn me for forcing Emilio to confess to Tempest?" Cord murmured as his gaze drifted toward the cave.

"He deserved what he got after what he did to you," Yellowfish declared. "The Mexican only understands violence, not kindness. He did not even apologize to the white woman for causing her such pain. He cares only for his own hide, no one else's. Besides, he would not have been able to face his own twisted pride if he had confessed without being tormented into it. He expected it of you because it is his way. You did not disappoint him."

"That's exactly the way I had it figured." Cord

chuckled as he glanced toward Emilio, whose eyes were like flaming arrows.

When Yellowfish rose to his feet to amble into the darkness, Cord stared pensively at the cave. He did regret putting Tempest through the anguish of watching him force Emilio to speak. But it had to be done, for her sake and for his. She wouldn't understand that and he could never convince her.

Restlessly, Cord found his footsteps taking him into the cavern. Squatting down on his haunches, he stared at Tempest's shadowed form on the quilt-covered pallet. Cord lifted long tendrils of her silky hair, letting them slip through his fingers like an elusive dream tumbling from his grasp.

"I have to let you go, princess," he whispered. "It's the only way . . ."

Ever so gently Cord braced himself on his arms and leaned down to press a tender kiss to her lips. It would be the last time he would kiss this lovely sprite. He would never forget how good she felt in his arms, how alive he felt when he touched her. But he had come to terms with reality. They had to part, even if it hurt like hell—which it did. It was better that Tempest went away, despising him. Perhaps she did love him a little, and perhaps not. But her feelings and his feelings changed nothing. Cord was letting her go, even if it killed him. He could already feel the ache in the pit of his belly. But he would compensate for that when he got his hands on Victor Watts. Having his long-awaited revenge on that scheming bastard would be his solace for losing Tempest. It *had* to be.

Tempest made a spectacular display of ignoring Cord when she awakened the following morning. Not only did she hurt all over but there was a throbbing emptiness in her soul and a hole the size of Texas in her heart.

"You are feeling better today," Yellowfish announced as he stuffed one of his remedies down her throat.

The remark wasn't an observation, Tempest decided. The old Apache was demanding that she recuperate immediately so they could travel. Yellowfish, like Cord, couldn't wait to have her out from underfoot—permanently.

"I've never felt better in all my life," Tempest declared with proud conviction. "I'll be ready to leave as soon as you are."

Yellowfish bit back a smile. Tempest's haughtiness was something he had objected to since he'd met her. But in truth, he appreciated her gumption, even if she was a white woman. Of course, he'd cut out his tongue before he admitted any such thing to her. Yellowfish had always asked that she speak and behave like an Apache woman, just to see if she would do it to please him. Tempest never had. She was definitely her own woman, a woman with strong resilience and indomitable spirit. She wasn't motivated by obligation, only by respect. Yellowfish had never tried to earn her respect and she forever balked at obeying his commands out of mere duty.

"I will be ready to begin the journey after you have washed our dishes and packed our supplies," he said, just to get a rise out of her. Sure enough, he did.

Tempest glared at the old coot. She had just crawled off her deathbed and he still antagonized her every chance he got. The word *ornery* had been coined just for this old buzzard!

Snatching the spoon from Yellowfish's crab-like fingers, Tempest pushed herself up—Indian-style—and began to eat.

"Apache women are not allowed to sit cross-legged," Yellowfish informed her. "They either squat on their feet or sit with their legs to the side."

"Good for them," Tempest replied with a toss of her tangled hair. "Thankfully, I can do as I please."

Yellowfish's joints creaked as he rose to tower over her. "You will be pleased to rejoin your own kind, white woman. It will be as it should be."

As the old Indian hobbled toward the mouth of the cave, Tempest peered at his proud profile and the wrinkles he'd acquired from his harsh life. Yellowfish was an old coot, to be sure, but she knew how deeply he cared about Cord. Tempest couldn't imagine why she felt sentimental all of a sudden, but she did.

"Yellowfish?"

The chief half-turned to stare at the lovely woman sitting in a shaft of sunlight that left her wild mane of hair aglow. "What is it, white woman?"

"Just so you know, I loved him, but not as an Apache woman who bows to her warrior or is a devoted slave to her master. I loved him for the tenderness he once showed to me, even if it wasn't truly a part of the man he is."

Yellowfish's obsidian eyes probed into her luminous pools of blue. "And do you still love him now, even after you saw his dark side last night?"

"It doesn't matter," Tempest assured him with a shrug. "It's over and I will give him what he wants—his freedom to do as *he* pleases. And I have given you what you wanted—*my* admission of love—a secret that only you and I share."

The old chief spoke not another word as he hobbled outside. There was a troubled expression on his face and a turmoil of emotion inside him. But Yellowfish had grown accustomed to keeping his own counsel. Only on occasion had Cord been allowed to know what he was really thinking and feeling. He was a master at cunning and illusion. But what the old chief needed most at the moment was to sort out his emotions. He did so while *he* packed the supplies. That was his concession to Tempest, one that provoked her to smile when she went outside and saw that Yellowfish had assumed the task. It was as close as a proud old warrior could come to making amends. Yellowfish was making it known that they would at least part as friends.

Annette Partridge glanced up from the crude table at the stage station when a tall, dignified gentleman trooped inside with four buffalo soldiers trailing at his heels. After she heard one of the soldiers refer to the first man by name, Annette blinked in astonishment.

"You're Judge Litchfield?"

Annette had pictured him as a plump, stoic man with a gavel in each hand. Litchfield was six feet tall, muscular and imposing. There was something distinguished about the sprinkling of silver hair at his temples, the firm set of his jaw, and the fire in his blue eyes. For a man who looked to be in his mid-forties, he was a striking figure.

Abraham wheeled about to survey the delicate blonde. She was extremely attractive but rumpled from her travels.

"How do you know who I am, young lady?"

"Because I met your daughter," Annette replied and then shrank back in her chair when the judge surged toward her like a locomotive.

"When and where did you meet Tempest? Do you know where she is now? When did you last see her?"

"Which question shall I answer first?" Annette replied with an impish smile.

Abraham dropped into a chair, braced his forearms on the table, and stared intently at the pretty blonde. "Why don't you just start at the beginning and tell me everything you know about my daughter," he suggested.

Annette collected her thoughts and explained her association with Tempest. "Your daughter came to my fiancé's *rancho* to question him about Cord MacIntosh. But then she was kidnapped right out of the *hacienda*. Victor Watts—that was my fiancé, but he isn't anymore—sent out his *vaqueros* to track Cord down. When they returned from the mountains, they said they had shot Tempest by mistake."

The color seeped from Abe's strained features. "Is she—?"

"I'm sorry, sir. I don't know her condition. I only know what I overheard. But I do know that my ex-fiancé has been deceptive in charging Cord MacIntosh with wrongdoing."

"Well, he sure as hell kidnapped my daughter!" Abe exploded. "And for that I'll see him rotting in jail until the end of his days!"

Annette winced at his intensity and then regained her composure. "Begging your pardon, sir, but—"

She didn't have the opportunity to complete her sentence. Abe clutched her hand and hoisted her out of her chair. "I want you to come to El Paso with me as a witness," he insisted. "Despite what I'll probably have to do to that rascal MacIntosh, I still owe a debt to his father. I intend to get to the bottom of this case, and you're going to help me find out what happened to my daughter."

Annette wasn't given the opportunity to accept or decline. When the stage conductor called for the westbound stage to lunge off, Annette was uprooted and dragged along with Abe's long, swift strides.

"Sergeant, you and your men ride back to the fort for reinforcements," he commanded as he bundled Annette into the coach. "And bring along the prisoners and those two clowns who call themselves bounty hunters. I intend to piece every bit of this incident together no matter how long it takes."

Having shouted from the window of the speeding coach, Abraham slouched back in his seat. "Forgive me, young lady. I was very abrupt, but I've been beside myself with worry. Now what did you say your name was?"

Annette smiled as she'd seen Tempest do—saucily. "I didn't say because you never gave me the chance."

A deep rumble of laughter rose from Abraham's chest. "No, I guess I didn't, did I?"

"My name is Annette Partridge," she replied, enjoying this new facet of her personality.

No more shy manners for her! She was going to do Tempest Litchfield proud. Annette only hoped she would have the opportunity to take a few more lessons in self-assertion from Tempest herself. The lively lady lawyer was an inspiration to the woman Annette strived to be.

"Partridge . . ." Abraham frowned thoughtfully. "Is Edgar your father, from down in Eagle Mountain country?" When Annette nodded, he eased back in his seat. "I tried a case for him several years ago—concerning some cattle thieves, as I recall."

Casting the thought aside, Abe turned his attention back to the topic foremost on his mind. "Annette, I want you to tell me everything you know about my daughter's ordeal—every insignificant detail. Don't leave anything out, no matter how irrelevant you think it might be. I want to hear your interpretations, as well as the facts."

Annette folded her hands in her lap and attempted to organize her thoughts. She proceeded as if she were sitting on the stand in a courtroom. She explained what Victor had told Tempest the day they'd met, and about his many mysterious jaunts to El Paso to confer with his "associates." She told Abraham how she had sneaked away from the *haci-*

enda during the night with three hired men who had agreed to accompany her. She didn't make any attempt to defend her ex-fiancé, either. In her opinion, Victor was mostly to blame for Tempest's plight, and Annette told the judge so in a straightforward manner that Tempest would have fully appreciated!

Cord couldn't help himself. He kept stealing glances at Tempest while they trekked around the craggy peaks toward Devil's Tank. Because of her fragile condition, he had taken the longer but safer route through the mountains. Tempest could barely sit atop her horse while the others ambled along beside her. In this wild tumble of mountains with its dangerous cliffs, she could faint dead away from exhaustion and plunge off a ledge. Cord wasn't taking any more chances.

When the unrelenting sun began to turn Tempest's splotchy face an alarming shade of white, Cord called a halt. "We'll rest here to eat and then travel through the night."

Although Tempest had refused to utter one complaint the past few hours, she was ever so thankful to rest beneath the shade of a ponderosa pine. She gasped in alarm when the clump of needles she assumed to be a variety of cactus suddenly scurried off. Tempest stared at the scraggly porcupine, surprised the creature hadn't decided to fling a few quills in her direction before retreating from its spot in the shade. Every *other* man and beast in these steep canyons and rock-choked ravines seemed to have it in for her.

"Tempest doesn't look well," Jefferson confided, dropping his cold shoulder treatment for the moment to speak to Cord. "I think you're pushing her too hard."

"Why do you think I stopped?" Cord asked as he

led Emilio over to a nearby mesquite tree to tether him.

"Probably because *you* got hungry," Jefferson said snidely. "I doubt you're all that concerned about her. You didn't give them a thought two days ago."

Cord scowled when Jefferson turned away to fuss over Tempest. That damned cousin of his was getting on Cord's nerves. Yellowfish's ponderous silence wasn't helping, either. No one had uttered a word for more than three hours, and Cord had spent all his time discreetly monitoring Tempest's condition. She hadn't even glanced at him. Didn't she know it was killing him to realize that every step he took led him closer to the inevitable moment when he had to tell her good-bye?

"I brought you some chokecherries," Jefferson murmured as he hunkered down beside Tempest. He extended the canteen he had filled at the spring. "This will make you feel better."

"I feel fine," Tempest insisted before gulping the water.

"Of course you do," Jefferson chuckled. "That's why your face is as white as paste and you can barely hold up your head. Indeed, pretty lady, I can't remember seeing you look healthier."

"Go away, Jefferson," Tempest grumbled grouchily. "Your sweet disposition is making me nauseous."

Jeff reached out to push the silky chestnut tendrils away from her blanched face. "I'm really—"

"Jeff!" Cord's low growl caused his cousin's hand to stop in midair. "Go tend the horses. They're as thirsty as the rest of us."

"You could have had *sweet,*" Jefferson said confidentially to Tempest as he stood up. "Instead you'll be stuck with *sour.*"

Jefferson's darting gaze left no question as to whom *sour* was. Cord looked as if he'd just bitten into a green apple.

When Jefferson sauntered over to grasp the reins of the two horses, Cord lurched around and wandered off. Hell's bells, he thought, he couldn't even tolerate watching Jefferson touch Tempest. It was a damned good thing he wouldn't be around in the years to come to watch other men with her. He was jealous and overprotective, even while he was making a heroic effort to forget the special magic between them. Suddenly Cord wasn't stewing about how he'd get through the rest of the day without aching for Tempest. He was worried about how he'd get through the rest of his life! *Caramba!* Sometimes he wondered if it wouldn't have been easier just to lie down and die rather than go on living when he felt so empty and dead inside.

Determinedly, Cord tried to remember all the platitudes about how he was doing what was best for the both of them. And of course, Yellowfish would reassure him that letting go was the right thing to do. This agony would be over soon, Cord convinced himself. They would reach the way station near the foothills of the Davis Mountains by mid-morning of the following day. Tempest would catch the stagecoach and she would soon be reunited with her father.

Mulling over that noble thought, Cord ambled back to camp to eat his meal in silence. When Tempest began to regain her energy and the color returned to her cheeks, he issued the order to move on. The fact that the pulsating heat and sticky humidity had caused the clouds to puff above the towering peaks prompted Cord to set a swifter pace. He preferred to reach the sloping foothills near Blue Mountain before a thunderstorm unleashed its fury. Tempest didn't need to be drenched while she was recovering from her wound.

Several hours later, when Tempest glanced skyward, she had the inescapable feeling that the weather wasn't going to cooperate. Clouds, like angry knotted fists, piled on the shoulders of the jagged summits. Thunder rumbled in the distance and lightning bolts danced against the rocks. The wind had picked up considerably, and her steed was stumbling over the stones in his path. Twice Tempest had come close to being catapulted from the saddle. Digging her hands and knees into the horse was all that had prevented her from being hurled through the air to bruise the bump on her forehead and rip open the stitches on her shoulder.

In grim anticipation, Tempest watched a curtain of rain sweep across the higher elevations. Any second, they were going to be in a downpour. She would have loved a cool bath to revive her deflated spirits and aching muscles, but a shower of icy raindrops and hammering hailstones wasn't exactly what she had in mind!

The thought was torn from her brain when Cord's brawny arm snaked around to lift her from her horse. Tempest was hoisted against Cord's chest and toted off before she had time to protest. Those old familiar sparks began to fly down her spine, and Tempest resented the fact that all her silent pep talks hadn't helped her recover from this impossible attraction. Even when she told herself she didn't care for him anymore, her traitorous body and foolish heart refused to listen. Even when she had seen the frightening side of his nature, momentary hatred couldn't overcome her love. Even when she had wanted to believe him guilty of thievery and murder she had kept on wanting him. It was hopeless! *She* was hopeless!

"Jeff, tie those horses up before they bolt and run," Cord yelled over his shoulder as he carried Tempest to an overhanging ledge that would shield her from the approaching rain. "Yellowfish, find some cover for Emilio and then tuck yourself away. This storm looks to be a cloudburst."

Tempest scooted back against the granite wall beneath the ledge the instant before the raging storm unleashed its fury. Silver streaks darted across the sky like bony fingers. A horrendous crack of thunder rattled the rocks in the mountains, causing echoes to reverberate around the canyon. Water poured down the slopes like rushing rivers, filling the ravines with frothy foam. The wind howled like a pack of coyotes, but Tempest was aware of nothing but the ruggedly handsome renegade who crouched in front of her. Her eyes were filled with him, memorizing each feature, each muscle on his magnificent body.

The realization that she would never be this close to Cord again tumbled over her like a rock slide. All her carefully guarded emotion came bubbling up like a geyser. Tempest reached out to trail her forefinger over his dark brows, high cheekbones, the angular slope of his jaw. She wondered if he could see the love shining in her eyes, if he could feel her affection in the way she touched him. This was her last chance alone with him to tell him good-bye—the others had sought protection in a nearby shallow cave. While the rain poured down like tears of longing, Tempest set her damnable pride aside. Just once more, she yearned to feel those fires of passion burning through every fiber of her being—fires so potent that even torrential rains couldn't extinguish them.

She couldn't love this wild renegade forever, but she could love him now. When she left him, she would have one last cherished memory to call upon during all the lonely days and nights to come. This would be her one shining hour, that glorious instant that made life worth living. She would offer Cord her body for his pleasure, but she would also give him her heart and soul for this short space of time.

And when the loving was over, she could only hope that her memory would linger in his mind like an eternal flame—a reminder of what might have been, if they had met in another life where there weren't so many obstacles in their way . . .

Twenty-six

Cord caught his breath when he gazed into those enchanting blue eyes. The feel of Tempest's trembling fingertips drifting over his face was the last straw. He'd known when he tugged her from her steed that he'd wanted them to be alone together to weather the storm. And he also knew that he'd wanted her so badly that he had even welcomed the storm as an excuse to have her all to himself this one last time.

Ah, how he longed to reassure her that she was the only woman alive who could bring out the tenderness in him. As if she were a fragile flower, Cord gathered her in his arms and drew her down on the clumps of grass beneath the ceiling of stone. Odd, how he wished that just once he could have made love to her on a feather bed with satin sheets and a velvet spread, allowing her to languish in all the luxuries a woman like Tempest deserved.

"For all the times I've hurt you, disappointed you, and angered you . . ." he murmured as his lips feathered across her forehead. "This last time I want to make it up to you . . ."

Tempest melted the instant his hands and lips whispered across her flesh, worshipping each inch of bare skin he exposed. She held nothing back from the very first moment he touched her. She responded instinctively, and with all her heart. While the stream of rain formed a liquid drapery over the jutting ledge, Tempest surrendered in total abandon. She lived for his practiced caresses and his breath-stealing kisses. She adored the feel of his body pressed provocatively against hers. She died a thousand times over, knowing she would never be this close to paradise again.

A gasp broke from her throat when his hands swirled over the dusky peaks of her breasts, sending waves of ineffable pleasure blazing through her. Her body quivered as he drew the throbbing crests into his mouth, his warm tongue flicking out to tease and arouse. When his bold caresses glided over her ribs to the small indentation of her waist, Tempest gasped. This seductive wizard had a magical touch. He could leave her dancing like a puppet on a string—dancing only for him. He could absorb her very spirit and create energy where there had been nothing but aching emptiness. He could make her body glow with rapture—he was her everything and she was about to lose him forever!

Cord couldn't seem to get enough of the taste and feel of her beneath his hands and lips. He wanted to devour her before the storm ebbed and yet, he longed to savor each wondrous sensation that making wild, sweet love to Tempest gave him. He was tender but impatient, hungry and yet strangely satisfied. Loving Tempest was sweet, aching torment. It was a fever without a cure. How in the world could he ever forget what he couldn't allow himself to remember in the months and years to come without driving himself crazy?

He touched her like a man who knew the torments of the newly damned, wanting to cherish each taste, absorb her sultry scent, yet knowing his moments were numbered and that the pleasure he had known with Tempest would never come again. Reverently, his palm whispered over her belly, seeking the soft heat that could burn him alive. Gently, his hand eased between her thighs and his fingertips caressed the silky flesh that concealed her molten core. He coaxed her responses until he felt the coil of feminine heat shuddering around him. The tender penetration of his tongue drew another trembling response that vibrated to the very depths of his soul, leaving him ablaze.

He could never possess another woman in the secret ways he possessed Tempest. What they shared was too magical, too private, too profound. He hungered only for the taste of her, yearned only for her hot, quivering responses. She was like a delicate rose and he was the sun, feeling the heat of his own hunger calling to her, feeling the fragile petals opening to burn around him. The exquisite fire knew only one name . . . Tempest . . . And even now, Cord could feel the memory of each unrivaled sensation. In the years to come, he would remember how it felt to *become* the fire that *consumed* him. The memories would ignite with the very mention of her name . . . Tempest . . . Wild wind, wild flame . . .

Tempest felt herself scaling one lofty plateau after another when Cord touched her in the most intimate places, and in the most intimate ways. There was no logic to this mindless passion. It was raw, turbulent emotion free from restraint, and Tempest couldn't contain the cry of ecstasy that burst from her lips when Cord brought her desires to such a fervent pitch. His caresses and kisses left no part of her untouched. The pleasure was so wild and intense that it demanded to be returned.

Gasping for breath, Tempest twisted away to caress his chest, feeling the pounding of his heart beneath her fingertips. She peered down into those tawny eyes that glittered with passion and she vowed to draw him to the very brink of abandon. Although she was no match for this formidable warrior on a battlefield, there was one place she could become his equal. He had taught her how to please him, and Tempest had come to know his body far better than she knew her own. And when they parted ways, she would leave him with this precious memory, bedevil him with the feel of her adoring hands and lips over the sleek contours of his body. He would know for a fact that he had been loved and loved well. Perhaps other women would provide him with pleasure, but none of them would feel the kind of love she felt for this Goliath of a man.

Cord groaned in unholy torment when Tempest's skillful caresses sensitized his flesh. She had practiced to perfection and her innovative techniques were driving him over the edge. Cord could feel his primitive instincts taking a fierce and mighty hold on him when her moist lips cruised over the muscles of his belly and her hand enfolded him. She teased and tormented him with her maddeningly tender assault of whispering kisses and caresses as light as the fluttering of a butterfly's wings. She tugged at him with gentle nips of her teeth that had him arching up to feel the moist recesses of her mouth enclosing him. Fingertips of silken fire glided over the throbbing length of him. Her tongue swirled around the tip of his manhood until he wept the warm rain of the desperate desire that only this one woman drew from him. Over and over, she excited and satisfied him, creating gigantic cravings that threatened to swallow him alive.

Then her body glided over him in the most agonizingly sweet caress of all, and she bent to share the taste of his own need that lingered on her lips. Cord could feel the tips of her breasts brushing against his laboring chest, feel her curvaceous hips moving suggestively against his. And when her petal-soft lips captured his once again, the world came crashing down like the hailstones that pelted the boulders above him. Cord didn't know if it was the hail that hammered so loudly in his ears or the frantic thud of his heart. All he wanted was to feel her silky body blending into his. He needed her as he needed air to breathe and nothing was ever going to be the same again until she was his, until she was a living, breathing part of him.

When Cord's lithe body arched toward hers and he guided her to him, Tempest felt the searing pleasure burn through her, streaming out in all directions like a wind-swept wildfire that fed upon itself. Suddenly they were clutching each other desperately, moving in perfect rhythm, riding the cresting wave of ecstasy that surged and swelled until it crashed like a breaker on a storm-tossed sea. Tempest felt as if she were drowning in an ocean of dark, sensuous rapture—plummeting, swirling, drifting with an undercurrent that dragged her toward infinity . . . and beyond . . .

A muffled groan escaped Cord's lips as he rolled over to bring Tempest beneath him before he lost that last shred of control. The pattering hailstones that danced around them were like impatient fingers drumming, taking him ever closer to the limits of his willpower. His hands slid beneath her hips, lifting her shuddering body to his as he drove into her. Cord knew he was like a wild savage, wracked with unrestrained emotion, but he couldn't help himself. This crazed hunger that gnawed at him demanded immediate satisfaction. When the last thread of self-control snapped, Cord didn't attempt to hold back the burgeoning ecstasy that consumed him.

Forgetting about her tender shoulder, the loneliness in all his tomorrows, and everything else that had any semblance to reality, he clutched Tempest in his arms. His body shuddered over hers, wracked with convulsive spasms of splendor. Cord buried his head against the swanlike curve of her throat and rode out the tidal wave of rapture. Even as the last pulsating throb of pleasure riveted his spent body, he couldn't let Tempest go because he knew exactly how far he was going to fall—all the way to the rock-hard bottom of his soul. When he withdrew, his arms would be instantly aching to reach out to her again. His eyes would absorb every detail about her—the way she looked with the afterglow of passion sparkling in her sapphire eyes, the way her dewy lips curved into a drowsy smile of fulfillment. Would she look and feel the same way in the arms of another man who could give her all the things Cord couldn't?

That distressing thought caused Cord to hold Tempest possessively to him, enjoying every last smidgen of pleasure. He didn't want to think such depressing thoughts when these precious few moments were all he had left. He just wanted to hold her, to recapture each wondrous sensation and store it in his mind and heart. He wanted to remember the way it had always been between them.

Tempest's wandering hand skied along Cord's shoulder to glide over his scarred back and down the lean curve of his hip. She couldn't have asked for more than she had received in their final rendezvous in the rain. It had been a glorious moment of passion, and she had communicated her deep abiding love for him in the way she responded, in the way she kissed and caressed him. Tempest had said all she could say without words. It was enough. If Cord couldn't hear her tortured confession of love then he wasn't listening to the whispers of her heart.

"It's stopped raining," she murmured, her voice still thick with passion.

"We better go," Cord rasped against her flushed cheek. But he made no move to leave because he hadn't mustered the will to pry himself loose.

"Yes, we definitely should," Tempest agreed as her hand absently caressed his sleek, muscular body once again.

When his hands framed her face, Tempest blinked back the hot tears that only this man could bring to her eyes and into her heart. And when his lips took firm possession, Tempest breathed in the taste and feel of him, savoring the maelstrom of tenderness that undulated through her. Her arms curled around his neck and she kissed him back with all the love bottled up inside her. Despite everything, he had to know how much she cared. How could he not?

"Good-bye, princess," Cord whispered softly.

"Good-bye, Apache . . ." Tempest bit her trembling lips. Achingly, she peered into those flickering amber eyes as he lifted himself away to gather his clothes.

Only the sound of raindrops and rolling thunder penetrated the silence. Composing herself as best she could, Tempest donned her tattered garments, wishing Cord could have seen her—just once—in an elegant gown and coiffure. Strange that she would wish something so whimsical. But she wanted him to remember her looking her best.

Ah well, that would only have served to remind Cord of the contrasts between her lifestyle and his. What difference did it make? Soon she'd be gone and Cord would put this interlude in the mountains out of his mind to devote himself to finding Victor Watts. She was already a fading memory. He had said his last good-bye . . .

"We will leave now," Yellowfish declared as he ducked under the overhanging ledge.

Whether or not the old Indian knew how they had spent their time, he didn't say. He simply peered at Cord with a meaningful stare, and then turned around and limped off. Dispirited, Tempest crawled from her niche and crept around the boulders to the place where Yellowfish waited with the horses.

"You had to have her one last time, didn't you?" Jefferson said with a sneer as he shouldered past Cord.

Cord's gaze narrowed on his sulking cousin. "She's still my wife. It's none of your business, Jeff. The way you're behaving one would think you're jealous because you're in love with her."

"Maybe I am," he muttered. "I wouldn't have traded places with you the past few weeks because I don't like the monster you've become. But right now, I'd give anything if she and I could have—"

Cord pounced on his cousin. His fist clenched in the front of Jefferson's shirt, jerking him up so that they were standing toe-to-toe and eye-to-eye. "Tempest and I—"

"Lobo Plano!" Yellowfish's voice cracked like a whip when he spied Cord and Jefferson at each other's throats. Their bodies looked as if they were about to break under the tension.

"We are leaving . . . *now,*" Yellowfish emphasized with a condescending glare.

Scowling, Cord loosed his fierce grip and retreated a step. "I'm sorry, cuz," he apologized but there was still too much venom in his voice to sound sincere.

"Yeah, so am I," Jefferson grumbled as he rearranged the shirt Cord had wrapped around his neck. "I should have taken Tempest back to El Paso when we discovered she wasn't who we thought she was."

Cord muttered at his cousin who had turned out to be a royal pain in the ass the last few days. Jeff suddenly saw himself as Tempest's knight in shining armor, her noble protector. Well, Cord wished that half-baked cousin of his would hightail it back to the Pinery before they came to blows.

Yellowfish was right. The old Apache was always

right about everything. When a man got too emotionally involved with a woman, he lost his common sense and perspective. Tempest caused trouble when she wasn't even trying and she was devastating when she *was* trying. Cord had let himself care too much for too long. But he had said his good-byes and now it was time to enter the next phase of his life. He had to concentrate on his confrontation with Victor Watts. When that bastard received his just desserts, Cord could put the past behind him and begin again. He had promised Victor a battle—Apache-style—and that was exactly what that conniving scoundrel was going to get!

Glumly, Tempest slouched in the rocking chair that occupied a dark corner of the adobe stage station nestled in the foothills. She was thoroughly exhausted after her rugged journey. Her shoulder throbbed in rhythm with her bleeding heart. Never in her life had she envisioned herself pining away for a man who had made love to her as if she meant something special to him and then deposited her on the road to the stage station and raced off with no more than the polite tip of his hat! Damn it, it had been such an impersonal farewell that Tempest felt as if she'd been crushed by a boulder.

Well, what did you expect? she asked herself crossly. Cord MacIntosh could never be accused of being overly sentimental and he wasn't one for public displays of affection, either. Only when they had been alone, riding out the storm, had he exhibited the tenderness she had come to love, even if it was only pretention. But when it was over, it was over. Done . . . Damn . . .

The sound of a bugle heralding the approach of the incoming stage filtered into Tempest's bleak thoughts.

"It's the westbound," the proprietor informed her as he wiped the table clean. Hensley twisted the cloth to swat at a pesky fly and then waddled over to the spittoon to send an arc of tobacco through the air. "Yer stage won't be here for another couple of hours. You want the wife to stir up some vittles while yer waitin'?"

"I haven't the money to pay for anything except my ticket," Tempest confessed. Cord had slapped the few coins he had left from his poker game in El Paso del Norte in her hand, which was all he had. *Except his heart and his love,* she mused despairingly.

"Well, I don't usually feed folks who can't pay their way. I ain't runnin' a charity house, ya know," Hensley declared. His gaze drifted over the ragtag garments that hung off her slender body like laundry on a clothesline. "But ya look as if ya could use some nourishment, little gal. The meal's on the house."

"You're very kind," Tempest murmured appreciatively.

"Naw, I ain't really. I just got a soft spot for little gals who look as if they ain't eaten in a week and just lost their best friend."

While Hensley bundled off to put his wife to work preparing food, Tempest laid her head back with a deep sigh. She had to get hold of herself. Her father would be even more distressed if he saw her like this. Wearing tattered men's clothes was bad enough, but Abraham wasn't accustomed to seeing Tempest's spirits scraping rock bottom. She had to get herself together before she reached the fort. Abraham would be asking questions that would require careful answers.

Abraham had always tried not to be overprotective of his fiercely independent daughter, but beneath that noble pretense, he pampered and fussed over Tempest because she was all he had . . .

Tempest blinked like an owl adjusting to bright

sunlight. Was that also why Yellowfish had disapproved of her? Was that his way of trying to protect Cord? By God, that had been the old codger's problem all along, Tempest realized. Cord was all Yellowfish had left in the world and he clung fiercely to his grandson. But surely the old chief didn't see her as a real threat. How could he . . . ?

Once again, Tempest's thoughts were interrupted, this time by the thunder of hooves. Absently, she glanced toward the closed door. She really wasn't in the mood for company. The westbound stage had arrived and she would have to make an effort to be sociable. Tempest forced a smile to greet the dusty travelers.

Her eyes bulged from their sockets when the door creaked open and Annette breezed through the entrance of the way station on none other than Abraham Litchfield's arm, as if *she* were his daughter . . . or something . . .

What was her father doing out in the middle of nowhere? He was supposed to be at Fort Davis. And what the devil was Annette doing with him? She was supposed to be enjoying Victor's hospitality. The girl's manner had changed dramatically since the last time Tempest had seen her. And Abraham was the epitome of gentlemanly attention. And worse, Tempest could swear the young blonde was giving Abe the eye! Good Lord, she had better be mistaken! The last thing she needed right now was a seventeen-year-old stepmother!

The instant Abraham Litchfield realized it was his long-lost daughter sitting in the shadowy corner, he let out a hoot of joy that rattled the rafters. Abe rushed to Tempest and scooped her out of her chair. He then proceeded to hug the stuffing out of her, as if she had returned from the dead. The judge had no idea how close he had come to the mark!

"Ouch!" Tempest sucked in her breath when her father very nearly split her stitches.

"My God, girl, I never thought I was going to see you again!" Abraham declared as he reluctantly eased his grasp on her. "Annette told me you'd been shot and I feared the worst. I was on my way to El Paso to hang every man involved!" He frowned when he noted the lack of customary sparkle in her blue eyes. "Are you all right, honey?"

No, she wasn't all right. Damn it, her heart was in splinters! "I'm fine. I'm just weak from my wound," she said instead.

When Hensley waddled back into the room, Abraham wheeled to face him. "I would like a bottle of your best brandy to celebrate my daughter's safe return."

"This ain't San Antone, mister," Hensley scoffed. "I got whiskey and that's all I got."

"Fine, we'll take it," Abe said with a wave of his arms. "And plenty of food. I'll gladly pay extra for larger portions. My daughter is recovering from a serious wound."

Hensley peered at Annette and then at Abraham before it dawned on him that the tattered slip of a woman was his daughter, not the elegantly dressed blonde who was his . . . Hensley didn't know *what* but he had a pretty good idea. Obviously the daughter had been cast aside to make room for the older man's . . . *whatever.*

"I promised this little gal a free meal," Hensley grumped, shooting Abraham a disapproving glare. "It looks to me as if she deserves it if that's how you treat yer own kinfolk."

Abraham blinked, startled by the remark and the disdainful glance. Before he could question the proprietor about his meaning, Hensley tramped off again.

Annette clasped Tempest's hands in a zealous squeeze. "I was so worried about you. All these weeks of never knowing what had become of you! Thank God you're alive and well. I prayed you would be. I wish I had half your strength of spirit, Tempest. I greatly admire you and how far you've come in this world. I'm so relieved that you survived."

Tempest peered at the blonde whose enthusiastic tone of voice and sincere expression set her back on her heels. Annette had changed drastically. But then, Tempest supposed anything was possible. Look how *she* had changed in the past month!

"I left Victor when I realized what a scoundrel he really was beneath all that gallantry," Annette explained with newfound self-confidence. "One certainly cannot tell a gentleman by the cut of his clothes! I learned that what's inside a man is far more important than what he pretends to be."

Annette had learned a few things, thought Tempest. The half-breed Tempest had come to know and love was certainly proof that manners did not make the man.

"Your father urged me to return to El Paso with him to testify to what I know about Victor's dealings. And I have decided to follow in your footsteps, Tempest. From now on I'm going to become as strong and as liberated as you are. You are my inspiration!"

"I hardly consider myself an inspiration to anybody," Tempest said. "But I thank you for the praise. You're doing wonders for my drooping spirits."

While the threesome sat down to take their meal, Tempest found herself impressed with Annette's remarkable transformation. Her first impression of Victor's fiance had been that of a dutiful, subservient maiden who had been instructed to stay in her place. Luckily for Annette, she had cultivated a mind of her own and had acquired enough gumption to use it.

"Annette has told me what she knows about Victor's activities, about the Salt Ring and Cord MacIntosh's jailbreak," Abraham remarked, cutting to the heart of the matter, as was his custom. "Now I want to know everything about your captivity."

Tempest had mentally rehearsed her colloquy while she was lingering in the stage station. Briefly and concisely, she explained what had transpired and why. However, she carefully omitted the part about the marriage for fear Abraham would go right through the roof. She, after all, had inherited her hair-trigger temper from her father and he knew how to use it as well as she did.

Analytical and methodical though Abraham could be on the judicial bench, he did have a tendency to explode in matters that affected him personally. It was always easier to be objective when one's emotions weren't involved. How well Tempest knew that! It was impossible to be objective in matters concerning Cord. She was worried sick about what he was going to do when he confronted Victor. After all, she had seen what had happened to Emilio Reynosa when he balked at telling the truth about Paddy MacIntosh's death.

Before Tempest could complete her story with all its unfortunate twists and tangles, the conductor directed them to the westbound coach. Although Annette had generously offered Tempest any gown in her satchel, there hadn't been time to change clothes. Tempest was left to make the first leg of the journey back to El Paso in her homespun garments. She would find time to take care of her frazzled appearance later. But it didn't really matter, so long as they reached Victor's *hacienda* in time to waylay Cord.

All Tempest wanted was to clear Cord's name before he did something rash, then she intended to head toward San Antonio. She wanted no more reminders of the man who had broken her heart. She just wanted it to be over so she could begin her life again—without Cord.

At least she wouldn't have to spend the next few years wondering if there was a man on God's green earth whom she could have loved. She'd already met him, loved him, and lost him. Tempest didn't plan to waste her time with any other man. She would dedicate her life to her profession, even if she got stuck with all the undesirable cases. And after all, she might even become the first female judge in the state, following in her father's footsteps. Maybe she could solve other people's conflicts better than she had solved her own.

Cord made it a point to take a wide berth around the well-traveled roads and trails that crisscrossed west Texas. His destination was the El Paso jail. The first order of business was to lock Emilio up in the same cell Cord had occupied.

Although Jefferson's animosity was still obvious, he had insisted on accompanying Cord since Myra had sent him to assist his cousin in any manner possible. Yellowfish, however, had drawn the line at venturing into the white and Mexican settlements along the Rio Grande. Tall and proud, the old Apache had bade them farewell and retreated to his domain in the Delaware Mountains.

Since Cord was still wanted for a variety of crimes, Jefferson had volunteered to escort Emilio into town and explain the charges against him. The law officials were Victor's associates and were hesitant to lock Emilio up. But Jefferson used some of Cord's power of persuasion—two loaded pistols and a threat:

he assured the sheriff and his deputy they would pay dearly if Emilio *accidentally* escaped.

When Jefferson returned to their meeting place along the Rio Grande, Cord lifted a brow. "Any trouble?"

Jefferson shrugged his broad shoulders. "Victor obviously has the town marshal in his hip pocket. He was reluctant to cooperate."

"I was afraid of that," Cord muttered. "No doubt the district judge also had his palms greased. I'll be lucky if I can bring Victor to trial at all."

Jefferson peered at his cousin as they headed south. "I thought you intended to scalp, stab, and shoot Victor and be done with him. That was the impression you left with the *vaqueros.*"

"Scare tactics," Cord explained. "I wanted Victor to sweat blood until I got my hands on him."

"Is that what you wanted Tempest to do, too?" Jefferson queried. "A more impersonal farewell between husband and wife I've never seen! You could at least have allowed her to keep her pride and dignity instead of shooing her off as if she meant nothing."

"Damn it, Jeff," Cord exploded. "What the hell do you think I was doing? It was never going to work between us. Look at me, for God's sake! What kind of husband would I have made for a lady lawyer? The esteemed judge's daughter? Can you see me in the fancy trappings of a gentleman? Rubbing shoulders with the upper crust of San Antonio society? Attending soirées and the theater?"

It was finally beginning to dawn on Jefferson why Cord had sent Tempest off in such a cold, abrupt manner. "No, I guess I can't, Tosh, especially since you weren't even willing to try to make the marriage work."

"Yellowfish says a man has to be careful he doesn't get what he *wants* but rather what he *needs.* He says the worst things in life are yearning for your heart's desire and then getting it—when it brings disappointment and disillusionment."

"Good God," Jefferson scoffed. "The next thing you'll be telling me is you did Tempest some noble favor by letting her go away thinking she meant absolutely nothing to you. Hell, even a blind man could see she cared about you, once she'd gotten to know you. She came back, didn't she? That in itself was proof enough that she was willing to bridge the cultural gap."

"For how long? A month? Six months? We would only prolong the inevitable. Ignoring our differences would change nothing." Cord scowled irritably. "And anyway, I'm through talking and thinking about it. It's officially over."

"Is it?" Jefferson questioned quietly. "Good luck trying to convince your heart, cuz. You sound like a man who's hooked, even if you want us both to believe otherwise. Your arguments sound more like excuses. You seem to forget I've known you all my life. There's never been another woman who got to you the way Tempest did. I wish I could find a woman who cared about me as much as I think she cares about you. If I ever do, I won't give her up."

"Since when did you become an authority on romance?" Cord muttered. "You're giving me advice, and your love life barely even exists!"

"I'm getting all the experience I'll ever need, just watching you botch yours up," Jefferson countered sarcastically.

"Curse it, Jefferson. Give it up!" Cord blared. "I'm tired of listening to you shoot your mouth off! It's none of your damned business."

"Okay, cuz. It's your life," Jefferson said with an indifferent shrug. "If you want to be a damned fool, it's no skin off my back. But would you like to know what I think?"

"Not particularly," Cord grumbled, but he knew Jefferson would have his say nonetheless. Sure as hell, he did.

"I have a hankering to give society a try, just to see what it's like. And as for you, you've got gold nuggets coming out of your ears. You could buy yourself a place in any social circle. You could own half of San Antonio and enjoy luxuries you've never imagined. Uncle Paddy didn't need money because he never really wanted to settle down, even when he married your mother. They just sort of satisfied certain needs in each other after Yellowfish felt obliged to give his daughter to the man who'd saved his life and become his friend.

"I think even Yellowfish knows they never came to love each other the way a husband and wife truly should. But marriage doesn't have to be like that, you know," Jefferson insisted. "My parents are still crazy about each other, even after all these years. You should see them kissing when they don't think I'm around. You could have had that with Tempest if you weren't so damned bullheaded, if your so-called noble intentions weren't so far out of whack."

"*Caramba!* Now you've turned philosopher," Cord howled in dismay, wondering if and when Jefferson would ever button his lip.

"There's something to be learned from watching you ruin your life," Jefferson continued, undaunted. "The only smart thing you ever really did was marry that gorgeous female. Letting her go was just plain stupid."

Cord reined his horse to a halt and glared at Jefferson. "For your information, Yellowfish could see I cared too much from the beginning. He knew it wouldn't work, either."

Jefferson rolled his eyes skyward. He may as well debate a stone wall, for all the good it was doing. "Fine, end of discussion. Have it your way, Tosh. But don't come moping around the Pinery, looking for companionship. Just buy yourself a bottle of rotgut and find a few señoritas to take your mind off the woman you love. Why, in a few weeks, you probably won't even remember how pretty Tempest was or how much you enjoyed having her around. For certain, there were no dull moments as far as I could tell. But she won't have trouble finding a man to replace you. On that you can depend—"

"I thought this discussion was over," Cord muttered crabbily.

"It is."

"Good."

"You're still every kind of fool, Tosh."

"Clam up, Jefferson!"

Jefferson stared into the distance. He wasn't saying another word on the subject, but he sure as hell thought Cord was a stubborn fool.

"Oh, and one more thing, Tosh," he added in afterthought.

Cord flung his cousin a withering glance. "Now what?"

"Am I going to get to help you bring Victor Watts to justice?"

"No."

"Then what the devil am I doing here?"

"Damned if I know."

But Jefferson knew why he hadn't returned to the Pinery. Despite his belief that his cousin had made a blundering mistake with Tempest, Jefferson still admired Cord. When Cord needed assistance, Jefferson would come. And Cord would do the same for Jefferson. The fact remained that they were much closer than cousins. They were like brothers . . . kindred spirits . . .

Twenty-seven

Jefferson groaned when he spied the beaming torches that surrounded Victor Watts's *hacienda*. Although some of the *vaqueros* had resigned after their month-long manhunt, Victor still had a small army in his service. They had been ordered to stand guard through the night, just in case Cord followed through with his threat.

"How the Hades are you going to get to Victor? This place is lit up like the Fourth of July," Jefferson grumbled.

Cord flung his leg over the saddle horn and hopped to the ground. He handed the reins to his cousin and extended his free hand. "I need your dagger," Cord said.

Jefferson retrieved the knife from his boot and handed it to Cord. "Anything else, cuz?"

"No. Go back to the Pinery," Cord insisted.

"I'm hanging around to see how this works out," Jefferson said with a wry smile. "I may not go back to the Pinery for awhile. Hell, I may even decide to move to San Antonio and court Tempest."

"That isn't funny," Cord growled.

"Maybe I wasn't kidding. If you don't want her, there are plenty of men who do. I wouldn't mind being one of them, if she'll have me."

Cord was annoyed with himself for letting jealousy nip at him. He had tried to adjust to the idea of other men in Tempest's future; knowing Jefferson could be one of them only made it worse. Jeff could be a regular Casanova.

Forcing himself to concentrate on his mission, Cord gathered up his saddlebags and vanished without a sound.

"Damn, I'd really like to know how he does that," Jefferson said to the darkness before he reined the horses around to find a secluded spot to wait.

Victor helped himself to another brandy and then circumnavigated his office for the umpteenth time. At irregular intervals, he flung apprehensive glances at the window. Since the *vaqueros* had returned with their message from Cord, Victor had been dodging his own shadow. He had scoffed at the threat to salvage his pride, but he had to give Cord MacIntosh his due after the elusive half-breed had led the bravos on a merry chase and stolen Emilio right out from under everybody's noses.

After swallowing another drink to calm his nerves, Victor paused to stare at the ring of torches that encircled the *rancho*. He'd had his men working twelve-hour shifts to guard the *hacienda*, but a week had passed and there had been no sign of the vindictive half-breed.

He was beginning to think Cord MacIntosh was charmed. There wasn't a cell that could hold him or horde of *pistoleros* who could kill him. Curse it, he should have had Emilio dispose of Cord when he'd been charged with cattle rustling. But he had feared Paddy MacIntosh would have been twice as difficult to deal with if his son had been lynched on the spot.

"Damned half-breed," Victor swore vehemently.

"Where are you, MacIntosh? I'm tired of this waiting game."

Victor had muttered that question for seven exasperating days, but he knew enough about the Apache and Comanche to know that outwaiting an Indian was next to impossible. They seemed to have the patience of Job and they instinctively knew when the enemy had his guard down. That's always when they struck.

When Victor had returned from El Paso earlier in the week to find that Annette had vanished, he was sure Cord had abducted her. No one seemed to know what had become of Annette. Part of her luggage was gone and so was she, along with three *vaqueros* who had ridden with Emilio. It was uncanny how people kept disappearing around him, leaving him to wonder if he would be next.

Heaving a sigh, Victor threw down another drink and headed for bed. He'd drunk far too much already. Keeping the vigil was a duty assigned to his hired men. As for himself, Victor needed his sleep so he'd be alert if and when Cord MacIntosh tried to take on this small army. Victor had resigned himself to the fact that the half-breed might very well defy the odds. After all, Cord had done it numerous times before. Victor would be ready and waiting, just in case Cord showed up to seek his vengeance . . .

Like a darting shadow, Cord moved from one spot to another, using trees and shrubs as protection against the torches and guards patrolling the perimeters of the *hacienda*. Following the same route he'd taken when he abducted Tempest by mistake, Cord homed in on his prey.

Escaping the attention of the sentinels had proved a simple task at four o'clock in the morning. Half the weary men were snoring while they sat propped beneath the torches. The other half kept nodding off, making it easy for Cord to maneuver around them. His only difficulty was preventing the vine-choked lattice from creaking as he climbed to the second-story gallery, but the chirp of crickets and cicadas muffled his approach.

With the stealth of a tiger, Cord crept across the balcony to the room Tempest had once occupied. The doors and windows had been locked for protection, but by using his knife, he pried open the window without so much as a squeak. Cord stepped over the sill and slipped noiselessly into the room, and that was where his footsteps stopped. His eyes fell to the bed—and Tempest's satchels. Impulsively, he plucked up one of the elegant gowns. Wistfully, he brushed the satin garment against his cheeks longing for that chestnut-haired beauty who still haunted his days and especially his nights.

Cord grinned when he spied a lacy blue garter among her possessions. He placed it around his forearm in a symbolic gesture. He was taking a little bit of Tempest with him, wherever he went. It was a well-earned keepsake, considering what he'd been forced to sacrifice for both their sakes.

Tucking those thoughts in the back of his mind, Cord headed toward the door and tiptoed down the hall. When he attempted to turn the knob of what Cord assumed to be Victor's door, he found it locked. But after all Cord had endured, he wasn't going to let a little thing like a locked door discourage him. Before he was through with that conniving weasel, Victor would be sweating bullets!

Reversing direction, Cord returned to Tempest's room to fetch one of the diamond-studded hairpins he had seen among her belongings . . . A wry smile twitched his lips. The hairpin would serve two satisfactory purposes. Not only would it trip the door lock, but it could be used to prick Victor's skin if he proved to be as stubborn about confessing as Emilio Reynosa had been. Cord was actually curious to see just how much of a man Victor really was. The deceitful scoundrel had surrounded himself with seasoned *vaqueros* to do his dirty work for him. Time would tell just how invincible Victor was.

Determined of purpose, Cord turned his thoughts and his footsteps toward the locked door that stood between him and long-awaited revenge . . .

When the golden fingers of dawn inched through the window, Victor moaned groggily and attempted to flop onto his side. But he found himself restrained in some manner that his fuzzy mind couldn't apprehend. At first he thought he'd become entangled in his bedding, preventing any movement. Half-conscious of the world around him, Victor tried to roll to his belly, but his body still refused to cooperate.

Grumbling over the fact that he'd drunk more brandy than he should have the previous night, Victor pried open one eye to determine why he was immobilized. With a startled gasp he spied the ominous form of a man crouched on the trunk at the foot of his bed.

Victor nearly suffered heart seizure when he saw the bare-chested savage spotlighted by shafts of sunbeams. A colorful *rebozo* encircled the Apache's raven head. An elk's teeth necklace, decorated with beads, surrounded his throat. Around one bronzed arm was a leather strap from which dangled a silver concho, several more colorful beads and feathers. His right forearm boasted a lady's lacy garter. But what terrified Victor most was the death threat stamped on the savage's bronzed features.

While Victor lay there, strapped spread-eagle to the bedposts with the cords from his own draperies, the menacing intruder rose from his crouch. Victor swallowed a roomful of air. Cord's only garment was a doehide loincloth that displayed the well-muscled columns of his hips and thighs to their best advantage. His moccasins and knee-high *botas* completed the rugged ensemble of the warlike Apache. White war paint was slashed beneath his glittering amber eyes and across his jaws. A lightning bolt had been painted diagonally across his massive chest. In one hand the looming savage held a pearl-handled revolver. A deadly-looking dagger was clasped in the other.

Victor knew he was staring death in the face. It would be a slow, torturous death that would leave him screaming for mercy—and finding none. Instinctively, Victor flinched when the muscular giant stepped off the trunk and onto the end of the bed. One moccasined foot was planted between Victor's legs, the other one was wedged against the outside of his thigh. For the life of him—what there was left of it, which didn't look to be much—Victor couldn't draw a breath. His heart was pounding like a sledgehammer against his ribs and butterflies the size of pigeons were rioting in his belly. He opened his mouth to speak but a grinding heel to his chest forced the last ounce of air out of him.

"In the Apache camp, cheaters are punished for their deceit by cutting off their noses," Cord growled in such an ominous tone that Victor shuddered like a sapling besieged by a lumberjack's axe. "Liars lose their fingers, one by one, very slowly so they will feel each tearing pain and never distort the truth again. That is why Apaches do not lie and why you will never lie again . . ."

Victor's eyes grew round as saucers when Cord laid the glinting steel blaze beneath his nose. "No!" he yelped, his voice breaking in stark fear.

Cord hunkered down, purposely shifting his knee

to Victor's crotch, causing his victim to grunt in pain. "A few fingers then, *gringo?*" Cord taunted unmercifully.

When Cord's knife glided toward Victor's doubled fist, he tried to protest but his vocal cords refused to function. A hiss of pain did, however, escape his lips when the blade sliced across his knuckles in a grim preview of what was to come.

"Don't kill me!" Victor croaked when he recovered his powers of speech.

A wicked smile curved Cord's lips as he watched beads of perspiration pop out above Victor's winged brows. It was just as Cord predicted. Victor was a yellow-bellied coward who hired men to carry out his strong-arm tactics. He was already begging and Cord had barely scratched the weasel's skin.

"I'm not going to kill you . . . *yet,*" Cord assured him with a devilish grin. "And if you tell me what I want to know, I might even decide to let you live."

Cord leaned over to nick Victor's left knuckle. It was obvious Victor had a low threshold of pain. He started squealing like a stuck pig.

"I'll tell you anything," Victor babbled hysterically, his adam's apple bobbing as he gulped for breath.

Cord cocked a dark brow. "Before or after I slice off your nose?"

"Before! . . . I mean . . . *instead* of! I had Emilio set you up for the rustling charge!"

"Tell me something I don't know," Cord said contemptuously. "Emilio confessed to that, but he was far more man than you are. It took days to drag the truth out of him. You're ready to speak in a matter of minutes." With a sardonic grin Cord waved the sharp dagger in Victor's face. "You're spoiling my fun, *gringo.*"

When Cord grabbed Victor's chin and tilted it up to the waiting dagger, Victor whimpered like a child.

"I gave the order to have your father killed," he choked out, staring cross-eyed at the knife that bore down on his flared nostrils. "I acquired the documents to your salt rights and land deeds! I'll even tell you who was in on the Salt Ring with me—the sheriff, the judge . . . ouch!"

Cord had barely pricked Victor's flesh again and already the man was howling as if he'd been stabbed through the heart. This lily-livered poltroon was ruining Cord's long-anticipated revenge. *Caramba!* Even Tempest had endured far more pain than Victor and she hadn't complained. Cord had waited more than six weeks for this moment and he wasn't getting much satisfaction watching Victor squirm like the worm he was.

Damn it to hell, Tempest's influence on him was even stronger than he suspected. Confound that woman. Even when she wasn't with him, he could almost see her standing in the shadows, frowning in disapproval. Blast it, he was having less fun than the chickenhearted Victor who was having no fun at all!

Jefferson frowned curiously when a buckboard came flying down the road at breakneck speed. He squinted into the sunlight to see two fashionably-dressed females and an elegantly garbed gentleman making a beeline toward the front door of the *hacienda.* When he recognized that glorious chestnut hair, he bounded into the saddle to intercept the wagon.

Abraham Litchfield stamped on the brake when a rider charged from the underbrush, waving his arms like a windmill. "Get out of my way! I have official business here," the judge shouted in his authoritative voice.

"Where is he?" Tempest demanded without bothering with a greeting.

Jefferson jerked his horse to a halt and shrugged a broad shoulder. Automatically, he tipped his hat to the dainty blonde next to the judge. "I can't say for certain, Tempest. He should have his hands on Victor by now, if everything went according to his plan."

Tempest surveyed the heavily guarded *hacienda*. "How in heaven's name did he get past all these men without being spotted?"

Jefferson grinned slyly. "He just did, or at least he must have. I haven't heard any shouts or pistol blasts."

Abraham gaped at the handsome young man on horseback who was alternately giving Annette and then Tempest the once-over. "This Cord MacIntosh character sneaked past all these armed sentinels?"

"I offered to go with him," Jefferson explained. "But you'd have to know my cousin to understand. He likes to work alone."

"It's just as well," Abraham huffed. "If he's taking the law into his own hands, he'll stand trial for it. I can guarantee that. By damn, there *is* law west of the Pecos and I'm here to see it enforced . . ."

Abraham's voice trailed off when Tempest snatched the reins and popped them over the horses' rumps. The steeds lurched into a gallop, forcing Abraham and Annette to grasp their seats to avoid somersaulting forward. Even Jefferson barely had time to rein his horse out of the way before Tempest took off like a human tornado.

The buckboard hadn't even screeched to a halt before Tempest clutched the hem of her borrowed gown and bounded to the ground. In a flash, she barreled through the front door, glancing every direction at once. She prayed she could find Cord before he did something so rash that he turned the judge against him to such an extreme that the courts would grant him no mercy. After she had given her father the details of the case, without mentioning the hasty marriage, her father had become sympathetic to Cord's plight. Tempest felt certain she could persuade her father to be lenient about the kidnapping charge after he'd calmed down. But if Victor was being tortured to death, Cord wouldn't be making a friend of the judge!

A muffled squawk caused Tempest's head to turn toward the staircase. She leaped up like a mountain goat, taking the steps two at a time in her haste to stop Cord before he took Victor's life. Without announcing herself, she burst into the room and skidded to a halt.

Her disbelieving eyes registered shock when she spied the ominous figure of a man dressed like an Apache on the warpath. The very sight of war paint and the skimpy loincloth was shocking enough to scare the living daylights out of anyone. Tempest staggered back. The scene hit her like a physical blow. She stood rooted to the spot, staring at Cord as if she'd never seen him before in her life.

Cord had been in midair when the door burst open. When Tempest breezed inside, he landed with both feet on Victor's belly, forcing a loud grunt from his victim. Cord was sure Tempest thought him utterly mad, considering the way he'd been carrying on by doing a war dance on Victor's body and his bed. The performance had been a good one, even if Cord did say so himself. He had assured Victor that he was performing the Apache dance of death—the last rite before Victor was launched into hell. Victor believed it.

Difficult though it was to tear her gaze away from the formidable giant, Tempest focused on Victor. The man was as white as flour, but there were only a few scratches on his hands and face. It looked as if Cord had only been toying with his enemy, using very effective scare tactics. He stood there looking like a sleek, muscular lion with his paw on a frightened mouse.

Cord stared at the vision of loveliness who burst into the room. Never before had he seen anything so bedazzling as Tempest in an elegant gown. She was positively stunning—the personification of sophistication, poise, refinement, and beauty. And here *he* stood, looking like a wild heathen—straight from the pages of a dime novel. If ever there was a time when he felt a galaxy away from this lovely lass, it was now. It drove home the point with such intensity that Cord actually grimaced.

"What are you doing here?" Cord croaked, his wobbling voice spoiling the terrifying effect he'd had on Victor.

"Oh, I just stopped by to watch you make a complete ass of yourself," Tempest said mockingly as Cord used Victor for a springboard to bound off the bed. Her blue eyes twinkled with wry amusement, causing Cord to shift self-consciously beneath her stare. "Do you have these fits very often, Mister MacIntosh? I can refer you to a very reputable hospital that deals with your kind of mental imbalance."

"Help me!" Victor shouted. "He's going to kill me!"

"Tempest! Where the devil are you?" Abraham's trumpeting voice reverberated through the hall.

Tempest wheeled around to see her father, Annette, and Jefferson rush into the room. When the judge screeched to a halt, Annette and Jefferson slammed into his back, knocking him off balance.

"Good Lord," Abraham gasped when his bug-eyed gaze fastened on the scene.

Jefferson shouldered past Abe to confront his cousin. "Cord MacIntosh, I would like to introduce you to Judge Litchfield." He shot Cord another amused glance. "You're making a splendid impression, cuz. Gee, I wonder if the judge is going to throw the book at you . . . if for no other reason than to cover up all that bare skin."

"Judge Litchfield?" Victor chirped in relief. "Thank God you arrived when you did. Get this murdering savage out of here! He tried to torture a confession out of me. *I'm* innocent of wrongdoing. *He* should be hanged on the spot!"

After shooting Cord a disdainful glance, Abraham marched over to the bed. "Victor Watts, you have been accused of conspiring to steal the legal rights to Paddy MacIntosh's Salt Lakes. You have also been charged with false allegations against one Cord MacIntosh and for the murder of his father. And I, representing the legal justice of the state of Texas . . ." He reached over to retrieve Cord's pistol and flipped it over in his hand. He slammed the make-shift gavel against the night stand, as if he were in a court of law. "I find you guilty of all charges and sentence you to twenty years in the state penitentiary."

"This isn't a court of law!" Victor spewed in protest.

"It is if I say it is!" Abraham boomed before lurching around to the skimpily dressed barbarian who was wearing Tempest's garter belt like an arm band. "You're fined for indecent exposure and you'll be sentenced for kidnapping as well."

"He didn't kidnap me," Tempest piped up as she wedged herself between Cord and her father.

"I went with Cord of my own free will," Tempest declared.

"No, you didn't," Abraham contradicted, giving her the evil eye.

"Yes, I did. Cord came to the *hacienda* and asked me if I wanted to go along and I said, 'Sure, why not?' Didn't I, Cord?"

Cord stared at the back of Tempest's head while she faced her father. When he lingered in thought, wondering why she was defending him after the rotten way he'd treated her, she gouged him in the belly.

"Didn't I?" she repeated.

Cord only grunted after having the breath knocked out of him.

Abraham's blue eyes narrowed on his daughter. He could not imagine why she would distort the truth to spare this wild savage. "Tempest, this is a court of law, such as it is. You know perjury is a criminal offense as well as I do."

"Very well then, judge, we will come at this from a different direction," Tempest parried. "You cannot pass sentence on a man if no formal charge is brought against him. If no formal complaint is placed, then in effect, there is no crime. And if there is no crime, there can be no punishment. And I do not wish to file charges."

"You want me to let him go scot-free?" Abe questioned in astonishment. "Why?"

"He's suffered enough. All I want is to go home as fast as I can get there." Tempest didn't dare turn to face Cord. Seeing him towering over Victor had already caused her heart to melt. "Tell Mister MacIntosh he is free to go—the sooner the better."

Abraham glanced over his daughter's head at the uncivilized brute looming behind her. It went against the grain to let this rascal walk away unpunished, but Tempest had that look about her; she wasn't budging from her stubborn stand.

"Very well then, you're free to go, but for God's sake, put some clothes on before you do!" Abraham grumbled resentfully.

There were a dozen things Cord wanted to say to Tempest, but there wasn't time and this wasn't the place. And he supposed it was a little too late anyway.

Soundlessly, he sidestepped Annette, who was all eyes and curiosity. Silently, Cord walked away without looking back.

Tempest battled the tears that threatened to cloud her vision. She stood as rigid as a flagpole until the door clanked shut behind Cord. Although the dam of emotions inside her threatened to burst, Tempest mustered her composure. She was not going to allow her father to know she was hurting. She would retain her dignity and survive. Falling in love with Cord had been her heaven and her hell. And she was *never* letting herself fall in love again.

Jefferson fell into step behind his cousin, who had detoured to the back of the *hacienda* to retrieve his saddlebag and clothes. When Cord swung onto his mount, Jefferson frowned curiously. "Now what, cuz?"

"I'm going back where I belong, after I see to one last obligation in El Paso," Cord declared.

"And what obligation might that be?"

"Compensation," Cord murmured ambiguously. "Well-deserved compensation . . ."

Jefferson didn't bother posing more questions. He could tell by the set of Cord's jaw that he was lost in thought. Jefferson didn't have to be a genius to determine what else occupied Cord's mind, either. It was written all over his rugged features. That blue-eyed pixie was torturing Cord far worse than he had tormented Victor Watts.

This was the kind of mental anguish that could drive a sane man mad. Cord's heart was warring with his brain, each one teeming with justifiable arguments about whether he'd done the right thing. Jefferson had tried to convince Cord that he was making a critical mistake, but nothing he'd said had influenced this billy goat of a cousin. Well, it was Cord's loss and he was already suffering for it, if the look on his face was any indication. Jefferson had the inescapable feeling that it was.

After Cord thundered away, Jefferson wheeled around to return to the *hacienda*. He had every intention of making sure the judge didn't have second thoughts about Cord's innocence. He also had every intention of making the lovely blonde's acquaintance. Just because Cord had passed up a chance at happiness with a bona fide lady didn't mean stupidity ran in the family. Annette Partridge might well be Jefferson's dream come true. He'd already learned that running away wasn't the answer, only part of the problem. And as Cord had recently reminded Jefferson, his love life was lacking . . . or at least it had been until now . . .

Twenty-eight

San Antonio, Texas

Abraham Litchfield opened the door to two young boys laden with packages. This was the third time in three weeks that anonymous gifts had arrived for Tempest. The first wave of packages had been filled with expensive jewelry. The second entourage of gift-bearing delivery boys had left Tempest with several elegant gowns, even though Abraham had always seen to it that his daughter's wardrobe was extensive. Now she had jewels and gowns galore, and he couldn't imagine who her generous and extravagant benefactor could be!

Since their return to San Antonio two months earlier, Tempest had refused to discuss her ordeal in West Texas. She had gone through the motions of living, throwing herself into her work and taking minimal nourishment. Although Tempest insisted she was in perfect mental and physical health, that old familiar sparkle was gone from her eyes. There was a certain sadness, even in her smiles.

Abraham hadn't had as much time to spend with Tempest as he wanted because of the excessive work load after his prolonged absence. He would have dearly loved to know what was wrong with his daughter and who the devil was lavishing her with gifts.

"Who was at the—?" Tempest pulled up short when she could see the answer for herself—another pile of presents that she didn't want or need. She had become annoyed by this constant barrage. She knew perfectly well who had sent her the gifts, even though she had refused to enlighten her father.

This was Cord's way of repaying her for everything she had endured, his way of apologizing. But Tempest wanted no costly trinkets—she only wanted Cord's heart and that was the one thing she could never have.

Damn him! Why did he have to torment her like this? She was trying to forget him and this wasn't helping one whit!

"My goodness, Miss Tempest," Herbert exclaimed when he stepped into the foyer to see Abraham overloaded with packages. "How many wealthy secret admirers do you have?"

"Several, obviously," she replied to the butler before scooping up several packages and heading toward the steps.

Abraham closed the door with his heel and trailed along behind his daughter. "Where is all this coming from?"

"I don't have the faintest idea," she replied without glancing at her father or Herbert, who was one step behind him.

Abe shifted his armload to clutch Tempest's elbow. "I think you know who it is. Now blast it, girl, tell me! Herbert and I are dying of curiosity. I can always check the boutiques and jewelers to find out who is footing the bill, if you insist on being closemouthed about this."

Tempest heaved a sigh as she dumped the packages unceremoniously on her bed. "It's Cord MacIntosh, if you must know."

Abraham blinked in amazement. "That penniless heathen? Where would he get enough money for such expensive gifts? He can't even afford a decent set of clothes!" His eyes probed into Tempest. "Or was he really a member of that outlaw gang who robbed the El Paso bank? I'm beginning to think I was too lenient with that rapscallion."

"It's obvious that Cord and Paddy MacIntosh *did* know the location of the legendary gold mine that was rumored to be somewhere in the mountains," Tempest responded. "I'm being showered with gifts as compensation for all my troubles. Now if you don't mind, I'd rather not discuss this any further."

Abraham gestured for Herbert to take his leave. Quietly, Abe closed the bedroom door and then turned to face his sullen daughter. For a long moment, he stared at Tempest, mustering the courage to broach a very delicate subject that had disturbed him since Tempest had been abducted. He hated to ask, but he felt he had to know.

"Tempest, did that man—?"

"Papa, please!" Tempest turned her back, refusing to meet her father's probing gaze.

Abraham had glanced at her in speculation too often the past two months for her not to know what he had intended to ask. Abe was dying to learn what had transpired between her and Cord while they were alone. She didn't want to answer her father's prying questions. Heavens! She had her hands full just getting from one day to the next without being expected to relive painful memories. She simply wanted to be left alone with her broken heart.

Tempest had once been an enthusiastic participant in life, teeming with an overabundance of joy. Now she was only an observer, sitting on the edge, never truly involved, never in control of her tangled emotions. She was so blasé and listless that she barely recognized herself. Even her legal obligations had failed to provide any motivation.

"Papa, I would really appreciate some privacy," she requested, showing him the door, as if he didn't know where it was.

Heaving a sigh, Abraham reversed direction and marched into the hall. It seemed to him that Tempest had suffered an emotional blow somewhere along the way. He had the unshakable feeling that she and Cord had become more than captor and captive. Of course, Tempest was too proud, independent, and stubborn to confide in him about such intimate matters. She had always believed in shouldering her own burdens and making her own way. But by damn, if she didn't share her inner feelings with him soon, he was going to drag them out of her—delicate subject or not!

The best thing for Tempest, Abe decided, was distraction. He would arrange a grand party to celebrate her return. She needed to involve herself with the city's elite once again. Thus far, Tempest had avoided prospective suitors like the plague and refused to make contact with her friends. Abraham vowed to eliminate this problem of self-imposed seclusion. He was going to make a dedicated effort to help his only daughter become her old self again. *Then* he would get the truth out of her about that wild heathen who went by the name of Cord MacIntosh. Abe wanted his daughter back. She was here in flesh, but not in spirit, and he had to resolve that problem posthaste!

Myra Jones pushed the heaping bowl of potatoes at her nephew, only to have it shoved away. "Tosh, you need to eat," she insisted. "It's not like you to pass up a second helping of my home cooking. And if I may say so, you're getting much too thin."

"You're being too kind," Jefferson told his mother. "Tosh looks like hell. I knew he'd come moping around here. And we all know why he looks and acts the way he does. But take my word for it, you can't tell Cord MacIntosh anything."

Cord shrugged off the insult and turned the legal document over in his hand for the umpteenth time since he'd sat down to his meal. He had received Tempest's annulment papers the previous month but he had yet to sign and return them.

Jelly Jones polished off another jam-filled biscuit and licked his lips. "I was reading in the newspaper the other day that all the restrictions have been lifted from the salt lakes again. Folks on both sides of the Rio Grande have been permitted to shovel all the salt they need—whether they're Mexican or American. Paddy would be glad you didn't let Victor and his Salt Ring take control of the lakes and charge the pants off every customer. He always said the salt in those lakes should be free for the taking."

Cord responded with another lackadaisical shrug, as had become his custom of late. He set the crinkled document aside to fiddle with his silverware.

"That Judge Litchfield must be extremely efficient," Jelly remarked when the conversation hit another lull. "According to the newspaper reports, the judge rolled into El Paso like a locomotive to have all Victor's conspirators fired from political office and jailed with Watts and Reynosa. It didn't take him long to see justice served before returning to San Antone."

Another stilted silence. Cord reserved comment. He simply shrugged—again.

"Do you remember the traveler we told you about who was here after you escaped from jail, Tosh?" Myra prompted her nephew. "The one who clutched his satchel under his arm as if it contained a fortune?" When Cord nodded in recognition, Myra rambled on. "Well, it seemed his luggage *was* filled with cash—all of which he embezzled from a merchant in Fort Smith. A federal marshal came through here last month, posing questions. He caught up with the culprit in Yuma and took the swindler into custody. The marshal returned last week with his prisoner in handcuffs. I thought there was something suspicious about that shifty-eyed rascal. Sure enough, there was."

More silence.

"I received a letter from Annette Partridge," Jefferson informed his taciturn cousin. "She has moved to San Antonio to live with the Litchfields. Annette has decided to enter college to follow in Tempest's footsteps. She greatly admires your *wife,*" he added emphatically.

No comment. Cord repocketed the legal document and stared at the far wall, as if it suddenly demanded his attention.

Myra cast her son a discreet glance and then refocused on Cord. "How is Yellowfish doing these days?"

"I haven't seen him for a week," Cord replied blandly. "He's been off on one of his ritualistic fasts, communicating with the spirits."

What the Joneses hoped would be the beginning of a stimulating conversation came to a dead end. Cord seemed to have said all he had to say. His attention turned once again to the document that he fished from his pocket to reread yet again.

Jefferson gave his cousin a withering glance, wishing he could shake Cord from his mood. Each time Cord came to the Pinery with another order for gifts to be delivered to Tempest, he was a lousy companion. This vital, dynamic man had turned sullen, and no one could draw any kind of emotion from him. He merely existed—like a hollow shell abandoned by a turtle.

A rap at the door caused Jelly to lift his rotund body from his chair. To his amazement, Yellowfish stood on the stoop, clutching a pouch of gold nuggets which he dropped into Jelly's hand. Without a word, the old chief limped inside. After a mute nod to each member of the family, Yellowfish motioned for Jefferson to accompany him outside.

Bemused, Cord watched his cousin scurry off with Yellowfish. The very fact that Yellowfish had come down to the trading post and stage station was baffling. He usually avoided contact with civilization unless it was an emergency.

When Jelly heard the stage conductor's bugle in the distance, he scampered over to scoop up his last biscuit before he dashed off for a fresh team of horses. While Cord slouched in his chair, Myra cleared the dishes. It was her duty to provide a meal before the passengers clambered back into the stage bound for El Paso. Myra intended to see that no one left hungry.

Cord supposed he should have offered to help his aunt, but he simply lacked initiative. These days he didn't feel like doing much of anything. Once he had traveled to El Paso, hoping to curb the craving for feminine companionship. But even an entire bottle of whiskey hadn't prevented him from being particular about which female he invited into his arms. None of them had looked quite right or felt quite right. His sex life had been completely ruined by memories of sky-blue eyes, chestnut hair, and a certain curvaceous body.

At least a dozen times in the past two months Cord had set to drinking to forget, and he always woke up remembering. He had thrown himself into breaking and training horses for the stage stations, but he kept getting distracted by thoughts of other times and other places. *Caramba!* How much longer would he be haunted by this unbearable longing, this aching emptiness? Nothing was the same without Tempest.

Cord very nearly fell out of his chair when his grandfather hobbled back inside the station. Or at least the man resembled Yellowfish—to some extent. The old timer had a flat-crowned hat atop his head and his gray hair had been tucked beneath it. A pair of black breeches replaced his traditional buckskin garments. He wore unscuffed leather boots, a stylish white linen shirt buttoned all the way to his neck, and a fashionable black waistcoat.

Cord braced himself for the worst. He knew the sky would fall in on him when a dyed-in-the-wool Apache like Yellowfish discarded his customary attire to step into white men's clothes. Judgment Day—the red man's or white man's or both—was upon them!

"Yellowfish?" Myra bleated, stupefied. "Is that you?"

At least *she* could speak. Cord had yet to regain control of his vocal apparatus and his tongue was still stuck to the roof of his mouth.

"Why, you look positively handsome," Myra added.

Yellowfish limped into the room on a hand-carved cane which completed his new image. With typical aplomb, Yellowfish parked himself on a chair. That was also a first. When the old Apache visited Cord's mountain cabin he had always insisted on sitting cross-legged on a pallet on the floor. Chairs, Yellowfish claimed, were another of the White Eye's useless contraptions.

Yellowfish frowned when he caught Cord staring at him as if he were a creature from the spirit world. "If you have something to say, Lobo Plano, then say it," he demanded.

The terse tone restored Cord's vocal cords to partial working order. "What the sweet loving hell are you doing?" he croaked.

There was no doubt about it, Cord decided. Senility had caught up with Yellowfish. The old chief no longer remembered who and what he was. He was suffering delusions, or an identity crisis. Cord wasn't sure which.

"Jefferson has agreed to take me to San Antonio," Yellowfish announced.

Cord did a double take.

Rising to his feet, Yellowfish gestured for his grandson to follow him onto the porch. Mechanically, Cord did as he was told.

Yellowfish braced himself on his cane and pivoted to face Cord. "I have been a selfish old man. I had been so set in my ways that I have placed my own needs and happiness above yours. I have practiced Apache cunning to influence you, but I have accomplished nothing. The white woman is still on your mind and in your heart. Her powers cannot be reversed."

Cord peered at his grandfather. At long last he knew he was about to hear what deep-seated problem had kept the old Apache from warming to Tempest.

"I watched you with an experienced eye, my son, while the white woman was underfoot. Day by day, I could see you falling beneath her spell. You had begun to treat her as your equal, not as your wife. You let her get away with murder," he added glumly. "She began to matter to you, not only as a woman, but in the same capacity as you would offer respect to another man. You came to love her too much for your own good, Lobo Plano."

"I—"

Yellowfish lifted his hand, palm toward Cord. "Do not deny it, my son. I knew you had even refused to admit your feelings to yourself and I persisted by telling you she was not right for you. But your deeds spoke louder than words. You risked your life to gain her respect. You risked your life again to steal her from the *vaqueros*. She made you happy, you said. You could not bear to see her perish."

"If it's all the same to you, I'd rather not rehash all this," Cord growled. "I let her go. It's over."

The old Apache gave his head a shake. "It is not over when she still speaks to you from your heart and whispers to you from your soul. It has been two months and still it is not over. It will never be over, my son. I have accepted what I cannot change and so must you."

Yellowfish sighed deeply and clenched his gnarled fingers around his newly acquired cane. "I was . . . afraid," he admitted at last, most reluctantly. "When I saw you look at the white woman I could see myself losing you. She was taking my place in your heart and your eyes, and I could see myself fading from sight. You are all I have left in this world, Lobo Plano. My wife was murdered by Mexicans. My daughter died of the white man's disease. I was afraid that if you followed this star-crossed love, you would go with the white woman to make a place in her world."

"But—"

Again, Yellowfish refused to let Cord interrupt. "You had already begun to put the white woman's needs above your own. If you left with her, I knew I would have nothing and no one, except the occasional bands of our people who travel through the mountains on their way back to New Mexico. I could not help the desperation I felt. The white woman had come between us, and I feared you would choose her over me and our natural way of life."

Cord gaped at Yellowfish in stunned amazement. For the first time in his life, Cord was seeing his grandfather from an entirely new angle. Yellowfish had always prided himself in projecting an air of invincibility and immortality. But now Cord saw the old man's vulnerabilities and insecurities. Yellowfish felt threatened and he had clutched desperately at every excuse imaginable to make sure Cord didn't slip from his grasp.

"You were jealous of her? Afraid of her?" Cord queried, still thunderstruck by the revelations.

Yellowfish nodded repentantly. "Jealous of her youth, of her spirit, her hold on you. I feared I had outlived my purpose, that you would forsake me and the way of The People to be with her. But when you let her go, as I urged you to do so many times, you died inside. I have watched your spirit wither away. You are not even half-Apache since you set the white woman free."

The old man drew himself up to full stature and lifted his chin. "Now you have become a man without purpose, without direction. I am going to San Antonio to find the white woman and live with her people until I understand them. At least she has spirit. I would rather enjoy a good argument with her than watch you stare into the sky. At least she fought back. You gave in to me and now neither of us can find happiness."

Cord couldn't believe what he was hearing! "It was you who assured me that I had made the right choice, you who said Tempest and I were not meant for each other. How can you possibly think it will work now when you didn't think it would work then?"

"The Great Spirit has shown me the way. I was . . ." Yellowfish steadied himself on his cane and forced out the distasteful word that very nearly choked him. ". . . *Wrong* . . ."

Cord glanced heavenward. The sky was sure to collapse on them. Until this moment, Yellowfish had never admitted to being wrong once in seventy years. *Wrong* was a foreign word to the stubborn old chief.

"It takes a great man to admit he has made a mistake, to admit that he was jealous and selfish and afraid," Yellowfish announced with great conviction.

Oh sure, now that old coot was ready to make amends, Cord thought sourly. But it was two months too late. Cord had broken all ties with the white woman—as Yellowfish persisted in referring to Tempest. She had even refused to glance in Cord's direction when they parted company after their final encounter at Victor's *hacienda.* Tempest had turned her back on him, closing the door on the past.

Caramba! Cord had been through two months of pure and simple hell, trying to forget how much that blue-eyed nymph had meant to him. He kept telling himself it was his place to care for and look after his aging grandfather. He had convinced himself, under Yellowfish's constant persuasion, that Tempest was better off without him, and vice versa. And like a bolt out of the blue, this old goat shows up at the Pinery with more than enough gold nuggets to buy himself a set of white men's clothes, traveling expenses, and a stage ticket.

What was Yellowfish trying to do? Erase all the pain and frustration they had caused Tempest? Hell, he and Yellowfish would never be welcome in Tempest's life.

"Take that ridiculous costume off," Cord demanded. "You aren't going anywhere and neither am I. Nor is Jefferson. It's too late."

"It is *not* too late," Yellowfish insisted, lifting his chin a notch higher.

Cord sighed deeply and leaned back against the outer wall. "I appreciate what you're trying to do, Grandfather. Your sacrifice is noble, to be sure, but I know my limitations. It is as you said. This is our home. Tempest is where she belongs. To see her again would open old wounds. She has suffered enough."

Yellowfish ground his cane into the planks of the stoop. "You fool yourself, Cord MacIntosh!" he erupted in protest. "The white woman sent the documents to you long ago. But you have not signed them because you cannot break the tie that binds. You cannot let go because you love her too deeply and she loves you."

"Does she really?" Cord scoffed as he snatched the wrinkled document from his pocket and brandished it in his grandfather's face. "Then why did she send this to me?"

"Because she believes it is what you wanted. You made certain she believed it was so," Yellowfish replied. "The day we left the mountains, the white woman told me she loved you."

Nonplussed, Cord peered at Yellowfish.

"It was not only in her words, but in her voice and in her eyes. Even when you tried to be cruel and you purposely shut her out of your life, her feelings for you would not change. She spoke of her love for you as if it was in the past. But she would not have spoken of it at all to me if it had not been so strong. Her love did not die. It is like the cactus of the desert, waiting for the thirst-quenching rain to nourish the blossom. And like the cactus, her love does not die, it only waits—forever, if that is how long it takes."

When the conductor signaled for the westbound passengers to board the coach, Yellowfish descended the steps. He rounded the corner of the way station and paused at the open door of the stage, silently commanding Cord to accompany him. Jefferson, however, did not need to be asked twice. He was already seated and waiting.

Cord stared at the crumpled document in his hand for a long moment. When the conductor made his final call, Cord strode purposefully toward the stage. If Yellowfish was wrong, they were going to look like a couple of crazy fools. But if the old buzzard was right . . .

For the first time in two endless months, a smile tugged at the corner of Cord's lips. He hadn't been to San Antonio since the outbreak of the Civil War. He wondered how much the town had changed. But most of all, he wondered what kind of reception awaited them at Judge Litchfield's. Cord certainly hadn't made a good *first* impression with the judge and he had left a very poor *last* impression with Tempest.

For the first time in years, Cord felt very unsure of himself. He was confident of his capabilities in these wild, untamed mountains, but he would be on shaky ground in San Antonio. Cord didn't like these vulnerable feelings that plagued him as he sat wedged like a sardine between Jefferson and Yellowfish. But he sure as hell was tired of being so miserable! If there was even a remote possibility that Tempest would find it in her heart to forgive him then he had to take that chance. Living with her memory was driving him crazy. The obstacles between them were still there, but if Tempest was willing to meet him halfway, perhaps they could find common ground—somewhere, anywhere!

Living in limbo certainly hadn't been the answer. Even after two months Cord could close his eyes and feel Tempest's presence. He could still taste those kisses. Yellowfish was right. Cord was no longer half-Apache or half-white. He was nothing at all without that spark Tempest had put into his life, a candle without a flame.

Cord pulled his sombrero low on his forehead and settled back to ponder their encounter with Tempest. Knowing how stubborn she could be, he'd be lucky if he got his foot in the front door. Just how did a gentleman woo his way back into a lady's good graces? Perhaps the gifts he'd sent had softened her up. Yes, Cord tried to reassure himself. Tempest would await him with open arms, having missed him as much as he had missed her.

It was a blissful thought. But totally erroneous, Cord imagined, as he settled in for a nap. Ah, but wouldn't it be nice if, *just once* in his life, something could be *simple?* He'd always found himself battling life the hard way. Would anything ever come as easy for him as wanting that sassy spitfire with the lively blue eyes? Considering his track record, Cord doubted it. But *just once* he would like to have something he wanted without a knock-down-drag-out fight!

Twenty-nine

Garbed in another newly purchased white man's outfit, Yellowfish strode toward the grand mansion in San Antonio, bookended by Cord and Jefferson. They had come dressed to kill, intent on making a good impression when they reached the Litchfield estate on the edge of town. Yellowfish hadn't expected to find the stately home surrounded with carriages and blazing with lights. A celebration seemed to be in progress.

"I think we've come at a bad time," Cord observed as he fiddled with the fashionable cravat that felt like a hangman's noose. "Maybe we should come back tomorrow."

Before Cord could reverse direction, Yellowfish and Jefferson caught both of his arms and propelled him toward the marble steps.

"We are two months late already," Jefferson insisted.

"We will wait no longer," Yellowfish declared with his customary authority. He cocked his head and listened interestedly when the orchestra in the ballroom struck up a fast tempo. "I have never seen the white man's dance ceremony. I wish to do so."

The old Apache marched into the spacious foyer without invitation. It was obvious the dance ceremony had been going on for some time. There were no servants to greet the latecomers, only the sound of music and the hum of voices. Curiously, Yellowfish moved toward the arched doorway where lights beamed and men and women in colorful apparel whirled in each other's arms.

"This is like no ritual I have ever witnessed," Yellowfish said with a snort. "Men and women should not touch in the presence of an audience! What kind of ceremony is this?"

Cord glared over his grandfather's head. Like metal drawn to a magnet, he focused on Tempest. For two months her image had been enshrined on his heart. And here at last was his fairy princess—the star of all his dreams—in another man's arms and smiling as if she hadn't a care in the world. Damn her!

The disturbing sight struck Cord like a doubled fist in the belly. For what had seemed forever, he had pined away for this dazzling temptress. But from the look of things, Tempest hadn't missed him one damned bit! If she wasn't having a good time then she was one hell of an actress! And to irritate Cord even more—if that was possible—the elegantly dressed dandy with Tempest was staring at her with a mouth-watering smile. Cord knew what that citified rake was thinking. He could almost *see* him thinking it!

"I'm getting the hell out of here," Cord muttered as he turned on his heel.

Yellowfish hooked the curved end of his cane around his grandson's neck and roughly dragged him back. "You will go nowhere. I have come too far and I have made too many sacrifices to turn back now."

With an amused grin Jefferson straightened the cuff of his black waistcoat. He rather enjoyed seeing Cord squirm and his self-confidence crumble. He deserved it after all the hell he'd put Tempest through. It wouldn't hurt Cord one damned bit. And from the look of things, he may very well have to get down on his knees and beg that gorgeous beauty to take him back.

Grumbling under his breath, Cord fell into step behind his determined grandfather. He was sure this was a disastrous mistake. The three of them could dress in fancy clothes and learn all the dance steps, but they still wouldn't fit in. Tempest was happy where she was. She had sent Cord the annulment papers because she had wanted to put the past behind her and begin a new life. He was the one who'd been living in a dreamworld and now he was about to humiliate himself in front of an audience of muckamucks!

The artificial smile plastered on Tempest's face cracked when she caught sight of the three men snaking through the ballroom. Her jaw fell when she met those obsidian eyes that singled her out from beneath the brim of a black, flat-crowned hat. She couldn't believe it! This couldn't possibly be the arrogant Apache war chief in white man's clothes . . . could it?

Tempest's heart slammed against her ribs when her astounded gaze focused on the muscular giant behind Yellowfish. Tawny eyes glinted down at her in extreme irritation, but she was too stunned to react.

She had been aghast at the sight of Cord in his loincloth, but his dashing appearance this evening was no less devastating. The whole room shrank to fill only the space he occupied. Two months of mental and emotional anguish seemed to evaporate in a second. The very sight of him had brought her senses back to life after they'd lain dormant for so long. Cord was a vision from her dreams, the very essence of her existence. The love she had fought so hard to deny burst into full bloom and Tempest was sure her heart would explode with happiness.

Cord felt every ounce of anger drain from him when those azure eyes met his. He had been afraid he'd lost Tempest to the dandy who clung to her so possessively. But he could almost hear Tempest calling out to him. He could see that lovable sparkle return to her eyes. Cord had feared he would find stubborn resistance or that Tempest had found another man. But the look on her face told a different story, one so fierce and intense that it knocked Cord for a loop. It was as Yellowfish had said. Tempest *did* love him. Her smile said it all and if he didn't get her back in his arms where she belonged—and quickly—he was going to disintegrate into a pile of smoldering embers.

"Is there something I can do for you, sir?" Marcus Davenport asked as he stood in front of Tempest like a shield. "I don't believe I have made your acquaintance."

"I don't believe I wish to make yours, white man," Yellowfish said rudely, using the butt of his cane against the human obstruction in his path. "I have come to speak with this woman."

"Now see here, old man," Marcus growled indignantly. "I don't know where you came from, but where *I* come from, it is most impolite to barge into a party as if one owns the place—argh!" Marcus doubled over when the ornately carved cane gouged him in the belly.

The commotion in the middle of the dance floor drew Abraham's attention. Pushing bodies out of his way, he scurried through the crowd toward his daughter and the three uninvited guests.

"Just what is going on here?" Abraham roared. His condescending gaze left the stoop-shouldered old man and riveted on the familiar face of Cord MacIntosh. "Good Lord! Not you!"

"Good evening, Judge," Jefferson said politely, drawing Abraham's attention away from Cord. "Nice party."

Jefferson's attempt to be cordial didn't faze Abraham—he refused to be sidetracked. "What do you want, MacIntosh?"

Although the question was directed at Cord, Yellowfish elected to answer it. "I have come to speak to my granddaughter-in-law," he announced.

"Your *what?*" Abraham croaked, aghast. His bewildered gaze bounced back and forth between Tempest and Cord, who couldn't seem to take their eyes off each other.

Abraham's question was followed by stunned silence. Nobody moved. No one uttered a word.

Cord drew himself up to his full height. "I have come for my wife."

Abraham staggered back as if he'd suffered a blow. "Good Lord Almighty!" he howled in disbelief.

Tempest barely noticed her father's astonished reaction. Her eyes and her thoughts were pinpointed on that darkly handsome face that was so close and yet so unbearably far away. Ah, how she'd longed for his touch, his kiss. It had been an eternity.

Dancing with the stuffy Marcus Davenport was like dancing with a limp fish. She had pretended to enjoy Marcus's company because her father had tried so hard to bring her back into society and out of her doldrums. But no one could ever replace this man, and Tempest wasn't about to waste precious time pretending to be angry.

Indeed, how could she be anything but flattered by this gesture that spoke louder than anything Cord could say! One look at Cord's and Yellowfish's attire assured her of the compromise they were prepared to make. Their appearance in San Antonio was a bold statement in itself. Tempest had never been more impressed! She had tried to fool her heart the past few months and it had caused her nothing but anguish. She had been through hell and now she was staring at the gates of heaven!

"Tempest, am I supposed to believe this outrageous statement?" Abraham asked incredulously. "You never said one word about being married to anybody!"

Tempest sidestepped Marcus, who still seemed to think it was his duty to protect her. As if he could! Marcus was no match for a man like Cord MacIntosh, not in any way.

"I said nothing because I wasn't sure my husband really wanted me," she explained to her father. Her gaze focused on Cord. "I sent him the annulment papers last month, but he never returned them. I thought he didn't even care enough to bother with the formality of mailing them to me."

Cord traced a trembling forefinger over Tempest's petal-soft lips. He wasn't sure where he found the willpower to restrain himself from scooping her into his arms for a long-awaited kiss. His pulse was racing like a runaway mustang.

"That worthless husband of yours couldn't sign that fancy-worded paper because it would have meant letting go of you forever. He gave you up because he thought it was best for you. But he could never convince his heart that it was the right thing to do," Cord murmured, his voice like a velvet caress that reached out to touch her.

Yellowfish poked Cord in the ribs impatiently. "Tell her you love her."

Cord had held in the words for so long that they leaped to the tip of his tongue the instant Yellowfish spoke. He didn't care who heard him. "I love you, Tempest, and I want you back. Nothing's been the same without you."

Despite the audience and in spite of propriety, Tempest flung her arms around Cord's neck with a kiss she felt clear down to her toes. In an instant her body was aching in all those familiar places. Passion burned through her and threatened to rage out of control.

"Tempest, for God's sake, remember yourself," Abraham blustered in embarrassment for himself and his bedeviled daughter.

Cord's arms surrounded her trim waist, pulling her against him to answer her hungry kiss with all the pent-up emotion that churned inside him. He didn't give a jot or a tittle what Abraham or Yellowfish or any one else thought of this public display. The judge already considered him daft after that wild episode in Victor Watts's bedroom. A man couldn't very well ruin his reputation with his father-in-law if he didn't have one, now could he?

Things were worse than Abraham had ever suspected! He'd never seen his standoffish daughter throw herself at a man. She'd kept them all at arm's length like a spinster. Now here she was, clinging to this barely civilized renegade as if he were her whole world. Tempest's self-restraint had cracked wide open and she was making a spectacle of herself. Abraham wasn't sure he liked this bold rapscallion as a man, much less as a son-in-law! Just what the devil did he plan to do? Drag Tempest back to his wickiup somewhere in the mountains, never to be seen or heard from again? Over Abraham's dead body!

"That's enough," Abe announced, prying the couple apart.

Yellowfish found the hand-carved cane very beneficial. Not only did it serve as a support and a weapon, but also as a hook. In one fluid motion, he had Abraham by the neck, pulling him out of the way.

"My grandson has found his destiny," Yellowfish assured Abraham with absolute certainty. "I tried to intervene before and I have brought them nothing but heartache and pain. You will not interfere!"

"Who the devil is this man?" Abraham muttered.

The old Indian drew himself up proudly. "I am Yellowfish, war chief of the Chiricahua Apache."

That certainly got everybody's attention! The crowd instinctively fell back a pace. They retreated another step when the Indian removed his hat, allowing his gray braids, adorned with beads and feathers, to fall over his shoulders. Yellowfish had shed his veneer, and his gaze burned like kerosene as he focused intently on the flabbergasted judge.

"I have come as one of you to make my peace with this white woman. But I will leave as an Apache if you try to stand in the way."

Jefferson stood in the wings, highly amused. Yellowfish did have a way of livening up a party. When Annette Partridge sidled up beside him, Jefferson clasped her dainty hand in his and flashed her his dazzling smile.

"Isn't this romantic?" she murmured dreamily.

"Not as romantic as it could be," Jefferson drawled seductively. Taking Annette with him, he made a discreet exit. "I told you I'd come . . ."

"And I've been waiting . . ." Annette assured him as she feasted on the handsome young man who had piqued her interest the moment he darted out of the underbrush to halt their wagon in front of Victor's *hacienda*.

While Jefferson and Annette slipped into the shadows, Abraham wrestled with a dilemma: how was he going to emerge from this predicament with some degree of dignity? It was obvious that Tempest was delighted to see this wild rogue who had become a legend in his quest for justice west of the Pecos. And although Abe hated to admit it, he did appear hopelessly in love with Tempest. A better match Abe was certain he could have found, but he hadn't been allowed to do the selecting. And Yellowfish seemed quite determined to see Cord and Tempest reunited.

Abraham directed his attention to the stoic chief whose very posture indicated he wasn't budging an inch without all-out war. "Tell me, Apache chief, do you really believe this was meant to be?" Abraham asked in all seriousness.

The old warrior nodded with great conviction. "I have consulted the Great Spirit. It is his will." He arched a graying brow and focused on Abe. "Now you tell me, white chief, has your daughter been happy since she returned from the mountains?"

No, Abe couldn't say she had. Tempest had been so listless that he had worried about her constantly. "Well, if the Great Spirit blesses this match, who am I to argue?" Respectfully, he offered his hand to Yellowfish in a gesture of friendship. To Cord, he said confidentially, "If you don't make my daughter happy, you'll have a noose around your neck, young man. And I'm just the person who can do it, too."

Cord was too beguiled by the love he saw in Tempest's eyes even to respond. All he wanted was to get her alone, to lose himself in the taste, feel, and scent of her. It had been ages since he had held her, loved her with every part of his being. She belonged to him, with him, and he wished to hell this crowd of sophisticated humanity would disappear.

"Dance with me," Tempest whispered, devouring him with her hungry eyes.

"I don't dance," Cord replied.

"I didn't ride mules or traipse along towering mountain peaks, either," she replied with a saucy smile.

When Abraham signaled for the orchestra to play, Cord slid his arm around Tempest. The dance steps didn't seem so difficult after all. He had only to drift in rhythm with the sway of Tempest's body and that had never been difficult for him.

"God, how I've missed you," Cord murmured as he nuzzled against Tempest's cheek.

Those words—sweet music to her ears—caused her to melt on the spot. "I've been miserable without you," she admitted, her voice on the unsteady side.

"Damn, if it wasn't for this crowd I'd strip you down and devour every delicious inch of you right here, right now," Cord assured her huskily. "Do you have a bedroom in this monstrosity of a house?"

"My boudoir, I'm sorry to say, is filled from wall to wall with furniture. Someone kept sending me jewels, gowns, sofas, and tufted chairs when all I wanted was his heart," Tempest replied with an elfin smile. "I'd almost given up on you, Cord."

"Is that why you were smiling at that stork-legged dandy?" he grumbled sourly. "Damned good thing I didn't show up a few days later, fickle woman."

"Marcus Davenport?" Tempest moved far enough away to stare bemusedly at Cord. Was he actually jealous? Of Marcus? What a waste of emotion. "I'll admit I've been lonely, but I'd never be *that* lonely." Her gaze narrowed accusingly. "And just how many females have helped you take your mind off *your* troubles, *my dear husband?*"

"Only one," Cord responded with a roguish grin. He chuckled when Tempest glared daggers at him. "Her name is Tequila. She and I drank ourselves blind a dozen times the past two months. Do you think I could touch another woman when the only one I've ever wanted was you?"

"Easy words for a man to speak when he's been conveniently absent," Tempest sassed. Lord, how she'd missed fencing with this sharp-witted renegade. How she'd missed everything about him!

"There was nothing convenient about it," Cord said flatly. "The man in me feels tied up in knots.

If I don't get you all to myself and pretty damned quick, I swear I'll explode." His body moved deliberately against hers, letting her know just how much he ached for her.

"My goodness, I think you may need to see a doctor," she teased as her hips glided provocatively toward the evidence of his arousal.

"What I need is a lover. Abstinence doesn't agree with me," Cord rasped.

It didn't agree with Tempest, either. From the moment Cord came into the ballroom she had become a shamelessly wanton woman. She yearned to spear her fingers through that mass of wavy hair, to peel away all this veneer and caress this muscled renegade who had haunted her dreams. She wanted Cord beyond bearing and dancing with him was only making it worse. It reminded her of other times—more intimate moments.

"We're leaving," Cord declared as he grasped her hand and headed for the door.

He screeched to a halt at the bottom of the staircase when Abraham zoomed out of the study and cut off their escape route.

"I've tried to accept the fact that my daughter is your wife as graciously as I know how," Abraham said vehemently. "But I draw the line here. I am not so old that I don't know what you're doing. There's a party going on here, and Tempest is the hostess."

"May I remind you that we've been married for more than three months," Cord countered. It was plain to see where Tempest had inherited her stubborn streak, Cord thought to himself.

"Abraham," Yellowfish called from the office door. "You have too much of the *English* in you, too. Perhaps another drink of this brandy will cure it. I will tell you the tale of how the Earth Mother and Sun Father came to be, before The People were brought here by the Great Spirit."

After trying to stare Cord down and failing miserably, Abraham threw up his hands in defeat. Why should he expect his daughter's husband to be less willful than she had always been? Muttering at the calamity that had befallen him, Abraham begrudgingly stepped aside.

"Make that two brandies, chief," Abe requested. "I've suddenly developed a powerful thirst."

Yellowfish smiled to himself. He well remembered how he had battled to stop this fierce attraction between this white woman and his grandson. Abraham had reservations, too, that was plain to see. But in time, he would realize that he couldn't win. For the first time in months, Cord was vital and alive again. Life had begun to matter to him. It was as if he had been wandering in darkness, searching for the sun. Now he had found it.

"You will adjust," Yellowfish assured Abraham before sipping the white man's brew. "Do not think I did not try to keep them apart. I did. But this love between them is stronger than both of us. My grandson is enough of a man to control your iron-willed daughter. You will come to like him as much as I have come to respect your daughter, even if she is white."

Abraham downed a drink and tried not to think about where Cord was taking Tempest. It would require several brandies and some serious adjustment, Abraham decided. For the life of him, he couldn't quite forget the sight of that savage hovering over Victor Watts. Abraham took another drink . . . or three . . . and listened to Yellowfish's tale of how the heavens and earth had come to be—Apache style.

Thirty

The instant Cord stepped into the resplendent bedroom he stared down at Tempest, making no attempt to conceal his ravenous hunger. She was so breathtakingly lovely, so utterly exquisite. It didn't bother him so much to see her looking so elegant when he knew he had sent her the expensive gown and jewelry she was wearing. Everything about her belonged to him—the diamonds, the blue satin dress, but most importantly, the woman herself.

Cord would have recognized this particular gown anywhere. He had sent instructions to the seamstress in San Antonio to create a garment to match the color of Tempest's eyes. Dainty white lace lay temptingly against the scooped neckline, displaying the generous swell of her bosom. The gold necklace, embedded with diamond tear drops, reminded him of the sun and moon and stars which had been missing from his life since she'd gone away.

He had visualized Tempest, just as she was now, hundreds of times since he'd ordered the gifts. But his mental image couldn't do her justice. She was the most gorgeous female he'd ever seen, and he longed to spend hours just savoring the sight of her. A sigh shuddered Cord as he reached out to touch Tempest's face. It had been so long.

"Oh, Cord, I love you so much," Tempest murmured with such genuine emotion that her voice trembled. "I don't care where we go or what we do, as long as I can be with you. Being without you was hell. I would even live in a cave in a cliff, as long as I have you. I would have been satisfied with that even before you sent me away. But I thought you didn't want me . . ." Her voice broke and Cord gathered her close to him.

"Not want you?" He laughed softly before he pressed an adoring kiss to her brow. "God, princess, I can't even remember when I didn't want you! I thought you would prefer your life in San Antonio to me, if you were given the choice. I didn't give you the choice because I couldn't bear knowing your lifestyle and career were more important to you than I was, fearing you would long for them eventually."

"Foolish man," Tempest whispered against his lapel, drinking in the masculine scent of him, drowning in the gone-but-never-forgotten memory of his muscular body meshed familiarly with hers. "My life is a disaster and my career is in ruin. I'm so boring in court I put the judge and jury to sleep. And one of those judges was my own father!"

"And Jefferson says I'm as much fun as a sunbaked snail," Cord confessed.

"Then it seems we should do something about all this," Tempest purred as her fingers skimmed eagerly over the buttons of his linen shirt, baring his broad chest to her greedy eyes.

While Tempest was brazenly relieving Cord of his jacket and shirt, he was working the stays on the back of her gown. He hadn't shown eagerness and impatience about anything in months, but he was eager and impatient now! He couldn't wait to remove anything that deprived him of touching and gazing upon what he had come to realize was the one thing he needed most to make life worth living. Tempest had become his source of energy, his inspiration, his amusement, his wildest desire. Without her, he wasn't even half a man.

His amber eyes flickered over her curvaceous figure like a starved man seeing a long-awaited feast. And in return, Tempest gazed upon him as if he were a magnificent work of art. They savored each other, aware of nothing but the sparks that danced between them, bringing their passion to a fervent pitch.

"You're beautiful," Cord breathed appreciatively. "I never could get enough of looking at you."

Tempest's hands splayed across his chest, feeling his heart leap. "Just looking at you never was enough to satisfy me," she admitted. "Even when I knew I should keep my hands to myself, I couldn't do it."

Effortlessly, Cord picked her up and walked toward the bed. He was so intent that he stubbed his toe on the leg of a hand-carved table. Before he could straighten up he sideswiped a tufted rocking chair and stumbled across the room to sprawl on the bed with Tempest held protectively in his arms.

Playful laughter gurgled in her throat when they landed in a tangled heap on the feather mattress. "We really must do something about all this extra furniture," she insisted as she moved suggestively beneath him. "A room with nothing but a bed would be just fine."

"All this furniture would look a damned sight better in my mountain cabin," Cord assured her as his wandering hands rediscovered every well-sculpted inch of her. "Would you mind that so much, princess? A castle in the canyon beneath High Lonesome Peak? I'll build you a mansion so you can have all the comforts of civilization. I don't think I can live in San Antone, but we could visit your father anytime you please, I promise."

Tempest drew his sensuous lips to hers. "Did you come here to talk or make love to me?"

"Both," he said, then kissed her soundly.

"If I have a choice, I'd much rather do the talking later," she murmured throatily.

With a roguish grin, he drifted his hand over her belly to caress the sensitive flesh of her thighs. "Whatever you wish, princess. I'm only here to please . . ."

And please her Cord most certainly did! His hands seemed to have perfect recall, as if it had been hours instead of months since he'd touched her. Her skin glowed under each masterful caress. Her body came back to life.

His fingertips swept over the throbbing tips of her breasts and she arched toward him, reveling in the tantalizing sensations. When his moist lips suckled each peak, Tempest clutched at him, holding him to her, needing more of the delicious magic that she had feared was gone forever. As his adventurous caresses skimmed her ribs to draw lazy patterns on her belly, Tempest gasped for breath. Cord had always had the ability to make her crave his most intimate touch. He left her quaking with the want of him, aching to satisfy the ravenous hunger deep inside her. As his knowing fingers found their way, Tempest felt the convulsive shudders of pleasure rock her very soul.

"Cord, please," she gasped when another wave buffeted her.

"In time," he murmured against the roseate bud of her breast. "I've waited so long to make love to you for as long as I want. I need to touch you, to savor you, to make sure this isn't just another dream."

"You're driving me mad . . ." Tempest gasped raggedly. She could barely catch her breath when the wild, tormenting spasms assaulted her again.

"Am I?" Cord grinned in pure male arrogance as he watched her writhe beneath his bold caresses.

Tempest squirmed away, gasping. He wanted to be seductively ornery, did he? Well, time would tell just how much of this sweet, maddening torture *he* could endure before he begged for satisfaction. With wicked delight, Tempest set her hands upon him, inventing new ways to arouse him until he groaned with the want of her. Her hands and lips were never still for a moment. She wove a spell of scintillating seduction over him as she raked her nails across the dark furring that funneled down the wide expanse of his chest to the taut muscles of his belly. Her lips followed the same path, setting fires that threatened to burn him alive.

"Good Lord, woman," Cord croaked. "Are you sure you haven't been practicing on someone else?"

Tempest smiled as her lips feathered over the sleek column of his hip. "I've been fantasizing," she confessed. "Shameful, isn't it?"

"Devastating," he said hoarsely.

"Wait until you see the finale, my dear husband," Tempest teased provocatively.

Cord wasn't certain he'd be around for the finale. His heart had very nearly beaten him to death already. Tempest was doing impossible things to his mind, not to mention the effect she was having on his body. His soaring blood pressure was about to spring a leak if she didn't stop what she was doing to him—and quickly!

When her hands and lips engulfed him, Cord sucked in a strangled breath and groaned. "Don't . . ."

"Don't *stop?*" she taunted as she stroked and excited him to the edges of his sanity. "I don't intend to. Only when I'm through with you, will you know how much I love you."

"I won't last that long, I swear it . . . Tempest!"

Cord was sure he'd been whisked into the vortex of a tornado as this skillful seductress invented new ways to drive a man to the brink and leave him dangling.

"Do you want me, Cord?" Tempest whispered

He wanted her all right, so much that his need to prolong their passionate reunion flew right out the window. He would have her now or he would die!

Like a rousing lion, Cord pinned Tempest beneath him. The muscles of his arms bulged as he braced himself above her to guide her thighs apart with his knees.

"You asked for this, vixen," Cord growled, his tawny eyes ablaze with barely restrained desire.

"I did, didn't I?" Tempest replied with an impish smile. Her arms glided over his powerful shoulders as she arched up to meet him. "I'm still waiting . . ."

Cord shuddered in an attempt to hold his ravenous desires in check. "I want to be gentle with you, but God, you always bring out the beast in me."

He reminded her of a bronzed lion—all meaty flesh and well-tuned muscle. "And you bring out my most secret desires," she whispered as he settled exactly upon her. "Love me, Cord, as you've loved no other . . ."

"I already do," Cord assured her as his body took complete possession to cherish the gift of love she offered him. "I always will . . ."

With a moan of surrender, Cord unleashed the savage instincts within him. When he made wild, sweet love to this witch-angel, there was no holding back. He let go with his body, his heart, and his soul. With each hard, penetrating thrust he felt the world slide out from under him, leaving him sailing through time and space. His hungry passion had reached a killing force. He was incapable of tenderness in the heat of such ecstasy. He was living and dying in the same indescribable moment.

Tempest clutched Cord to her as the world teetered off its axis, leaving her filled with ineffable pleasure. At long last, experiencing these remarkable sensations that transcended all physical bounds. Only when she was in the magic circle of Cord's arms did she have a will and a purpose. Life without him had been torment. But this . . . ah, this was paradise!

A convulsive shudder wracked Cord's body when the dam of fiery passion burst inside him. His mind and soul were numb with splendor, blotting out everything but the wild sensations that converged from all directions. And even when he collapsed, in an exhausted state of bliss, those tumultuous feelings lingered like an echo in a bottomless canyon.

If there had been even the slightest doubt about where Cord belonged, it had disintegrated the instant Tempest's body united with his. He had never known such wild passion tempered with such a sense of inner peace and fulfillment. This lovely temptress was what had been missing from his life. He had never felt as if he had truly belonged anywhere. But now he knew for certain that he belonged *anywhere* at all, so long as Tempest was by his side.

In the aftermath of love, Tempest reached up to trail her index finger over the dark angles of his face, enjoying his expression of contentment.

Cord nibbled at her fingertip and then took his time kissing her. *"Caramba!* For all that prim-and-properness, princess, you do know how to knock a man clean off his feet," he drawled lazily.

"Whah, thank ya kindly, sah," she replied in her best Southern belle accent. "Ah do aim tah please."

"And you please incredibly well, ma'am."

Tempest sighed in pure satisfaction as she combed her fingers through his dark hair. Hesitantly, she glanced over at their discarded clothes. "I suppose we really should make an appearance downstairs," she said unenthusiastically.

Cord cocked a brow. "And risk having your father refuse to let me come up here again? Not bloody damned likely I'll take that chance!"

"You shouldn't take offense," Tempest admonished. "Your grandfather was every bit as possessive of you as my father is of me."

Absently, Cord toyed with the lustrous chestnut tendrils that cascaded over the pillow. "Yellowfish regrets keeping us apart," he told her. "It was he who insisted on coming to San Antone to find you." When she blinked in surprise, Cord nodded affirmatively. "I had resigned myself to living death, convinced that it was my obligation to send you back home and remain with my grandfather. He's an old man, Tempest. He was afraid of losing me, afraid he'd be left alone in his world. But beneath all that gruffness, he admires your spunk. I guess his conscience bothered him to see me so miserable without you. He swallowed his Apache pride and even dressed in those clothes to come here. And believe me, he wouldn't do that for just anybody!"

"I couldn't believe what I was seeing," Tempest tittered. "We'll make a place for him in our cabin."

"In a home that doesn't breathe?" Cord asked with feigned shock. "Walls suffocate him. But I think he's coming around, despite his complaints. He took a fancy to the soft bed at the hotel, even if he didn't want me to know he enjoyed a good night's sleep." Cord smiled as he moved suggestively above her. "As for me, I couldn't wait to make love to you on a real bed. It's a first, if you recall."

"I recall," Tempest replied with a provocative grin. "A first, to be sure, but hardly a last . . . There are a few luxuries I would like to keep. This bed is one of them."

"Done," Cord replied. "You'll have a grand home in High Lonesome Valley and Yellowfish can have the cabin."

"After you add a few more windows for Yellowfish," Tempest replied.

"I'll make you happy, Tempest," Cord promised with a kiss that verified all the love and devotion he felt for her.

"You already have," she whispered, her heart in her eyes. "You came back for me . . ."

The love that burned between them blazed anew when their eyes met. Tempest could feel it straight through her, obliterating all other emotion. Now she understood why the old Apache had been so intolerant of her, so adamant in keeping them apart. But she would make Yellowfish realize that her love for Cord was a blessing, not a curse.

That was the last sane thought to flit through Tempest's mind before Cord once again wove his spell around her. She gave herself up to sheer pleasure and then returned it—caress for adoring caress, kiss for worshipping kiss. She and Cord would make a new beginning in the plush valley beneath High Lonesome Peak. There would be no more doubts, no obstacles. Tempest had discovered that she had become as restless in the confinement of civilization as Cord had always been. She had developed an appreciation for wide open spaces herself. Life in the city was too predictable to suit her anymore. Ah yes, she and the old Apache would get along just fine. They both had Cord's best interests at heart . . .

"I love you, princess," Cord whispered as he nuzzled her swanlike throat.

Tempest blinked back a tear and pressed a kiss to his cheek. "I know," she murmured. "At long last I believe it's true."

"And you'll never have cause to doubt it again," Cord assured her softly.

Sure enough, she didn't. Tempest hadn't really thought she would. When a man like Cord MacIntosh loved a woman, she knew she was loved! He was the magnificent, remarkable man who had taught her cautious soul to sing, who had stolen her carefully guarded heart. And at last, Tempest had found her destiny whispering in the wild Apache wind . . .